Philippa started to speak, but Ryan's face lowered to hers . . .

The kiss was inevitable. It encompassed weeks of empty loneliness. Their lips meshed into a perfect oneness as their hearts matched each other, beat for rapid beat. She no longer had tingling sensations, she had earthshaking tremors flowing through her.

Ryan's tongue began to trace the outline of her lips, slowly, gently, intimately. She opened her lips a fraction and his tongue crept inside her tempting mouth to explore . . .

DESTINY'S INTERLUDE

Also by
Jan Lesoing

Forever Yesterday

Published by
PAGEANT BOOKS

and smoky dust from wiping her neck and fore-head. It was enough to make a brass monkey weep! Here she was, she fumed, an eighteen-year-old graduate of the Hansen-Tawzer Academy for Young Ladies, and she was in the most impossible of predicaments. She'd been well schooled in English literature, she spoke French proficiently, and she had been plied with piano lessons, needlework, the art of haute cuisine, and all the other accomplishments her esteemed aunt had thought necessary to be a lady. But it seemed she had not learned any common sense at all.

Why hadn't she questioned how readily that bald-headed little man at the Fitch Employment Agency had given her this teaching position? He himself had said they wanted an experienced *schoolmaster*, yet he'd eagerly hired her. Now she knew why. No educated man would come to this desolate place where the sun was scorching hot; where there were no towns, or houses, or trees; where the railroad dropped you off in the middle of a prairie; and where the reception committee from the school board were late to meet you. If only she hadn't been so desperate to leave St. Louis!

The afternoon sun was merciless, so she began to trudge slowly toward the shade of the water tower, wishing she hadn't packed her parasol in her trunk.

Her trunks!

An alarm went off within her. The conductor had put her off without her trunks! On the heels of this followed another alarm, one even more dreadful.

Andrew!

Of course! She should have guessed, for she knew he owned railroad stock. Maybe this was part of some macabre scheme of Andrew's. He must have discovered her plans to escape St. Louis and arranged all of this. How long would he leave around in dismay. She saw no one: only a dark red wooden water tower and a cattle chute. Never had she felt so forsaken. She wanted to scream at the top of her lungs to the receding train, "Stop, oh please, stop! I have money to buy another ticket—" but it was too late. The screech of the whistle as the engine gained momentum was deafening, and yelling after it would be silly.

She watched the snakelike train move across the endless prairie until it faded to a small dot in the distance. Then she looked around pensively. This was nothing like St. Louis. Not even a tree was in sight, just an expanse of nothingness. Determined not to panic, she perched her brimless feathered hat on her head and anchored it with hat pins. She should have worn a wide-brimmed straw bonnet instead of this stylish confection, she thought with annoyance. Dear Heaven! Her ignorance would fill a volume, beginning with taking a teaching position she knew nothing of, in Bluffsview, a place she knew even less about. She hadn't even been able to find the town in her atlas. One by one Philippa began to tally all the blunders she had made since she began this adventure. No woman of perspicacity would have worn this heavy blue moire suit for traveling in the August heat, nor would she have forgotten to don a protective straw hat. Even one of the meanest intelligence would have realized she should bring food with her when she noted the ticket the agency had given her was stamped "Coach Fare Only." Why hadn't she remembered that her aunt, the eminent Clara Rose Van Arder, always traveled with a packet of rosewater-scented damp cloths to wipe away the soot?

Disgustedly Philippa looked down at her once-white gloves. Now they were smeared with grime clared, "Miss Marquette, you have to get off here. This is as far as your ticket takes you."

Philippa presumed the man was joking, making her an object of ridicule because she was the only female passenger in this car. She knew how unusual it was for a young lady to travel unchaperoned, or for one dressed as elegantly as she was not to be traveling first class. But, drat it, she'd had no choice. And she was tired of all the traveling salesmen's sly innuendoes. Refusing to be baited, she looked directly at the conductor and staunchly pronounced, "The middle of a field is most assuredly *not* my destination, sir!"

"It's a water stop and the train will pull out again as soon as it takes on enough water. You must get off quickly," he autocratically informed her.

As she peeped out the open door opposite her, she saw there was nothing on the other side of the train either. "I don't understand," she argued, a little less assertive now. "Why would you put me off here? My ticket was for Bluffsview."

"This is the junction where Bluffsview passengers get off, miss. Bluffsview's only a few miles from here; no doubt someone is waiting to meet you."

Apprehensively Philippa grabbed her hat and handbag and followed the man to the door. Almost before she was off the bottom step, the train started chugging up its head of steam and began to move slowly forward. The conductor set down her valise beside her, tipped his hat, and then swung aboard the moving train.

Timidly she waved back to his curt salute, all the while hoping the person who was assuredly here to meet her was on the opposite side of the track, for there was certainly no one visible on this side. She waited for the caboose to pass.

But when the train had gone, Philippa looked

Chapter One

✦✦✦✦

Nebraska—1898

"THE TRAIN IS now arriving at its first Nebraska junction. It is three thirty-six P.M. and we are a record-breaking two hours and ten minutes ahead of schedule. All off who are getting off." The conductor sang in his singsong chant. He stepped up beside Philippa Marquette's seat and lifted down her valise from the overhead rack as he repeated, "All off who are getting off."

The train had stopped so many times on the journey from St. Louis that Philippa no longer paid attention to the conductor's formal announcements. Instead, she continued to stare out the window, praying for a vendor to come aboard hawking tamales or apples as they did in St. Louis, for her hunger pangs were becoming unbearable. Here she did not see a vendor, or even a depot. Pressing her nose to the glass, she looked left and right, but there were only fields of native grasses stretching to the horizon. With a deep sigh of disappointment she turned around as the concerned conductor de-

1

DESTINY'S INTERLUDE

For Meredith, a dozen roses,
all vintage Trifari

PAGEANT BOOKS
225 Park Avenue South
New York, New York 10003

Cover artwork by Pino Daeni

Printed in the U.S.A.

First Pageant Books printing: January, 1989

10 9 8 7 6 5 4 3 2 1

DESTINY'S INTERLUDE

JAN LESOING

PAGEANT BOOKS

her alone out here before capturing her and forcing her to return home? she wondered. All night? Two or three days? Who knew what Andrew would do? Perhaps he planned never to rescue her. No, he needed her to fulfill the stipulations of the will. It would be just like him to make her suffer before forcing her to return to St. Louis with him.

As if she hadn't suffered enough at his hands. Everything was his fault—his and his mother's. Philippa still couldn't believe her aunt's perfidy. The woman had taken her in as a child when Philippa's parents died, raised her in a luxurious Victorian home as her own daughter, and given her every reason to believe she would have a happy, secure future. Then Aunt Clara Rose had died and her will had disclosed the truth. She wanted Philippa to be an exact replica of her—in short, to be her son's wife—or Philippa would be left homeless and penniless.

Brokenheartedly Philippa had accepted her changed status and her poverty. But Andrew had not. The will stated that all of the late Mrs. Van Arder's vast wealth would go to the Temperance League of St. Louis if Philippa and Andrew, her cousin by adoption, were not married at once. And so Andrew had insisted they wed. She still didn't know how he had convinced that judge to marry them without her consent, for she had refused vociferously. Andrew was much older than Philippa and much cleverer in the ways of connivery. He was selfish and greedy, degenerate, a heavy drinker, and . . . she could go on and on blasting his character, but that wouldn't help solve anything now.

Immediately after the ceremony he'd had to leave St. Louis on business and she'd managed this escape. Until now, she'd been very proud of herself, pleased at this venture. . . . How long had she been waiting? Could it possibly be getting hotter, or was it her imagination? All this must be her imagination. Andrew couldn't have traced her here, could he?

The school board members would be arriving any minute to welcome her, any minute . . . Was it always this hot in this foreign state of Nebraska? Did trees grow here? Why, oh why hadn't she bothered to check on such things before coming on this . . . wild-goose chase?

Her gloves, which had been soiled beyond repair, were now damp from wiping the perspiration off her forehead. Damp? She could probably wring water from them. It would serve these people right when she offered them a soppy wet hand in response to their welcoming handshakes. She giggled aloud at the thought. They deserved such a reception for being so late.

Philippa had been sitting slumped against one of the posts that held up the water tower, trying to take advantage of the little shade it afforded, but her nerves were too shattered to let her sit still any longer. She got up and began to pace back and forth. Something was wrong, very wrong.

Had the school decided not to hire a teacher this year after all?

Had the employment agency remembered to telegraph the school board president she was coming, as they'd assured her they would?

Had that railroad conductor played a cruel trick on her after all? Why hadn't another train come by?

Had Andrew plotted this?

Or had the sun addled her brain?

Frantically she scanned the horizon again and again, until fear in combination with the heat left her disoriented. At long last she thought she saw a lone horseman coming toward her. No, it must be an apparition, appearing as he did out of nowhere. He seemed to be leading another horse. From deep within, a pinprick of fear warned her it was no apparition. If it was someone from the school board they would be driving a carriage; therefore, it must be someone Andrew had paid to ambush her and bring her back. Was Andrew going to punish her by having her brought back tied onto a horse like a sack of meal? The hateful creature knew she did not know how to ride horseback!

If he was angry enough to arrange this, Philippa genuinely feared he'd imprison her when he got her back to St. Louis. Philippa had always known how evil Andrew was—it was the reason she had preferred to be penniless than married to him. Thinking of this, terror filled her and she turned and began to run across the prairie, away from her would-be captor, but the ground was rough and her new high-heeled kid boots were too stiff to run in. Her valise kept bumping her leg, becoming heavier with each step, so she dropped it, hoping she'd be able to run faster. Hairpins and hat pins were popping out so fast they no longer held her toque nor her hair in place. Her heel caught and tore her lace petticoat ruffle, nearly tripping her, but she managed to keep running.

The sound of galloping hooves was coming closer, but she kept on, desperately hoping to retain her freedom. Maybe the villain would fall and injure himself before he was able to capture her. It surely sounded as if he was galloping fast enough to do so.

He was close enough now that Philippa could hear him shouting to her, "Hey, lady, stop! Ma'am, you shouldn't be running in this heat!"

Then the man was beside her, reining his horse to a halt, giving it a gentle, "Whoa, boy! It's all right," as he quickly dismounted in Philippa's path. She tried to run away from him, but his tall, muscular body moved over in front of her again and she was blocked. He did not grab her and throw her up on the horse as she expected him to. In fact, he did not touch her at all, so she took several steps backward, her heart still pounding from fear.

He must be biding his time, she thought. Was there another way to elude capture? She studied the tall man in front of her. He was almost as short of breath as she was, she noted, so perhaps if she hit him over the head with her coin-filled purse, she could knock him out and run again. But where?

As the stranger scrutinized her, no doubt preparing to make his move, she glanced from side to side. There was simply no place to run to. Still, if she evaded him, it might be possible to hide in the tall grass growing beside the railroad tracks until another train came along. Maybe if she could render him unconscious long enough to tie him up with the rope hanging from his saddle, she could thwart his evil plans. This might be her only chance! She had to take it, for the idea of being returned to Andrew was insufferable.

The stranger was shaking his head in disbelief and staring at her. He pushed back his hat on his head, and asked disgustedly, "What did you think you were doing, running away like that?"

Philippa wasn't about to give Andrew's hireling the courtesy of answering his question. Did the idiot think she'd be waiting for him with a gracious welcome? She pretended to be looking at her scuffed new boots, and inched closer as she inspected the sides of first one and then the other, until she was within close range of his head. She steeled herself, remembering her whole future depended on this single opportunity.

Wham! With all her might she brought the heavy pocketbook smack against the side of his head. The blow landed on his temple, causing him to stagger temporarily with surprise and then fall forward. *Wham!* She gave him another blow right on the back of the head as he went down. After the second whack, his strong body dropped limply the rest of the way to the ground.

He had continued to hold the reins of his horse when he'd jumped down to stand in front of her, but as soon as he fell he released them, and the excited animal reared high on its legs, giving a screaming whinny. Fearing the horse was going to kill her for harming its master, she hurriedly backed away. Cowering with shock, she watched the animal bring its forefeet back to earth, while it continued looking wild-eyed and malevolent. When nothing further happened, the animal edged forward and nuzzled the man on the ground.

There was no way on God's green earth that Philippa was going to risk her life by going near enough to that beast to undo the rope attached to its saddle. In fact, the proximity of the horse to the man precluded any thought of tying him up.

Her victim was lying very, very still, and a sudden horrifying thought gave her goosebumps. What if she had killed him? Dear God! She'd never intended that. She only wanted to escape Andrew, not be a murderess! What could she do now? She couldn't leave him lying here, not knowing if he was dead or alive. Her natural compassion quickly conquered her fear of being taken prisoner. Keeping an eye on the horse, she sidled closer to the man and cautiously started to kneel beside him to search for a heartbeat or pulse. One knee hadn't even touched the ground before a sinewy arm snaked out and grabbed her wrist, yanking her down beside him.

With a rapid lunge, surprisingly fast for someone she thought was dead, he immediately loomed above her as he pinned her shoulders flat to the ground.

Momentarily paralyzed by the swift maneuver, Philippa lay there looking up at him through eyes filled with a combination of surprise, dismay, and fear. His green eyes stared back at her with undisguised anger.

She didn't know what to expect next. She certainly didn't expect him to scramble to his feet and then yank her up beside him. The stranger was the first to break the silence, growling at her through gritted teeth. "Why did you run off like a rabbit if your aim was to knock me out and pick my pockets, huh, lady?"

"Why, the gall of you, sir!" Philippa retorted, genuinely, shocked. "I had no intentions of anything of the sort. I only wanted to make sure I hadn't hurt you seriously. I was hoping," she confessed, "that you were unconscious."

"Why would you want me unconscious if not to rob me? Were you going to steal my horses too? Have you got an accomplice hiding out in this tall grass?"

He looked around very cautiously, and Philippa noticed his hand went to the gun strapped in his holster.

Taking a deep gulp of air, she pleaded hoarsely, "I swear, I've never stolen a penny in my life. Mercy, do I look dressed as a pickpocket? As for having an accomplice or taking your horses, why, the idea is ludicrous!"

"Well, since this isn't the most likely of places for a light-fingered lady to ply her trade, guess I'll have to take your word for it," he replied, still studying her wanly. "But then why did you run away, much less try to knock me out? Where are you headed?" He looked back over his shoulder and gestured. "The Villers' place? Was John to meet you?"

Why was he asking these questions? Philippa wondered, still dazed. Someone hired to apprehend her surely would not be asking questions! For the first time she looked at her enemy, the man she had so frightenedly run from and then hit over the head. Philippa was tall, but she had to look up several inches to see his deeply tanned face. He looked like the pictures of cowboys she'd seen in the penny dreadfuls as he pushed his brimmed straw hat back off his forehead. His eyes were a deep silver-green in that dark-skinned face.

The shock of dark auburn hair that fell from under the brim of his hat looked slightly unruly and almost red in the hazy sunlight. He was indisputably handsome in a rugged sort of way. While he did not act friendly, neither did he act like a villain.

What could she say? Beginning to stutter slightly, she made up what she hoped was a plausible story as she went along. "Oh, sir, I am dreadfully sorry. I was frightened by the sight of an unexpected stranger coming toward me. It made me feel so alone and helpless . . . that's why I ran away and then hit you. I was afraid you'd harm me. My train was to have been met here but the carriage is late, you see, and . . ."

The man looked skeptical. "I s'pose it's understandable. Don't know why you'd be afraid, though, not with that wallop you pack!" He rubbed his head and grinned at her before continuing, "You *are* visiting the Villers, then?"

This sounded more like a statement than a question, and she hastened to correct him. "Oh, no. I'm the new schoolteacher for Rural District Number Three near Bluffsview. I am to live with the Horace Belden family."

"*You're* Phillip Marquette?"

"Philippa Marquette," she corrected, wondering how he knew her name.

"*Philippa.*" He started to laugh uproariously, spitting out between peals of laughter, "Philippa! And the agency sent you here to teach *this* school!" He was stricken again with roars of glee.

She began to feel very frustrated. "I don't see anything funny about the situation. Is there something I should know?" she asked curtly, trying to diminish his humor and retain her dignity.

He wiped the back of his hand across his eyes, now tear-filled from laughter. They looked like pools of clear green water. He was even more handsome when he laughed, for small weather crinkles appeared at the corners of his eyes, and his straight white teeth were revealed by lips that curved upward as if laughter were inherent to them. Being this close to him made her feel a little strange. Since Philippa had seldom been in the presence of men during her young life, she was not at all sure what was causing her reaction. Her body felt hot and cold at the same time, jittery and excited. She told herself the feelings were a consequence of hot weather and hunger, but toe-deep she knew it was being so close to this man.

He had stopped laughing and was answering her strangely. "Not some*thing* you should know. More to the point, some*one*. Namely, Alvena Belden. All hell is going to break loose—excuse m' swearin', ma'am—in that house when you get there tonight. You will be back on the train tomorrow."

"*No!*" she cried indignantly. "I can't possibly be! Why would you even suggest that? I have a signed contract. The agency said my credentials were very good. Why, I took a course in Latin and advanced mathematics, and I speak French. I always excelled in English literature and history. Won't that be enough to qualify me? I can't understand why you say I won't meet with her approval."

"I say it because there is no way Alvena Belden is going to permit a looker like you to live near an old rounder like her husband, Horace. I doubt if she even gets around to consider your qualifications before she dismisses you; she'll do it on sight."

"A rounder?" Philippa pondered the word aloud. Were school board presidents out west libertines?

The cowboy quickly reassured her, "Oh, he's harmless enough. Just an old rogue, but Alvena is insanely jealous. God, when she sees you . . . excuse the profanity, ma'am"—he shook his head dismally before he continued—"well . . . We had best be gettin' on our way to Belden's place now. It's a few miles beyond Bluffsview."

Deep inside Philippa had begun to suspect he was the one they had sent to meet her, but it was still hard to accept a lone man on horseback as the welcoming committee she had expected. Harder still to admit was that she had made a fool of herself by first running away from him and then hitting him over the head, causing him to think her a thief. How humiliating!

Flustered and embarrassed, she could only stammer, "You are going to take me there?"

"Yeah," he answered bluntly.

Still puzzled, she stammered, "No one is coming for me?"

"I'm here for you."

"I mean a carriage!"

With an exasperated look he answered, "That's what I've been trying to tell you! The Beldens were coming for you, but their team is old. Horace was afraid the heat today would be too much for 'em, so he asked me to come get you."

The look on his face and the condescending tone of his voice ignited Philippa's taut nerves. He'd let her stand here in the heat for hours, scared her to death by not immediately identifying himself, and then implied she wouldn't be accepted—and *he* was exasperated?

Tartly she snipped, "I hope it didn't inconvenience you too much, sir."

"Not at all ma'am."

"Enough that you found it necessary to be several hours late."

"Late?"

"Did it occur to you how uncomfortable I might get standing in this unbearably hot sun?" she continued.

"Well, no, because—"

"Because you were too—"

"Now hold on, lady!" he interrupted, taking out his pocket watch as he spoke. "It's exactly *five forty-five!* The time the train's due. Hell—I mean, shoot! I expected to have a good hour's wait. This is the first time in months the train's been on schedule."

"On schedule," she chirped. All of a sudden she recalled aloud, "This wretched train was a record-breaking two hours and ten minutes early!"

"Early? Two hours early? The regular westbound? That's remarkable!" He looked as pleased as the conductor had sounded when he'd announced it.

Philippa felt a little remorseful, but still, she'd been stranded here. "Quite remarkable, especially since it left me in this godforsaken place, in the hot sun—"

Once again he caustically interrupted, "Ma'am, tell me: How could I know this train would be early for once?"

That truism stemmed her temper, and she admitted, "I suppose you couldn't." Suddenly she felt very guilty for lambasting him, as he looked so sincerely contrite, and she apologized. "I'm sorry. I'm sorry for blaming you for my long wait. In truth I'm very thankful you are here. I was feeling quite deserted."

"No doubt," he granted her before adding, "The few miles won't take long on horseback." He looked toward his second horse, grazing near Philippa's valise, and continued, "But if we don't start now we won't be there before dusk."

"I can't ride."

"You mean without a sidesaddle? I can prob'ly rig the stirrups—"

"No. I mean I have never been on a horse in my life."

"Never been on a horse?" He stared at her with astonishment. "Where do you come from?" he asked, amazed at her confession.

"Sai-Cincinnati. My . . . father thought girls should be very genteel."

"I see . . . I reckon. Seems strange he'd let you come way out here alone."

"He died recently." Philippa wondered if she would ever be able to tell the truth again about anything. Probably not. She hoped she could keep all the lies straight. "What are we to do?"

"There's sure no time to teach you now, ma'am, but if you stay out here you'd better learn to ride. It could be important someday. You'll have to ride up behind me," he told her. He'd turned away and didn't see Philippa's face blanch in horror. He walked back, got the other horse, and tied her valise onto its saddle. Then he led the mare to where Philippa was still standing, looking apprehensively up at his large chestnut stallion. When it snorted restlessly she practically tripped trying to back away from it.

This was an impossible situation, Philippa thought as she stood wondering how she was going to get on that huge beast, let alone *stay* on it. He'd said she could ride behind him. Did he mean for her to hang on to him? Goodness, no! She couldn't hang on to a strange man. Especially not *this* man, who was already making her feel quivers she'd never felt before.

"You better take your hat off before you lose it," he told her matter-of-factly.

Remembering the loose hat pins, she hurriedly took it off, asking, "What shall I do with it?"

That was a good question. They stood looking at one another, each waiting for the other to suggest something. She wanted to put it in her valise, but he had just finished carefully tying that onto the horse, so she didn't suggest it.

At last she said, "I don't suppose I'll have much need for such a formal traveling hat out here. I have another one."

"Nope! Don't think you'll need two of 'em."

"Well, the . . ." She started to drop the hat, but he quickly grabbed it from her and flung it into the air with playful abandon. They both watched, fascinated, as it flew high like a bird in flight, then suddenly plummeted to earth. The action seemed to release some of the pent-up tension for both of them, and she asked, "How do you propose to get me up onto that animal? I'm frightened silly of it."

"I've come to the conclusion, ma'am, in that skirt you can't ride astride, so I'm going to mount and then lift you up in front of me."

"Oh!" was her only reply. She was even more hesitant about being held in his arms than hanging on to his back, but she had to agree there was no other way. He mounted swiftly and then told her, "Turn around." She cautiously backed up close to the horse and watched out of the corner of her eye as his broad shoulders leaned down toward her, while his muscular arms reached around her. They brushed her breasts and made them tingle with funny sensations, then large hands grasped her waist and lifted her easily up onto the horse.

He settled her comfortably between his arms before clicking his tongue, urging his horse to go. She tried to be careful to sit bolt upright and not touch his tempting shoulder. The bounce, bounce, bounce of her body made this impossible, and she found herself leaning against him to stop the jolting motion. His body seemed to be going up and down with the movements of the horse; this was better, so she snuggled a little closer, hoping he wouldn't notice.

"I don't even know your name!" Philippa said suddenly. Here she was, riding in this man's arms, and she didn't even know his name—a man she had practically killed! Oh, what a story this day would make to tell her lifelong bosom friends, Lee Ann and Dottie. They would never believe it. She could hardly believe it herself.

"I'm Ryan Murphy, ma'am," was his brief reply.

Philippa wanted to know more, so she quizzed, "You live near the Beldens, I assume."

"Down the road a piece. Across from the school."

"Are you a farmer, then?"

"Kind of. I run a feeder cattle operation."

Philippa wondered what feeder cattle were, but she didn't want to seem ignorant. More important, she was anxious to find out a certain other fact about her rescuer. Evasively she asked, "Will you have children in my school?"

"I don't have any kids."

So much for roundaboutation. "Are you not married, then?" she asked bluntly, holding her breath for some reason until she heard the answer.

"No, ma'am, I'm not."

He didn't say any more, and Philippa felt she had already been too inquisitive. He was certainly a man of few words. Was he annoyed because he had had to come and get her; was he the quiet type; or was he just disgusted because she had acted like such a ninny? Probably the latter. She vowed to be very circumspect and as wordless as he was for the rest of the trip. That vow lasted two minutes.

Abruptly she sat upright, beseeching, "We must turn back! We have to get to the nearest telegraph station and send a wire to stop that train. My trunks are still aboard it. All my clothes and school-books are in them. I just have to have them. Won't you please take me somewhere to wire a station or two ahead so they can put them off for me?" She hated to ask him to do more for her, but those trunks were vital. The agency had made it very clear that she had to furnish her own textbooks. Fortunately Aunt Clara Rose never threw anything away, so she had all her books, from her first primer to her last English grammar. Hopefully this long-legged horse would be able to get them to a telegraph station before her trunks ended up at the train's destination in California.

Chuckling at her sincere dismay, Ryan explained, "They never unload freight at the junction 'cept on Mondays, when Sam gets his supplies for the store. The rest of the week, all merchandise and trunks come over by freight wagon from the depot. They'll lock your stuff up there tonight. You'll get it tomorrow if there's a full load— If not, in the next day or two."

"Gosh! That's a relief," Philippa exclaimed, forgetting for a moment that she was now a dignified schoolteacher. She hadn't even gotten over the embarrassment of uttering such a childish expression when she was embarrassed even further by the demanding, loud growl of her empty stomach. She hoped he hadn't heard it, but she was afraid he had. Of course, a gentleman would be too polite to comment on such a thing.

"When did you eat last?" he asked, ignoring politeness.

She was so hungry she ignored it too and proceeded with this conversation they shouldn't even be having, according to the Hansen-Tawzer code of propriety. "Not since yesterday. I didn't know I wouldn't be allowed to go to the dining car."

"Alvena sent you a *coach fare?* That figures. We'll have to get you to Beldens' faster so you'll be there for chow." He gave his horse a kick in the ribs and ordered, "Git moving, Thunder."

The horse began to gallop, and Philippa was too apprehensive to ask what he meant: *chow?* Now the horse's hooves seemed to be rapidly going high off the ground, then down again so fast that she pushed closer against him where she felt safer.

When he felt her curl tightly into his chest, Ryan tightened the arm circling protectively around her side and continued reining his horse with one experienced hand. When next he looked down at her in his arms, it was easy to recall how young and inexperienced around horses she was. He could feel her tenseness. Her face was blanched, her blue eyes enormous, but her lips were stubbornly pinched together. He smiled to himself and slowed his horse to a smooth gait.

Chapter Two
✦✦✦✦

ALVENA BELDEN STRAIGHTENED the corner of the crisp white tablecloth, admiring her good crystal glasses and the company china as she did. Too bad there were only zinnias for the Dresden vase in the center. Everything was so dry this year. She supposed it was fortunate zinnias were hardy, or there would be no fresh flowers at all for a centerpiece.

It was nice to be setting the table for a guest again. Other than the preacher and his wife, they hadn't had company all summer. Oh, there had been the threshing crew and an occasional hired hand, but they didn't count. One did not use the dining room table nor the bleached white linen for the likes of them. They ate on an oilcloth-covered table in the kitchen, using the mismatched everyday dishes.

Tonight the table was set to impress the new schoolmaster, so it pleased Alvena's notion of gracious living. She wanted him to know this was no ordinary farmhouse he was staying at, but a house where refinement was cultivated. The last young man had been so appreciative of her efforts that she had continued to use the dining room with her good things every Sunday for the entire five terms he had boarded with them. Alvena still resented that the superintendent had transferred dear Alexander from District 3 to teach at a town school at the opposite end of the county. To her, Alexander had been the son she had always wanted but never had. She hoped his replacement would be as sociable and mannerly. Once more she pulled back the stiffly starched lace curtain to look down the road, while her fingers habitually tried to loosen the scalloped edge made by the nails that had held the curtain to dry in its stretcher.

No one was in sight. She was still annoyed that Horace had sent Ryan Murphy to meet the train instead of letting them go to meet it themselves. Horace claimed his team was getting too old and the heat would be too much for them. Alvena knew he was only hinting they should buy some Thoroughbred horses like that Murphy fellow owned. Horace always had been too easily influenced.

"Ha!" Alvena muttered half aloud. As if anyone should pay attention to that cowboy who had moved into the old Carter place. The man hadn't fixed the house up in the least but spent all kinds of money on Thoroughbred horses and crossbred cows and new barns and fancy farming equipment and such. Thank goodness she and Horace had built this house twenty years ago and moved farther up the road, so Horace wasn't constantly influenced by Ryan Murphy's extravagance.

Originally the Beldens had lived next door to the school, across the road from Ryan's kin. Why, the Belden family had even donated the land the school was on to the county, and here Horace was, trying to ape some unsettled Irishman! She could only hope the man hadn't made too bad an impression on the refined new schoolmaster.

It was nearly dark by the time Ryan reached the Belden farm. Philippa was still curled tautly in his arms, so he spoke to her softly before the house came into view. "Ma'am, we're at the Beldens' . . . ma'am!" He spoke louder and nudged her slightly.

Ryan's gentle shaking brought her back to reality with alarming suddenness, and for a moment everything was a blur of unfamiliarity. It took a few seconds to acquaint herself with her surroundings, especially at finding herself curled in such an unfathomable place as up against a man's firm, warm chest on top of a horse! Once alert, Philippa could not believe she had actually allowed herself to press so close to him. True, she had been exhausted from lack of sleep on the train and the frightening ordeal this afternoon, but still—to have relaxed so comfortably in this stranger's arms! What must he think of her immodest behavior?

"Mr. Murphy, I am so sorry. I never meant to . . . I don't know what to say. What must you think of me? I've never done anything like this before in my life!"

"Don't fret, ma'am," he said, dismissing the subject.

Horace Belden hurried toward the approaching horses, blinking his eyes as he walked. Maybe Alvena was right—he did need glasses. For all the world it looked like Ryan had a lady on the horse with him and just a suitcase on the horse tied behind. He walked a little faster to get a better look.

Sure enough, it *was* a lady, and from all he could see in the twilight as they came closer, she was a young, pretty one. This couldn't be the school-teacher. The schoolteacher was a man, and probably a prissy, prosing one like Alexander. But what if she was?

"Welcome, welcome!" he called out enthusiastically. "Glad to see you made it back in good time, Ryan." He tipped his hat to Philippa. "Ma'am, would I be right in assuming you're our new schoolmarm?" There was a hopeful note in his voice.

"That is correct, sir. I am Philippa Marquette."

"Philippa?" Horace asked.

"Philippa," Ryan affirmed.

"Philippa," Alvena shrieked as she bustled out of the house to join the trio. "There has been a ghastly mistake! The wire distinctly said *Phillip!"*

"Oh, no, ma'am. There's been no mistake." Philippa tried to sound convincing, but she was certain now the Fitch Employment Agency had intentionally erred just so they could collect their fee. She wished there was some graceful way to get off this horse so she could hurry and appease this lady. This was obviously the woman Mr. Murphy had warned might want to send her back. "I have my signed contract right here in my pocketbook, and my diploma is in the trunk with my books; I graduated with honors from high school and also from a women's fine arts academy. I was hired by the Fitch Employment Agency to teach at Rural District Number Three." After completing this speech she once again looked for a way down.

Ryan must have sensed her discomfort, for he asked genially, "Horace, will you give her a hand down, please?"

"He most certainly will not!" came the scathing

answer from Mrs. Belden as she continued to glare at the attractive young woman. "Take her into town for tonight. She can go back on the train tomorrow. You, Mr. Murphy, can take her back to the junction. You should never have permitted her to get off!"

Philippa wondered what bizarre thing was going to happen to her next. Here she was on a horse, in a stranger's arms, being rejected by a woman, if Mr. Murphy's guess was true, only because a man might flirt with her?

"Now, wait a darn minute here, Mrs. Belden." Ryan let go of Philippa and swung himself angrily down from the saddle. "You know the rooming house in town is already filled, and the hotel is sure no place for a lady. Hell—excuse me, Miss Marquette—she hasn't eaten for two days because *some* stingy individual in this district only sent a coach fare. She's tired and hungry, and you want me to take her the four miles back into town?" Ryan's angry tirade did not even cause Mrs. Belden to flinch, but her husband did.

"Alvena!" Horace said, aghast.

Philippa watched wordlessly as husband and wife glowered at each other. What could she do or say to change this woman's mind?

Before she thought of anything, Mr. Belden spoke up. "The fee has been paid to the agency and the railroad ticket used. If she goes back, the board would have to come up with money to pay another fee and buy another railway fare!"

Ryan rubbed his chin as he added fuel to the argument. "In addition, all of us on the board would have to pay Miss Marquette's food and hotel bill in town, buy her a return ticket, and pay her a month's salary just for coming here. That'll all add up."

Philippa felt a thud inside of her as if her heart

kicked an extra beat at Mr. Murphy's words. She had wanted him to argue on her behalf, help convince them she had good credentials and should be allowed to stay, not just agree that it would cost them a pretty penny to send her back. The man must not only be tight with his words but with his purse strings as well. This wasn't the romantic way she'd been thinking of him as she rode in his arms, and she chided herself for her foolishness.

Horace looked pleadingly at his wife and in a wheedling tone continued, "The biggest landowners have to pay the lion's share, 'n' that's us, dear, 'n' of course Murphy here. Perhaps we should think about this. School opens Monday. If we can't get anyone else before then . . . well, I might not be reelected!"

Philippa did not know at the moment which of her fears were causing her to tremble. Foremost was the alarming thought that if she was not allowed to stay here, she had nowhere to go. Returning to St. Louis was too abhorrent to consider. Equally dreadful was her fear of sitting alone on this horse. She tried to stop shaking and listen as her fate was discussed. The stares of unmitigated dislike she was receiving from the older woman were making her feel most self-conscious. She felt even more so when she compared her disheveled hair to the neat knot at the top of her adversary's head; it was skintight with not a hair out of place.

At last Mrs. Belden spoke. To Philippa it sounded as though she said, "Harrumph." She seemed to be reconsidering.

If only I could get off this beast, Philippa thought, but she was too afraid of falling to try. Pleadingly she looked at one man and then the other. Ryan caught her look and hastened to help her down. He stepped nearer and held out his arms. She leaned forward and felt his strong hands carefully grasp her at the sides of her waist and lift her down.

He seemed to hold her in midair a moment longer than necessary, and her foolish heart started doing those flip-flops again as she looked into his eyes. They seemed to be twinkling—with pleasure maybe? Did he feel something too, or was he just eager to be rid of her?

He quickly stood her on the ground when Mrs. Belden cleared her throat loudly, showing her distaste at this spectacle, and commented, "A *lady* would have ridden the other horse."

Oh, no, Philippa moaned inwardly, another thing to put me in her black books.

"Not if the lady has never been on a horse in her life," Ryan said crossly, defending her.

"Never been on a horse!" Mr. Belden sputtered. "You don't say!"

They all seemed so shocked. Didn't they know about trolley cars? She had always traveled on the trolley or in a private carriage.

It was the weapon Alvena needed. "The teacher is required to ride from here to the school and back everyday—*on horseback*."

"I'll walk. I'm used to walking a lot," Philippa assured them hopefully.

"I can take her over in the buggy," Horace offered without thinking.

Alvena exploded. "You can *what?*"

Quickly Ryan said, "I'll teach her to ride."

"Yes, yes, that's a good idea," Horace assented nervously. "Why don't we all go in and eat? We can discuss this later. You'll join us, won't you, Ryan?"

"The table is set for three," Mrs. Belden hissed loudly to her spouse before Ryan had a chance to answer.

Philippa noticed Ryan stifling a smile as he replied, "Nope, I need to get home and tend to some things. Thanks anyway, Belden."

He raised his hat a few inches off his head as he looked at Philippa. "It was a pleasure meeting you, ma'am. I hope you'll be happy here."

As she met his steady gaze, Philippa was hoping she would simply be staying. *Happy* seemed an irrelevant word, but she answered, "I'm sure I will be. Thank you so much for . . . everything."

"I'll be sayin' good night to all of you, then," Ryan said as he mounted his horse.

"Good night, Mr. Murphy," Philippa said in her soft, husky voice.

"Thanks for helpin' out, Ryan. Good night to you, too," Horace boomed.

Philippa felt awkward as she watched Mrs. Belden turn and stomp toward the back of the house. Mr. Belden motioned for her to follow Mrs. Belden, but he didn't even offer to carry her case for her. It seemed rather strange to her to enter someone's back door, but she determined it must be customary here and remained silent. The kitchen did have a homey appearance and the food in the warming ovens smelled heavenly. If only one or the other of the Beldens would say something to her! She paused nervously in the dining room doorway, still clinging to her valise, while Mrs. Belden fussed with the flowers on the table and Mr. Belden stood on first one foot and then the other.

Alvena was waiting for the teacher to comment on the lovely table. Perhaps if Miss Marquette was extremely complimentary and appreciative, Alvena would consider letting her stay. Of course, she wouldn't give her the big front bedroom upstairs. The small one under the eaves would do fine. Most assuredly, this would be the last time they ate in the dining room and used the company dishes. It was obvious this girl didn't appreciate refinement. She still hadn't said a word commending the Beldens' new Eastlake dining room set or the stylishly laid table.

Philippa wished she knew what to do. "The host and hostess always speak first to welcome a guest," she had learned in deportment class. What she hadn't learned was what one did if they *didn't*. Aunt Clara Rose had insisted courtesy, culture, and propriety were essential. Each night she and Philippa had dined at the lovely antique Hepplewhite table on which Sadie had placed a lace tablecloth with Aunt's beautiful china, crystal, and sterling silver pieces. Philippa mistakenly assumed they followed the same custom here. Bewildered, she looked toward Mr. Belden. He did not suggest she could go to freshen up, nor did his wife, so she pulled off her soiled gloves and surreptitiously used them to wipe her face before wadding them up and putting them in her pocketbook.

When she finally got up the courage to speak, it did not occur to her to compliment Alvena's personally set table. Instead, she made a fatal mistake. "The dinner smells delightful, Mrs. Belden," she pronounced.

The dinner the hired woman had cooked! Alvena was so put out she practically pulled the petals off the zinnia she was rearranging. Wordlessly she stormed to the kitchen and began clanging around pots and pans as she served up the meal Mrs. Olsen had prepared before she left. This girl must be one of those immigrants, she thought to herself as she dished up the vegetables. It was obvious she'd never before been in a refined, cultured home. Talking about the smell of food, indeed! No, Alvena knew she would not be able to tolerate Miss Marquette around the house—nor around her husband, with those roving eyes of his. Those clothes she was wearing were much too fancy for a schoolteacher! They looked as if they came right out of one of those *Women's Home Companion* magazines, those French couture styles, which meant the girl must have stolen them—or worse!

Mr. Belden didn't say a word to Philippa as they stood listening to the cacophony coming from the kitchen. She wondered what faux pas she had committed—she'd only been trying to be polite. The poor man just shrugged his shoulders and looked at her apologetically. Finally, he did reach out to take her valise and set it by the stairway.

The meal was eaten in complete silence after a brief prayer of thanks to the Lord. Philippa felt miserable. The food was so good she wanted to praise it over and over, but she was afraid to say another word.

After dinner, Alvena lit the wick on an arc-handled kerosene lamp and told her, "I'll show you your room and the way to the outhouse and pump now," and without another word led her upstairs to a small bedroom and then back out, down through the kitchen to the backyard, where she pointed out the water pump and the privy. She then handed Philippa the lantern and went back into her kitchen to resume angrily banging things about.

As she settled into the scratchy sheets, Philippa wondered about this strange household. Until she finally fell asleep from exhaustion on the lumpy, narrow bed, Philippa heard loud arguing from downstairs. She could not hear the words, but she was afraid her champion, Mr. Belden, was losing the argument. It sounded as if he got only one word in to every ten of his wife's. Surprisingly, the last thing she thought of before she fell asleep was, "If she doesn't let me teach the school, I'll probably never see Ryan Murphy again!"

Ryan Murphy had a difficult time getting to sleep that night too. Every time he tried to close his eyes, the vision of Philippa Marquette crossed his memory again. Her beautiful golden hair enchanted him. Her light-to-dark, dark-to-light brown eyes haunted him. But it was her mouth that possessed him. The sensual lips that curved up so sweetly when she talked or smiled and curved down so suddenly if she was vexed—how he would like to feel those lips pressed against his, venture inside that mouth with his tongue to explore its alluring secrets. . . .

She was tall, almost skinny, but he had felt her high, firm breast pressed against him as she had curled up in his arms. How he'd like to see her hips without that bustle! He envisioned a seductive roundness. The innocent look of shock and fear in her eyes when he'd thrown her to the ground was fixed poignantly in his mind. He still had a lump on his head where she'd clouted him. Why had she done it? Somehow it seemed more than she had explained, but he couldn't say why. It had almost been worth it to look down into her eyes as she lay there beneath him . . . Damn!

Angrily he punched his pillow into a different shape and commanded himself to get some sleep. It was foolhardy to let a mere girl torture him this way. . . . But he suspected that under that prim, youthful exterior there was a warm, sensuous woman. Why did she have to be a city-bred schoolmarm?

After a restless night Ryan wasn't in the best of

moods when he awoke to the sound of hammering and loud banging. He pulled on his pants and walked to the front window to investigate. Across the road Horace Belden and his hired hand, Knute Olsen, were on the roof of the ramshackle old house next to the school. Hurrying back to the bedroom, he quickly put on his shirt and sat down to pull on his western-style boots. Most farmers wore striped denim overalls and heavy work shoes with laces, but Ryan continued to wear the clothes of a cowhand, the comfortable garb he'd grown up wearing.

Within minutes he was striding across the road to offer his help if they needed it. Why on earth were they fixing the leaky roof? Horace had been talking recently about tearing the house down and using the lumber for a hog shed on his own farm.

"Hello up there," he called out as he approached the house through the overgrowth of dried weeds. "What are you up to this morning? Need a hand?"

"Murphy, good to see you." Horace came lumbering down the ladder and walked to where Ryan was standing. "We're getting the old place all ship-shape for the new teacher."

"You're *what?*" Ryan was sure he had misunderstood. This house was beyond repair. It was ready to tumble down.

"We're sprucing the place up a bit for Miss Marquette. She's going to move over here next to the school."

"You're kidding me, aren't you? That house will cave in on her. You can't put a lady in a place like that!"

"Now, now, Ryan. Don't get your dander up. As Alvena says, the kitchen and the back bedroom were added on years after the house was originally built. They're not too bad and she won't need more room than that. Why, the kitchen's huge!" Horace sounded as if he was giving a well-rehearsed sales pitch, but Ryan wasn't buying any of it.

"What's wrong with her living at your place like the committee agreed? You're getting paid for boarding her!"

"Oh, we're going to do it, too," Horace hastened to assure him, "but since she doesn't ride horseback . . ." He stopped midsentence, shook his head in dismay, and then admitted, "Oh hell, Murphy. Alvena don't want the girl at the house. Some silly damn notion of hers that she's not pious enough. Alvena thinks she's one of them damn educated immigrants who come from them tenement houses in the cities nowadays and, well . . . she don't trust her. I know it's a lot of folderol, but there's no persuading that woman once she's made her mind up. Since we've already paid out the money for her train fare and everything, Alvena decided we'd put her over here. We'll stock the larder with supplies for her."

"No!"

"What do you mean, no?"

"I mean, I'll pay her train fare back and donate another fee and ticket. You can't put her here."

"But Ryan, she don't *want* to go back. She's downright stubborn about it. Says this place will be fine, sight unseen. They say the poor are starving in the cities. The way she ate last night, I can believe it! Ate more'n any hired hand I ever saw. She won't go hungry here—Gertrude is sackin' up flour and sugar and canned goods from our pantry right now. Ole is going to bring over a cow so she'll have milk and a few chickens for fresh eggs. When I butcher later on after this hot spell is over, I'll salt her down a crock of pork. Nope, she won't starve here like back in Cincinnati in those tenements."

Ryan was torn between his sympathy for the girl and his dismay at the thought of having her live this close to him. Last night he'd decided to keep his distance from her. Now they wanted to move her in across the road from him! Ryan had suspected Alvena wouldn't permit her to live with them. Philippa Marquette was much too beautiful and Alvena Belden much too jealous. And it was a well-known fact that no one else in the district had an extra bedroom. If the girl was as determined to stay as Horace intimated, this was probably the only solution. Ryan suspected when she saw the ramshackle house and the primitive school, she would turn tail and run. He'd got the impression yesterday that, far from being a starving immigrant, she was a highborn, aristocratic lady. She had mentioned her father's dying. Perhaps his death had left her penniless. Ryan went up the ladder to help with the shingling, telling himself that she could live here and he would ignore her.

Andrew Van Arder was glad to be home. Not just home from Chicago, where his business venture had turned out to be a huge disappointment, but home to the place of his roots. He didn't pretend it had been a happy home, nor that his childhood had been memorable, but the house itself had distinctive class. It bespoke wealth and prestige and an aura of luxury. None of the lodgings he had rented since he left it had ever given him the satisfaction this house did. The feeling of success and self-worth filled him today as he bounded up the steps and across the veranda to the massive front door.

He gave the bell a quick twist, then turned to look out across the perfectly manicured lawn, twirling his cane as he did. His mother had never found a gardener who had suited her and thus had always directed the care of it herself. Just as she had maintained imperious control indoors. While he'd despised his mother, Andrew had inwardly approved of her methods. It was to be hoped Philippa was trained to follow her pattern. He wanted the aloof tranquillity of this house to prevail.

But when the door was opened, prevailing tranquillity was *not* what met him. The housekeeper, Mrs. Carpenter, began to shriek something about how she wasn't at fault and couldn't be held responsible, while two other servants stood chirping just as incoherently.

"Ladies, please, stop this caterwauling at once. None of you are making any sense. Stop it, I say. Where is Mrs. Van Arder? I prefer to have my wife explain whatever has you so hysterical."

"That's what we're trying to tell you, sir," Sadie, the cook, managed to blubber. "Little Miss . . . she's gone . . ."

"Gone?"

"Yes, yes!" Mrs. Carpenter composed herself enough to admit.

"Are you telling me she has been abducted? Kidnaped? Has there been a ransom note? Stop your blithering and answer!"

"No . . ." Mrs. Carpenter's voice was weak and small with fear. "She must have run away."

"Perhaps to find you," Sadie offered hopefully. "Did she turn up in Chicago?"

"Of course not. What have you fools done? Allowing her to escape! I warned you . . . I told you . . . didn't I?"

At the sight of the unbridled anger evident on his face, all three women began to cower. Sadie bravely ventured, "But why would a new bride want to run away?"

Mrs. Carpenter added, "You only told us she wasn't to have visitors because they'd upset her, and that's why you didn't want her out—people would cause her grief. You never said we should guard her like a . . . a prisoner!"

"Yet you knew what I expected of you. Well, didn't you?"

"Y-Y-yes, sir. I suppose."

" 'I suppose,' " Andrew sneered. "You knew damn well what I wanted and you . . . Hell, I should discharge the lot of you! In the future you will follow my dictates—explicitly! Do you understand?"

"Yes, sir."

"Yes, Mr. Andrew . . . er, Mr. Van Arder—"

"Out of my sight! All of you! Now I have the embarrassing task of going to the parents of Philippa's friends, Lee Ann Narin or Dottie Marshall, and retrieving my errant bride. Damnation!"

Chapter Three
✦ ✦ ✦ ✦

ONCE AGAIN PHILIPPA found herself in a wagon with high boarded sides just like the dray wagon she'd hired to take her things to the depot back in St. Louis. How shocked those draymen had been when she had practically sneaked into the back of their cart to hide on the floor behind her trunks. This time, however, she was not on the floor in the back; she was up on the seat between Mr. and Mrs. Olsen. Extra slats had been added to the sides to keep all the food and household goods from falling out as the wagon bounced over the rutted road. A crate holding several chickens had been secured onto the tailgate and a very displeased cow was tied on behind. The cow liked neither being tied nor having to walk at the pace of the horses, and she made her displeasure known by incessantly bawling.

Philippa had liked the Olsens on sight. Their warm, cheerful faces had greeted her when she first came downstairs this morning. Mrs. Belden had continued to look pinch-faced and belligerent and Mr. Belden had still been distant, so the warm welcome of the Olsens was most appreciated. Mr. Belden had cleared his throat several times and had finally managed to offer her the choice of returning back east or living in his parents' old house next door to the school. Even though it sounded as if the offer was halfhearted at best, there had been no choice—she could not go back.

One of Philippa's first plans for escaping St. Louis was to stow away on one of the few wagon trains west that still embarked from there, but she had never imagined it was remotely possible. Yet here she was, heading west on a wagon loaded with everything needed for living on the prairie. Of course, she was not going to a log cabin or an isolated soddy where civilization had not yet reached. She wouldn't have to be afraid of Indians and wild animals, would she? She looked around at the desolate prairie. Thank goodness Ryan Murphy lived across from the school. For some reason, just thinking of him made her feel this would be a safe refuge.

Gertrude Olsen confirmed Philippa's thoughts as she continued her chatter. "I still can't believe

Alvena! Sending you to this ramshackle old house ven she and Horace just rattle around in that big empty place. Thank the good Lord Ryan lives just a stone's throw away. If it veren't for that, Horace vould never have let her move you here. He's a good man in spite of the fact he lets her vrule the vroost!"

"Yah," her husband seconded. "Horace told me so himself. He thinks highly of Murphy. Ve all do. Still, this just don't seem vright to me. Have you ever lived out in the country like this, ma'am?"

"Oh, yes," Philippa told him, trying to sound persuasive. She wanted to put the Olsens' minds at rest. It was evident they were upset with this idea, but they had not dared to reprove their employers.

"In truth, living with Alvena might be vorse than an old farmhouse. Some days I think the five or six hours I vork for her vill get the best of me!" Gertrude confided.

"Yah, and she's not afraid Horace vill give you the eye!" Ole winked at his wife as he teased, "You're too old and too fat! Now, a girl like Miss Marquette! That's something else! Alvena vould be mighty touchy. You'd be vorse off, all right, ma'am!" He nodded his head to emphasize his words.

Philippa wasn't quite sure what he meant by all this. Mr. Belden did not seem to be at all what she had envisioned as a libertine. He was extremely proper, just somewhat unsociable.

She decided to change the subject back to one which interested her decidedly more. "I take it you know Mr. Murphy quite well, then?"

"Oh, indeed ve do," Gertrude assented. "He's a fine man. He hasn't lived here long, but about every neighbor hereabouts has reason to thank him for one thing or another. He even gave a whole beef to the Parkers last vinter ven Rafe got laid up for a spell."

"You should have heard him vrant at Belden this morning because he vas moving you over here!"

"He doesn't want me to live here?" Philippa found this thought extremely disturbing.

"It's the house, ma'am. He don't think it's a fit place for a lady, and he's right about that. He helped all day to make it just as snug and tight as ve possibly could for you." This information caused Philippa's heart to soar. It did not soar very high, however, before it came down with a plop as they crested a hill and she had her first glimpse of the schoolhouse and its neighboring residences. The schoolhouse was a small white frame building with a bell in its cupola. The two houses had probably been white at one time; now both of them were weatherworn gray.

The house next to the school was a plain, rectangular dwelling, which had had an addition tacked on to the back and a porch on to the front. The porch had not remained attached. Its roof had pulled away and lay partially on the ground, at an angle from one broken and one unbroken porch post.

The house on the opposite side of the road was a square, wood-shingled structure that appeared solid despite its need for paint. Its yard and driveway were not overrun with weeds as the other one was, and behind it were two huge new barns.

Gertrude shook her head in dismay. "It's even vorse than I thought. Ve never vorked for the Beldens ven they lived here, and not having children, ve had no call to be over here. You can't stay, dear. Vatever your circumstances back home, they can't compare to this!"

Little does she know, Philippa reflected as she, too, despaired at the necessity of leaving her beautiful home for this monstrosity. Then her mind conjured up a picture of Andrew, and she promptly began to assure the tenderhearted Mrs. Olsen, "It can't be as bad on the inside as it looks from here, and as you yourself promised me, I'll have plenty to eat, for it seems you packed enough food to last me for years! Once you've gone hungry, you really appreciate meals. I think I can stand almost anything as long as I'm not starving!"

Mrs. Olsen did not know Philippa was only referring to the two days on the train, and her compassion was at once aroused for this skinny, half-starved girl. "You poor little thing," she commiserated, "I vish I could take you home vith us. I'd have you as vround as Ole an' me in no time, but our house is small. It's owned by Knute's mother, who lives vith us."

"Looks like Ryan sickled a path here after ve left," Ole proclaimed.

"I thought I'd better cut a few brambles or we'd never get the furniture moved in!" Ryan welcomed them from beside the wagon, where he stood nearly obscured by the tall weeds. His eyes were warily watching Philippa. Her colorless face told him how shocked she had been at the sight of the house. He knew he was waiting to hear her renounce living in such a shack. Waiting and hoping that she . . . would? . . . wouldn't?

"Good afternoon, Mr. Murphy," she said, her voice softer than usual. "Mr. Olsen tells me you helped to repair this house for me, and I want you to know how much I appreciate it."

Even as she said this she was wondering what had been fixed. The tumbledown house still looked to be in need of complete rebuilding.

Sensing her anxiety, Ole rushed to explain, "Ve boarded the front part up from inside, ma'am, an' fixed the kitchen and bedroom vindows so they'd go up and lock down. Mr. Belden is in town vright now gettin' a new lock for the back door. I'll be over and put it on for you tomorrow. Ve fixed the vroof and put in some new screen. You'll be safe as a bedbug here."

"A bedbug vould not liff here," Gertrude pronounced disgustedly as she proceeded to climb down off the high wagon seat. "Good afternoon to you, Ryan."

"Same to you, Gertie," he replied, "and you, too, Miss Marquette." He had not yet taken his eyes off Philippa. She was wearing the same shiny blue dress she had worn yesterday, but today its jacket was open and he could see the high-necked white silk blouse underneath. The open jacket gave an even more revealing outline of her delectable breasts. Her hair was not piled up on top of her head but braided into a neat plait, which hung to the center of her back. If he had been hoping his memories of her had been inaccurate, one look denied it. The teacher was even more lovely today in spite of her pallor.

He wanted to reach up, lift her down, and try to console her, but he restrained himself. Gertrude and Ole probably would not be as critical as Alvena, but they wouldn't understand. Hell, he didn't even understand himself, he mused as he watched her climb down. Her long legs easily reached the step with only a brief glimmer of her ankles before her skirt fell back into place. Ryan found himself still wishing for a view of her behind without that bustle. Chiding himself, he remembered that a proper little schoolmarm from some big eastern city wasn't his type at all.

Gertrude was moaning in back of him, "Ole, come in here. Look at this vrubbish! It's all over everywhere."

"Now, Gertie! Ve hauled most of it out and burned it. There's just a little sveeping left."

"A little! You can call this a little, you'd call an elephant an ant, Knute Olsen. Ve need to scrub, too," Gertrude declared as she rolled up her dress sleeves. "Get that box of lye soap an' rags unpacked first thing . . . no, first thing give me the grain broom that's tied on the side of the vagon."

Philippa had now reached the kitchen door and was looking around unbelievingly. Had she honestly been the one to pronounce it couldn't be as bad on the inside? It was worse.

Chunks of ceiling plaster had fallen to the floor here and there and most of the paper was peeled off the walls. The oilcloth tacked up behind the small black cast iron cookstove had yellowed with age. She was afraid to venture on into the bedroom for fear of what she might find; instead, she took off her jacket so she could start helping Mrs. Olsen and looked tentatively around for a place to lay it.

Through the back door she heard Ryan telling Gertrude, "It's lucky a couple of the cats from my barn have been slinking around here. They've kept the place from being completely destroyed by mice."

Mice! Philippa shuddered at the thought. She laid her jacket on the crook of the stovepipe, causing some of the previously undisturbed dust to fly. This seemed a good place to begin dusting with one of the rags Ole had just carried in, so, holding her jacket in midair with one hand, she dusted with the other, nearly choking as accumulated dirt flew in every direction.

"You mustn't do that in your good dress, Miss

Marquette," Gertrude interposed. "You vill vruin it!"

"My trunks haven't arrived yet; this is all I have. If the train's coal dust didn't harm it, then I don't think this will."

"At least put my apron on," Mrs. Olsen insisted as she took off her big white apron and put it over Philippa's head, bringing the waist ties around to her back and then around front again before tying them. "My own dress is vashable, but that moire of yours von't vash. I have some naphtha I use for cleaning Mrs. Belden's church dresses. I vill send some over. Just be sure you hang the dress out in the air after you clean it t' get rid of the smell." She was sweeping up a storm as she talked and the air was black with dust motes.

The stovepipe was already dust-covered again. Perhaps it would be more efficient if she went into the bedroom and started there with the new broom Ole had just brought in, Philippa determined.

Pushing the bedroom door ajar, she cautiously peeked in. It wasn't as bad as she had imagined. While it was a far cry from her lovely rose-mauve sanctuary at home, it was not an impossible room. The ceiling plaster had given way in only a few places and the wallpaper was intact. Even the linoleum on the floor seemed to be in fair condition, so she enthusiastically went to work with her rags and broom. She didn't hear Ryan when he walked in until he asked, "Where d'you want me to set this washstand?"

Philippa turned to him from the pile of dirt she had just gathered on the floor. He had rolled up his sleeves and unbuttoned the neck of his shirt before starting to unload the wagon, and the fine brown hair visible on his forearms and upper chest drew her attention. For a moment she just stared, forgetting his question. She'd never seen a man's shirt unbuttoned before, and the thick mass of hair it revealed intrigued her. Quickly she recalled herself and stammered, "I suppose over there by the window, against that wall."

Tentatively Ryan suggested, "Wouldn't it be handier, ma'am, to have it just inside the door here so you won't have to carry the water so far?"

Of course it would! Having never carried pitchers of water in nor basins of water out herself, she had not thought of the convenience. Once again he was going to think she was a complete idiot. She had done nothing but stupid things since they met. What a hen-wit he must think her!

Wanting very much to correct his impression of her, she told him, "You are definitely right. There are just so many things on my mind today." She tried to give intelligent thought to the placing of the rest of the pieces. "The chest should go next to the closet . . ." Belatedly she looked around. The room did not have a closet, and Mrs. Belden had not sent over a wardrobe press. She tried to gloss over her blunder. ". . . I mean, by the hooks there on the wall, and the bed can go by the window—"

"If you can call it a bed!"

His conversational tone made her forget she was trying to sound knowledgeable. "Isn't it awful? I slept on it last night, or I should say, I tried to. Between the lumpy bed and loud voices I didn't get much sleep."

"They must have thrashed it out, all right, but I still can't believe Belden actually let Alvena put you over here. He generally stands up to her on the important things."

"It *was* important to get me out of there," Philippa told him. "Mrs. Belden took an immediate dislike to me before we sat down at the dinner table and has barely spoken to me since. They offered me a return ticket, but I ca—don't wish to go back. I like the challenge a country school offers." She quickly tried to cover her near slip.

Ryan admired her pride. She didn't want to admit she couldn't go back now that she was an orphan. Ole had told him what she had said about being able to stand almost anything except having to go hungry. It wasn't fair that this house was her reward for such tenacity. Even the shabby, all-male domain he had grown up in was not a hovel like this. He felt so damn sorry for her that he unthinkingly offered, "The school is one thing, but this house is something else. My place may not look like much, but it's sound and Grandma had it fixed up real cozy-like inside. You're welcome to live there and I'll bunk here. I'm not in the house much anyway."

Philippa was stunned by this offer. He scarcely knew her, yet he was willing to make such a sacrifice. A warm shower of affection flowed over her body, a closeness with this handsome stranger, but she didn't quite know what to say. How could she refuse and show her appreciation at the same time?

In the end her shyness only permitted her to murmur, "That's a very generous offer, Mr. Murphy, but of course I can't accept. This house will suit once it is cleaned up. Thank you so much for thinking of it."

Ryan looked down into her eyes, now dark with emotion. Was she angry at him for suggesting such a thing? Of course she was! No proper lady would allow herself to be beholden to a stranger. It was not suitable at all, and Miss Marquette was being extremely polite about it. Damn! He could kick himself for making such an unthinkable suggestion. He turned and rushed from the room, thoroughly disgusted at himself. It wouldn't happen again, he vowed.

Long after the wagon was unloaded and the Olsens and Mr. Murphy had gone home, Philippa continued to clean her new home. She used vinegar on her windows as Aunt Clara Rose had instructed the cleaning girls to do. It made the leaded glass back home sparkle; here it made it possible to see dimly out of the cheap distorted glass. Thank goodness her aunt had called every one of the servants into the dining room each morning to give them explicit instructions for the day. If Philippa had not overheard those orders, this would be an even more dismal situation, she reflected.

She wished she had paid closer attention to details. Mrs. Carpenter, Sadie, or the day girls who came to wash, iron, clean, and help in the kitchen had taken care of everything. Philippa had been responsible for keeping her room neat, but not for its weekly cleaning. All the menial tasks like carrying water had been done by the hired girls. Even the care of her clothing had been turned over to the Quality Garment Cleaners Company.

Sometimes, the loneliness of the silent rooms in that big house had prompted her to slip away to the detached summer kitchen in the backyard, where she could listen to the jovial banter of Sadie and the hired girls. She was never permitted to help them, though, no matter how eagerly she begged. Everyone knew as soon as Philippa was missed, Mrs. Van Arder would come to take the girl back to her piano practicing or to work on bright cross-stitch samplers.

Tasks for a lady, Philippa thought disgustedly as

she tried one more time to scour the layers of grime off her windows. Now she would be doing all the work she had wanted to try to do back in St. Louis. Ironically, the companionship she had craved that had made her want to help with the chores was still to be denied her.

Only the time she had been allowed to spend with Lee Ann and Dottie had been filled with true comradeship, fun, and laughter, for at school and church she had been shy and uncomfortable. What a strange creature I am, Philippa chastised herself. Craving companionship but frightened of crowds. Hopefully she looked forward to finding a solace for her loneliness in teaching school. Her lifelong dreams of a caring love and laughing companion-ship were forever going to be denied, she feared.

Chapter Four

+ + + +

PHILIPPA DECIDED THE cow must be lonely here, too; it was mooing so piteously now that it had gotten dark outside. She knew just how it felt. To be away from everyone you knew, everything beloved and familiar, was a miserable feeling.

Her own loneliness dissipated somewhat when she thought of Ryan Murphy, to be replaced by a longing for something . . . ?

After he had been so kind as to offer her his own home this afternoon, he had seemed to avoid her the remainder of the day. He hadn't even stayed long enough for her to thank him for all he had done.

The cow was getting louder and louder by the minute. Would it moo like this all night long? Philippa knew she was going to get very little sleep in this creaky old house, and if the cow kept it up she wouldn't get any at all.

Suddenly a loud banging on the door startled her. Outside it was completely dark now, and the back door was locked only by a chair pushed under the doorknob. Would it keep an intruder out? Stop being foolish again, she tried to tell herself. Invaders with evil intentions wouldn't knock. She called out timidly, "Who is it?"

"Ryan Murphy! Why are you letting that poor cow bawl?" came the angry reply.

What did he expect her to do for a homesick cow? The man was impossible. She was so dirty and disheveled from cleaning she didn't want to open the door and let him see her, so she answered curtly, "There is nothing I can do for that cow, Mr. Murphy."

"You might try milking it, *Miss* Marquette!" he replied in a mimicking voice. "I would like to get some sleep tonight!"

Milking it! God in heaven! She had never even seen a cow milked. No one in their neighborhood had kept cows. A dairyman had brought around jugs of milk and crocks of butter twice a week, which Sadie kept in the big old icebox on the back porch.

How could she admit any more ignorance? She just couldn't, so instead she asked sweetly, "Would you consider milking it for me tonight? I've hurt my arm."

Grabbing the tea towel she had been using to polish the silverware, she quickly tied it cornerwise around her shoulder to make a sling for her supposedly injured arm. Philippa inwardly wondered if there was any demand for professional liars. She was really getting to be an expert.

"You hurt your arm? How?" His voice was no longer sarcastic but concerned. "Open the door."

"I must have wrenched it moving furniture. It's very sore." She carefully removed the chair and opened the door using only one arm.

He stepped inside and practically jerked her arm from the sling, moving it this way and that. "Probably just a sprain," he finally pronounced. "I'll do the milking. Where's the milk pail?"

The milk pail? Philippa looked around, hoping it wasn't the bucket she had used to scrub with. She was relieved when she saw the shiny metal pail on the big open shelves that filled the end wall of the room.

Ryan took the pail from her, trying not to look at his nemesis. No darn teacher should look so cute and pert and vulnerable. How could she be so desirable with that too-big apron on and her hair falling loose from its once-neat braid? He stomped off to the barn, holding his lantern high to pick his way through the undergrowth. Philippa trailed his steps. She had to watch and learn about this milking business.

When Ryan realized she was following, he tried to rush her back to the house. The last thing he needed tonight was to look at her in the moonlight; that would be his final undoing. He tried to be cross to curb his overwhelming desire to take her into his arms. "I'm capable of milking a cow without any help, ma'am. Just scoot on back to the house. When I'm done I'll put the lid on the pail and drop it in the well for you."

"Drop it in the well?"

"Yep."

"But why would you?"

"So you don't have to, miss. It might be rather difficult to tie a knot onto the bucket with one hand."

"Oh!" Philippa breathed a sigh of relief. She would be able to pull the bucket back up again and use the milk. "But I mean, not *why*, but to what purpose would you drop it in there?"

"To keep it cool, of course."

"Oh!" This time her "oh" was even more enlightened.

"How did you keep milk fresh in Cincinnati?"

"We put it in the icebox."

"You had an ice cave, then?"

Now it was Ryan's turn to ask the questions. His grandfather's place had an ice cave, but Ryan hadn't bothered to fill it last winter. He hadn't known the men hereabouts well enough then to ask for the help he would have needed to cut the blocks from the creek and haul them back by sled to pack down the cave.

"Ice *cave*? No, we didn't have anything like that. The ice man's helper brought blocks of ice to the back door for Sadie, our cook."

"Oh!" Now Ryan was enlightened. Poor people in tenements didn't have ice delivered to their door, nor cooks. He had been right. She had been of the upper class back in Cincinnati, or at least until her father had died.

He turned away from her to head on to the barn, away from this conversation . . . away from the moonbeams shining on her hair and the reflection of the lantern light in her eyes . . . away from those too-tempting lips.

Stubbornly, she didn't go back as he'd told her to, but kept following right on his heels. If he stopped and turned suddenly, she would be right in his arms.

He was tempted. Then he remembered she was the *schoolmarm*, so he started taking longer strides and told her gruffly as he walked, "Said I'd take care of the cow. Don't you trust me to do it?"

"Yes, yes, I do." Philippa was trying to think fast to cover her milking inexperience with a convincing lie. "It wouldn't be very polite of me to ask you to help and then not even accompany you, would it?"

Her manners were impeccable, as always. He couldn't dispute her, so he only replied, "S'pose not."

Pushing open the shed door, he reflected that the cow had a sturdier place to live than the girl did. He hooked the lantern over a nail and took down the three-legged stool Ole had hung there this afternoon. The miserable animal continued to throw its head back and moo until he had milked enough to relieve the pressure on the udder.

Philippa could hear the *squish-spurt-splat, squish-spurt-splat,* but she couldn't see exactly what Ryan was doing, so she bent down and inched her head closer and closer. When he turned unexpectedly toward her, their mouths were only a breath apart. Each wished the other's eyes were readable in this dim light.

What was she trying to do to him? Ryan wondered. Did she have the least idea how she was affecting him? He didn't think so. In fact, he didn't think the prim and proper little schoolmarm had ever been kissed. There was an innocence about her that provoked and intrigued him at the same time. He was provoked because if she was one of the girls from the neighboring ranches he had grown up with, he would *know* what to do. They had been as earthy as he himself was, and in these circumstances he would probably kiss them.

He was even more intrigued because she remained innocently close to his face. Their mouths were so close they were sharing breaths. Once again, he could smell that hint of fresh meadow flowers combined with her own musky scent.

He was trying so desperately to keep his actions under control that he was squeezing the teats of the cow too rapidly. The momentum became *squish-squish, spurt-spurt, splat-splat.*

Their close proximity made Philippa forget to watch Mr. Murphy's hands. She was too busy trying to confine the accelerated flutterings inside her chest to that immediate area. It was a futile task, for the disturbing tingles persisted, spreading all through her. Her mouth felt as if it was in the grip of a magnet—closer, closer, and then her lips met his with a reverent softness. It was a gentle, sweet kiss that neither of them was prepared for. It awakened too many sleeping qualms. Each of them knew this should not be happening, but neither of them was willing to end the tantalizing responses vibrating between them. Ryan instinctively started to deepen the kiss just as the cow mooed for him to continue milking. It brought both of them back to reality.

What was she thinking of, standing here in a shed encouraging a man who was practically a stranger to kiss her? She found she was both wanting the kiss to stop and wanting it to continue. She stepped away just as Ryan quickly turned back to his milking.

An awkward silence followed. This situation certainly hadn't been covered in any of her lessons on proper etiquette between ladies and gentlemen, so Philippa was at a total loss to think of a polite comment. Ryan was wondering how in the hell he'd ever got himself into this and how he was going to get out of it without saying something that might embarrass her or show himself up for the fool he was.

Out of the blue, Philippa admitted baldly, "I was trying to learn how to milk a cow."

The humor of the ludicrous scene and Philippa's disarming comment struck both of them at the same time and they broke into gales of laughter. Ryan jumped up and jubilantly grabbed her in his arms, swinging her around and around within the crowded confines of the shed. Philippa was so lost in hilarity that she didn't even realize it when her swinging feet tipped over the stool, which fell against the milk pail, spilling all the milk. Weakened by laughter, Ryan staggered and fell, crumpling both of them into the pile of new hay.

The laughter had released their tense emotions. Weakly they lay there trying to regain their breath. They were lying on their backs, but his arm was still under her waist; he could feel the warmth of her through her silken blouse and chemise. Turning his head to look at her, he found she was staring at him with eyes full of questions. They glowed in the flickering light of the lantern hung from the rafter above them.

It was by far the most difficult task Ryan Murphy had ever had to do: to remove his arm from underneath Philippa Marquette's warm, inviting body. There were too many questions in her eyes, and he knew the answers.

Slowly he rose to his feet, reaching down and taking hold of the arm that wasn't in the phony sling. As he helped her to stand, he apologized, "Sorry I got a little carried away with my hilarity, ma'am. It was just so dang funny the way you were watchin' me and . . . " He didn't want to embarrass her by mentioning the kiss, so he merely added, ". . . the way you said how you were tryin' to learn to milk a cow."

Philippa was angry with herself. It wasn't bad enough she had been flat on her back on a pile of hay under most unladylike circumstances . . . it was worse. Much worse! She had actually been disappointed when he'd stood up so quickly. Her own unruly body had wanted to remain in his arms for some reason. How humiliating! Why, he must think her an absolute trollop! She had to disabuse him of that impression at once.

Resolutely she adopted her aunt's no-nonsense voice and proclaimed, "It *was* rather uncouth of you to grab me that way, sir, but I admit the circumstances may have warranted it. Be that as it may. I seem to give your sense of humor a real treat, don't I? From my name, to the fact that I can neither ride a horse nor milk a cow, I am just one laugh after another!"

Ryan was torn between being angry at her recriminations and sorry that he had laughed at her. He wasn't as sorry as he was angry. In the future he'd be sure he never came within fifty feet of *her* again. That was for damn sure! Hell, she'd been laughing as hard as he had, and as for the kiss—! She had initiated it just as much as he had!

"I told you once to git in the house, lady! None of this would have happened," he lashed out at her accusingly. "Ole can teach you to milk tomorrow and every other thing a dumb city girl needs to know to get by out here. Now git!" He yanked the stool and pail upright and plunked down to finish his interrupted task.

Shamed and totally embarrassed, Philippa ran out into the dark, fighting the tall weeds as she

tried to make her way toward the dim light showing through her kitchen window. It wouldn't have
mattered if it was broad daylight, she still wouldn't
have been able to see her way through this dense
undergrowth, for her eyes were stinging with
tears. Once she fell over some snarled vines, but
she quickly picked herself up and continued to
stumble on toward her new home, this desolate
shack out in the middle of nowhere. How she hated
it now!

All night Philippa had remained wide awake,
curled in a tight, stiff ball on her narrow, uncomfortable bed. Each new groan and creak of the old
house petrified her. She had never been alone in a
house after dark; even the silence of the night was
frightening. There were no occasional sounds of
carriages or wagons, no katydids singing in the big
trees around the veranda, and no clocks chiming
the hour and half-hour.

The hours were passing, of that she was certain;
hours in which she tried not to think of Ryan Murphy or Andrew Van Arder. Men! Men were hateful
and cruel. She was glad she had a teaching position so she could remain independent forever and
pledged herself to become such a good teacher that
the Fitch agency would place her in a school every
year for the rest of her life. But *never* back at Rural
District No. 3, the district where a man made you
quiver and feel warm and fluttery inside and then
yelled at you to git!

Along with her mixed emotions about Ryan she
struggled with frightening images of Andrew Van
Arder. The fears that he might find her became
even more vivid in this dark, spooky room. Had
she really escaped him? Had she arranged every-

thing so perfectly it would be impossible for him to find her? Carefully she examined each step she had taken and tried to convince herself he could not trace her. Still, the fear persisted in haunting her, just as the intoxicating kiss in the shed tonight did, and she tried to dispel these terrifying qualms and befuddled emotions by seeking solace in recalling poetry memorized long ago.

It was a ruse she had often resorted to when dilemmas plagued her, and over the years it had served her well. Diligently she tried to think of poems or verses about sleep. A line from Longfellow seemed most appropriate: "Oh sleep, sweet sleep! Whatever form thou takest thou art fair." And another, from *Evangeline:* "Silently, one by one, in the infinite meadows of Heaven, blossomed the lovely stars, the forget-me-nots of the angels."

The house groaned and creaked continuously, and before she was aware of the tangent her mind had taken, some of the words from Mr. Poe's "The Pit and the Pendulum" stole forward. "It was not that I feared to look upon things horrible but that I grew aghast lest there should be nothing to see. With dread I unclosed my eyes and my worst thoughts were confirmed. The blackness of eternal night encompassed me. The intensity of such darkness seemed to oppress and stifle me . . ."

In the dark of the house the words were so frightening that a sudden scampering sound sent her from the bed like a bolt of lightning. Groping shakily in the dark, she managed to light the lamp beside her bed in time to see a mouse scurry across her kitchen floor. Bounding across the room, she slammed her door and wedged a towel in the crack beneath it, hoping she had made a firm enough barricade to keep that creature from her bedroom. For the remainder of the night the lamp was kept burning to keep all her enemies at bay: The mouse. The gruesome words of Edgar Allan Poe. The menacing tyranny of Andrew Van Arder. Most of all, the tormenting tingles that the memories of Ryan Murphy conjured up inside her.

The next day Ole came over to put the door lock on, warning Philippa to keep it locked always. Not wanting to frighten her, he said it was because once in a while tramps or a band of roving gypsies moved through the area, and while they wouldn't harm her, they'd steal everything that wasn't nailed down or locked up tight.

Ole also taught her how to milk the cow whose name was Tilly, and he told her how to take care of it, as well as the proper way to tend chickens and gather eggs. By some lucky quirk, Philippa was not afraid of the cow. In fact, she felt an easy kinship with the lonely, docile creature. However, it was *not* easy to extract milk from her. It took several tries, even with Ole's expert instructions, for Philippa to get even a few splatters of milk in the pail. The thought of never having milk for drinking or cooking made her determined to learn. Recalling Mr. Murphy's expertise and his final comment about a "dumb city girl," she became even more determined to master the chore. Surely a girl who had conquered piano concertos could accomplish this! When she finally had the bucket half full, Ole offered to finish milking for her. She gladly let him, wondering if the poor animal's teats were as sore as her fingers.

While Philippa wasn't exactly *afraid* of the chickens, she found tending them made her feel very uneasy. They watched her with their beady eyes, keeping a far distance from her while she filled their watering trough. However, as soon as she opened the grain bag to fill their feeder, they hopped all over her and each other unafraid, causing Philippa to spill a lot of feed on the ground. The chickens didn't seem to mind; they eagerly pecked at the spilled grains, making it difficult for her to walk from their midst without tripping over them.

While the chickens were eating, Ole told her to go into the coop and gather the eggs. She nearly dropped the first one she scooped from the nest when she discovered it was warm.

At the end of the morning Philippa persuasively assured Ole she would get along fine now that she had had her memory refreshed on how to tend the cow and chickens, but she suspected he was still skeptical about her knowledge and abilities when he left. He promised that he and Gertrude would come by and take her into town with them on Saturday.

Saturday was two long days away.

"If you haven't found her by Saturday," Andrew told the men standing around him at the rear of the saloon, "every damned one of you is fired—and you're not getting a lousy penny from me for your worthless efforts! And you call yourselves experts! Can't even locate one simpering schoolgirl!"

"The lawmen ain't doin' no better, not even them Pinkerton fellas you sent for," a shrunken man with a bristly gray beard reminded him.

Another old man with a patch over one eye added, "We've outdone any official search, Van Arder, and you owe us—you promised us a handsome fee. No John Law could have checked out all them brothels for you nor made sure she didn't get shanghaied by some white slavers. You owe us, 'n' nothin' was said about a Saturday deadline, neither—nothin'—so don't be figgerin' you'll be let off."

"All right! All right! You'll get the damned money, but Hellsfire, the lot of you should have found that girl by now! She's got to be in St. Louis somewhere. But keep checking ways she might have left town, just in case."

With this warning Andrew turned and left the building. He had driven his new automobile to-night, for he didn't care to have his coachman know he was familiar with the dives on Wharf Street. Servants were the worst gossips. That was all he needed—more gossip. The whole town was agog with it already.

If only he hadn't published the damned notice of his marriage in the paper. It made him look bad, having his bride run away and every inveterate snoop in town talking about it. The fool girl! Where the hell was she, anyway?

He'd paid to have the Marshals' and Narins' houses watched, but there had been no sign of Philippa. Where could she be? She had no known relatives.

Andrew gave the crank on the car an extra hard twist and the motor began to growl and sputter. He climbed in behind the wheel and pushed hard on the gas pedal, wanting to get away from this neighborhood fast. He didn't fear the men in the saloon—they'd been on his payroll off and on for years—but around here anyone might be stabbed just for the coins in their pocket and the watch they carried. He'd hoped that in her eagerness to flee from him, his bride hadn't wandered this far from home. Of course, if she had, his men would have ferreted out that information by now.

No, the witless girl was . . . but Philippa wasn't

witless, he recalled abruptly. She was extremely intelligent. For the first time, Andrew actually began to fear he might not find her within the next day or two—but find her he would!

After Mr. Olsen went home, Philippa explored the schoolhouse and found it was in good condition, compared to the house. It had a nice teacher's desk, a recitation bench, and a big double pedestal chalkboard. There were two neat rows of student desks on which seats folded down from the sturdy metal sides that held the top of the desk in back of them. While this tiny little one-room clapboard building did not remind her of her own two-story, well-equipped grammar school, its desks did. How well she remembered: if the person in the seat got up suddenly, it always jolted the desktop of the person behind. Sally Mae Jenkins always used to jar the seat intentionally during penmanship just to get Philippa in trouble for ink stains on her paper.

It didn't take Philippa long to clean the schoolroom, but she realized it would take quite some time to air out the closed-up smell of hot summer. This was probably why the school board had sent the train fare and insisted on her early arrival.

Much later, when she found the list of students' names and their grade levels, she understood the real need for the teacher to arrive early. It was necessary to prepare assignments for thirteen children in seven different grades. Once again she began to wonder about her trunks. What would she do for books and lessons if they didn't arrive? Mrs. Belden would gleefully dismiss her. Even if she did get her trunks in time, she began to question whether she could possibly prepare this many assignments. Escape, not proving her ability to handle the job, had been her only motive in accepting this position. Somehow she'd manage, she promised herself as she locked the schoolhouse.

Returning home, she saw the large scythe sitting by the fence that Mr. Murphy had used to clear a path from the road to her house yesterday, and she decided to rid her yard of some more of the tallest weeds. She took several swipes with the tool, but not a single weed fell beneath its blade. Finally she tried swinging it in an arc almost to her shoulder and found that worked quite well. Such a hefty swing clipped down weeds with each swath of the scythe. Pleased that she had finally figured out something on her own, she began chopping industriously.

It was a hot, humid day, and in a matter of minutes her back ached and her blouse was clinging to her perspiring skin. Occasionally she stopped and wiped the moisture from her forehead, then continued to sickle down weeds. After almost an hour of cutting she had a narrow path cleared to her outhouse and the cow shed. Next she decided to make one across the yard to the school grounds so she wouldn't get cockleburs on her good dresses.

As she thought of her good dresses, Philippa ruefully looked down at the blue moire traveling costume that had been so stylish yesterday. Now it was destined for the rag bag as soon as her trunks arrived. It was ripped from falling over the vines last night, snagged in innumerable places, and covered with these awful, clinging cockleburs. Even the naphtha Gertrude had promised to send over could not save it now.

By late afternoon Philippa had chopped a wide

path toward the school grounds, but her shoulder muscles and back ached so badly she could not finish. Maybe she would come back to it later, she contemplated, when it was cooler. Even to herself she did not admit her hopes that if she went out then, perhaps she would see Mr. Murphy doing his evening chores and she wouldn't feel so isolated.

She had heard him leave this morning just shortly after that one big chicken of hers had made its loud cock-a-doodle-doo noise. The sound had scared her senseless after the stillness of the night. Full of fear, she'd run to her window to see what the startling blast was.

There that colorful chicken had stood on top of a fence post, just crowing as loudly as it could. She had wondered if it needed attention as the cow had, but after a few minutes it flew off the post and went back to the chicken coop. Later, Ole had chuckled and told her to expect it every morning.

Somehow, despite her aching muscles, she milked the cow and tied the milk pail to the rope and dropped it down the well to keep cool. She was delighted with the eggs her chickens had laid and made herself a fluffy omelette to eat with the watermelon pickles Mrs. Olsen had sent over with Ole. By now Philippa's back and shoulders were throbbing and she felt stiff from head to toe. She actually cried out at the sharp pains as she pumped the water to wash the dishes, and groaned when she picked up the bucket to carry it inside. She decided she needed to lie down and rest a minute before she washed the dishes or herself. She was so exhausted she fell into a deep, dreamless sleep before dark, before her house started creaking, before Ryan Murphy rode back into his yard.

Chapter Five

✦✦✦✦

Ryan felt a twinge of worry when he returned from his fields that evening because there was no lamplight visible from the schoolteacher's place, no sign of anyone around at all. Concerned, he went over and pounded on the door, but no one answered. In the twilight he could see the newly cut paths leading from the back door; Belden had obviously let Ole spend the entire day helping Philippa out. Since the cow was quiet, she had undoubtedly been milked. He tried the back door, thinking that if it was locked, Ole had probably worked here today and then taken her to his place for supper.

To his surprise he found the inside hook on the screen door was latched. He tried banging louder but still got no answer, so he went back home. Obviously she was still angry at him for last night. She had every right to be—he was angry with himself. No doubt that was why she wouldn't answer the door, but why didn't she light the lamp?

At dawn he got up to watch for signs of life across the road, deciding if he didn't see her moving about over there soon, he was going to bust into that house. Any number of things might be wrong with that know-nothing city girl. Bleary-eyed, he watched as the rooster flew up onto a fence post across the road and began to crow. Then to his astonishment the teacher stepped out from behind her house, took dead aim at the rooster, and hit it with a rock. The rooster gave a wounded, angry croak as it flew down off the post and ran back to the coop. Miss Marquette brushed the palm of one hand back and forth against the other in a pleased gesture, then picked up the milk pail and headed jauntily toward the barn. Soon he could only see the top of her head over the weeds. She was all right!

At first he was relieved. Then he was furious. She had made a fool of him, sitting in her darkened house refusing to answer the door. Ryan had planned to hitch up his team today and go into town to get her trunks for her, but damned if he would now. Not after *this*.

She could go into town on foot and tote her trunks home piggyback, as far as he was concerned. For that sight he'd ride into town himself, he chortled as he went about doing his morning chores.

Philippa tended her cow and chickens, straightened her house, and then went back to cutting weeds. Her muscles still ached, but she was resolved to finish the path to the school and widen the one to the road. Adding to this resolution was how agreeable it had been to fall into bed so exhausted that she had heard no noises, for that way she hadn't been too frightened to sleep.

Soon her back and shoulders were throbbing again and the blisters on her hands from yesterday had broken open to plague her. The blouse and chemise she wore were so wet with perspiration they clung to her. Even her hair was damp. Frequently she had to stop to wipe her cheeks and forehead, but her path was now widened almost to the road. The Olsens would be surprised when they came after her tomorrow.

She tried to swing the scythe higher and faster so she could get done. Today she wanted to have time to soak in a hot tub and wash her hair. If only she had one of her good dresses to wear to town tomorrow . . . Why was the sun getting so hazy? She began to feel dizzy and lightheaded and the sun became hazier.

Ryan knew he would be glad, when winter came, for all the acres of prairie hay he had cut and stacked to feed his cattle, but after his sleepless night last night he never wanted to see another haystack. Most days he didn't take time to go to the house for lunch. Today he needed to fortify himself with some strong coffee. Hurriedly he unhitched his team from the hayrake and led them to the water tank. Then he headed for the side porch. As he neared the door he heard a *swish-swoosh* that made him glance across the road. There was the teacher cutting weeds, swinging that scythe with a strength he would never have guessed she possessed, as skinny as she was.

Amused, he stopped to watch her a minute or two. The little scamp sure wasn't favoring that hurt wrist now. He had to smile at her clever ruse to get him to do the milking for her. Then, as he watched, she collapsed onto the scythe. Instantly, Ryan jumped over the end rail of his porch and raced across the road.

When he approached her, he saw the girl's skin was white, blotched by the red, sunburned nose and cheeks. Ryan could barely detect a heartbeat when he knelt beside her and picked up a clammy wrist. A bloodstain on her skirt was spreading rapidly. He gently turned her over onto her back and pulled up her skirt to look for the source of the bleeding. She had a wide gash on her leg above her high shoetop where she had fallen across the scythe. The cut didn't look too deep, in spite of the fact that her stocking was ripped to shreds. Urgently he tore a big square out of her white petticoat to try and stem the flow of blood. He folded it and pressed it onto the wound, tying it in place with his own red cotton neckerchief. Then he scooped her up into his arms to carry her to a cool place.

There were no trees in Philippa's yard, so he quickly carried her across to his house and placed her under the big old walnut tree near the well. Then he drew up a pail of water and carried it over beside her. Unhesitatingly he ripped off his shirt and dunked it into the bucket to sponge her off, knowing how important it was to bring her body temperature down as soon as possible. Damn, this city girl was too thin and frail for this type of work. Roughly he slapped her cheeks, trying to bring her to consciousness. With vigorous sweeps he sponged her face and arms and legs, dousing her blouse sleeves and stockings as he went. When she still did not respond, he unbuttoned her high-necked blouse and tried to pull it away from her shoulders so he could saturate some more of her body. Her mounded breasts were well defined by her perspiration-soaked chemise, and he sponged water as low on her chest as he could without taking the blouse completely off.

The sponging caused him to have very mixed emotions. He was most concerned for her welfare, of course, but a part of his mind drifted to the sheer pleasure of holding her in his arms this way as he'd dreamed of doing. There was a spark deep inside that inflamed him and refused to be squelched. It relished the task of sopping the water onto her beautiful face, her slender legs, her tempting breasts. He was shocked from his fantasy as he turned her wrist to dampen her forearm and saw the open blisters on her hand. Lord! She didn't have a lick of sense.

After eternal minutes she began to roll her head from side to side, murmuring. While he was filling the second bucket of water, Philippa began to come around and looked slowly at her unfamiliar surroundings. Only Ryan, coming toward her, was a recognizable part of the blur. She was so thankful to see him through this unreal haze that she cried out unthinkingly, "Oh, Mr. Murphy . . . I don't know where I am . . . what happened? I was cutting weeds . . . the sun became all hazy . . . I got dizzy, and now . . ." The dizziness was receding, only to be replaced by a fierce headache. Philippa tried to rub hard enough on her forehead to relieve some of the pressure, turning her head from side to side more rapidly to get away from the pain.

Ryan slid one arm under her shoulders and pulled her head up against his chest as he continued to sponge her with only one hand, saying soothingly, "Please, ma'am, you must hold your head still. We have to get you cooled down. Just relax, you're gonna be fine."

Philippa began to feel better from the combination of the soothing tones of his voice, the coolness of the water, and the support of his chest for her aching head, but she was still puzzled about what had happened. She looked up at him to ask, just as the dripping shirt was lifted to sponge her forehead again, and her eyes and nose were inundated instead. She spluttered and tried to wipe away the water with her sleeve just as he realized what had happened and threw his shirt aside to wipe her face with the back of his hand. Their hands collided over her face and two sets of fingers automatically intertwined while two pairs of eyes simultaneously met and locked magnetically.

Philippa slid her other arm up to bring Ryan's face close to hers where she wanted it. She had been so lonely, so frightened, so insecure for the last few days that she desperately needed this secure feeling she had right now. Once again she wanted the shocking hot and cold tremors to shoot through her as they had when he had kissed her in the barn. With no thought at all to her aunt's pious teachings, Philippa raised her face to Ryan's.

The kiss began as sweet and surprising as the one in the barn but changed within seconds. Ryan untwined his fingers from hers so he could use that hand to hold her closer to his bare chest. Only the thin, wet fabric of her blouse and chemise separated their wet bodies. All his warm sensations from sponging her returned to seemingly set his body on fire.

The kiss was everything Philippa had hoped it would be. The hot and cold tremors returned to her body in full force, and she tried to snuggle closer to him as their mouths dueled for control of the kiss. He turned his face slightly so he could crush her begging lips with more force. Urgently she compelled him to continue by the pressure she exerted with her lips to match his. It was a kiss neither of them wanted to end.

Ryan raised his head and looked into those beautiful deep brown eyes. They were bright with surprise and promise. He wanted to kiss her again and again but suddenly remembered who *she* was! Worst of all, she'd nearly had a heat stroke and she had a bad cut on her leg that might still be bleeding. What the hell was he thinking of? He practically dropped her like a hot stove poker, grabbed his now dirty, wet shirt, and pretended to sponge her forehead.

Disgusted with himself, and cross with her for not knowing about noonday sun, he began to mutter, "You darn near got heat stroke, Miss Marquette. You should never have been out here in this heat, especially not without a hat. We need to cool you down, ma'am." He dipped the shirt in the bucket, wishing he could dump the whole damn pail over his head to cool himself down.

Once again, Philippa knew she had acted stupidly. She had lived all her life in a hot, humid climate where shades were drawn by eleven A.M. all summer long. Sit-down tasks were saved to be done at this time of day, and visitors were entertained on the shady sides of verandas or in dim, high-ceilinged parlors. Ladies chatted over elegant lace or feather fans waving leisurely back and forth. Men argued while cardboard advertising fans with wooden handles swiftly moved the air around. No one risked heat stroke! Why hadn't she remembered?

Even more demeaning was that she had forced him to kiss her. The strictly-brought-up Philippa Martin had forced Mr. Murphy into an unwanted kiss, just as she had forced him to kiss her in the shed. Had she become a "chit with no principles," as Aunt Clara Rose had defined one of the many hired girls she had dismissed? This man, whose high regard was so important to her, whose respect she especially wanted to have as the dignified new schoolmarm, now probably thought her to be a stupid, ignorant . . . trollop. He was still berating her.

"—you fell plumb across the scythe. Lucky you didn't gash more'n your leg. That's some cut you got."

"Cut?" When he mentioned it, she did feel a throbbing in her leg. It had been previously overshadowed by her severe headache and the emotional demands of her body, but now she rose up to look down at her leg. What she saw was her skirt hiked far above her knees! Feeling the shoulder of her blouse slip down as she rose up, she reached her hand to straighten it and found her blouse unbuttoned so low that her shoulders and neck were bare. Hastily she tried to pull the two gaping sides together while staring at Mr. Murphy, her eyes huge with misunderstanding.

Seeing her outraged expression, Ryan tried impatiently to explain. "You had fainted from the heat, lady! I had to cool you down as fast as possible. I also had to try and stop the bleeding on your leg . . ." Damn! Why was he stammering and stuttering like a guilty schoolboy? Hell, he had probably saved her life, and this prim little miss was making him apologize for it! Miss Goody Two-Shoes had evidently forgotten the way she had kissed him while she was still semiconscious, a kiss that had left his loins aflame.

To cover his feelings, he growled as he stood up, "Why were you out there working like a farmhand during the heat of the day when you're not used to it? Any five-year-old would know better!"

"I was out there, Mr. Murphy, because it seems I have innumerable weeds to scythe before Monday when the students arrive. Rural School District Number Three may not feel the necessity for a teacher's home to have a respectable appearance, but I do." Her voice was so cold it froze on the syllables of each word. "It is also important for the teacher to arrive at said school without snags and cockleburs all over her dress. Hence, I must cut a path to the school grounds. It is most imperative for a teacher to look very dignified at all times."

Philippa knew she looked anything but dignified right now, sprawled out on the ground in wet, dirty, bloodstained clothing, but somehow she had to make Mr. Murphy see that she was a lady, not like an immoral hired girl. To convince him she mimicked her aunt Clara Rose's icy voice, which had been known to put even the mayor in his place. "I have not received my trunks, so I will have to spend the entire night trying to make this dress presentable to wear into town tomorrow. I can only hope I am able to hobble to my house and draw enough water to heat for a bath. If you don't mind, I shall be on my way, as I have myriad things to do before nightfall."

Ryan Murphy just stood glaring at her, not saying a word. He watched as she tried to stand and failed, dropping limply back to the ground, rubbing her forehead once more. At that point, he scooped her up into his arms, marched across the road to the kitchen door of her house, opened it with one hand and an elbow, then carried her through the kitchen to the bedroom, where he plopped her down onto the center of her awful bed. Then he sailed back out of the room.

Philippa heard the back door slam, then the squeak of the old water pump. The door slammed again and she recognized the slosh of water as it was dumped into the big copper boiler. This pattern was repeated several times until the boiler must surely have been full. It was, for she heard the metal scraping noise of stoking the fire, then the rustle of the basket as he added more fuel to make it burn.

The house vibrated as he slammed back out of the kitchen. She peeked out the bedroom window to see if he went toward his yard. He didn't. He fed and watered the chickens and cow for her, then he strode back into the house, letting the door bang again.

She identified the clang as her round galvanized tub was pulled from behind the stove and plunked into the middle of the kitchen floor. The noise resembled a waterfall as the copper boiler was emptied into the bathtub. Open, shut, open, shut went the drawers on the old chest until the third open, which was where she had put the two towels Mrs. Belden sent over. Finally it shut too. Then her bedroom door opened and once more she was scooped up into his powerful arms. He still did not say a word, and Philippa was too aghast to speak as he took her back to the kitchen and sat her on a chair he had pulled over by the tub. He watched for a minute to make sure she had regained enough strength to sit. Content that she could, he went back out the door with a final slam. Minutes later she heard his team and wagon taking off down the road at a fast pace.

Slowly Philippa managed to get out of her clothes and into the tub of water. It felt heavenly to soak in such nice warm water. She scooted down into the tub so the warmth could reach every possible aching muscle. After allowing herself the luxury of relaxing several minutes, she soaped her hair and rinsed off before the water got too cold. Somehow she managed to drag herself to the bucket of water on the worktable and pour a little into a fruit jar, to which she added some vinegar, then she painfully knelt back over the bathtub and poured the rinse over her hair to cut the soap and leave it shining. After tying a makeshift bandage over her leg, she put on her gown and wrapper.

Too tired to make an omelette with the crated eggs on the shelf, she merely sliced a large piece of bread and put the rest of the jar of jelly on it. The crock of butter was down in the well now, too, and as much as she wished for butter on her bread and a nice cool glass of milk to drink with her meal, she knew she was too weak to make the trip out to the well. Reluctantly she decided she would just lie down until she felt better. Later she would get up, empty her bath water, milk the cow, and, most importantly, attempt the impossible task of making her dress look respectable enough to wear to town. Once again she fell into an exhausted slumber.

The doctor's buggy pulled into Philippa's sickled lane and around to the back of her house. Dr. Eberle climbed down, black bag in hand, and went to the door. He knocked a couple of times but got no answer, so he opened the screen enough to knock on the inside door and yelled, "Anybody home? It's Doc!" Still he received no answer. He looked around the farmyard but saw no sign of anyone. Ryan said the girl had fainted from the heat and had lost a lot of blood from a surface gash on her leg. Could she be unconscious in there?

He was banging on the door very hard when Ryan's wagon pulled up, loaded with the teacher's trunks. Doc had heard Murphy had fast horses. Now he believed it. Ryan had picked up the new schoolmarm's baggage after Doc had left town, and he still pulled into her driveway only minutes after Doc himself had arrived, and he was pulling a heavy farm wagon. Doc hadn't spared Nell, either, in spite of the heat.

"I can't rouse her, Ryan." Doc's voice was anxious. "I think we'd better break in. She may have fainted or had a relapse from the heat."

"Doubt that. She just thinks it's me and won't open the door."

"No, I told her it was me, and—hey, this door isn't locked." Dr. Eberle stuck his head inside and called once more, "It's Doc. I'm here to have a look at that leg."

There was still no answer. Without hesitation, Ryan stepped in front of Doc and rushed in. She could have passed out in the water and drowned! Why had he ever left her alone? Relieved to note the tub was empty, he walked warily to the bedroom door and rapped softly as he said in a pleading voice, "Ma'am, I've brought the doctor to tend to your cut. Ma'am?" There was still no answer, so he reluctantly pushed open the door and surveyed the room. Their patient was lying perfectly still on that terrible bed. Her skin was very red against the white sheets and white nightgown, and her unbraided hair was splayed all over the pillow, shining like golden straw as the last rays of the afternoon sun beamed through the narrow window. She looked like an angel, he thought, a stab of conscience pricking him for staring at her this way when she was in her nightdress, but she was so still, it alarmed him.

Dr. Eberle pushed Ryan to one side and ambled to the bed, prattling to himself in his gruff voice. He sat on the edge of the bed and examined Philippa, saying, "Lord, it's hot in here! I still don't see why Horace let her live in this run-down old place. It's even worse than I remembered. Belden came into the hardware store and told Vernon she insisted on it, and since she couldn't ride a horse, he and Alvena had finally agreed to let her stay here. Something about her not wanting to go back and starve with the rest of the immigrants."

"That's a bunch of hogwash, Doc," Ryan interjected. "This girl is no more an immigrant than you or I. In fact, I think she comes from wealthy folks. She lost her pa, so she took up teaching school. I offered to teach her how to ride, so that wasn't it. Nope, it was just Alvena. Well, take a look at her for yourself."

Doc chortled and agreed, "I don't think Alvena needed to worry about this one taking a second look at Horace. Why, a little beauty like her will have her choice of every unmarried buck within fifty miles of here once the word about District Number Three's schoolmarm gets around."

Doc kept rambling as he pulled his spectacles down on his nose to take a closer look at her leg.

"Nasty cut, all right. It's good you came in for me. Wouldn't want it to get infected. If anything happened to her, the single fellows hereabouts would probably form a vigilante posse and string me up to the nearest tree. Lucky you seem to be first in line, boy!"

The garrulous doctor administered treatment to Philippa as he continued. "She sure sleeps through anything. I know this stuff burns like all get out."

"She sleeps sound, all right," Ryan agreed. "I couldn't get her to wake up last night when I came to see if she was okay over here. But you're wrong about one thing though, Doc. I'm at the tail end of the line." Ryan ruefully thought to himself that Miss Marquette always seemed sweet and friendlylike until she eventually recalled she was dealing with a plain old cowpoke. Then she quickly put him in his place with that hoity-toity voice: "It was uncouth of you to swing me around." "Schoolteachers must always be dignified." "Riding horseback is not genteel." "A very generous offer, Mr. Murphy, but of course I can't accept." "I have myriad things to do." Things that *didn't* include the likes of Ryan Murphy!

Well, she'd put him in his place for the last time. From now on, he *was* going to stay far away from her, no matter what. Let all the other bachelors fight over her! At this last fragment of thought, he gritted his teeth with displeasure and told Dr. Eberle, "I'll get her trunks in, then milk the cow for her. Lock the door and just push the key back underneath it."

"Yes, I'll do that. And thanks for coming in to get me. She'll probably be fit as a fiddle by tomorrow. You young folks bounce back fast.

"Oh, and Ryan, I wouldn't count myself *too* far down the list if I were you. You're a handsome devil and a big landowner around here."

But she's a *schoolmarm*, Ryan silently added before saying, "Night, Doc. Thanks for coming."

When she awoke the next morning, Philippa could not believe she had slept straight through the night. Why wasn't her cow bellowing? she wondered. Looking out the window, she saw the shed door latched and the chicken pen gate blocked shut. Mr. Murphy must have come back and milked and closed in the chickens after she fell asleep.

Turning over to stretch her legs, she spied her trunks and with a joyous exclamation started to jump out of bed to open them. The pain that shot through her leg when she took her first step reminded her of the cut. Pulling up her gown, she saw the neat bandage wrapped around her leg. Could Mr. Murphy have put it on her without waking her? He must have; he'd carried her trunks in.

Tingles ran through her body at the thought of her handsome neighbor bandaging her leg while she was asleep. She could almost feel the heat of his hands on it. He had done so very, very much for her and she had never been able to let him know how grateful she was to him. If only he didn't think she was such a stupid city girl!

Most of all, she wished she hadn't behaved so immodestly around him. Whatever had made her act so uncharacteristically? *Especially* when he had let her know by the way he had rejected her in the shed that he did not approve of such forwardness.

She resolved that in the future she would be very circumspect around him, so she could prove to him she was a respectable lady, and she'd show him she was not an incapable dolt, either! In the meantime she would find a way to repay him for all his kindnesses to her.

Chapter Six
✦✦✦✦

BLUFFSVIEW HAD BEEN established before the Midwest land boom of the 1880s. Because of its location, it had missed most of the rapid growth and prosperity that had so dramatically altered many nearby towns. Therefore, Nebraska's dry years of the nineties and the bypassing of Bluffsview by the railroad lines had left it practically unchanged since its original founding. Hawkins's General Merchandise Store was still its mecca, although the store was now in the capable hands of Samuel Jr., its second-generation owner. Vernon Timmons ran a hardware store next door and did the town's blacksmithing; nearby were a bank, a two-story brick schoolhouse, and two churches. A few professional men rented some offices over the bank. The feed and seed store marked the end of the business district at one end, and the saloon with the hotel above it, the other. The residences of Bluffsview's population were two blocks each way off of the main street. Only two houses, George Moore the banker's and Sam Hawkins's, were two stories tall.

As they pulled down the main street to Sam's store, Ole's team kicked up a lot of dust. Philippa wondered why the water wagon didn't go around more frequently to keep the dust under control. Could it be that they didn't have a huge, barrellike wooden spray tank here? She resolved not to ask. From now on she was going to learn everything quietly without asking questions or admitting her ignorance.

One thing that was certainly different about Bluffsview was the way people stared openly at passersby. Men were lined up along the fronts of buildings and on the wooden sidewalks, and every one of them was looking at Ole's wagon. Philippa took a peek at the back of it herself in an attempt to discern what made it so interesting.

Noticing her puzzled expression, Gertrude explained with her usual Swedish frankness, "Vell, it's plain to see Mr. Horace Belden's big mouth has told the whole countryside ve're bringing the new teacher in vith us this veek. They've all come over town t'get a look!"

"Yah! And not just the town folks are here. I've

vorked on threshing crews vith some of these men, fifteen, tventy miles away!" Ole chimed in.

"To see me?" Philippa was so surprised she forgot her resolution not to ask questions.

"Yah," both of them chucked in unison. Ole continued, "Ve have six, maybe eight unmarried men for every girl. An unmarried vun—vell, ven she is comely like you, Miss Philippa—oh, they'll be lookin' you over all vright!"

"I vager vun month, she has a proposal already," Gertrude pronounced to her husband, then turned to Philippa. "You look so fine today, dear. You vill truly turn their heads."

Philippa knew she should not be nervous; she certainly looked presentable in her russet gown with its ecru lace capelike collar. It had sleeves that were puffed stylishly full above the elbows and then pinched into tight cuffs down to the wrists. The skirt was closely gored at her slender waist but flared gradually to her ankles.

But she was worried, not because she was afraid she would not make a good impression, but because of what Mr. and Mrs. Olsen had said about the marriage-minded young men. It reminded her of the awful ceremony in Judge Timpton's office and of her grotesque husband.

Fearfully she began to wonder if one of these staring strangers might recognize her. By now Andrew must have given her description to lawmen throughout the country. The thought of being returned to him made her shudder. Did an unconsented marriage ceremony give Andrew legal rights over her? Could she be apprehended? She wished she knew more about the laws concerning a man and his spouse. She knew all of a woman's property became her husband's upon marriage, but did the woman, too? She remembered a piece of illicit information Dottie had told her and Lee Ann when they were children: that a marriage was not legal until it was consummated—and she'd brazenly informed them she knew consummated meant sleeping with a man. Heaven knew Philippa had never slept with Andrew, so surely she was not bound to him by law!

Growing more confident with each passing minute, Philippa felt her optimism return. Her conviction grew that she *was not legally married*. The certainty pleased her.

Perhaps she could have the wooing and courting she had dreamed of, after all. Both Lee Ann and Dottie had implied courtship would be very exciting. Yes, Philippa was thankful she had escaped Andrew and found a place he most assuredly would not find her—not in this small, off-the-map town under her new name. Providence had certainly blessed her.

Shyly she looked under her lashes at all the men on the front stoop of the store as she sat on the wagon. Was it her imagination, or could she feel the appreciation in their eyes? Irrationally she wondered if Mr. Murphy was among them and furtively hoped he was. It would be nice for once to have him see her in a clean dress with her hair all neatly in place.

Big Sam Hawkins himself came down the steps in front of his store to greet the Olsens. Knute and Gertrude had traded here for years and had never before received such distinction. Gertrude muttered so only Ole and Philippa could hear, "How old is little Sammy now?"

"Tventy-vun, tventy-two," Ole told her.

"Yah! No vunder his papa vants to greet us!"

"Ole! Gertrude! Good to see you!" boomed the voice of Sam Hawkins. "And this must be the new schoolteacher we've all heard so much about. The doc sure was right about you, ma'am. He told us you were a right attractive young lady." Sam guffawed with good humor as he reached his beefy hand up to assist Gertrude and Philippa from the wagon.

"Yah, she's the new teacher, Miss Marquette. Ma'am, this here's Mr. Samuel Hawkins, Jr. He runs the store here vere you vill be getting your supplies." Ole made the introductions.

Sam Hawkins kept hold of Philippa's arm after he helped her step down from the wagon seat. He led her up the steps, proclaiming jovially, "Here's somebody who couldn't even sleep last night after Doc Eberle told us about you 'cause he was so eager to meet you! Miss Marquette, this is m'boy, Sammy. Son, this is the new teacher from District Three you've been dyin' to meet."

The red-faced, bespectacled youth looked as if he would die of mortification long before he died from not meeting her, Philippa thought. From his astonished expression, he might never have heard of her or of Dr. Eberle. She had never heard of Dr. Eberle, either, and yet Mr. Hawkins kept implying the doctor had seen her. The doctor must have her mixed up with someone else, she decided as she hurried to put the boy at ease. His face had paled from livid red to ash white.

"How do you do, Mr. Hawkins. I am very pleased to meet you. Perhaps you would be so kind as to direct me to the grocery section of your father's store?"

"Oh, yes, ma'am!" Sammy exclaimed. No one had ever before referred to him as "Mr. Hawkins." And this beautiful creature had said it in front of all these people! For this plaudit he would gladly give her the whole grocery section if she desired it. He opened the screen door extra wide for her while Big Sam stood back, beaming.

Several men who had also been waiting on the porch were not nearly as shy as young Hawkins. They weren't about to stand idle while Sammy whisked away this prize.

Calvin Lawrence was the first to step up to Philippa and introduce himself. Hamilton Fields and Jasper Clough were close behind him. They quickly stepped between Philippa and her would-be escort.

Jasper Clough stood head and shoulders above everyone else. He must be over six and a half feet tall, Philippa surmised. He had the palest blond hair she had ever seen and the bluest eyes. His eyes seemed to twinkle with amusement at her discomfiture as he asked, "Do you want to know what my mama fed me to make me grow, or do you just want to know what the weather's like up here?"

"She's not going to ask you either of those stupid, worn-out questions everybody else asks you, Clough, because she could not care less. Now that she's met me, the rest of you may as well run along home. Her eyes will only be for the estimable Mr. Lawrence!" Calvin took her arm in a very exaggerated manner and led her into the dim interior of the store as he continued, "Allow me to introduce you to our local grocery store. Also the dry goods store, the shoe-repair shop, the catalog order mercantile, and the drug and sundry emporium, alias Sam Hawkins's place. Just present me with your list and I shall endeavor to fill your order for you. In fact, I'll fill any orders you give me, ma'am!"

Philippa was enthralled by these two teasing, bantering men, and her eyes sparkled as she looked from one to the other. Although, she was not used to any sort of teasing, their good-naturedness delighted her. Then she was drawn to look into the dark eyes of Hamilton Fields. His eyes were a much darker brown than hers—in fact, they were almost black—but they were serious, intent. His hair was black and his mustache was full and luxuriant. Even though he was not much taller than she was, he had broad shoulders and narrow hips, truly a handsome man.

She quickly looked back to Mr. Lawrence. He was taller but lean and spare, with hair that was a nondescript brown. His eyes might be blue with brown flecks; she couldn't be quite sure. What he lacked in handsomeness, though, he made up for by his confident personality. He was now telling her, "You will never know, Miss Marquette, how lucky you were the day fate decreed you be a schoolmarm in Bluffsview, Nebraska!"

"Oh, yes, I agree the stars must have been in my favor that day!" Philippa said, thinking how fortunate she had been to have the Fitch agency help in her escape from Andrew.

"Only because the stars could see the lonesome Jasper Clough was out here at the end of nowhere, just waiting for a dream to come true. That's why the fates sent you here. They're great at matching up dreams," Mr. Clough told her with mock seriousness.

Before she could answer, Calvin was rebuking his compatriot, "Give a listen to that 'star-crossed lovers' tripe! Always trying to impress everybody with that poetry stuff! Well, I warn you, Miss Marquette is a very discriminating lady. I can tell by looking at her. She won't want any part of a poem-spouting lawyer. Now, a congenial feed and grain store owner would be ideal for her."

"Come, Miss Marquette." Hamilton Fields held

out his hand. "We aren't all overzealous barbarians here. Perhaps we really should find the things on that list you are holding so tightly."

He separated Philippa's fingers from the wrinkled piece of paper and tried to straighten it out before handing it to the clerk. Sammy had stood without saying a word through the entire encounter with Philippa's would-be beaux.

"Perhaps you can help us, lad." Hamilton smiled.

Lad. Sammy took the list and clomped over to the grocery shelves. Big Sam was waiting there, hands on hips, wishing his son had half the flair of his local adversaries. The boy would never win the hand of any eligible young lady if he didn't exert himself a little. Sam himself had married a lovely young French teacher who had come from New Orleans to Bluffsview High School twenty-three years ago. His fondest wish was for his son to follow in his footsteps and marry the girl everyone else in town had their eyes on.

The only drawback to Sam's marriage was that Babette wasn't happy in Bluffsview. She'd always wanted him to take her back to New Orleans. He had managed to keep her reasonably content by building her the biggest house in town and constantly buying her newfangled things.

This girl looked softer, more tenderhearted. She might not be as unreasonable and mercenary, Sam reasoned. If she wasn't, she would do nicely for Sammy. However, the boy was going to need some help, he could see that, so he pitched in. "We Hawkinses always aim to please, ma'am. We'll have everything on your list boxed up for you in no time. What's first there, son?"

"Lemons, Dad."

"Lemons? We don't carry lemons, Miss Marquette. We get a few in cold weather, around Christmas. What's next?"

"Pork chops, roast beef, and chicken."

Sam Hawkins shook his head. How could he keep meat fresh here in the store in this heat? The place would smell rancid before the day was over. "I don't know where you've been doing your shopping, Miss Marquette, but we can't stock fresh meat."

"Where do people get their meat here?" Philippa asked, forgetting her stern resolution not to ask questions. She was already getting tired of eggs at every meal, and had made up a list from her Hansen–Tawzer culinary cooking class recipe book.

"Why, they butcher when it's cooler. This time of year they eat a lot of chickens and smoked hams or beef they've cold-packed. A few have ice caves they can keep fresh meat in year round. Where do you come from that you put meat on the staples list?"

Philippa felt embarrassed, and everyone was waiting for her answer. She hoped no one here was from Cincinnati and that they did things there as they did in St. Louis. "I come from Ohio. Cincinnati, Ohio. We had meat markets where a butcher went into the ice house behind his store and cut the meat we wanted on hot days. In cooler weather he just had it in a meat case and we picked out chops or roasts."

Trying to change the subject, she asked, "Do you carry fresh produce here? I need some fruits and vegetables."

Sam was getting more than a little aggravated with this girl. He wasn't at all sure someone who discredited the family business this way would be an asset to his son, after all. "People raise it in their own gardens around here.

"Give me that list, Sammy. I'll pack up anything we have that's on it." Grabbing the list, he shoved a box to the center of the counter, which he began to fill.

This left his son standing idle, trying to apologize. "I expect you'll find a lot of things different out here, miss."

"Yes," Philippa agreed. "Things are very different."

"And much better," Calvin added. "Next Saturday is the Grange Dance. That will give you a chance to see how much better it really is. May I escort you to it, Miss Marquette?"

"He can't dance a lick, ma'am. You'd better go with me," Jasper Clough told her.

"Jasper, you big lummox, I can dance circles around you!"

While the two of them argued, Hamilton Fields stepped up beside her and suggested, "Until you know us all a little better, maybe you'd rather just ride over to the dance with the Olsens. They always come. They attend the Methodist Episcopal church, too. I'd like to invite you to come to services tomorrow with them, unless you plan to go to the Lutheran church with the Beldens."

"No! I mean, I want to come with the Olsens," Philippa quickly assured him. "That is, if they don't mind."

Gertrude, patiently waiting nearby, agreeably insisted they had already planned on it. Things here were going about as she had expected them to. At the Grange Dance, Miss Marquette would be even more besieged by would-be suitors, but for now, Philippa looked a little overwhelmed, so she suggested, "Ve had best get the rolls of vallpaper and oilcloth ordered ve talked about. The catalog is back here."

Philippa welcomed the diversion. While it was very flattering to have all these men talking to her and flirting with her, it made her apprehensive. She had not grown up in the constant presence of men, and she did not know what to do or say. If only she were clever and witty like her flirtatious friend, Dottie Marshal, or smilingly coy and self-assured like Lee Ann Narin, but instead she was the wary and tongue-tied Philippa Martin/ Marquette. Mr. Murphy was the only man she had met so far whose mere presence did not intimidate her, but then, in front of him she was always embarrassing herself, she recalled miserably.

Oh, dear! Was that coquettish creature she turned into around him her true self? Surely not! She quickly picked out wallpaper, oilcloth, curtain material, and a new roll of linoleum for the floor to distract her mind from these disturbing ideas. For the remainder of her shopping expedition, her mind was solely on her purchases, hoping their cost would not deplete her finances too much.

They arrived back at Philippa's after dusk. It had taken Ole a long time to pick up the mail and load Belden's feed onto the wagon to bring back, because so many people stopped him to visit and to be introduced to his passenger. It was not too dark, however, to see that every weed had been mowed around Philippa's house. They had all been raked up and a fire was still smoldering where they had been burned. Even the cow was in the shed with the door latched, which meant she had been milked and the gate to the chicken pen was closed.

Philippa's heart soared. He had done all this for her! She wanted to go and thank him, but there were no lamps lit at Mr. Murphy's house. Ole told Philippa that Ryan always went into town on Saturday nights. Unreasonably disappointed at this piece of news, Philippa thanked Gertrude and Ole for taking her with them as he carried her box of supplies inside. Then the Olsens went home to do their own evening chores.

As Philippa took off her dress that evening, she felt a twinge of disappointment that Mr. Murphy had not seen it. Somehow the house seemed much more deserted and lonely tonight, knowing there was no one across the road. Unfortunately Philippa was not exhausted enough to fall asleep amid the creaks and muffled noises her house resounded with. In addition, her trip to town had given her too much to think about.

She tried to decide whom she liked the best: the shy young grocer, Sammy Hawkins; the tall, blond good-looking lawyer, Jasper Clough; the fun-loving owner of the feed and grain store, Calvin Lawrence; or the extremely handsome and mannerly Hamilton Fields. He hadn't told her what his occupation was. He was probably a farmer. He seemed so kind and caring and serious, like Ryan Murphy, who was also a farmer of sorts. Serious and yet fun-loving, the way he smiled so frequently. Even the memory of Ryan's smile warmed her.

She still could not believe that he had spent his entire day cutting the weeds for her, and almost wished she had stayed home so she could have watched. Perhaps he would have stopped and talked to her and she could have tried to thank him for everything he had done for her. Just thinking of him made her ache very strangely.

Why hadn't any of the men today made her feel that way? None of them acted as if they would reject her as Mr. Murphy had. Of course, she certainly would never do foolish things around them. Only around Ryan Murphy did she seem to forget all about her staid upbringing.

Finally she heard his horse galloping down the road and listened as it turned into his yard. At last she was able to drift into sleep.

Chapter Seven

✦✦✦✦

RYAN HAD GONE into town to get rip-roaring drunk. He had planned to drink so much that he would come home and fall into bed in a drunken stupor. Tomorrow's hangover would be worth it just to get a good night's sleep.

This morning, Ryan had watched the Olsens take Philippa Marquette into town. He had seen her climb daintily up onto the high wagon seat wearing her fancy dress. It was some sort of a whiskey brown color that brought out all the gold nugget sparkle in her perfectly arranged hair. She had sat so prim and ladylike on that seat, clinging to her pocketbook with both hands, that he had watched, fascinated, until she was out of sight.

Then he had hitched up his team to the flat wooden mower with its crosswise blade and gone over to her place to cut down every weed in sight. After that, he had come back and put the team to the high, curved rake. He'd piled the weeds and burned them. He'd even pulled the crumbling porch roof off with his team, laid the posts behind the cow shed, and burned what was left of its shingles. He decided the house looked better without it. He did her chores, as well as his own, before diving into the creek that ran through his pasture to wash up. Then he'd put on his clean clothes and headed for town.

He had arrived just in time to see Philippa being gently assisted into Ole's wagon by Jasper Clough while Hamilton Fields and Calvin Lawrence doffed their hats respectfully to her as they wished her good day. As far as Ryan could tell, young Hawkins was falling all over himself to get her attention, while at least a dozen other men were hanging around Hawkins's store gawking.

Ryan thought highly of Clough, who had represented him in some land-boundary legal matters, and he'd always felt Lawrence was fair and square in their feed dealings. He didn't know young Hawkins or Fields, but tonight he hated all of them equally. Them and all the others in the saloon this evening who couldn't talk of anything but the beautiful new schoolmarm. He'd made up his mind he'd punch the first one who made a ribald joke or remark about her. He was waiting to pummel somebody—anybody!

But there had been no jokes. Men didn't make those types of comments about a *lady*. And Philippa was a lady, a lady who made marriage foremost on the bachelors' minds.

Ryan had drunk until he shouldn't have been able to stand up; still, his mind wasn't numb. When he'd thought of how far her place was from any other farms and how vulnerable she was out there alone, he'd stormed savagely out of the tavern and come home early. Come home only to toss and turn in his bed once more.

Oh, she was going to have her choice of men, all right. Educated men such as lawyers and merchants. He'd expected that, hadn't he? Then why in the hell did it bother him like this? He recalled the way she'd felt as he held her by the well—remembering clearly how he hadn't been wearing a shirt and her unbuttoned blouse had been all wet . . .

Dammit!

Back out of his house he tromped, not even bothering to shrug on his jeans or light a lantern. He cut across the corner of his pasture and jumped into the creek. He swam fiercely for several minutes until exertion and all the whiskey he had drunk caught up with him. The combination relaxed him as he hadn't been relaxed for days. In fact, he hadn't felt so good for a long, long time.

He floundered to the bank and eventually managed to climb out awkwardly after three or four attempts to grab hold of a branch failed. He staggered toward the farmyard singing at the top of his lungs, singing the yodeling songs the cowboys always crooned back home when they moved the herd or rode night watch at roundup. The night seemed friendlier now, more peaceful. It was so nice outside he decided to cool off in the old hammock in the front yard for a while. He tumbled into it and started it swinging back and forth, continuing his concert.

That wretched chicken! Philippa silently cursed. It was up earlier than ever and making a much worse noise. No, that couldn't be the chicken. It had to be the cow. Whatever was wrong with the dratted thing now? Sleepily she put her head closer to the window screen to listen.

It was not the cow, but a very human noise, and it was coming from Mr. Murphy's house. Merciful saints! He must be hurt! Philippa hurriedly put on her wrapper and unlocked the kitchen door, wishing as she ran that she had taken time to put on shoes. The freshly cut weed stalks were very sharp on the bottoms of her feet, but she would not go back for them. This was her chance to go to Mr. Murphy's aid as he had come to hers so many times.

As she crossed the road and went through his gate, she hoped she would know what to do for him. It sounded as if the agonized groans were coming from the yard, not the house. Maybe his great beast of a horse had thrown him.

There was a little moonlight, and her eyes had adjusted well enough by now that she could make out the swinging hammock at the corner of the house.

Rapidly she raced toward the moaning sounds of "Yip-e-i-o, Yip-e-i-ay." She stopped a split second before she reached the hammock. Good Lord in heaven—Mr. Murphy did not have a stitch of clothes on! It was very plain to see, the way the moonbeams were shining down between the branches of the two trees. Perhaps he was burning up with fever!

For a moment Philippa just stared, fascinated at her first sight of a naked man, but then she remembered she had come to help him. What, oh what could she do? His eyes seemed to be closed now and the cries of anguish had stopped.

For once Philippa swore to remember Decency, Decorum, and Dignity, although it was difficult to adhere to such tenets at a time like this. Before she could go closer and check his forehead for fever, she would have to cover him, but with what? Only her wrapper came to mind. Since she would still have on her heavy cotton nightgown, it seemed the most decent thing to do. She took it off hesitantly, then gently placed it over him, allowing her fingers to brush through the thick mat of soft hairs on his chest before she decorously felt his forehead. Relieved to find his skin cool to the touch, she gently lifted his arms, then his legs, looking for a sign that a bone was broken. At first she thought his leg was quivering a bit, then she realized it was only her own hands shaking as they held up this very interesting part of her patient's anatomy. Her whole body seemed to be engulfed with cold tremors. Cold tremors that made her feel warm—and guilty. She decided it was best not to examine further. Besides, now her patient looked rather peaceful, almost as if he had a smile on his face.

Tentatively she asked softly, "Mr. Murphy, are you in pain?" But there was no answer. If he had been thrown from his horse he wouldn't be here like this, would he? He must have had a touch of food poisoning, she decided, and the pain had caused him to wander outside. Maybe he had been feverish earlier and thrown off his . . . his . . . whatever men wore to sleep in. He was breathing in a rhythmic snore now.

Illogically she was tempted to lightly kiss his smiling lips good night, without waking him, of course, but she refrained and instead watched him as the back-and-forth, back-and-forth swing of the hammock slowly hypnotized her. As if in a trance she walked up beside him and gently tiptoed her fingers across his chest, mesmerized by the sensuous feel.

As she stood there daydreaming, Philippa was not prepared for strong arms that reached up and pulled her down across Ryan's naked body. Only her nightdress and thin wrapper separated them, and even then in the unexpected movement her own nightdress was hiked indecently high.

She hadn't even recovered from the fall or had a chance to exclaim when warm, moist lips sought out her own waiting ones. Her daydreaming had been too filled with yearning as she brushed the hairs on his muscular chest to resist his demanding kiss. She felt no qualms when the kiss became deeper, more insistent. After a few moments, Philippa opened her eyes to look deeply into Ryan's, but his were *closed. Tightly closed!*

"Ryan," she spoke softly, drawing herself away. "Ryan!" She shook him gently.

But his eyes never opened—the insolent cur was sound asleep!

He had given her the kind of kisses she'd always yearned for, and it was so common to him he'd done it without even waking up! She quickly disentangled herself from his arms and her awkward position lying across the hammock, to stand beside it once again.

In anger she pulled back her hand to slap him for his rudeness. Then she recalled she was the one who had incited *him*. Besides, how would she explain the slap . . . or anything else to him, if she woke him? Angrily she ran through the stubble back to her own dark house, hating herself . . . and maybe Ryan Murphy too.

Ryan felt like hell when the first rays of dawn woke him. The dawn and that damn rooster across the road! He pushed his hands up to press his aching temples as hard as he could and uncurled his long legs, which prickled with cramps from sleeping in this too-short hammock. When he started to swing out of it, a flimsy piece of fabric fell off him to the ground. His head ached unmercifully as he bent to pick it up and examine it. What the hell—a lady's pink-flowered wrapper! A wrapper just like the one he had seen hanging on a hook in the schoolmarm's bedroom the night he had carried her trunks in for her!

Damn! What had he done before he'd passed out last night? The last thing he remembered was diving into the creek to cool down.

He looked up from the wrapper to the house across the street. There she was, out throwing rocks at that rooster, as usual, and he was standing naked in the middle of his yard. He dashed into the house, wondering if she had seen him and wondering again just what he had done last night. How had he got this wrapper and how could he get it back to her? He was pretty sure he hadn't actually done anything wrong. His body still felt an urgent need at the thought of Philippa Marquette.

The Bluffsview Methodist Episcopalian Church was already crowded when Ole, Gertrude, and Philippa drove up to the hitching rail.

"Gonna have to tie the team to the picket fence today, I reckon," Ole remarked, looking for a place to pull up with his wagon. "Never saw a crowd like this exceptin' maybe ven there's an ice cream social or somet'in'."

Children crowded around the Olsens' wagon and gaped up at Philippa. Some of them were smiling shyly, and Philippa smiled back at them, anxious to become acquainted with each of them, especially the ones who would be attending Rural District No. 3.

However, she was not given the opportunity. The minute she stepped to the ground, Jasper took one of her arms and Calvin the other, greeting her good-naturedly and speeding her toward the door of the church.

Sammy Hawkins dogged their footsteps after a nudge from his father, while the stylishly gowned lady standing beside Big Sam assessed Philippa from head to toe. Many of the other ladies who were standing in the shade of the building studied her just as intently. Since it was summer, no one went into the hot, airless church until the last possible minute. Some of the ladies wore neat, unfaded calico dresses as Gertrude did, while others looked as if they might perish in warm gabardine or heavy serge dresses, probably their one good dress.

"A lovely treat for the eyes, that's what you are, Miss Marquette," Calvin pronounced.

Jasper was not to be outdone. "This county—no, this whole state—has never beheld such a fair damsel!" He bent closer to her ear and whispered, "I think you should know you have smitten the town's most eligible bachelor!"

"Yeah," Calvin hurriedly assured her, "me!"

"You! You'd be considered eligible only by a rodent that would like to feast in your grain bins!"

"Ha! At least I don't have to constantly shoo birds out of my hair that think they've found straw already in a tree for a nest!"

Philippa could not help quietly laughing at these two. She wished she could think of a clever rejoinder, but she could only reply politely, "Please, gentlemen, I thank you for the compliments, but you must not ridicule one another."

"Why not?" a disgusted voice echoed from behind them. "They're tellin' the truth."

Philippa turned to face the panting young grocer who had been trying to keep up with the fast pace the others had maintained. When he had Philippa's attention, he added, "My family would be proud to have you sit in the front pew with us this morning, ma'am. It's our regular pew—"

"My sister has already gone on into that stuffy church to hold places for Miss Marquette and myself," Jasper interjected, trying to turn Philippa back around.

Calvin informed them, "My mother wants Miss Marquette to join us and then come to dinner after the service."

"—but my father said she would prefer the front row!"

"He's wrong. She's eager to meet my sister."

"Both of you are wrong. It is only fitting she sits with Mother and me, since she is joining us afterward."

Deportment class to the rescue, Philippa thought. She knew a lady should resolve this situation either by sitting with all three gentlemen, sitting with the one who had asked her first, or sitting with none of them. Eeny-meeny-miney-moe!

Hamilton Fields stepped in to rescue her. He looked even more handsome today in his black frock coat, vest, and trousers, with his wide white clerical collar. Why, he was the minister!

His black eyes glittered as he saw the surprised expression on her face. He greeted her by taking her right hand in both of his, and she could feel the warmth of his palms through her white silk glove. "Good morning, Miss Marquette. Welcome to my church. With your permission, I have placed a guest's chair in the front by a window. Would you be so kind as to sit there? Then, while all the congregation stare intently at you, I can pretend I have their undivided attention during my sermon. The topic is 'Love Thy Neighbor,' which I believe will please them, don't you?''

"Oh, yes. 'Love Thy Neighbor' is an excellent choice," Philippa assented, trying not to think of Ryan Murphy. She quickly turned her eyes and her thoughts back to Reverend Fields, flushing slightly when she saw him looking at her. She felt as if he might have read her mind. She began to stammer, "I . . . I can sit in front if you wish me to, but I do not understand the furor over a new teacher."

"Not only a teacher, a lovely, *unmarried* young lady," the reverend told her, his eyes still twinkling. "Most of the children in Rural District Number Three have never had a woman teacher before. They're very taken by the idea."

"Amen!" pronounced Calvin, and Jasper did not dispute him for once. "Yes—Ay-men!" he agreed.

At the end of the service, Pastor Fields stepped down from the pulpit to where Philippa stood and said, "I could drive you home in my buggy and resolve your dilemma of whose guest to be for dinner today, if you wish."

"Yes, I'd like that very much. I can't accept these invitations when I barely know these people! Also, it will save Mr. and Mrs. Olsen from driving out of their way to take me."

"Splendid! I shall wish my flock God's care for the week and then I'll be with you." He stood at the front door and shook hands with everyone, encouraging them to come back again.

Jasper Clough and Calvin Lawrence had also driven their buggies the short distance to the church, and Sammy Hawkins had his parents' roof-shaded surrey. All of them had made plans for the new teacher, so she was glad to have a plausible excuse for declining their invitations. She thanked each for his kind offer, but told them she had lessons to prepare for the first day of school tomorrow. Little faces beamed all around her. Strange, Philippa thought as she recalled how she, Lee Ann, and Dottie had dreaded the start of the school year. This might be a good omen if her pupils looked forward to its beginning.

It was pleasant riding in a well-sprung buggy again after a farm wagon, a train coach, and horseback. Hamilton laughed when she told him so, saying, "I had the feeling this was all quite new to you. Where is it you come from?"

Did one lie to ministers? Would it be a deadly sin? She hesitantly told him, "Back east," and quickly tried to change the subject. "I have never taught school before, and I am very pleased because the children seem quite happy school is to begin for the year."

"They get out of a lot of work during school hours. After a summer of hoeing weeds, picking fruit and vegetables, and any number of other chores, school is a welcome vacation."

"Oh!" Her disappointment was obvious in her crestfallen expression.

Reverend Fields hurried to give her back her confidence. "The fact that the teacher is young and pretty helps a great deal, too. I don't recall that they were very eager to go back to the strict Alexander last year, and none of our students who will attend town school want it to start."

"Why ever not, if they get out of so much work?"

"Sometimes work is still preferable. Miss Penelope, Miss Grace, and the long-widowed Mrs. Trafalgar have passed over the hill, so to speak. They are too old to teach but not old enough to retire. They complain, nitpick, and lay on a lot of unnecessary rules and disciplinary procedures. The truth is, they bully the children."

"Bully the children! Sir, you do not sound like a minister at all! But," she hurried to add, "you do when you are in the pulpit. I was in awe of you."

"I never want you to be in awe of me, Miss Marquette," he told her in a soft voice. "I am a man, you know, not a celestial being."

Once again Philippa found herself blushing and did not know what to say. Hamilton quickly sought to put her at ease by talking about something else. "I think you should be aware that personal relations move much faster here than . . . back east. All manner of relations. You will know all your students very well after only a few days. It is not considered improper for you to go to families' homes for meals on very brief acquaintance. I can only caution you to try and keep tight rein on your emotions. Courtship should always be given enough time to mature naturally. True love may arise instantly, but so can infatuation. It is very important to wait until you're sure of the difference. There will be any number of hopeful swains trying to rush you into marriage."

Philippa appreciated his plainspokenness. They had pulled up to her back door as he finished the sentence, and he stepped down to help her out. He held on to her arm until they reached the door. Then he stepped forward and pulled open the screen for her.

A flimsy, pink-flowered piece of fabric fell out from where it had been stashed between the screen and the inside door. Red-faced, Philippa scooped it up so fast Hamilton was unable to make out what it was at all. She stuffed it under her arm and murmured in embarrassment, "Thank you very much for driving me home, Reverend Fields."

"Hamilton, please, and the pleasure was all mine, Miss Philippa," he told her, trying to look into her eyes. She avoided meeting his by lowering her lashes and then turning her head to put her key in the lock so he could not see her flaming face. They both said "Good day," he reluctantly, she with blessed relief. What must he be thinking? The pastor, finding her wrapper stuffed in the door this way!

Chapter Eight

✦✦✦✦

RYAN WATCHED DISGUSTEDLY from his front window as the shiny black buggy with the pure white horse turned into Philippa's driveway. He watched the handsome young pastor jump out with athletic grace and assist Miss Marquette gallantly by taking one of her daintily gloved hands in his own. He did not take his hand off her, either. He very gentlemanly assisted her to her back door by holding her arm oh, so correctly. They vanished from sight behind her house, and Ryan just stood there envisioning the teacher asking the pastor in to . . . to tea, maybe?

He wished he hadn't mowed the weeds. Then when Fields had climbed down he would have been covered with cockleburs from the thickets in that backyard! Weren't ministers supposed to be celibate or something? How come this one was courting Philippa Marquette? No, he recalled, that was priests. His ma had told him a little about religion, and a priest had usually made it out to their spread to celebrate mass once a year, but after his ma had died the visits had dwindled, and he couldn't recall the last time he'd seen one. He didn't even suppose he was properly a Catholic anymore. Around these parts, it was better to downplay coming from a Catholic family anyway.

He glared back at the house across the road. Protestant pastors married just like anybody else. This one wasn't like just anybody else, though. He was handsome and agile and mannerly, and probably well educated.

Angry at himself for staring out the window like a schoolboy, Ryan turned to go back to the kitchen. He looked in on the roast beef he was baking and was starting to mix some biscuits when he heard the buggy leave. Inadvertently he heaved a sigh of relief as he watched it top the hill from his kitchen window. She hadn't had the pastor in to tea. His relief dimmed as he recalled that decrepit house she lived in. Of course, a lady like her would not ask anyone inside a hovel like that.

The sudden, unexpected knock surprised him. He'd never had anyone come to the front door since he'd lived here.

As he walked toward the front, the pane of glass in the upper half of the door, which was covered by one of his grandma's hand-crocheted lace curtains, revealed the teacher, pink-flowered wrapper in hand; and she looked madder 'n a hornet. Damn! He must have done something inexcusable last night.

Slowly he opened the door. It was just as well he hadn't thought of what to say; she wasn't going to give him a chance anyway.

Without preamble she began her attack. "How dare you? How could anyone be so low and vile? And after all I went through for you last night, too. I tried to be good to you because you've done so many nice things for me. I wanted to repay you, and this . . . this is what I get in return!" She was waving the flimsy pink thing at him.

Low? Vile? All she went through? She had only been trying to repay him? He remembered how sweetly innocent her kisses in the barn and under the walnut tree had been. Had she given him one of those beautiful, sweet kisses and he had . . . had what? How *had* he gotten the wrapper?

Once again she didn't wait for him to say anything. "Can you imagine my chagrin when I opened my door and this . . . this wrapper falls out at the feet of the pastor! What must he think of me? What possible reason could one have for such a thing? He probably suspects I'm a . . . a loose woman. And he was so nice to me, too!"

Ryan hated his thoughts, hated the plaintive tone of her last words, but since he didn't recall anything he didn't know how to defend himself or console her. All he could do was try to put her on the defensive, instead of himself, so he growled, "Now wait a darn minute! What was your wrapper doing on *me* this morning, anyhow?"

He watched as her cheeks flushed a very becoming color of rosy pink. Then she took a deep gulp as if finally at a loss for words.

Pushing his hoped-for advantage, he asked, "Well?"

"Well," she repeated meekly. "You see . . . I

mean . . ." Then she stopped and bit her lip. The action must have revived her ire, for she resumed spunkily, "Mr. Murphy, you put me in the most embarrassing of positions last night. Why, I've never been so humiliated in my life. Don't you remember anything?"

"No, ma'am," he confessed. "I don't."

And he didn't even sound contrite, Philippa noticed, a little disappointed that he hadn't even remembered. "You, sir," she snipped, "were ill. Quite ill, in fact, unless you have a habit of moaning piteously over a mere stomachache."

"Moaning? Piteously? Me?"

"Yes, you. You sounded in dire need of help . . . in the middle of the night. I ran through the stubble, barefooted, to assist you, only to find you . . ." She couldn't go on.

She didn't have to. Ryan knew exactly how she had found him, dead-drunk in the hammock without so much as jeans on. He almost laughed at the thought of her maidenly shock. He had to quickly turn his head so she wouldn't see his smile as he managed to say, "So you discovered I was lying in my hammock, quite ill. That still doesn't explain your robe, does it?"

"Mr. Murphy! As you probably already know, you were . . . you didn't . . . Why, you were in the altogether! I had to cover you before I could see if you had been thrown from your horse and broken any bones or if you were feverish. Why, I was the epitome of propriety," she insisted, relieved he didn't remember anything and that she didn't have to admit to running her finger sensuously across his chest or her reaction to his sleep-induced kisses.

"So," he continued to push, "you thoroughly

examined me from head to toe and found me to be suffering from only a bellyache?"

"That must have been it. You weren't feverish and you obviously have no broken bones."

"Quite obviously. I am only upset because I wasn't awake for the examination. I might have found it quite . . . pleasant."

"You dolt! Why do you always have to make me seem . . . I mean you have a penchant for . . . Well, really, sir, I am not in the habit of kissing strangers in sheds or . . . or I certainly don't go out seeking men without a stitch of clothing on so I can examine them . . ."

"You found it distasteful, then?"

"No. I mean *yes!* Yes, very! I am not what you think me, a . . . a coquette or something!"

Her voice sounded too upset now, so Ryan changed to a quieter voice. "I've never thought any such thing, ma'am. I have the highest regard for you."

Relieved, she quickly asked the last question to which she needed an answer: his opinion of her inadequacy as a country girl.

"You don't consider me too stupid, do you?"

"Oh, you've done some stupid things, all right, I'll grant you that!" Undeniably relieved, Ryan was once again his usual teasing self.

When Philippa heard the hint of teasing disdain in his voice, she immediately put up her own defenses. "I may have done some stupid things in the past, but I have now come to terms with the differences between life here and in Sai—Cincinnati. You'll see! I will cope very well in the future."

There she goes again, Ryan thought with a wince, in that highbrow voice! Well, he would just tell her to git again. That would fix her wagon.

But before he could speak, she was asking in her

own soft, husky voice, "What is that delicious aroma?"

Ryan inhaled deeply. It was her. That flowery perfume she wore.

She went on. "It smells like a beef roast."

"Oh, that! Yeah, it's a roast."

"Roast! Where did you get it? They don't sell any meat at all in town."

"Jake Radcliff has an ice cave. He lets me keep beef in it in exchange for some of the meat. I rode over this mornin' and picked up a big rib roast. I'll bake it today, then it'll keep all week in a covered crock in the well. I just slice off a hunk to fry for breakfast or supper."

"Oh, I see," Philippa said winsomely, sounding like the starved little waif from the city the Olsens had told him she was.

"Want to stay and eat with me? I'd be right proud to have you," Ryan asked skeptically, afraid he'd be rebuffed and informed it wasn't at all proper.

It wasn't, of course, but Philippa was not going to stand on propriety way out here, especially when the minister had told her it was not considered improper and when roast of beef was offered. She disregarded Reverend Fields's stipulated "families."

With delight she exclaimed, "Oh, I'd love it! I'll go back and get a jar of fruit and some vegetables to go with it that Mrs. Olsen packed."

"That sounds real good. I'm gettin' pretty sick of biscuits and gravy."

They both enjoyed their meal immensely. It seemed easy to talk to each other as they were preparing the food and eating. After the kitchen was cleaned up, Philippa knew she should leave, but

Ryan came up with a perfect reason to keep her longer.

"Are you ready for your first ridin' lesson now, ma'am? Even though you ain't staying at Beldens' and can easily get to and from the school, I still think you should learn to ride and to drive a team, too."

"Do you think I could—learn to drive a team, I mean?" Philippa was gratified she had a reason to stay, but she wasn't quite brave enough to venture up onto a horse alone. She would prefer a wagon seat, with Ryan beside her. "This dress is one of my new ones. I don't think I should ride horseback in it."

"Oh, no, ma'am, of course not. I'll hitch up the team."

"Do you have to call me ma'am? I feel fifty years old when you do!"

"What would you like me to call you—Miss Philippa?"

"Heavens, no! I'll probably hear enough of that from my students. Can't you just call me Philippa, or better yet, Pip? That's what my friends at home called me."

"Pip . . . I like that. You're a pip, all right! If I agree, will you stop with the Mr. Murphy? I keep thinkin' my pa's been brought back from the grave. Ever'body calls me just plain Murphy, or Ryan."

"I like the name Ryan. Is it Irish?"

"You bet. My granddaddy came over here in 1820 and Pa came west in the fifties.

"What's Marquette? French?"

"It is, but I'm not. I mean, my father's family was French a long time ago, but they lived in England for years before they came to America. He was born there. My mother was Dutch. I get my dark eyes from him and my light hair from my mother."

They were standing very close as they exchanged these confidences. Philippa wanted to move a little closer, but then she recalled how furious he'd gotten before when she acted so forward. She wasn't going to risk making him angry again. It was pleasant, having someone to talk to.

Ryan became quite brusque too as he reached behind her and opened the door, announcing, "We're off, then. Your first lesson is at hand." He reached back and grabbed both his wide-brimmed straw hats off the deer antlers hanging by the back door and handed her his good one, pronouncing, "No more overheating, Miss—Pip. Wear this!"

She hoped a hat would help. She did feel overheated walking side by side with him.

"You just wait here in the shade. I'll go on in the barn and get the horses." The memory of lying on the fresh hay in her shed brought a blush to her face. He must be afraid she would confront him with her fast behavior again. She determined to change his opinion if she had to act as proper and dignified as Aunt Clara Rose for the rest of her days. Instinctively she froze her voice and words into an imitation of her aunt's. "Why ever would you assume, *Mister* Murphy, that I would go into a smelly old barn if it wasn't absolutely necessary? I shall gladly remain here in the shade as you have ordered me to." Rebelliously she plunked her hat over the nearest fence post.

"Ordered you to!" he snapped, angered at her superior tone.

He didn't get a chance to say anything else, for as they stood there, hands on hips, eyes locked in combat, glowering, the sound of hooves echoed from the hilltop. They both looked toward the approaching horse and buggy.

It was Mr. Clough, Philippa realized disappointedly.

Hell, it's that lawyer, Ryan thought angrily. He wanted to continue this argument with the teacher because he wanted to tell her once and for all that if she kept on lighting into him, she could git on over to her side of the road and stay there. No matter how hard he tried to act like a gentleman, she always ended up putting him in his place by using that glacial voice. Down deep inside, he admitted what he really wanted was to grab her and kiss her hard enough to melt that ice and discover if there really was a warm, responsive woman under that stone mask, as he suspected. Not that he would permit himself to do that, of course. Firmly ingrained in his mind was his own stubborn, independent nature. And he did not want to have fantasies about a young, city-bred schoolmarm like Philippa Marquette.

Jasper Clough had seen the two of them by now and was hailing as he turned into Ryan's driveway, "Good afternoon, Miss Marquette, Murphy. Lovely day, isn't it?"

Lovely? It was hotter than Hades, Ryan fumed as he nodded his head while Philippa pleasantly greeted the newcomer, now using her lovely modulated voice. "Why, good afternoon, Mr. Clough. Yes, it is a beautiful day. Are you out for an afternoon's drive?"

"No, no. Not just for a drive—I was sent to bring an apple to the teacher. Not an apple, singular, but a bushel of them. When I told my sister how dismayed you were at not finding fresh produce in the store, she insisted I bring these apples out here to you."

"How very nice of her."

"Just set the apples out for Miss Marquette here, Clough, and I'll carry them over for her later. I was about to give her a driving lesson. She can't ride horseback or drive a team, so it's important she learn to do one or the other, living way out here." Ryan hoped his reasonable, matter-of-fact explanation would send the lawyer back to town.

It didn't. Jasper Clough was used to winning legal arguments and debates, and he wasn't about to give an inch to this handsome Irishman. "Great idea, Murphy, but your horses are all much too spirited, and a team would be more difficult to manage than a single horse. I'll just take her up here in my buggy and teach her to drive Habeas Corpus. He's fast, but gentle as a lamb."

Philippa felt torn. If only there was some magic solution! She knew she would be much too ill at ease to learn to drive while Mr. Clough flooded her with flirtatious compliments, but she couldn't tell them that she preferred to have Ryan teach her. She even had to ask herself why she found him so appealing, when he always rejected her. He wouldn't have invited her to dinner if she hadn't taken the initiative.

Trying to be polite, she suggested a compromise. "Both Mr. Murphy and I will join you. Perhaps I will learn faster with two teachers."

The idea did not seem at all reasonable to either gentleman.

Ryan looked daggers at her and warned, "You'd just get confused."

Jasper was quick to sense his opponent's anger and hastily made use of it to further his own suit. "He's right, of course. It would be too crowded to learn with three in the buggy. You and I will take a turn around the section and—"

Another buggy topped the hill. It was passed by a horseback rider before it got to Ryan's lane. The rider was Radcliff's oldest boy, who carried a basket for Philippa with some freshly dressed chickens in it and three jars of plum jelly.

The buggy was driven by a vexed Calvin Lawrence. He, too, had brought a bushel of apples, along with a bag of feed for Philippa's chickens. He was perturbed to discover his idea had not been original . . .

As was Sammy Hawkins when he arrived minutes later.

Greetings were exchanged. Insults were exchanged. Compliments were tendered. Conversations were stilted. Calvin and Sammy remained vexed. Young Radcliff remained awed. Ryan remained angry. Philippa remained frustrated. Only Jasper Clough remained unemotionally optimistic.

It was late afternoon before anyone left. Each of them had hoped to outstay his adversaries. Somehow all the bushels of apples had been left by Ryan's back door. Philippa had excused herself long enough to take the dressed chickens home and put them in the five-gallon crock suspended down into her well by its bales. She was not going to risk having her only meat spoil.

As the last buggy went out the gate, Philippa walked over to the apples, thinking, An apple for the teacher. *The teacher*. She had not prepared a single assignment for her students. Thirteen children would arrive tomorrow and what would she do with them? What would she do with all these apples?

"Have an apple, Teacher?" Ryan questioned teasingly. He liked it when she got that lost look on her face. Then he felt in control. This afternoon's visits by the buggy-driving town men in their three-piece suits had made him feel out of sorts and out of place in his jeans and boots. They had taken off their jackets and loosened their ties in the hot afternoon sun, but he'd still felt out of place.

They had all treated him congenially, but hell, he couldn't even argue about apples. Horses and cattle he knew, not about growing apples! Or wheat, or corn, or any of the other topics the conversation had swung around to. If it hadn't been his own yard, he would have left.

One thing he had noticed, though: the teacher had been as quiet as he had. They all tried to include her, of course, but she only answered their questions and had not volunteered to continue the conversations. Maybe she shared his dislike of crowds.

"I may never want to see another apple again!" Philippa exclaimed. "I should preserve some of them and make some apple butter. I watched our cook make apple butter once, so I'm sure I can . . . And the rest, well, applesauce is probably made about the same way. If only I had some canning jars!"

"There's plenty of jars in my cellar over here. Grandma must have canned a lot." He walked over and lifted up a big plank door that seemed to be lying on a small embankment in his backyard. When he opened it, a stairway appeared down into the ground. Philippa peered into the cavelike hole. It was full of cobwebs. Mice and ground squirrels scurried this way and that as light entered their dark domain.

"Goodness, what kind of a cellar is that? I couldn't possibly go down there. I'm scared to death of spiders and rodents."

"Tell you what," Ryan offered. "I'll brave the

rodent hole and fetch up some jars. I'll willingly carry them, and all the apples, too, on over to your house, in exchange for some fried chicken. I don't know when I last had any."

"I'll even make some apple cobbler," Philippa volunteered.

"Then I'll even do your milking."

"Oh, this offer is sounding better all the time," Philippa declared as she picked up the box with Mrs. Radcliff's gift of plum jelly and held up a jar. "If I add one of these, will you bring in the eggs and shut the chickens in for the night?"

"For plum jelly? Yes, ma'am!"

Her ugly, awful kitchen seemed more warm and cheerful as Philippa sorted through her book trunk for the recipe folder she had compiled in culinary arts class. Apple cobbler was near the front. It had been considered elementary compared to the difficult angel food cakes and puff pastries they had advanced to after only a few lessons. Basic baking, boiling, and frying had been omitted by the French chef who had taught the class. He had deemed—rightly, in most cases—that the young ladies under his instruction would only be dabbling in their kitchens, leaving the normal food preparation to servants. Philippa had learned the basics by watching Olga, the Norwegian cook at the Narins' house.

In St. Louis, a guest had never been served on unmatched crockery dishes, but that was all Mrs. Belden had sent for Philippa's use. She had also packed only one knife, fork, and spoon. Alvena had evidently wanted to ensure that the teacher washed the dishes after each and every meal—and ate by herself. The knife and fork were placed for

Ryan to use, while Philippa put the spoon by her
plate. Should she tell him this was all she had, or
should she just let him think she was too witless to
set a table correctly? Maybe she wouldn't say anything and just hope he didn't notice. She filled her
spatterware coffeepot and set it on to boil, wishing
she had some good coffee to serve instead of this
bitter Hawkins Special Blend.

All the time he was doing his chores, Ryan whistled a snappy tune. Tonight he wasn't going to eat
a lonely meal, a meal he'd cooked himself of beef,
biscuits, and gravy, or beans, which was about the
extent of his normal supper cooking. For breakfast
he usually fried eggs, which he purchased by the
crate in town. Occasionally he had griddle cakes or
cornmeal mush with molasses. It was the fare he'd
grown up on after his ma died, and he was getting
mighty tired of it.

He kept trying to convince himself it was only
the thought of the food . . . but it wasn't, it was
eating across the table from Pip again. Lunch had
been special just because she was there in his
kitchen with him. Tonight they'd be across from
each other at that little table in her kitchen. He
worked faster as the tempo of his whistling
speeded up. When he finished he washed up at his
pump, ran his fingers through his hair to push his
unruly cowlick back, and sauntered across the road
and around to her back door.

As he started up the back steps, he could hear
her singing and stopped to listen to her melodious
voice before knocking. She sure had a beautiful
voice. Ryan hated the yearnings that suddenly
poured over him from the song she sang, the aroma
of the food, and the knowledge that the beautiful,

vibrant Philippa Marquette was on the other side
of the door. What the deuce was he doing here?
Tempting himself with something that could never
be. Oh, there would be a wife for him someday,
but not a beautiful, youthful schoolmarm—not one
who sounded like an angel. His wife would be
quite different.

He dropped the hand he had just lifted to knock
with and stepped back. He was plagued enough by
wanting her without going into that candlelit
kitchen. Her hair would be glistening with lamplight reflections and her eyes would be a dark,
polished hickory color. That mouth—those
lips—could he go in there and calmly sit across the
table from her and remember she was not for him,
a stubborn, unworldly cowhand? Why, she had
her pick of every eligible bachelor in town. Hell,
no, he couldn't do it! He turned and went slowly
back to the black shadow that was his house across
the road.

Philippa heard the footsteps go back down the
porch steps, watched as the dark silhouette passed
the window going toward the road, and wondered
what he could have forgotten. She put the food on
the table, took off her calico apron, and looked at
herself in the small, cracked mirror beside the
kitchen door while trying to re-pin her hair and
fluff up the wilted ruffles at the neck of her blouse.
Whatever was taking him so long?

She looked at her little gold locket watch, thinking how fortunate it was she had remembered to
pack it. How would she ever know the time out
here without it? Then, as the minutes ticked by,
she wished she didn't have it. Nothing could take

half an hour to get or do. No. He just wasn't planning to eat with her. He had only asked for the food, hadn't he? Not her company at a meal again. Philippa had thought sharing lunch was delightful, but he had probably been bored. Once again, she wished she had a flair for stimulating conversation and coy cleverness.

Hurt, angry, and disappointed, she scooped the food onto his plate and covered it lightly with a tea towel. He had kept his part of the bargain; she would keep hers. By the time she reached his door, tears were streaming down her face. She couldn't let him see that he had upset her this way, so she set the plate by the door, knocked, and fled back into the darkness.

The Saturday deadline Andrew had set for his men had come and gone without any progress in their search. Today had been a revelation to him, for he'd had a great deal of time to think. Even the scurvy bunch he'd hired did not work on Sunday, nor did either of the two Pinkerton men. If the local law officers were on duty, and most of them probably weren't, they'd reported nothing to him.

Of course, he'd attended church this morning, playing the role of the bereaved son, the bereft bridegroom, but throughout the long afternoon his thoughts had run rampant. Some of his anger of the past days had shifted to a grudging admiration for the girl he'd been forced to marry. She wasn't as timid as he'd thought. To the contrary, she was spunky, conniving, clever, and filled with determined deceit, qualities Andrew admired. He'd never encountered them in a woman before. She had become a challenge to him. He'd always intended to find her for the sake of his inheritance; today the girl herself had started to become important.

And going off to Chicago! Andrew was not a man prone to finding fault with himself, but that had been a blunder. He'd known she didn't want this marriage. Hadn't she told him so in the judge's office? Somehow she'd found out about Lil, too, not that she'd seemed to mind about his having a mistress. In fact, she'd sounded quite pleased when she'd asked, "Then ours will be a marriage in name only?"

Yes, she'd given him plenty of clues as to her feelings and he hadn't heeded them at all. He'd assumed his mother had taught the girl to obey the law, no questions asked—the moral codes and all that. A wife did not leave. She was her husband's property, to be dominated by him for the rest of her life. His little adopted cousin was more like him than he'd ever suspected. He, too, had rebelled to escape the confines of dictatorship.

Philippa must have carefully and cautiously planned this scheme to embarrass him—and to cheat him out of a fortune. She knew how the very idea of the money going to the ridiculous Temperance League upset him.

Giving his mother's things to the hired help to get them out of the way while she had draymen carry out her things had been a shrewd maneuver. The way she'd outsmarted Madame Marquette, the modeste he'd hired to make her a suitable wardrobe for a wife of the esteemed Andrew Van Arder, was cunning, too. The wily girl had gotten herself a wardrobe suitable for any number of middle-class occupations: a companion to an elderly spinster or widow, or a governess, or maybe a seamstress.

Mrs. Carpenter said Philippa could sew a little; perhaps she had become a teacher in a girls' school like the one she'd attended? She'd be qualified for that, or even a clerical worker in an office, or a store clerk. Possibilities were becoming quite numerous for women with educations.

Damn his mother for educating the girl so thoroughly! Grammar school would have been sufficient. But no, Clara Rose Van Arder had been determined to make Philippa a pattern card of the current trend for wealthy young women. She had wanted the girl to become a prominent social figure in St. Louis, as Mrs. Andrew Van Arder.

Andrew had to concede that Philippa could easily become just such a paragon, with her intelligence, her looks, and him to guide her. Finding her was becoming imperative to him. He had seldom been outwitted by any man, and by God, he sure wasn't going to be by a woman—a mere girl! If only they could find out how she had gotten all her things from the house. Someone had taken her *somewhere*, and that person was the key figure to unsnarling this coil. Before he went to bed that night, Andrew rewrote the WANTED posters, upping the ante for any information.

Chapter Nine

✦ ✦ ✦ ✦ ✦

ONLY TEN OF Philippa's thirteen enrolled students arrived for the first day of the new term. Four of them were from the same family, Rafe Parker's. The little sister of Will Radcliff was the oldest one in the class; Lydia Radcliff was fourteen, followed closely by Rafe Parker's eldest, Alice Ann, who was thirteen. Her brother Isaac John was eleven. The Hubbard twins, Herbert and Henrietta, were ten, but Henrietta was several inches taller than her brother and far advanced in her schooling. Emma May Parker and Lars Gulickson were nine and Ella Gulickson was eight. Paul William Parker, who vigorously iterated he was "Pee Wee" Parker, was seven, and the youngest student was six-year-old Susan Murray. After Philippa identified each student, Susan asked in her impish little voice, "And what us be to call you, ma'am?"

"Miss Philippa would be just fine."

"Miss Pippa. What a purty name!"

Philippa did not have the heart to correct the little girl, so she became "Miss Pippa" to all of them.

Since she had been far too exhausted last night to prepare lessons, she proclaimed the first day of school to be Get Acquainted Day. She had them take turns reading aloud from the readers and going to the chalkboard to do sums so she could try to determine where to place each one in the reading and arithmetic primers. She gave them a morning and afternoon recess and then read a story to them to fill the rest of the day. Needless to say, the students of Bluffsview Rural School District No. 3 all went home in love with their new teacher.

Philippa went home to apples and more apples. The crop must have been a really good one this year, because almost every one of her students had brought along an extra one in his or her lunch bucket for the teacher.

She heated water in the boiler and then dumped it into her bathtub to wash the cobweb-covered jars. While the water heated, she peeled apples and peeled apples and peeled apples. Every crock, bucket, and bowl was full of them, awaiting their turn in the copper boiler, which was the only thing she had to use as a canning kettle.

It was when she was on her knees in the middle of the kitchen floor, washing jars in the bathtub, that the cow began its incessant reminder it had not been milked. She grabbed the pail, rinsed the apple juice from it at the pump, and practically ran to the shed, for she didn't want Ryan Murphy to come over and scold her for not milking. Indeed, she did not want him to come over here at all, ever again.

As soon as Ryan finished feeding his horses, he started to go to the teacher's house to milk her discontented cow, but before he reached his gate he saw her headed for the shed on the run. Now there was no excuse to go over.

He had thought maybe if she was canning, he could pull the filled jars out of the boiling water and seal them tight for her. His ma had always had one of his big brothers do that when she canned. After last night, he couldn't just go over and volunteer. It was probably better not to go over at all after the inexcusable way he had run home lastnight. Whatever had made him do it? The old cowardice had taken over, the inane fears and insecurities that had bound him since childhood.

Ryan Murphy presented himself to the world with swaggering bravado, as a devil-may-care fellow who, while he never started a fight or a brawl, never walked away from one either. He'd set out to prove himself the best in every way, fair in all dealings with everyone, faster on the draw, a topnotch horseman, victorious in any skirmish, a man who could outwit, outdrink, and outsmart every crony in his hometown. As he grew older he'd also become the best cardplayer, the best cattleman, and the best judge of horseflesh for miles around. He'd also proved his prowess with women time after time. Somehow in the process of all his triumphs he'd become a very wealthy man.

Then one day he realized it was all a front because, dammit, he'd never learned to read or write. His ma had taught his three older brothers a little about readin' and cipherin', but she'd died when his younger brother was born. Ryan was five at the time, and it had never occurred to anyone he needed to learn the three R's. So he proved himself in every other way, but laid low around anyone with a lot of learning.

Maybe that had been part of his reason for moving here to his grandpa Carter's place. It was a place to start over. He was tired of constantly having to prove his skill at cards, with his fists, and with a gun. He wanted to settle down to a simpler life where he could concentrate on his business acumen, his knowledge of horses and cows. In Bluffsview no one knew or would ever find out the shameful secret of his illiteracy. It had been working out as ideally as he'd hoped until now. With that provocative teacher getting under his skin, things had changed. He'd rather pack up and leave than to have her find out the truth, and of his past too. But if he left, she'd be out here alone, unprotected.

It was more than not being able to read and write much. It was the blow his pride would suffer if anyone knew his secret. His pa and his brothers had always laughed when he'd tried to explain this to them. They told him flat out that he was big and tough and had plenty of bucks in his pocket, so he never needed to kowtow to anybody. He wished he felt as confident about it as they did. The Murphys were highly regarded for a hundred miles or more in every direction from their ranch, so his brothers must be right. That was regard by other cowmen and business contacts, though. Probably most of them didn't have much more education than the Murphy boys did. None of them had the polish and cavalier manner Ryan hankered for. Dismally he crammed his hands down deep into his pockets and turned back toward his grandpa's empty old house.

The Saturday night Grange Dance rated in the category of a minor catastrophe in Philippa's mind. Wanting to look her best, she wore the fanciest dress she had selected from Madame Marquette's designs, one of the few Andrew had ordered that she had considered suitable enough to bring with her. It was a beautiful heliotrope taffeta that appeared iridescent when its wearer moved and twirled about. She had taken extra pains to put her hair up into a mass of small curls that cascaded down her neck in back.

The dress was much too warm for the hot Grange Hall, and as the night progressed the pins fell one by one from her artfully arranged hair until it was tumbling down around her ears and shoulders. It didn't seem to matter in the least to the gentlemen who asked her to dance. They proclaimed she was "lovely," "a vision," "beautiful," "purty," or "nice-lookin'."

However, the ladies were not using the same adjectives to describe her. Alvena Belden whispered words like "educated immigrant upstart," "jade," "flirt," and "insolent" loud enough for Pip to overhear, while Gertrude Olsen and Mrs. Rafe Parker made a counterattack with "stylish," "best teacher ever," "beautiful," "cultured," and "well educated." The three teachers from the town school had their own terminology. They expounded on the inadvisability of having someone so young for a teacher and questioned loudly her qualifications.

All three teachers were attempting to accuse the Fitch agency of deception when Philippa danced close by in the arms of Jasper Clough. Pretending to talk to Philippa in his loud courtroom voice, he asked, "Did I tell you I plan to bring a bill before the next town meeting that will require every teacher in the county to pass the State Board's rigid test for graduating teachers? Pass it each and every year before we sign their annual contracts."

The three women fell silent so abruptly Philippa almost giggled aloud, and Jasper went on talking as if he had not even noticed the three ladies standing there.

Once she overheard Sammy Hawkins defending himself to his father and mother. ". . . but how can I dance with her? Somebody always sweeps her out onto the floor before I get there."

"Use perseverance," his father told him.

"Use prestige," his mother added.

Young Sammy must not have been familiar with either tactic, because Philippa never did dance with him. She did dance with every other male there, it seemed, from Big Sam Hawkins's father, who was an eighty-five-year-old master of perseverance and prestige, to young, athletic Pee Wee Parker. Even Horace Belden twirled her around the floor. If looks could kill, Philippa was sure both she and Mr. Belden would be dead from the murderous glares Mrs. Belden was giving them.

The dance should not have been a catastrophe, it should have been the most exciting night of her life, Philippa mused. She was undeniably the belle of the ball this evening. She remembered the talks she, Lee Ann, and Dottie had had with Lee Ann's sister Florine during her "season." The day after each ball or party, Florine had had three excited young faces gathered around her wanting to hear all the details. She had gone off each evening with her mother when there was a ball and had often not returned home until nearly dawn. (Mrs. Narin had said she was glad she only had two daughters to go through "seasons" with and more than once wished the two of them were twins!)

Florine had told of the marvelous waltzes played by real orchestras and of all the girls seated primly in salon chairs along one wall, twittering and giggling behind ornate fans or lacy handkerchiefs held elegantly in gloved hands as they were surveyed by all the dashing young men, some in formal attire, some (the most exciting, in most of the debutantes' opinions) in military uniforms. According to Florine, every eligible young officer from the military establishments in St. Louis attended the cotillions. Usually it was the young officers who began the early dancing, while the young civilian men, too shy to call attention to themselves, stood in groups opposite the young ladies.

This did not seem to be the case this evening. Every one of the younger people started to dance the minute the fiddler got his strings tuned and began to bounce the bow rhythmically across them. There was a sprinkling of older citizens dancing too. Many of the farmers stood in clusters discussing the weather and crops, while farm and town wives gathered to discuss the endlessly fascinating subjects of childbirth and local gossip. Young men, outnumbering young women considerably, gathered at the punch table or near the door, watching the dancers and waiting for a chance to steal a partner (preferably Philippa) away. Instead of being elated, though, each time she was asked to dance Philippa felt like moaning. It was difficult to smile sweetly and say, "I would love to," when one was totally exhausted.

All week she had stayed up almost all night long to preserve apples and prepare her students' lessons. The canning had given her a rare sense of accomplishment. Only two of her jars showed evidence of air bubbles that would let the contents spoil. This made her very proud, because it had been hard to screw those lids tightly onto those hot jars. Her wrists still ached, but she had proved she could do something she had often yearned to do in her aunt's summer kitchen.

Preparing apples had been easier than preparing lessons. Philippa had always been an excellent student, and this helped; it also helped that she could vividly recall many of her favorite teachers and imitate their methods and mannerisms. Still, she was not at all confident in her ability to teach.

She would have stayed home tonight if Mrs.

Olsen had not assured her everybody would be there. Her pulse raced at the thought of dancing in the strong, muscular arms of Ryan Murphy, and she had dressed eager to attend. She wanted not only to dance with him, but to show him that not all men rejected her as he did. She had been telling herself she would treat him with disdain and ask him if he had enjoyed his fried chicken.

If all she wanted to do was make him angry, then why was she so bitterly disappointed he had not come?

"I seem to have lost you, Miss Marquette. Perhaps I should retrace my steps," Calvin Lawrence was saying politely. "I dislike the idea of losing even your thoughts for a few moments."

"I'm very sorry. I was thinking about . . . about some of my students," she prevaricated quickly. "They have not been at school all week."

"The two Murray boys?"

"Why, yes. How did you know?"

"Their father keeps them working in the fields until all the crops are in. That's why they are over sixteen and still in grammar school. Their mother always insists they continue each winter."

"Over sixteen?"

"Yes. We've wondered what you'll do with them; they're a handful. You'll also have Bessie June Hendee starting then."

"She works in the fields too?"

"No. She doesn't like school much, but she does like the Murray boys!"

"Oh, I see what you mean. I may have a problem."

"I'm thinking you may need a man out there for a couple of days to get things under control. This is my slack season at the store; I can come out and lend a hand."

"Thank you, but I'm sure I'll be able to deal with them. If not, Ryan is just across the road."

As soon as she said it, Philippa realized how presumptuous this must sound. Calling Mr. Murphy "Ryan" and acting as if she knew she could count on him! She hoped Mr. Lawrence didn't notice.

Since no one liked the idea that Horace Belden had moved the new teacher into close range of the well-to-do cattleman, Calvin immediately took inventory of her remark, thinking the move was obviously giving Ryan Murphy an unfair advantage.

"Ryan, is it?" he finally asked pointedly.

Philippa was baffled as to how to answer. She finally decided just to tell the truth for once. "He asked me to call him that because he said 'Mr. Murphy' reminded him of his father."

"I heartily agree with him, Miss Marquette, but only provided you call me Calvin."

"All right, and would you please call me Philippa?" She did not offer him her nickname. It reminded her too much of Ryan's saying, "You're a pip, all right!"

"Where is Murphy tonight, anyway?"

"I haven't the least notion. Why, I haven't even seen him since last Sunday, when you were there."

Without thought, Calvin pronounced, "That's a relief!" and held her a little tighter in his arms.

The dancing went on and on until Philippa thought she would surely disintegrate, she was so tired. She wasn't sure she could make it around the floor again when she recognized the kind voice of Hamilton Fields.

"May I have the pleasure of sitting out this dance with you, Miss Marquette? I would love to dance with you, but I might be condemned by some of my congregation. However, since I have dutifully visited with all and sundry, I am sure they will allow me to sit down and have a glass of cider with their blessings."

"I will add mine to theirs. I do indeed want to sit down!"

Reverend Fields led her to the big, long table at one end of the room, found a seat for her, and then obtained a tall glass of cider for each of them.

"Apple juice!" Philippa winced. "I have seen so many apples this week, I fear the teacher may *become* an apple!"

"Flooded you with them, did they? It's the chief crop this year. The fields dried up, but the old trees had their roots deep enough to survive, so people eat them, can them, and give them to teachers and ministers."

"You too?"

"Oh, yes. Most of my salary is paid in foodstuffs."

"Do you can them?"

"My housekeeper does."

"On a salary of foodstuffs, you can afford a housekeeper?" she teased.

"A former pastor's widow, she comes with the house they furnish me. I am lucky to have an inheritance that provides me with an adequate amount for other expenses."

"Yes, you are. I had hoped for an inheritance too, but . . . it never materialized, so I became a teacher."

"I'm glad. You might never have come here if you had inherited the money."

"Yes, I'm glad I came here too. It has been quite an experience."

"For all of us."

She knew he had her blushing again. Ministers weren't supposed to talk this way, nor to look into one's eyes as if they could read all the way to a person's soul. It was unnerving.

Ryan found himself lying in the hammock await-ing Philippa Marquette's arrival home. It was as if he was hog-tied there against his will. Why was it so almighty important just to see who drove her home tonight? The handsome minister? The tall, brilliant lawyer? Any one of a dozen others would have driven their buggies to the Grange tonight instead of walking or riding on horseback, each in hopes she might accept his offer to see her home.

Ryan had never missed a Grange dance before, but he knew he had to stay away tonight. Philippa probably wouldn't even speak to him, let alone dance with him, after last Sunday night. He had it coming all right, but still, he could not go to that dance and not even be able to hold her in his arms for a set or two, nor could he watch her being whirled around by all the eager suitors she had already acquired. He cursed himself for the way he felt, but it changed nothing. He began to whistle softly as he set the hammock into a swinging mo-tion.

Chapter Ten

✦✦✦✦✦

INDIAN SUMMER IN Nebraska was beautiful but short that year. Soon the cold, crisp mornings of early fall sent Philippa scurrying to milk the cow and feed the chickens as rapidly as possible so she could return to the warmth of her stove. She and her students frequently left their coats on for the first hour or two of classes. There was a potbellied iron stove stored in the small shed where the Hubbard twins stabled the pony they rode to school. She hoped someone would put it up before winter. Perhaps she could ask Ryan about it.

Except that now she was reluctant to bother him; for he seemed much too busy from early morning until late at night to be bothered with being neighborly. Sometimes she neglected to correct a recitationist's spelling error or mispronounced word because she was watching him out the schoolroom window. How she loved to watch him get on and off his horse, loved to watch him ride. The strong muscles in his legs were so evident when he stepped into the stirrup and threw his leg over the saddle. He sat tall and straight on his horse, and yet his body looked completely relaxed when he rode, as if he and the horse formed one fluid motion. A month or so ago he had switched from a western-style straw hat to a felt one, but he still looked rugged and a little rakish, the way that tuft of hair always escaped down onto his forehead.

Philippa did not realize the extent of her daydreaming until she overheard Lydia, Alice Ann, and Henrietta chattering in the schoolyard at lunchtime one day. After opening a window to air the room for a few minutes, she noticed the girls must be sitting propped against the wall underneath it. At first, she didn't pay any attention to their titters and giggles, but when she heard her name mentioned, she couldn't resist listening to what they had to say.

"Did you see Miss Pippa watching him again today? I told you, she's sweet on him," Alice Ann said with a giggle.

"She likes Pastor Fields. He drives her home from church every Sunday."

"She likes my brother, I know she does." Philippa knew this was Lydia speaking. She told Philippa everything her brother said about "the beautiful teacher" every day. She was a born matchmaker and a loyal supporter of Will Radcliff. "He picked her up and took her home in Papa's wagon the night she had dinner at our house!"

"You know your mama had you ride along." That sounded like a chiding Henrietta.

"So? They still looked at each other a lot. She likes him, all right."

"Does not!" This was Alice Ann's firm statement. "She likes Mr. Murphy. I can tell by the way she gazes out the window every time he rides in or out of his yard. Your brother is too young for Miss Pippa anyways. He still lives at home. Mr. Murphy has his own place, and he's handsome and rich."

"You're just saying all this 'cause you like Will yourself. He's going on eighteen now and he doesn't even know little old you is alive. Why, you only just turned thirteen!"

"I don't like your brother!"

"Do too!"

"Do not!"

"I know you do, Alice dumb Ann."

"Please don't get mad at each other!" This was Henrietta, pleading. " 'Cause you know what will happen if you do. You two won't speak to each other and I won't know *whose* friend to be!"

Philippa tiptoed over and silently closed the window. The three girls reminded her so much of herself and Lee Ann and Dottie. How she missed them! She suddenly felt very lonely. Obviously she was going to have to stop watching Ryan Murphy out the window, and this thought made her feel even more desolate. Close on the heels of this came an even more sobering thought: what if her students learned she was married?

No! She *wasn't* married! That awful ceremony was not even vaguely related to a sacrament like taking one's marriage vows. She forced the abhorrent thought from her mind by returning to grading papers with fervor.

One Sunday Philippa had dinner with Calvin Lawrence and his mother. Mrs. Lawrence was as personable as her son, and the two of them had provided a delightfully humorous mealtime conversation. Philippa had not been able to think of any funny or interesting things to contribute, so she had remained quiet and enjoyed listening to them.

Then Jasper Clough and his sister Cecilia had asked her to join them for a Saturday picnic, and the two of them had gotten into the most stimulating discussions of religion and politics. It had been pleasant and enlightening to hear a brother and sister state opposite viewpoints on everything.

At the Parkers' house, where Philippa had been invited to supper on a school night, everyone in the family talked constantly. It had given Philippa an entirely different view of family life than she had ever had before. She loved being a guest there. It was just the opposite the night she had dinner with the Radcliffs. No one said very much at all because they wanted Will to do the entertaining. Poor Will was too awestruck to stammer more than a few sentences during the entire meal.

Philippa was thankful she always knew the polite and proper thing to say. She knew her manners were faultless because of Aunt Clara Rose's exemplary training and her deportment classes. She just wished she could be a stimulating conversationalist like Calvin's mother or Jasper's sister. She envied the Parker children, who were growing up so articulate. Meals had been very formal at Aunt Clara Rose's house—formal and silent. In fact, in all her life the only people she had really been able to talk with were Lee Ann and Dottie, and as she recalled their talks in more detail, she realized the two of them had done most of the talking, while she had listened.

Every night after she prepared her students' lessons she sat by the warmth of her cookstove and read the Gothic novels she had brought with her. There in the lamplight of her own kitchen she could pretend to be the clever heroines who were never at a loss for words. She even tried to memorize their coy phrases, but they never seemed to fit just right into a real conversation.

Philippa did not think she could eat one more egg. Not fried, boiled, baked, or even scrambled into a fluffy omelet. She was hungry for meat.

Her only source of meat was her chickens, and she became determined she was going to kill, clean, and cook one of them. Even her students were able to do it; she knew this from classroom discussions. If a ten-year-old was able to do it, then *she* should be able to.

The biggest problem was catching the chicken to kill it. If she tried to sneak into the coop when they were sitting on their nests and grab one, they pecked her arms and hands until she gave up. Once, she had tried to sneak in at night when they were on the wooden roost, but they all flew every which way, including at her. Her best opportunity, she decided, was to sneak up on one in the yard while it was busy pecking away at the ground for a worm. However, she never could get close enough before it ran, squawking, back to tattle to the other chickens. She found a long old board and planned to hit an unsuspecting one over the head. She wouldn't have to get so close to do that, she had rationalized. However, the chicken always darted to one side or the other just as she took a swipe at it, and she only managed to clip a wing or loosen some tail feathers. This just caused it to squawk louder. She would end up chasing the thing, squawking all the way, until it got under the shed or porch where it was out of her range. Once more she would go in, defeated, and cook eggs for supper.

The first Saturday in November, Philippa was enjoying being able to fix breakfast leisurely, knowing that she did not have to get into her clothing, rush to milk the cow and feed the chickens, then make haste to the schoolhouse. It was a pleasant emotion until she picked up the egg to crack it into the skillet. Eggs—she was so sick and tired of eggs!

Bang!

The reverberation of a shot echoed through her kitchen.

Bang!

The sound repeated. It was a gun, she was almost certain, but where and why? The noise seemed to be coming from across the road by Ryan's house.

Ryan!

Unhesitatingly she forgot her own fears and ran out of her kitchen door, down the back steps, and over to the path, where she could see across the road, blessing heaven when she saw that no one was shooting at Ryan. Instead, he seemed to be shooting at birds. She watched, fascinated, as he picked up some dead pheasants from the ditch down at the end of his pasture, then walked back up onto the road again with his gun over his shoulder.

Here was the answer to her dilemma! Without recalling the impropriety of it, she went running down her driveway, her flannel wrapper flapping loose in the wind, her long hair flowing around her shoulders.

"Ryan! Ryan!" she was shouting at the top of her lungs, afraid he would turn to go back toward the lane of his house before he heard her.

Ryan turned and looked at the vision flying toward him. Her hair was flying softly around her face and shoulders. The early shades of a dawning sun deepened its color to a rich, burnished gold, and she looked devastating as she came running, calling his name. He had been working from dawn to dark every day, trying to keep too busy to think of her. He hadn't succeeded.

Now he quickly laid down his gun and dropped the birds so he could run to meet her, fearing something terrible had happened. It must be a disaster to cause her to be outdoors in her wrapper, calling to him as if her life depended on it!

"Pip, what is it? What's wrong?" Anguish and

concern were heavy in his voice as he reached out to stop the hurtling figure. She practically tumbled into his arms, she was so breathless from running. He held her around the waist to support her as she stood there gasping for air. "Are you all right?"

"There's . . . nothing . . . wrong!" she tried to assure him breathlessly as she took several deep gulps of air to fill her lungs. At last she had her wind back, but she did not move away. Instead, she stood very close in his arms, looking up into his eyes, and pleaded, "Will you *please* shoot some chickens for me?"

Ryan had heard of lots of animals getting rabid and having to be shot, but he didn't recall ever hearing of a chicken with rabies. "What happened? Did one attack you?"

"More than one!" She held out her hands so he could see the peck marks.

Ryan examined first one arm and then the other, unable to believe this had been done by attacking chickens. He was sure it couldn't be rabies, because a lot of the beak marks looked nearly healed. She would be deathly ill by now if her flock was rabid. But he hated the thought they were hurting her.

"I'll shoot every damn one of them."

"Oh, no, Ryan, not all of them! I need *some* eggs. I just want you to shoot two or three so I'll have some meat to eat. I'm beginning to hate eggs. I don't need you to shoot them all."

Ryan threw back his head, and peals of laughter rang all around them. She had been trying to kill the chickens to eat! With a board! With a rock! He laughed all the harder. He couldn't draw enough breath to explain himself when she pulled loose from his arm, screaming, "I should have known you wouldn't help me! That you would just laugh at me as always!" Then her voice dropped from a near shriek to a pathetic query. "Why do I always have to make such a fool of myself around you?" She turned to walk away.

Her forlorn voice sobered Ryan in a hurry, and he reached out for her retreating form. He could not stand to see her this way. The icy barrages he could endure, but not this complete loss of confidence, for he knew that feeling too well himself.

"Here, now." He pulled her back into the circle of his arm and brushed her hair out of her face with his other hand so he could see if she was crying. Her big brown eyes were darkest agate and lightly misted with tears. "Please, darlin', don't be feelin' bad just because I laughed. I sure never meant to make you mad or hurt your feelings. I saw you chasin' your chickens with the board and throwing rocks at them. I never dreamed you were trying to kill them!"

The humor of it touched her, too, and she began to chuckle softly. "I probably did look funny, chasing my squawking chickens around! They peck me if I sneak up on their nests, and I don't know how to catch one. I'm not even sure I'll be able to kill it if I do catch it, but if Alice Ann and Isaac John Parker and Lydia Radcliff can kill and dress chickens, then their teacher should be able to too. It's awful having students who can do so many things I can't. They all know how to ride horseback and . . . Oh, I wasn't trying to kill that biggest chicken with the rocks, just trying to break it from its habit of making that *awful* noise. It's the first one I want shot!"

"But that's your rooster!"

"Whatever you call it. It's the worst nuisance, and it's going to be the first to go."

"You have to have a rooster, Pip."

"Why?"

"Well, you just do, that's all."

"Is the rooster different from the others?"

"Yeah, it's the male. The others are hens. You need a rooster," he finally told her bluntly.

"I see." Philippa knew she was blushing more shades of red than the early-morning sun was turning the dawn sky. She put her head down so Ryan wouldn't see her flushed face. Why hadn't she read some books about poultry and livestock, or information about life in the country, instead of her secret cache of Gothic novels? Why had all of her teachers only assigned memorization of poets such as Keats and Longfellow and never facts from *The Farmers Almanac?*

The two of them were standing so close that when she tipped her head down in embarrassment, it collided with his hard, muscular chest. Before she could pull away, his hand began to stroke her hair, and he was saying softly, tenderly, "Come on now, don't fret. I'm going to teach you to ride a horse so well that you'll be able to ride circles around those kids. Wait and see. As for killing chickens, that can wait until another day."

He knew she was too disconcerted this morning to learn how to pluck a chicken and pull out its innards, even if he did wring its neck for her. "I'll give you a couple of pheasants after I clean 'em, and some beef, too."

Philippa started to look up to tell him how wonderful it was of him to offer to teach her to ride, to give her the meat, but before she spoke a word she met his face looking down. The kiss was inevitable. It encompassed weeks of empty loneliness for each of them and grew out of their frequent thoughts of one another; a deep, soul-searching kiss. Their lips meshed into a perfect oneness as their hearts matched each other, beat for rapid beat. Philippa no longer felt tingling sensations; she had earth-shaking tremors flowing through her. Ryan's tongue began to trace the outline of her lips, slowly, gently, intimately. She opened her lips a fraction and his tongue crept inside her tempting mouth to explore. His hand slipped lower onto her hip to pull her closer to him. He did not have to pull, for at the first pressure she snuggled up against him. Her own arms were around him now, sliding up and down the back she loved to watch as he sat so straight on his horse.

The touch of her fingers washed away all Ryan's intent to be gentle. His tongue was now plunging, and his arms were crushing her as if he wanted to make her a part of himself. One kiss led quickly to another and then another as they stood there in the middle of the rutted dirt road. Their arms shifted, their hands changed positions, but their bodies remained solidly together. Hardness against softness; softness against hardness.

Philippa had never even imagined all that was happening to her body. One feeling washed over her followed by another and another as Ryan deepened the emotion he poured into his kiss. He had called her "darlin'." He had spoken to her in such gentle, tender tones. He must not feel like rejecting her anymore. Philippa quivered slightly in his arms at the pleasant speculation.

When he felt her quiver, Ryan slowly released her lips. The quiver had aroused his desire to a fervent degree, and he wished he could gather her up into his arms and carry her into his house, into his bedroom. He wanted to continue to love her until she was in flames as he was, wanted to feel her melt completely in his arms. He craved to ignite every inch of her beautiful body. Desired to see the breasts, hips, thighs that he could feel pressed so close against him. Instinctively he knew he had awakened her awareness to passion for the first time. In her innocence, he was sure, she would respond to her new desires as he wanted her to, as he had dreamed she would.

Forcibly, he remembered who she was. He could not betray this innocent woman whose ardor seemed to equal his own. She was responding to him because she was lonely and inexperienced, and he had managed to make her forget her modest maidenly veneer for a few minutes, but when she recalled herself to reality she would hate him, and herself too, if they continued. Guiltily he admitted he could not just let her go. She needed him; today had proven that. Oh, not as the lover he desired to be, but as a friend. Someone to teach her to catch chickens and ride horseback, to cut the wood for her house and the school this winter. Ryan looked forward to filling the emptiness of his own life with taking care of this innocent from the city.

He kissed her one last time lightly, briefly, then forced himself to wrench free from her lips again, saying, "Little darlin', I could stand here in the road and kiss you 'til the sun goes down, but maybe we'd better mosey on back." Liar, he thought. Two more kisses like those and he'd be forgetting all about the restraint he was determined to maintain.

After Ryan drew his lips away from her for a moment, Philippa stood dreamily thinking, her heart still thrumming out of tune from Ryan's kisses, the words "little darlin' " still ringing in her ears. But when he said nothing more, she became furious with herself. She'd acted the *fool* again! Running down the road, in her wrapper yet, her hair not up and only her knit boots on her feet. The strictly brought-up Philippa Martin was in the road in garments she had not been allowed to leave her boudoir in, back at her aunt's mansion.

Worse still, she had literally thrown herself into this man's arms. Wanting him to shoot a chicken, of all things. She was an imbecile!

Just maybe, this one time, she had not initiated the kisses, but she had certainly participated most willingly. Participated in kisses that probably were too passionate to be permitted an engaged couple back in St. Louis.

But she wasn't back in St. Louis. Here in Nebraska things were very different. Not different in that respect, however, she suspected, but Ryan Murphy *was* different. He wasn't at all like any of her swashbuckling or insufferably moody heroes in her novels. He was a real man who aroused unbelievable real emotions inside her. Emotions she liked. No one here knew her as the staid, prissy, adopted niece of the stalwart Clara Rose Van Arder. She liked her life much better now, and she loved having Ryan talk to her, hold her, kiss her, and touch her. He was no doubt used to "real" women of the world, and to please him, she vowed she'd become one.

Although Ryan had stopped kissing her, he pulled her close beside him, and arm in arm they walked to pick up the forgotten gun and the pheasants. After he retrieved them, he no longer had a free arm to put around her waist.

This was easily solved by squeezing her under the arm with the gun and moving the gun onto her own shoulder, where she had placed his hand. This was most agreeable to Ryan. He tucked her tightly against him once again as they continued to the point where his gate was on one side of the road and her lane on the other.

They paused to go their own ways, but neither turned away. They just stood looking into one another's eyes until at last Ryan said, "I'll bring you a pheasant when it's cleaned."

"I could cook yours, too . . . and bring it over to you."

The offer was soft, hesitating, but his answer was firm. "I'd like to just come over and eat it at your house, if you'd let me."

"You would?" She wondered why he would come now when he hadn't before, and the question echoed between them. Belatedly an answer dawned on her. "My kitchen is not so unpleasant as it used to be. Ole fixed the plaster on the ceiling and Gertrude helped me paste up the wallpaper and hang the oilcloth. I made some gingham curtains and we rolled down a new piece of linoleum. It isn't so unappetizing anymore."

"You think I didn't come over because the kitchen wasn't fixed up?"

"I didn't know. I thought maybe . . . I just didn't know. It was pretty awful!"

Ryan was appalled. How could he answer a ridiculous question like this? She was so earnest about it; he knew he had to be truthful so he wouldn't hurt her feelings again, so he admitted, "I stayed away, Pip, not because the room was unappetizing, but because you were . . . too appetizing."

Genuinely puzzled by his answer, Philippa could only mutter, "Too appetizing?" Here she had just been thinking she would have to become more worldly to attract a man like Ryan, and it seemed he might already find her appealing.

"Maybe I worded that wrong, honey. You're most attractive, and as you've no doubt been told many times, you're also very young and innocent. Hardly my type."

"And what may I ask is 'your type'?" Philippa stormed, trying to cover how deeply his words had hurt her.

"*You are,*" Ryan felt like storming back. "*I love you for your youth, and innocence and beauty, but your damned education stands between us like an insurmountable boulder.*" Making his voice gruff and convincing, he insisted, "Soon I'll be marrying a woman much like myself. Why, I've known her for years. She'll be joining me here any day now."

Personally Ryan felt this improvisation was an excellent solution. He could invent a pretend bride-to-be, someone to arrive in the far-distant future, and in the meantime be the friend Pip needed now, to look out for her.

Philippa was appalled. "You are *engaged?* To be *married?*" She was shaking so violently she was afraid he would notice, and the lump in her throat made her words sound guttural. It felt as if her heart might have dropped to the pit of her stomach and was forming a painful knot there.

"Yep! I'm an old engaged man, I guess. Dixie and I were all set to get hitched a long time ago, but we had a spat and broke up. A few months back, she wrote me, and I wrote her, and well, we've sort of worked things out now. I guess you could say she'll be one of those 'mail order' brides." He chuckled, hoping he'd made the story sound plausible. He and Dixie had been engaged once, had broken up, but it was a rift that would never be mended.

Aghast, Philippa stammered, "But the way you just kissed me? Held me? Called me endearing names? May I ask what all that was about, *sir?*"

"A paltry kiss or two? Come on. Even you aren't

too prudish to enjoy a little dalliance, are you? As for 'honey' and 'darling,' why, they're just commonplace friendly-like names, aren't they?"

"Commonplace, friendly-like names"? Such endearing words meant nothing to him, and those kisses! To him they were just dalliance. Ryan Murphy was an *engaged man!*

No! He couldn't be! He just couldn't! A mail-order bride was exactly like a wedding ceremony in which the bride had not said "I do." Things could be worked out . . . and somehow they would be, Philippa made a solemn vow to herself.

The first thing she had to do was to learn all she could about her adversary, she determined. That way she could fight her. Trying to sound indifferent, she asked, "Tell me about her."

"Dixie and I grew up on neighboring ranches. She knows horses and cattle about as well as I do. She'll be a big help running my cattle-feeding operation."

"Does she ride a horse?" Philippa asked, managing to sound casual.

"Like the wind."

"And can she drive a team?"

"Can she ever! She drove a six-horse rig in a race with my brother once and beat him!"

Resignation had subdued some of Philippa's anger but not her resolutions. She was thankful once again for her aunt's rigid training as she said in habitual formality, "Congratulations, Ryan. I hope you and . . . Dixie . . . will be very happy. I apologize once again for my behavior." She looked down at her gown, sorely embarrassed now as she noted her wrapper was not even tied tightly about her, and continued, "I seem to have a penchant for forgetting myself around you. Now that I know you are about to be married, I assure you it will not happen again.''

Her words were dripping icicles again, Ryan noticed, so he implored, ''We're neighbors, Pip. Can't we be friends . . . and do neighborly things for one another? Like I can chop wood for you and you can—''

''I could iron your shirts and mend them.''

''Noticed, did you?'' He held up his arm where the elbow was completely ripped out.

She laughed and assured him she hadn't, but promised if he would just help her put the stove up in the school, she and the children would be eternally grateful. This unseasonably warm spell wouldn't last for long. He promised he would that very day—after her first riding lesson.

Each turned to go to their own home with deep regret for the way things had to be, but feeling an undeniable thread of excitement weaving itself between them. They were going to enjoy being friends.

Chapter Eleven
✦ ✦ ✦ ✦ ✦

PHILIPPA HAD MADE one of her serge skirts into a culotte for riding, in hopes Ryan might offer again to teach her. As she had sewn it, she'd anticipated feeling elated at such an event. Today she donned it rather dejectedly with one of her Hansen-Tawzer uniform middy blouses and her old school coat, deciding it was no longer important to look her best since he was going to marry someone else. Someone who could already ride a horse like the wind, knew all about horses and cattle, and won races as a wagoner. The thoughts were most defeating, but Philippa was buoyed with confidence for the first time in her life. She was no longer the timid, dominated, Philippa Martin of St. Louis. She was now Miss Philippa Marquette, schoolmarm, lady of the house—her *own* house—a woman many men took a second look at . . . and she was exceedingly clever.

She had escaped the despicable Andrew and his forced marriage. She'd been strong enough to refrain from saying "I do" even when he had forcefully twisted her arm and she had adamantly refused to sign any papers. That judge Andrew had under his thumb had nonchalantly turned the other way when Andrew had forged her name, but that had nothing to do with her. She'd only been present at that sham ceremony, not taken any part in it, and she *would not, would not* accept herself as a married woman.

Nor would she accept Ryan's mail-order bride as an insurmountable impediment. He wasn't married yet!

Horseback riding turned out to be much easier than Philippa had ever imagined. She wondered why she had been so afraid to try it. Nearly every day Ryan rode over on his stallion, bringing his beautiful mare, Lightning, for her to ride. His horse was called Thunder for the noise of his galloping hooves, and the mare was named for her speed. Thunder and Lightning: Philippa loved the names, loved riding through the fields, and especially loved spending the time with Ryan. Frequently, after their rides, she would cook for them while he tended his horses and milked her cow for her.

Methodically she heated her sadirons on the stove each Saturday morning and painstakingly ironed Ryan's shirts and then mended them or sewed on buttons. In turn, he kept her wood box full, as well as the one at the school. Alvena had sent Ole over with a load of corded wood and instructions to teach Philippa the proper way to chop it into stove lengths. Ole chuckled when she informed him Ryan would chop it. He said he'd be most pleased to give the message to Mrs. Belden. When Philippa watched Ryan swing the ax, she could see the muscles ripple across his back, even with his shirt on. The way he held the log in place with one booted foot while he chopped made her realize how lucky she was that he was doing it for her. Her foot actually cringed at the thought of doing it herself and chopping off a toe.

The best part of their new alliance as neighbors was that it staved off loneliness for both of them. Where she had previously been reserved and quiet around everyone, Philippa suddenly found herself taking the initiative in conversations with Ryan. Animatedly she told him of incidents from her new schoolteaching experience and her indoctrination into living in an isolated area. She loved it when she made him smile or laugh, now that she realized it wasn't ridicule.

While Ryan was still afraid of revealing his illiteracy, he, too, began to confide in her, finding Pip to be an avid listener when he talked of his cattle-feeding venture and raising purebred horses. And she was delightful to tease. It was irresistible fun to watch that vexed look cross her face and then to listen to her soft chuckle when she discovered he wasn't serious.

Only occasionally did their conversation hit snags. When anything concerning her past was mentioned, Philippa immediately became pensive and changed the subject. For her, the reason behind the times Ryan clammed up remained a puzzling mystery. It seemed to happen in the midst of the most innocuous conversations.

One night when he came over to eat with her, Ryan brought along a handsome long-haired cat and proclaimed, "I'm giving you the best in the lot. She's by far the gentlest of the barn cats that hang around my place, and a superb mouser. This cold weather is bound to drive a few field mice indoors around here, I'm afraid!" He didn't mention that this ramshackle house was a haven for them. He didn't want to unduly alarm Pip.

"Oh, Ryan!" she'd exclaimed. "She's lovely. A really beautiful cat, and yes, oh, yes, I need her, for I do have mice. I can hear them in the walls and in the attic at nights, and once I actually saw one in my kitchen, and I envisioned the hundreds of rats in that awful pit of Poe's at Toledo."

"Pit of Poe's at Toledo," Ryan mumbled dubiously, wondering what terrible thing might have befallen her. She was keeping something in her past hidden, and he hoped to discover what it might be so he could try to help her forget it. "Toledo, Ohio," he mused aloud, remembering finally a wrangler they had had on the ranch for a while during roundup one year who hailed from there. "What awful kind of pit is there?"

"No, silly!" Philippa softly giggled when she surmised he was teasing her again. "You know I mean that torture chamber in Edgar Allan Poe's 'The Pit and the Pendulum.' Remember that gruesome place? The way he described it made it seem so real, don't you think?"

"Yeah, I guess," Ryan muttered, turning his head so she could not see his face. A story he'd never read by an author he'd never heard of.

Now he was the one desperately wanting to change the subject before Pip decided to try to get into a discussion about this Poe from Ohio. "Well," he sighed heartily, "what do you think you'll name this little lady?" He softly rubbed the cat's ears, generating an audible rumble of pleasure.

"Oh, I've never named a pet before. My . . . father was uncomfortable around animals. I'll have to think about that for a minute. Do you have any suggestions?"

"My pa thought it was silly to name the cats that hung around the barn—said it wasn't any good gettin' attached to them. But my kid brother did have a special one for a while; seems he called it Fluffy."

"Oh, I want to name her something a little more special." She thought for a moment, then looked up at him with a grin on her face. "I know! I'll call her Endymion."

"Endy-what? What kind of name is that for a cat?"

"You remember—Mr. Keats's wonderful allegory, 'Endymion.' "

"Oh . . . yeah . . ."

"Here, Endymion—here, kitty, kitty, kitty . . ." The tawny longhair stretched magnificently, then leaped from the rug in front of the stove into Philippa's lap, butting its head against the young woman's hand, begging a stroking. Philippa obliged willingly, murmuring, "Beautiful Endymion" as she petted the long fur. Ryan just shook his head, wondering when all of this was going to come to a head. He couldn't continue indefinitely to just change the subject whenever she mentioned book learning.

Calvin Lawrence came out from town to take Philippa to the two-act play the high school English class put on. The play was rather boring, but, as always, Calvin's comments kept her very amused. Was sharing laughter with someone infatuation or love?

The question of infatuation or love was equally pertinent when Jasper Clough took her to the courthouse in Nebraska City to hear him prosecute a lawsuit. All the way to the county seat, riding in Jasper's well-sprung buggy, they discussed their favorite poets. Things she had read and enjoyed were easy for Philippa to talk about. Jasper had commended her on her choice of a name for Endymion, and the cat, knowing she had an admirer, rubbed against his leg affectionately as he assisted Philippa into his buggy.

She was impressed by his brilliant presentation of the facts in the case and his courtroom demeanor. Afterward, as she stood waiting for him in the hallway of the courthouse, she tried insisting to herself that she did feel more than infatuation for Jasper; he was handsome, brilliant, loved books and poetry as she did—and he hadn't sent off for a mail-order bride, either.

However, try as she might, she could not convince her contrary heart to feel more than friendship for him. Only Ryan made that stubborn heart of hers skip beats and sent shivers climbing up her spine. If those were signs of true love, then she must be a flighty piece of baggage to feel them only for a man who had told her point-blank he belonged to another, that she herself wasn't his type. Disgusted with herself, she turned and strolled down the wide, door-lined hall to help pass the time and control these wayward thoughts.

At the end of the long hall was a built-in bulletin board, and Philippa stopped to glance casually at the announcements and WANTED posters tacked to the cork. The light at this end was rather dim, but the printing on the signs was large and easy to read. She shuddered at some of the crimes and descriptions of the renegades whom the law was hunting, but bravely went on reading them since Jasper had not yet come out of the courtroom. One on the bottom row caught her eye because of the large reward being offered, and she began to peruse the details without really thinking about them until the words "St. Louis heiress" popped out at her.

Shaking uncontrollably, she reread the posted notice from the top:

WANTED:

*INFORMATION ON THE WHEREABOUTS
OF A MISSING ST. LOUIS HEIRESS*

It listed Philippa Martin Van Arder's name, age, and description and then Andrew's business address to apply for the $5,000 reward if she was found.

Oh, Lord!

She had practically managed to forget the existence of Andrew the Ogre, the obnoxious beast who had turned her world topsy-turvy. How she hated him—and yet, if it had not been for him, she never would have left St. Louis, never would have become acquainted with all the people of Bluffsview, nor known her challenging students, would never have felt the sense of accomplishment in being on her own . . . nor would she have met Ryan Murphy.

After furtively looking up and down the hallway for any witnesses, she quickly yanked the poster down and stuffed it into her pocketbook. With numb fingers and hands still shaking, she carefully altered the position of two other notices so the empty space was not so obvious. Proud of her strategy for rearranging the board and having the nerve to steal the poster, she heaved a deep sigh, then prudently ran to the other end of the corridor before she was noticed.

Surely the reward poster was an old one. Andrew wouldn't still be looking for her—would he? she thought hopefully. Then she realized she was being foolish. It had not been that long since she had escaped his repellent clutches. It had only seemed a long time because so much had happened to her.

Even Philippa had to marvel at herself: a girl who had always lived in the city, who had been waited upon by others, and who had never taught a day of school in her life, was now able to milk the cow, tend chickens, wash and iron clothing, can apples, teach school, and so much, much more. It hadn't been easy, but she had done it. Perhaps it was because she had been so determinedly working to accomplish all these things that she had been able to dismiss Andrew and St. Louis from her mind so completely. Or perhaps it was because when that mind wandered from duties, the silly thing wandered in the direction of devil-may-care Irish eyes and a smile that made one's stomach do cartwheels.

In the future Philippa determined to be even more careful to keep her door locked at all times. When she was outside doing her chores, she'd listen carefully for the sounds of a horse, a buggy, or possibly an automobile, for Andrew owned a new one. It was an ugly black thing, and from the way it growled and chugged and spluttered when he cranked it into action, she did not think it could possibly make a tour all this way to Nebraska. Would her loyal students protect her from him? Would Ryan? Perhaps she could borrow Ryan's gun . . .

This was all nonsense, Philippa told herself firmly. She had the wanted poster tucked away now and would burn it. He'd never find her, not in Bluffsview, and she wasn't going to spend endless hours worrying about something that would probably never happen. Nonetheless, she was relieved when Jasper joined her in the empty hallway and escorted her to the large hotel dining room down the street for luncheon.

On the way home she urgently wished she could ask Jasper about the legality of a wedding in the judge's chambers when the bride did not say the vows or sign the certificate, and also about the validity of a mail-order bride, but she did not have the courage to bring up either subject; the conversation might get too personal.

The following Sunday, as he drove her home from church, she found it was not easy to avoid personal discussions with Hamilton Fields either. It always seemed as if he were reading the thoughts behind her words when he asked her politely about Calvin, Jasper, and Ryan, and sometimes about her past. However, he was careful not to press her, she noted thankfully.

Only with Ryan could she converse freely. Not about her aunt's betrayal or Andrew or St. Louis, of course, but about things she had never actually shared with anyone: things like being raised by her aunt, not remembering her real mother, or never having the brothers or sisters she had wished for. She wished he would tell her more about his past, but he rarely mentioned his family or his childhood.

Susan Murray was a very jittery little girl the day before her big brothers were to start their brief school term. She confided her childish concerns to her very own special Miss Pippa. All through recess and the lunch hour she prattled, "Freddie and Roy ain't mean, Miss Pippa. They just tease a lot. You mustn't pay any mind to the things they say. They're just funnin'." Then she asked, "You *will* let my brothers come to school, won't you? Even if they are too big? Mama will be so sad if you send 'em home like Pa says you will." And, "I tol' Roy you are the nices' teacher he ever saw an' he promised me he'd try his darnedest to behave. So did Fred."

If the rumors she had heard about the Murray boys before did not frighten her, their little sister's remarks did. It was with serious trepidation Philippa approached the schoolhouse the next morning. The Murray brothers were standing outside the door when she walked up. Each of them appeared to be over six feet tall, and they towered above their five-foot-six teacher. Both were brawny and solid-looking and both wore frowning sneers of disdain.

Philippa pasted her sweet, no-nonsense Teacher's Smile firmly into place and greeted first one, then the other with a cheerful "Good morning." She got a grunted "Mornin' " from the younger-looking of the two and an abrupt nod from the other.

Susan was chirping animatedly, "I tol' you they was comin' today, Miss Pippa! See, here they are!

All the corn is in an' shucked, so Pa let 'em come. Ain't—isn't it grand?"

Philippa was not certain that was exactly the word she would use to describe the situation, but she had to agree. "Yes, Susie, it is very nice to have your brothers join us at last. Will everyone please come in and take your places now." She raised her voice as she gave the order, for most of the children were standing at the far side of the schoolyard instead of near the door where they usually waited for her each morning.

"Y'all still got just them little seats, Teacher?"

"Sh-h, Freddie," Susan shushed him. "That's not Miss Pippa's fault."

"Fourth- and fifth-graders have to sit in the middle of the room," Lydia Radcliff informed the brothers haughtily as she and Alice Ann walked to the door, their heads held eighth-grade high.

"I'm teacher's assistant," Isaac John bragged. "I start the fire in the stove and bring over the fresh pail of water from her pump every day."

"So who gives a hoot if you're teacher's bootlick?" Roy growled.

"He's a seventh-grader," Lars defended him.

"Lars 'n me are in fifth grade now," Herbert said to no one in particular.

"My brothers can build better fires and carry more water, an' they're prob'ly in *sixth* grade this year!" Susan defended.

Philippa thought, We are going to have a war: the Murray family versus the rest of the student enrollment. This must be averted before it can begin.

The Murray boys were big and tough-looking, but Philippa suspected underneath they were just two frightened boys with chips on their shoulders because they felt inferior, having less education than most of the much-smaller children. It was something in their demeanor that she couldn't pinpoint, but it gave her a clue as to how to proceed.

"Roy and Fred will be given special lessons in addition to their regular lessons so they can catch up on the work they have missed. Because of the special work, they will be considered the same as eighth-graders. Since it will soon be much colder and we will have snow, I shall ask that Roy take over the stove from Isaac and Isaac will be in charge of scraping the frost from the windows each day. Fred will take care of scooping the snow from the paths. On the days it is heavy, Lars and Herbert will help him."

"It won't git that heavy, ma'am," Fred obligingly informed her.

"I'll chop the wood as well as bring it in. I'm fast at it," Roy assured her.

The other children seemed to have developed a certain respect for these two boys who would now do the worst jobs willingly to be considered eighth-graders. Hostilities ceased as everyone marched in and took their places. Philippa devised a desk for her two new students by putting the recitation bench and the library table behind the eighth-grade desks. Two small desks were shoved against a wall to be used as a library table, and Lars Gulickson offered his mother's old wash bench for a future recitation bench to sit beside the teacher's desk.

Philippa was very pleased at how smoothly this transition was progressing. Her pleasure was brief. Just as everyone calmed down and began to pick up their readers, the door opened and a latecomer entered.

Bessie June Hendee looked even less like a grammar school student than the Murray boys. She was not much over five feet tall, but she was a well-

developed sixteen-year-old. Every curve was em-
phasized by her tight dress. Philippa was not sure
if it was a dress the girl had outgrown or a new
one either with the seams taken in or made a size
too small. It did not look very faded. The Murray
brothers' sneering frowns were preferable to the
haughty glower of hatred Bessie June gave her new
teacher. It was as if she dared Philippa to comment
on her tardiness.

Philippa was not brave, but lifelong friendship
with Dottie Marshall had prepared her to always
take a dare.

"You are our last enrolled student, I believe.
Bessie June Hendee, isn't it? You do not have an
excused absence for the first eleven weeks of
school, and you now have a tardy mark that must
also have a written excuse from your parents or be
made up in time spent after school," Philippa ad-
monished. She did not have any sympathy for this
girl who had not come to school because she just
didn't care to—a girl who had obviously come in
late because she had taken time to crimp her hair to
impress the Murrays.

"Well, la-dee-dah!" was Bessie June's only answer as she scanned the room. When she spotted
Fred and Roy, she walked over to their desk, wig-
gling every part of her body possible, and asked
suggestively, "Can you make room for lil' ol' me
on that bench too?"

Philippa noted happily that neither boy budged
an inch. It gave her the opportunity to take control
without controversy. She told Bessie June firmly,
"Your records show that you are reading at a fifth-
grade level. Since you are not taller than many of
the other students, you will sit in a regular desk.
This one." She pointed to a desk behind Pee Wee,

a desk at the opposite corner of the room from the Murrays'.

Rebelliously the girl flung herself down into the seat, her burning anger obvious.

At least she sat down where I ordered her to, Philippa thought, breathing a deep sigh of relief. She had turned to walk to the blackboard when she heard the scraping of a desk on the floor. She turned to see Pee Wee pulling his desk far to the front of his row.

"What are you doing, Paul William?"

When the teacher used his full name, she was angry, Pee Wee knew, but he was plenty mad himself. He announced, "She stinks like lavender salts. I ain't sittin' close t' her. Lavender salts makes me sneeze. Ma never puts 'em in my blankets."

"He's right, Miss Pippa," Emma May vouched. "Ma just leaves the nasty ol' camphor smell in his comforter all winter, 'cause lavender makes him sick, Doc Eberle says."

"Good. I'll move away from the little snot," Bessie June countered. "I never wanted to sit here in the first place." She began to pull her desk back in the direction of the eighth-graders.

Philippa had to step back into the fray. "You may leave your desk up front today, Pee Wee, but tomorrow you will move it back. Tomorrow Bessie June will not wear any lavender water cologne."

"Won't I, now?" Bessie June asked, but not as viciously. The teacher had implied Bessie actually had on cologne, not just a pouch of salts wrapped in fabric tucked down the front of her dress, as she actually did. This pleased her enough to stop dragging her desk and she relented. "Oh, okay! So tomorrow I won't wear lavender, but Miss Pippa, if

I bring my own chair, can't I please sit at the back table?"

The girl was giving tit for tat, and Philippa knew that she should, too. Instead, she bargained. "If you catch up on all your missed assignments, you may move your desk to the back of your row."

"I won't ever catch up, and you know it." The girl was belligerent again.

"You can if you try." Philippa stood firm. Once again the girl plunked down in her seat, causing Herbert's chalk and slateboard to fall off the desktop behind her.

"You cracked it!" he shouted. "Miss Pippa, she broke my slate!"

Things were going from bad to worse, and Philippa began to wonder if this bedlam would ever end.

"Take mine, you big baby." Bessie June had turned and given Herbert her slate without being asked. From the look of it, it was brand new, Philippa thought, and she was sure of it when she saw the smile on Herbert's face.

It was progress, at least, so Philippa decided to encourage it. She opened the drawer of her desk and took out her own school slate, which had pink roses painted on its wooden edge. She walked over and handed it to Bessie June, saying, "I know you will take good care of mine for me. I'll let you use it, since you are older."

Bessie June was a very attractive girl when she smiled.

/

After school that day she told Ryan the entire story while they rode across his pastureland. She was still telling him the details when he came in to eat after he finished the milking. He had killed and dressed a couple of chickens for her while she was at school. When she found them soaking in a pan of salt water on the table, she was so pleased she immediately invited him to eat supper with her—as he had hoped she would.

"Fred and Roy are really intelligent boys; they just need a chance to catch up. I can't believe a father would keep his sons working when they should be in school. It's unthinkable!"

Ryan hoped she didn't notice the flush on his face as she continued. "As for the Hendee family. Letting Bessie June stay at home except when she wants to come! Why, it's like encouraging her to look for a husband instead of getting an education. What if she turns out to be a spinster like me? She won't even be able to support herself by teaching school."

Philippa was used to Ryan's mirth by now. In fact, she liked the easy way he broke into laughter. There was merriment and teasing in his eyes as he laughingly asked her, "Then you're all set to be an old-maid schoolteacher, Miss Spinster?"

Philippa didn't answer. She knew her riding had improved, but she hadn't even started to learn to handle a team. In addition, it seemed Dix (as Ryan referred to her) had no problem cooking for all the drovers at roundup time and could even handle the branding iron, if need be. Since Philippa was not sure this paragon would remain away long enough for her to accomplish all these feats, she decided she had better convince Ryan of her alternate intentions.

"I'm going to be the best schoolteacher the Fitch agency ever placed. They will be able to find a school for me year after year, and I'll always be independent and not need anyone."

"Will you come back here next year?" There was no laughter in his voice now.

"That depends on a lot of things."

"Such as?"

She could hardly tell him, "Such as whether your bride arrives before then," so she only answered nonchalantly, "If they offer me the school or not." When she thought of her circumstances, she went on, "If they were to offer it and let me stay here through the summer, I could raise a garden and can some fruit and vegetables and things . . ."

At the next board meeting, Ryan determined to push Miss Marquette's contract through for next year, no matter how much opposition Alvena Belden offered. He couldn't make the promise to Pip yet, so he changed the subject.

"What you are doin' for those Murray boys is darn nice. Makin' them feel big and important by givin' them the hard work and a table to sit at. It's great how you figgered out how to handle them. They dealt Alexander a fit for the last five years, I hear. I had to go out one night last winter and rescue him after they put him in the girls' outhouse and nailed the door shut. All the others skeedaddled home. They were afraid of the Murrays if they helped him and afraid of Alexander if they didn't. It was Susie who tattled to me. She'd only tell me if I 'promised true' not to let her brothers get expelled for it. I had to promise her and then convince Alexander not to do it!"

Philippa was laughing with him now. No one had ever made her laugh as much as Ryan did. Was this kind of sharing true love? If only she could convince Ryan she would be a big help with his cattle and horses, maybe he'd fall in love with her and forget she was not his type, provided she could make him forget about Dixie.

She looked up from her crockery plate at Ryan's smiling face. As always, she thought, How handsome he is when he smiles! His complexion had faded from its dark, ruddy brown summer color to a lighter shade. His hair was darker now, without as many reddish highlights in it, but his eyes were still the same clear, silvery green with little weather crinkles at the corners, and his grin was as infectious as ever. She loved his straight white teeth. Just once she would like to run her tongue over them as he had done to her the day on the road. Just one time, she wished Ryan would forget about his intended and kiss her again . . . but he never did.

Wishing Andrew and their marriage to perdition gave Philippa no qualms, but she felt a little guilty for wanting Ryan to betray his bride-to-be. She began to eat quickly, as if to swallow her thoughts. At least now she had a fork, too. Ryan had brought over a box of his grandma's dishes and silverware when he found out why she always ate with a spoon. It was nice to have matched dinnerware, even it it was only crockery.

"Thanksgiving is next week," Ryan observed, attempting to break her reverie.

"Yes, the children reminded me they will have a day's escape from school."

"How many asked the teacher to come and eat turkey with them?"

"Several, but I won't be going. I wouldn't dare choose one invitation above the others.

Ryan felt a happiness steal through his chest and take a grip on his heart as he tried to say casually, "I could buy a turkey from Radcliff. He raised a few extra. If you wanted to roast it . . ."

Philippa couldn't contain her excitement at the possibility of spending a holiday with Ryan.

"Oh, yes, I will! I'll start saving bread crumbs for the stuffing, and Gertrude gave me some yams she dug late. I can make sweet potato pie."

"And apple pie?"

"Of course I'll make your favorite. It used to be one of mine, but now I'm getting almost as tired of apples as I was of eggs."

"You still have beef, don't you?"

"Yes. You're much too generous."

They were both through eating now and sitting companionably at the table, just looking at one another. If they put off getting up from the table, they could put off the time of Ryan's departure. He always insisted on drying the dishes for her. Then he emptied the slop bucket and brought in kindling for the night. After he banked the fire for her, there was no longer an excuse to stay.

Each night they sat at the table talking just a little later. They both wished they could say what was in their hearts, but instead they spoke of school and cattle and weather. Only their eyes said more.

Chapter Twelve

◆━◆━◆

EVERYONE BROUGHT BASKETS of food to church on the Sunday before Thanksgiving. Philippa wished she had known of this custom of giving to the poor and the elderly in the township on holidays; she could have brought some jars of applesauce and apple butter. When she tried to explain to Hamilton how much she regretted not bringing anything, he protested, "The nicest thing you could give these people, Philippa, is yourself. Come with me this afternoon to deliver the baskets. All the shut-ins have heard of you and you'll be a delightful surprise for them."

Ryan had told her last night they would take a long ride on his horses this afternoon while the weather still held. Her serge culotte and reefer were already laid out to put on as soon as she arrived home from church, and it was with deep disappointment and resignation that she agreed to go with the minister to deliver the baskets. "One must always do the proper thing" had been deeply ingrained into Philippa by her aunt's strict teachings.

The task proved rewarding, regardless. Philippa found she enjoyed visiting with the sick and elderly, and they seemed to be as pleased to meet her as Reverend Fields had promised. All of them acted quite thankful for the food baskets. More than ever she wished they included some of her apple butter. Perhaps she and Ryan could come to their homes on one of their afternoon rides and bring a jar or two of it.

At the thought of Ryan her heart sank. By now he would be wondering where she was, and she could only hope he'd understand.

"Where do those deep daydreams take you, Philippa?" Hamilton was questioning. "Back east to your home? Did you leave loved ones behind to come out here?"

The reverend was reading too deeply into her thoughts for comfort, and she tried to think of an answer that would not be an out-and-out lie.

"I was thinking of home, but no, I didn't leave

any loved ones behind. Only two very dear friends I had gone through school with, from primary to academy graduation."

"Which academy is that?"

"Ha—Hawthorne. Named after Nathaniel Hawthorne, I believe." Her first lie to the pastor. Her aunt had sternly instilled the commandment—"Thou shalt not bear false witness"—into Philippa's mind, and she had broken it over and over again these past months. Nervously, she looked away. Then she looked back again and asked anxiously, "Do you believe one can be forgiven for telling lies? I mean, if the lies can't be helped—"

Hamilton's lips twitched slightly at the way her actions betrayed her, and he turned his head to clear his throat. He knew she was running from her past; he had tried to encourage her to confide her problems to him, without asking her directly. "Philippa," he said kindly, "it is best to seek help so one doesn't need to lie about anything."

Philippa considered her problems. Everyone had been so good to her; she was sure someone could help her with this dilemma. But who? The thought of Ryan Murphy leaped to mind, but what could he do? Perhaps Jasper Clough could at least unsnarl any legality, but then Andrew would find her. Hamilton could help her by praying for her soul, but he already had so many requests from the people they had called on today, and she couldn't add her petty needs to such real burdens.

Seeing the distress on her face, Hamilton gently tried to help her. "Tell me about yourself. How are things going for you?" When she still seemed lost in far-off thoughts, he tried again to put her at ease. "Are you getting used to our small community? Do you like it here?"

"Oh, yes, I like it very much now," she hastened

to answer, realizing her mind had been elsewhere. "Especially since I learned to ride horseback. I've adjusted to most things."

"You do ride horseback? Did Horace and Alvena finally supply you with a horse, as they were supposed to, then?"

"No, I don't think they know I've learned to ride. I ride one of Ryan's horses—a beautiful black mare named Lightning. She's a treasure."

"I'm sure she is. Ryan Murphy raises excellent horses." Hamilton wished that Murphy did not own this choice horse and that Philippa did not love to ride it so. He had been with her long enough to know she would be the perfect wife for a minister: compassionate, polite, courteous, and genteel. He knew the minister in question loved her dearly, but he also knew she did not love him. He had vowed not to rush her, but Jasper and Calvin talked of her constantly, and now it seemed Ryan was courting her, too. He must at least get her to consider him as a suitor, not just "the preacher."

"If I might suggest, Philippa, you wouldn't find things so primitive in town, or as lonely. Have you considered marrying one of us who have offered our hearts to you, and remaining in Bluffsview permanently?" There, he thought, I've clearly included myself in the category of suitor and planted the thought of marriage in her mind. Surely she will choose to marry one of us before the term is up. It did not sound as if she wished to return to wherever, whatever, or whomever she had escaped from. Knowing her as he did, he knew the escape was not a criminal one.

Philippa was puzzled as to how to answer him. She had been surprised by his suggestion, "marrying one of *us*." Did Hamilton Fields include himself when he told her to be sure if it was love or infatuation? A minister would not fritter with infatuation, would he? Did he love her? She quickly repeated the story she had told Ryan.

"I have decided to be a permanent schoolteacher. I love it, and I am becoming more capable all the time. I am sure the Fitch agency will be able to place me year after year, and I hope to prove myself by having at least four students take their eighth-grade exams this year instead of just the two scheduled. Maybe five."

"Five students out of the few enrolled—you won't have anyone left to teach!" Hamilton commented as he slowed his team so he'd have more time alone with Philippa. "Who all do you think can pass the superintendent's oral and written tests?"

"Lydia Radcliff, of course. She could probably have passed last year, she is such an intelligent girl. I'm sure she waited for Alice Ann Parker to catch up so they could brave the town high school together. Then there's Roy and Fred Murray, who should be able to pass if their father doesn't pull them out too soon for spring planting. Surprisingly they have kept up with their reading at home nights, and I am giving them double mathematics and spelling lessons. I hope the superintendent will forgo stringent geography and history tests. Susie tells me this is the last year their father is going to let them 'waste time in school.' I want them to have diplomas to please their mother. Bessie June Hendee could pass the tests too, if she would apply her mind to it." Today the ride home seemed to be taking longer than usual, Philippa noticed, thinking of Ryan guiltily as she turned to concentrate on what Hamilton was saying.

"You do sound like a very dedicated teacher,

Miss Pippa, but what a waste it will be if you do not give some of this understanding and caring to children of your own. Perhaps you could go back to teaching later in life as Mrs. Trafalgar did, or you could always fill in when teachers are ill, or teach Sunday school."

"No, I'm afraid I'm destined to be a dedicated spinster schoolteacher as I planned. I may or may not teach another term at District Number Three. I may ask to be transferred to someplace different. A large town where you can buy meat and produce, maybe," she speculated wistfully.

She could not tell Hamilton that she did not wish to stay here even one day after Ryan's mail-order bride arrived. Reluctantly she knew she should consider staying as a married lady in town. A lady married to a minister or a lawyer or a store owner would have a good life, and she seemed to be safe here from Andrew, whereas she might be found in a big city. He may have stopped looking for her by now, but her instincts warned that Andrew Van Arder would not be the kind to give in to defeat easily, especially when it meant his inheritance was going to the temperance society.

But Philippa knew that even if her marriage were declared null and void, she still could never commit a deceitful act like marrying one man while loving another. No, somehow after she had solved the problem of Andrew, she had to make that stubborn Irishman see that he wanted and needed her, even if she couldn't brand his cattle. Otherwise, she had to accept being a teacher forever . . . elsewhere.

"I hope you'll let me try to convince you to change your mind about this, Philippa. I do not wish to interfere with your plans, but would it be all right for me to try to dissuade you?"

"Perhaps, but I must warn you, it is most unlikely."

Hamilton was not so sure. He felt certain that under her proper, pious, ladylike demeanor, Philippa Marquette had a sensuous and passionate nature. If only the right man came along, she would forget her extreme reserve. There was no way he could envision this warm, beautiful girl as an old-maid schoolmarm.

"Perhaps you would join me for Thanksgiving dinner this Thursday. As you may have noticed, the largest of the six baskets was for Mrs. Vail and myself. I am sure it contains someone's second-largest turkey, a pumpkin, some yams, and a jar of Mrs. Parker's excellent mincemeat for a pie. You would make the day very special for me."

The pumpkin and mince pies sounded tempting, but Philippa knew that she would prefer plain old apple pie and sharing the meal with Ryan. However, it had been nice of Hamilton to ask, and she wanted to refuse politely without hurting his feelings. "Ryan bought a turkey from Mr. Radcliff, but I don't believe he knows how to make dressing or sweet potato pie, so I am going to cook it for him and share it with him. Thank you very much for asking me to join you; perhaps another time."

Murphy must be starting to court Philippa seriously, Hamilton noted to himself, and if she was having him over to eat a meal with her she must be amenable to it, so he pressured, "Next Sunday for dinner, then?"

Philippa could hardly say no to Hamilton now, when she had been the one to suggest some other time.

"I would like that." She lied to the pastor again.

* * *

As soon as she arrived back at her house, she changed into her riding clothes and hurried across the road, hoping there would still be time for at least a short ride, and to explain to Ryan what had happened. When he did not answer the door, she ran to look inside the barn and her heart fell. Thunder was gone. Lightning nickered at her invitingly.

"If only I could saddle and bridle you, you beautiful thing," Philippa told the horse sadly, "we would have our ride and perhaps find your owner. That will be my next lesson—how to prepare you for riding." She stroked the horse's nose for a while and then walked dejectedly back across the road.

Before she got to her door she heard horses' hooves and eagerly ran back around to the drive to call to Ryan, but it was Calvin Lawrence who came into view astride his frisky palomino horse. He turned into her drive, glad to see her at home and outside. Every time he had dropped by after school, he'd found her gone. He waved at her, reined up to where she was standing, and jumped down to stand beside her.

"Philippa, you look beautiful. You make the tedious ride out here more than worthwhile by your loveliness."

"Calvin! How you do carry on. I'm beginning to suspect you are Irish, the way you always sound as if you had kissed the Blarney Stone!" For once Philippa was prepared with a retort for Calvin's superfluous compliments.

"Oh." It came out subdued, abashed. "Then does your Irish neighbor fill your head with his blarney?"

"Ryan? Mercy, no. All he talks about are his cattle and horses." She recalled the Irish way he called her "little darlin'," but she didn't confide that to Calvin.

"Yes, he's a dyed-in-the-wool cowman from out in the western part of the state. Lives 'em and breathes 'em. Always has and always will. Why, the only girl he'll ever think of marrying will be a cowgirl, wearin' boots and a pants skirt." At that moment Calvin noticed for the first time that Philippa had on a pants skirt, and he stumbled on quickly, "One who can break a bronc, rope a calf, and probably butcher a steer in time for breakfast."

"To be sure" was Philippa's only answer. Now she had bronc breaking, calf roping, and butchering to add to her list of future accomplishments. The feat was becoming more inconceivable all the time. A hopeless cause, maybe.

"I see you are wearing a riding skirt. Does this mean you have now learned to ride horseback?" Calvin questioned hopefully.

"Yes, I've finally managed the art."

"Do you have a horse? We can go for a gallop."

"No, I ride one of Ryan's mares, but he isn't home, so I guess I won't be riding today after all, as I had hoped."

"Well, now, we can't have you disappointed. Here—up with you. We'll ride double on Sloan. You can show me how well you've learned. Sloan isn't too easy to handle, I should warn you; however, I'll be right here to take over if he gives you any trouble." During this nonstop monologue he had helped Philippa up into the saddle, climbed up behind her, and handed her the reins, not giving her a chance to issue a refusal before he kicked his horse in the flanks.

The minute the palomino started moving, it took all of Philippa's concentration to direct the feisty animal down the drive and into the road without allowing it to rear up and sidestep as it was trying to do. Calvin's hands were on her waist, but when she continued to have problems with the animal, he reached around her and took a firm hold on the reins himself, immediately bringing Sloan under control. He gave the animal an extra-hard kick in the flanks and at once they were galloping down the road—so fast that Philippa had to hang on to the pommel tightly with both hands. Concentrating so hard on keeping her seat, she did not even see Ryan until they were almost upon him.

He was coming from the opposite direction, loping along slowly on Thunder, carrying a large pumpkin. The sight of it almost made her lose her balance, she was so delighted. They were going to have pumpkin pie after all! Philippa suspected he had made the effort to find one because she had mentioned it, but Calvin did not slow down his galloping steed for her to ask.

Instead, he hollered, "Hey there, Murphy. Nice day for a ride, isn't it?" and continued at full gallop. When they got to the crossroads, he turned back and slowed the lathered horse to a walk.

"Why did you run your horse like that?" she asked crossly, not even trying to hide her perturbation.

"I wanted you to see how fast he is, lovely lady. I wanted to thrill you as you rode at breakneck speed in my arms."

"Thrill me? You scared me half to death! And why didn't you stop and speak to Ryan? It was the polite thing to do."

"I'm sure Murphy understands that when a man takes his best girl for a gallop he does not wish to share her with anyone else."

"Is that what you were doing?" she demanded, her voice fraught with agitation.

"Of course. Is there anything wrong with that?"

Everything was wrong with it. Philippa did not

want Ryan to think she was Calvin's "best girl" or that she had willingly gone for a ride with him, when she was supposed to be riding with Ryan. What if he got the idea that was what she had been doing all afternoon? Since she could not tell any of these things to Calvin, she merely said, "I suppose not. I must get back now. I have some lessons to prepare for school tomorrow. Thank you for the ride."

"It is I who am thanking you for the ride, Philippa. It was wonderful." He squeezed his arms a little tighter around her. "I'm glad I didn't bring another horse; this is much better. Unfortunately, it made me forget my purpose.

"Mother is fixing her usual feast for all our relatives for Thanksgiving Day. We want you to join us. All my aunts, uncles, and cousins are eager to meet the girl I hope to marry."

Hope to marry? She must get him to dismiss this idea immediately. "There you go with the blarney again, and you not even Irish! Why, Calvin Lawrence, you hardly know me. I would die of mortification to be looked over by all your kinfolk."

"I don't know why. They'll love you, and you have to meet all of them sooner or later. Please say you'll come."

Relieved that there would *never* be a reason for her to meet all of these people, she answered politely, "I am very sorry to have to refuse you, but I can't. I'm cooking a turkey Ryan bought from the Radcliffs, for he doesn't know how to prepare one."

"Then I shall join you. There will be so many people at my house I won't be missed." He had to break up this dinner for two. Now he knew for certain that Belden should never have moved her here. It was giving Murphy the advantage. Calvin was determined to take desperate measures, even impolitely inviting himself to dinner if necessary.

This created a terrible predicament for Philippa, for she did not want to be rude, but she was going to have enough trouble explaining today to Ryan, without having Calvin interrupting their Thanksgiving dinner.

As they crested the top of the hill, Philippa's lane came into view, relieving her considerably. This conversation would soon end. "You must not even say such things, Calvin," she rebuked as they turned into her drive. "Of course, you know I would never dream of taking you away from your family on Thanksgiving. Why, that's a day especially for families, and your mother would hate me. No, you may not join me, and that's that." She used the same firm tone she used on her seventh- and eighth-graders. It left no room for argument.

Calvin reluctantly put her down by her back doorstep. He was tempted to hold her for an extra moment, wanting to kiss her delectable mouth, but he knew he should not rush her. Still, he knew he had to speed up his courtship. Fields always seemed to be taking her up in his buggy to drive her home or to deliver baskets, and now Murphy was going to have a meal alone with her.

Maybe he should try a different tack. "Philippa, I still have a little trouble with my arithmetic once in a while. My account books at the store are rather a botch. Could I get you to help me straighten them out, say, maybe Saturday? I could drive out and get you in the morning, and after we're through we'll go and let Mother prepare us one of her lunches from the leftovers. It's almost as good as the Thanksgiving dinner itself!"

Philippa was hesitant, but accepted. "I could help you for a little while if you need me. You've been so kind to always sell me my chicken feed at a discount, I owe you the favor.''

Calvin didn't exactly want her to come because she owed him the favor, but at least he would have some time alone with her.

If they all got such shocked expressions that Philippa was going to share Thanksgiving dinner alone with Ryan, she wondered what they would think about the meals she and Ryan frequently shared in the evenings. Tonight, for one. As soon as Calvin crested the hill out of sight, Philippa ran across to Ryan's, in a most indecorous fashion, to invite him for Sunday-night supper.

But he was nowhere to be found. Only the huge pumpkin sitting on the back porch testified he had been there.

Disappointed, Philippa picked up the heavy pumpkin and lugged it across the road. As soon as her chores were done, she would scrape it out and strain out the seeds. She wanted to get the pulp into a crock with the spices so it would be tasty for Thursday. She had watched Sadie go through this ritual every fall, hoping each time that Aunt Clara Rose would change her mind and allow her to carve the shell into a jack-o'-lantern. Belligerently she made up her mind to do it once in her life, even if Halloween *was* past. In the end, however, she didn't, for it turned out to be such a large batch of pulp that she had to hurry and can two jars of it so it would not go to waste. Endymion prowled around, protesting that Philippa was not preparing something with tidbits for a cat. Although she was up very late, she never heard Ryan come home.

Chapter Thirteen

❖ ❖ ❖ ❖ ❖

ALL OF PHILIPPA'S thirteen pupils were unruly the three days before Thanksgiving. The excitement of the holiday had infected each one of them. She might have joined in their merriment were she not so worried about Ryan. Roy and Fred Murray had gone over and done his chores, and had even chopped the kindling at her house as well as at the school. All they could tell her was that Mr. Murphy had dropped by late Sunday afternoon, saying he was going to be gone for a few days, and hired them to take care of things for him. Mr. Murphy had insisted that they sleep at his house, too.

On Tuesday, after school, Jasper Clough rode out from town to see her. Philippa was still at the schoolhouse when she heard his horse on the road, and for an eager moment she thought it might be Ryan. Even in her disappointment, she noted Jasper looked very much at home on his big bay horse, which rather surprised her since she had always thought of him as a buggy-driving lawyer wearing a suit and hat. Today he was bareheaded and his light-colored hair looked almost white in the sun. He was a man who would be handsome even when he was old and gray-haired, she thought. Apprehensively she watched as he looped the reins of his horse over the outside rail. With his long legs, it took only a few strides for him to reach the door and open it.

"Good afternoon, Teacher. I have a problem I need solved: Does one or does one not knock before entering a schoolhouse? If it is proper etiquette to knock, please tell me! I shall exit at once, for I am on my best behavior today."

Philippa tried to keep from laughing at his mock seriousness. "Miss Cauly, my deportment teacher, said one always knocks except when entering a public building. I believe we could call this one room a public building, don't you?"

"Whew! That's a relief. They did not have deportment class at Bluffsview High School, so I am always in doubt."

"Jasper, your manners are impeccable, and you know it. Why, you are a perfect example of everything a lawyer should be—and a gentleman, too," she added, recalling the way he rode his horse and the many things he could discuss: religion, politics, poetry, even the growing of apples.

"Do you really think so, Philippa?" He was standing very close now and looking down into her eyes.

Philippa was becoming flustered under his sensitive gaze and struggled to turn this conversation around. "Yes, I certainly do." She hastened to her desk and began putting away books and stacking already neat piles of papers. "In fact, I've often wondered how you know so much about farming, and where you learned to ride a horse so well."

"You find those things impressive? I thought it was my love of poetry you would find endearing."

This was the kind of question that completely baffled Philippa, and she suspected Jasper knew it. It was as if he was trying to get her to divulge a private thought.

"I find your love of poetry easy to understand,

for I love it so much myself. No, it is something like horseback riding that always fascinates me, since I did not grow up around horses."

"I see. Excellent horsemanship intrigues you, then, because it is new to you?" Jasper thought unwillingly of the way Murphy could ride a horse, almost as if he had been born riding one. He supposed it might impress this girl, who had grown up in a city where she had probably never seen anyone ride hell-bent-for-leather before. He hoped she would not let this adolescent hero worship affect her choice of a husband.

Jasper Clough intended to go to the state legislature and perhaps on to Washington, D.C., someday. With a wife like Philippa Marquette beside him, things would be perfect. She had all the poise and polish a politician's wife would ever need, and he knew she would be a distinguished dinner hostess at the most elegant functions. That she shared his love of poetry and literature was an unbelievable bonus. Still, her most compelling asset, in his esteemed opinion, was that she was beautiful.

Hoping to cast aspersions on her idol, he continued, "Horseback riding is a very simple thing, my dear Philippa. I learned as a child. Cecilia and I lived on a farm with our parents until our father died and Mother decided she preferred the conveniences of even a small town like Bluffsview over this primitive rural life. I could teach you to ride horseback in no time at all, if it appeals to you so much."

"Oh, thank you, but Ryan taught me to ride quite some time ago, and I frequently ride his mare, Lightning. I can't keep up with Ryan, of course, but at least I'm no longer left in the dust when we race. I suspect he holds Thunder in a little, but I am improving every time we ride."

Damn! Jasper thought, but aloud he said, "I am glad to hear it. My sister never uses her horse anymore. I could bring it out here for you."

"No, that is much too generous of you, and the shed is barely big enough for the cow. With the cold weather coming, I could not keep a horse, but thank you so much for your kind offer. Besides, Lightning needs the exercise, Ryan says. It's good for a mother-to-be—she is to have her colt in the spring. We have already decided it must be called Rain. Thunder is the name of Ryan's stallion. Thunder, Lightning, Rain. Isn't it the perfect name?"

"Yes, I suppose so." Jasper's discouraged "I suppose so" had nothing to do with the name of the horse. It was the familiar way Philippa talked of Murphy. If the two of them had ridden horseback together frequently and even discussed such an improper subject as the breeding of horses, they must be on very friendly terms.

He knew exactly the intentions of his friends, Hamilton Fields and Calvin Lawrence. Somehow the inarticulate, quiet Murphy had not concerned him overmuch. As a trial lawyer, how could he have overlooked such powerful evidence? The man lived right across the road. He probably chopped firewood and did all sorts of little favors that she would appreciate, in addition to teaching her how to ride. Curse Horace Belden for not keeping Philippa at his house as he was supposed to! This was one time when he should have stood up to Alvena. Philippa should not be living out here alone—alone across the road from Ryan Murphy, who also lived by himself. Jasper hoped he could resolve this situation to his personal satisfaction before it was too late.

"Even if you can't keep Cecilia's horse out here, I shall bring it out Thursday morning for you to ride. We'll go for a gallop before we go into town for our Thanksgiving dinner. I'll even be very gallant and let you win a race." He smiled at her in his most winning fashion. "What time shall I call for you so that we will have plenty of time for our ride first?"

Spending Thanksgiving alone out here was the most intolerable thought Philippa could imagine. Would Ryan be back by then? Where was he? In the past she'd sincerely enjoyed the company of Jasper and his sister Cecilia, and since she hadn't ridden for several days now, it would be fun to go horseback riding again. However, she had refused both Calvin's and Hamilton's Thanksgiving invitations. She could not be so rude as to accept Jasper's after declining the others. Besides, she was still holding desperately to the trust that Ryan would come back before Thursday.

When she thought of Ryan's return, pins and needles riveted through her, and she hoped her deepest fear would not be coming true also: that he would be bringing his bride with him; that Dixie was the reason for his long, unexplained absence.

"I'm so sorry, Jasper," she said with a note of regret in her voice, "but I can't come to dinner. Ryan bought a turkey from Mr. Radcliff, and I am going to roast it for him. He doesn't know how to make dressing to stuff it with, or pumpkin pie. Please give my regrets to Cecilia."

Cecilia, Jasper ruminated. Could she be his answer? She was always commenting on the handsome Murphy. No. Not his sister and the quiet

Irishman . . . his sister and his best friend were predestined. Jasper knew, even if Calvin and Cecilia didn't, that the two of them were made for each other. Without knowing it, they had been in love for years. If Cal would stop thinking of Ceci as Jasper's little sister and she would ever realize he was not a second big brother! The Irishman wouldn't spend hours debating with her as Calvin would. Murphy wasn't the intellectual type, Jasper speculated. Sooner or later this would become evident to Philippa, too. All Jasper had to do was find a way to make it happen sooner.

He stood looking down at her. Her expressive eyes weren't quite as sparkling now as they had been a few minutes ago, almost as if she had had a distressing thought. He wished he could determine what it was.

"Cecilia is going to be disappointed, but not nearly as much as I am. I realize your duties as a hostess will not permit you to accept, but promise me that I may at least come out late in the afternoon to sample your pumpkin pie."

He had now set up a new dilemma. She did not want him to come and see Ryan familiarly drying the dishes, but she could not tell him this. Nor could she tell him she was looking forward to having dinner instead of supper with Ryan, so that for once he might not just bank the fire and hurry home.

On the other hand, if she was alone—or worse yet, had been accosted by newlyweds—how welcome Jasper's presence would be! Her mind reeled with the dilemma.

Then Jasper broke into her thoughts. "You're off on a cloud again, my angel. May I come out for celestial pie? Just seeing you will be heavenly."

"I . . . don't know what to say." He had her

completely befuddled now, and she knew he was aware of it.

"Say yes, Philippa." He was crowding her again, trying to look too deeply into her eyes. She wished she had kept some of her unruly students after class today. This room was closing in on her. Aware of Jasper standing so near, she had the feeling that her answer had nothing to do with eating pie. Dare she say yes when he had such a beseeching look on his face? She subconsciously bit her lip as she deliberated her answer.

"I'd love to bite that lip for you," Jasper offered. He knew it was a most shocking, improper thing to say, but he was afraid these tangents her mind seemed to spring off on were distractions caused by Ryan Murphy. Cold shock often brought the truth out of a witness. Perhaps it might work now.

When she looked up at him she was as surprised as he had expected her to be. Her big brown eyes were as dark as rich French chocolate creams. He wished he could kiss her to obliterate that stunned look, but it would be most unfair to add inexpedience to shock.

Philippa didn't know what to say. She practically said "Do!" when he offered to bite her lip for her, for she needed to compare someone else's kisses to Ryan's. Ryan's kisses left her whirling like the tail of a tornado cloud, feeling as warm as the July sun and as high as a hawk could soar. It was unfair even to think of kissing someone for such a degenerate reason—only to compare a kiss. She really *was* becoming an unchaste vixen! Quickly she tried to compose an answer for Jasper.

"I have a desk back there in the corner for students who misbehave. I believe you are headed for it, Jasper." She tried to lighten the mood that had developed between them.

"I deserve the dunce cap, Philippa. I should never have said that."

"I don't believe in dunce caps. The desk is only a threat; I have never been able to bring myself to actually seat a child there. But right now, I had better finish grading these papers, or my students will be justified in seating the teacher at it! I shall bring you and Cecilia one of my pumpkin pies so that you can taste it. I have to come into town Saturday to help Calvin straighten out his account books."

"Straighten out Calvin's account books!" Jasper began laughing so hard Philippa was afraid he would harm himself. She was still concernedly wondering what she should do when he caught himself enough to blurt out, still chuckling, "He was a straight-A mathematical genius!"

"He was?"

"He was. His accounts are apple-pie perfect, unless he has boggled them intentionally."

"Oh" was Philippa's only answer, but Jasper was figuring several.

Everything began to close in on Philippa as she watched Jasper ride away. What she had taken for the light flirtations she had never been permitted—and was enjoying now, to a degree—was getting out of hand. All three of her most interesting friends wanted to be more: They wanted to become her suitors . . . *had* become her suitors. Somehow, she had to disabuse them of their notions. She *could* admit to the absurd tale of Andrew. That would end their courtship, but it would also end any chance she might have with Ryan; and since it wasn't a true tale anyway . . .

well, she'd just have to find another way to discourage them.

Chapter Fourteen

+ + + +

WILL RADCLIFF BROUGHT the turkey to school just at dismissal time Wednesday. Ryan had paid him extra to dress it, Will confessed when Philippa expressed her appreciation.

The Parker children had proudly presented her with a jar of their mother's renowned mincemeat, and the Murrays generously gave her a bag of cranberries. Their grandparents were visiting for Thanksgiving and had brought a bushel along from Wisconsin.

Philippa now had all the trimmings for a festive meal worthy of her aunt's table and groaning sideboard in St. Louis on the holidays, but there had still been no word from Ryan. She had pointedly asked the Murray boys if they were to have dinner with their grandparents or to stay another night at Mr. Murphy's. They had reckoned they'd "do up his chores in the mornin' and then skedaddle home in time for dinner." She wasn't to worry. If Mr. Murphy didn't get back, they'd be there to do chores and sleep over. She needn't be frightened that she'd be left all alone out here at night.

That of course was not what frightened her. Admittedly she felt safer when someone was in the house across the road, but if she slept better when she knew Ryan was there, she would not admit it to the Murray boys or to herself.

With a heavy heart she made the cranberries into a sauce that night and cooked the turkey giblets to put into the dressing, laughing in spite of herself at Endymion's antics to have a taste until she finally gave in and dropped her part of the liver. "Well, you greedy darling," she told her pet as the cat dragged the bit of meat to the rug in front of the stove and then consumed it swiftly, "at least if nothing else I'll have you to share tomorrow with!"

It seemed as though she had just dozed off when the pounding began at her door.

Ryan was back! Opening her eyes, she found she had fallen asleep in the rocker. Brushing the tense cat off her lap, she ran and nearly unlocked the door before she remembered to ask, "Who is it?"

"It's us, ma'am! We came to see why your lamp's still lit. Is anything wrong, Miss Pippa? Mr. Murphy will have our hides if we let anything happen to you!"

With dampened spirits Philippa tried to calm their youthful concern. She assured them she was going to bed just as soon as she put the turkey in to bake. It would take eight or nine hours to cook in a slow oven. They went away placated.

Philippa took out the three pies she had baked—pumpkin, mince, and apple—and set them on a shelf to cool. Endymion rubbed against her leg sleepily and sniffed, then disdainfully returned to her regular sleeping spot on the rug beside the stove leg. Philippa shoved the turkey into the oven, blew out the lamp, and went to bed.

Since Philippa had not expected to sleep at all, she was most perturbed to wake up late, and then only because of Endymion's screeching demands to be let out. Her cow was bellowing and she had banked the fire too much—it had gone out. It took time to restart it with cobs before she could tend to Tilly. As soon as she had the fire crackling she grabbed the milk pail and started for the shed on the run.

Halfway there, she happened to glance across the road. The sight stopped her dead in her tracks.

There, sitting in Ryan's yard, was a shiny new buggy. Not just a plain, ordinary buggy, but one with yellow wheels and a leather fold-down top that was now up in place to protect its passengers from wind and cold. Oh, how she wished she had been awake to see who had climbed out of that buggy when it had arrived! On second thought, she was glad she had been asleep, for inwardly she knew that she could not have stood there and watched Ryan help his bride alight from that buggy and welcome her to her new home. The sight of such a tender scene would have been intolerable.

Try as she might, Philippa could not think of a single other reason for that new buggy sitting there. Its horses must already be stabled in the barn. Guests did not stable horses except in the bitterest weather.

No. There *was* no other explanation. Now she was forced to accept what she had always known was to be. How utterly stupid she had been to let her feelings for Ryan carry her beyond her sense of reason. Of course, his bride would arrive eventually. She was the one Ryan had chosen, wasn't she? Any girl would practically give her right arm to be married to the handsome Irishman. To be around him all the time and know his teasing and his caring and his incredible kisses. To listen to him talk in that slow western drawl about his cattle and horses, and all his plans. His cattle-feeder operation was already large and prosperous. Now he was going to raise thoroughbred horses as well. With his knowledge and abilities, he'd make his plans realities.

Oh, yes. Any girl would want that, all right. Philippa could not help but wonder why this one had taken so long to get here. Perhaps she wouldn't come until he'd bought a new buggy and a matched pair of horses for her. Foolish Dixie! Philippa knew she would have walked barefoot from the Bluffsview junction if marriage to Ryan awaited her at the end of her journey.

Stop this nonsense, she tried to tell herself. You, Miss Pippa, are a schoolmarm and always will be, now. Admittedly she knew there would be other suitors, but after her feelings for Ryan she didn't think she could ever face marriage with anyone else. And not only because of that, but because she quite possibly already had a husband.

Thoughts tumbled back and forth in her mind. Was he still planning to share dinner with her? Would he bring his bride? Of course he would bring her along—if he came.

Hastily she washed away her tears, then changed into her Irish green waist and a pale, cream-colored skirt with a small bustle. She fussed with her hair for so long she nearly forgot to boil the yams for sweet potato pie. Should she be gracious and set the table for three, or should she only set it for herself and feign surprise when Ryan brought his Dixie over?

When the knock she had been sadly anticipating finally came, Philippa literally jumped. She had to steel every nerve in her body to walk over and open the door. There at her door stood Ryan, looking so unmercifully handsome that she wanted to cry at the sight of him. He wore a brown pinstripe suit and a green-and-brown-striped tie. The green in his tie exactly matched his eyes. His brown boots gleamed with their well-polished look. Were these his wedding clothes?

She looked beyond him, trying to see the new Mrs. Murphy, but saw no one. There was a long, awkward silence before they both said "Hello" at the same time.

Finally Ryan asked shyly, "Are we still having Thanksgiving dinner together?" All he could see from the partially open door was the unset table.

"Just the two of us?" she asked tentatively.

"Unless you've invited someone else."

"No, I haven't, Ryan, but I will if you want me to. There's plenty of food for one more."

"Why would I want you to? Who are you thinking of asking—your friendly feed and seed dealer?" Ryan steamed every time he thought of her galloping that way with Lawrence, but he'd convinced himself these last few days that he had to accept seeing her with all her suitors. It was what he wanted for her, wasn't it? Not for her to spend her life all alone, teaching school here, there, and everywhere.

"Why would I ask Calvin? I was referring to . . . don't you have . . . someone . . . at your house?"

"Not that I know of."

"But the new buggy . . . and the suit!"

"I've been thinking about gettin' a buggy and a new team for a long time, so I finally up and did it. Don't you agree it's about time I bought a new suit? Can't very well come to Thanksgiving dinner in my dungarees, can I?"

"Oh, Ryan!" Overcome, Philippa threw herself against him and wrapped her arms around his neck. "I'm so glad you're back!" Endymion came up to inspect the visitor, sniffing warily, then, deciding Ryan was welcome, she brushed by and went immediately to her warm spot, where she curled contentedly, ignoring the two people's strange behavior.

"Now, this is more like a welcome-home should be, little darlin'." He folded her into his arms and gave her a tight hug. A friendly, neighborly hug was all he had intended it to be, but when he pulled her up against him, it turned into so much more.

Her body was warm against the coldness of his jacket, and her rounded softness fit perfectly against the hardness of his chest. She was quivering slightly as he reached out to tilt her face up to his. Her eyes had tears in them. Had she really been this lonely? He never should have gotten angry and left the way he had without even telling her good-bye. He wanted to tell her how sorry he was, but he didn't know how to say it, so instead he kissed her, softly. He meant it to be a gentle welcome-home kiss, but her lips were moving softly against his with a faint clinging motion. He pulled her to him and closed his eyes and violently poured his heart and soul into the tempestuous kiss he gave her.

The embrace was no longer just friendly. Ryan now held her as tightly against his body as he could mold her to it, and she responded to his every movement with one of her own. Her fingers were twisting a lock of hair on the back of his neck one minute and gently massaging his cheeks the next as she held his face up against hers.

A week's loneliness and her relief that Ryan wasn't married yet freed Philippa of all the inhibitions she should have possessed. She put her hands inside his jacket and let her fingers stalk across the smooth satin fabric on the back of his vest. The feel of the material sensitized every part of her.

Ryan had initiated his own exploration. His hands were low on her back under the bustle, cupping her buttocks, pulling her tightly against him.

The kiss was progressing at a rapid-fire, out-of-control intensity. Each of them parted their lips slightly to feel more of the sensuous part of the other's lips. The kiss had turned into a yearning duet when they heard wagon wheels in the driveway.

Since they had been only fractionally into the kitchen, Ryan quickly stepped on into the room and sat down at the table. Philippa tried to smooth her hair, her ruffled collar, and her disarranged bustle all at the same time. Her mind tried to blank out the possibility that Calvin or Jasper had come out after all, even though she had refused them. Ryan looked enraged. He was probably sure it was her friendly feed and seed dealer.

At last the dreaded knock came at the back door. Not a confident rapping, but a timid *tap, tap, tap.* Thank heaven, Philippa thought: it must be one of her students. She quickly opened the door to a quaking Sammy Hawkins.

Damn! Ryan thought.

Drat! Philippa thought.

Sammy didn't wait for her greeting or look beyond her into the room. He only breathed a sigh of relief and expounded, "Thank goodness you're here, ma'am. Please get your coat. I have to hurry and take you to my house."

"Whatever for, Mr. Hawkins?"

"Well . . . you see . . . I was supposed to be sure to invite you to join our family for dinner today. Maman has been telling everyone you'll be there.

Papa's delighted because he heard you turned down the preacher, Clough, and Lawrence."

"I thought maybe they'd forget. I sort of forgot, myself. I didn't tell them you were coming, but I never got around to telling them you weren't. Now our table's all set for four with the company china. Shoot! I thought if you turned everybody else down. . . . But since you're here, please just come on. I'm gonna be in a peck of trouble if you don't." Sammy's face was beaming with his usual boyish smile, with a hint of smugness that he'd succeeded in his mission.

Philippa felt sorry for Sammy's predicament, but Ryan's presence diminished her sympathy for the young grocer. Stepping back from the door, she motioned toward where Ryan sat at the table. "I'm not alone, Mr. Hawkins. Mr. Murphy has joined me for dinner."

Ryan nodded a greeting as he stood to shake hands. Sammy was obviously shaken, and he blurted, "I don't dare go home! Maybe I could just eat here."

"Certainly not! Your parents will be very worried if you do not return soon. In fact, I suspect you should hurry along. You'll think of some reason I am not with you, I'm sure." She was using her effective Teacher's Instruction Voice and ended with a firm, "Good day, now, and thank you so much for asking me. Give your parents my regrets." As she spoke, she had practically moved him out the door.

Sammy looked like a spanked puppy. "Well, good day to you, then." Then his expression changed to one of delight as he added, "I think I'll just drive the rig on over to the Hendees'. I just bet Bessie June will come into town to have dinner with me. At least Maman will have her guest."

"I just bet she will too!" Philippa agreed.

Happily, he ran down the steps and leaped into his surrey, leaving at a much faster clip than that at which he had arrived.

Ryan and Philippa burst into laughter. They knew that little Bessie June Hendee might appeal to Sammy, but his parents were going to dissemble when they saw their dinner guest! Old man Hendee didn't farm much, just fished and hunted and lived off the land. Mrs. Hendee was a hard-working woman, but she was also a hard-drinking one; she made her own corn likker and sometimes a keg of beer or two, if her sometime garden yielded any hops. The lackadaisical way Bessie June attended school would not endear her to the Hawkinses, either.

Humming a Thanksgiving hymn, Philippa hurried around to set the table. The turkey had turned out perfect and her sweet potato pie looked just right. With the thrill of Ryan's homecoming, that distracting kiss, and the intrusion of Sammy Hawkins, though, she had forgotten about the warming dinner rolls. They were like rocks when she opened the skillet.

Disappointedly she exclaimed, "Oh, no—my rolls! I used the last of my yeast to make them light and fluffy, and now they're ruined."

Ryan did his best to ease Philippa's chagrin over the leaden dinner rolls, even as far different matters occupied his thoughts. "The rolls are fine," he insisted, but gut deep he knew that Philippa should be in town, having dinner in any one of those handsome dining rooms. She should be sitting at a big table set with linens and china instead of here with him, using cast-off dishes on an old oilcloth-covered table in the kitchen. Still, he couldn't deny how he loved having her here, singing, hurrying around with that little bustle he had loosened flipping this way and that.

This past week he had met two of his brothers in Omaha to arrange some cattle shipments back east. They had tried to get him to stay and eat Thanksgiving dinner with them at the posh Blackstone Hotel; it served great food in its main dining room, they said. When he'd refused, they had been surprised.

"Thought you said Bluffsview was like a morgue," Stuart huffed.

"The town is, but now he's sweet on a little schoolmarm," his kid brother, Halfpint, quipped. "I've even got a list of stuff I'm s'posed to git for her in Chicagey."

"Hot damn!" Stuart exclaimed. "Courtin' a schoolteacher when you ain't never been to no school. If that don't beat—" He hadn't even finished the sentence before Ryan slammed his fist into his older brother's jaw.

"What'd ya do that for?" Halfpint asked, reaching down to help Stuart up. Stuart started to take a swing at Ryan but thought better of it and rubbed his aching jaw instead.

"You mighta broke it, you snake-in-the-grass. What the hell's gotten into you? I was only makin' a joke!"

"Sorry," Ryan had muttered half apologetically. "This teacher is a very proper, genteel girl. My neighbor. She's a high-class lady, the kind you don't make jokes about."

"You mean she thinks she's too high-falutin' good for you?" Halfpint asked. In his own opinion, nobody was good enough for his idol, Ryan, and he took an instant dislike to this prudish little teacher.

"I mean she has several suitors already," Ryan informed them through clenched teeth.

"Sounds like you better come up to Frenchie's with us, after all," Stuart stated. "She's got a Spanish girl you won't forget! I heered she also got in some fancy new mirrors in the upstairs rooms."

Sitting here in Philippa's kitchen, Ryan surmised that Stuart had probably been right. It was no doubt exactly what he'd needed. After watching Pip gallop off with Lawrence last Sunday, he'd wondered which of her suitors she would eventually choose. But today was not the time to think about that.

In the end, neither Ryan nor Philippa could remember eating a better Thanksgiving dinner in their entire lives. Afterward, they rode the horses despite the cold, cloudy day. It had turned dark and ominous by the time they returned. Philippa asked him to come back in and eat some leftovers with her, but he had to pretend he was too full. He knew the only leftovers he wanted now were the emotions still hanging fire from that kiss this morning. They told one another good night as they carefully stood four feet apart.

Chapter Fifteen

✦ ✦ ✦ ✦

THE DAY AFTER Thanksgiving, Phillipa awoke to a world of white. Snow was inches thick on the shed roof and on top of the chicken coop, clinging to the fence wires and post tops. Even the sky was a leaded, grayish white.

As she dressed to go out to milk her cow, she wished she had added some more items to her stack of merchandise on that long-ago day at Madame Marquette's. The coat she had chosen was a beautiful Paletot, which at $37.50 had been the most expensive on the rack. It was three-quarter length and made of warm genuine seal plush. Its collar and lapels were trimmed with marten fur. The upper sleeves ballooned fully, but from the wrist to the elbow they fit tightly, as did the waist. It was not exactly a coat suited to milking cows. Nor had she thought of anything but styles that made her appear older when she had picked out hats; warmth had been far from her mind, which meant the only thing she had to wear now was a tea towel tied over her head. A matching marten fur muff that went with the coat would only be in the way while tending chickens.

The snowstorm made her wonder where Ryan was this morning. There were no sounds at all from his farmyard. With the stillness all around, Philippa wished she would hear some kind of noise; even her chickens seemed glued to their roosts when she filled their feeders and watering pan.

After tending to her animals and clearing up her few breakfast dishes, Philippa sat down in her rocker. Endymion, curled up close to the stove, looked up at her with intelligent amber eyes.

"Well, Endymion, what should we do today to pass the time?" she asked the cat, who merely blinked and continued to watch her. "The County Superintendent told me last month that none of the children are expected to attend classes during any sort of bad weather, so we have the whole day."

Once each month the superintendent "happened" in on their school, always without warning. Philippa was sure this was intentional, so that the teachers had lessons prepared each day for each student and did not get behind in grading papers. So far he seemed very pleased with Rural School District No. 3.

She wished her social life was going as well as her school-teaching venture. Since Calvin, Jasper, and Hamilton had all three openly confessed to courting her, she'd become insecure and wary. If only it were Ryan, with whom she already felt so at ease, who wished to marry her, how wonderful things would be.

No, unfortunately, she had to admit things would be worse, for if he was courting her, her predicament would be unbearable. Still, wasn't it unlikely that Andrew would find her after this long, and wouldn't it be even more impossible to locate a married lady? No lawman or detectives would be searching for the wife of anyone other than Andrew Van Arder. A marriage would definitely put a seal of safety on her escape. Why, then she'd *never* be found.

With nothing else to do, Philippa finally heated some water in the copper boiler, got out her washboard, and scrubbed her laundry clean before she remembered she would have to wade in the snow to hang it out. The sheets and towels would freeze dry, but she did not want her clothing frozen stiff.

She pulled two chairs close to the stove and put her broom over the backs for a drying rack for her undergarments. Her fingers were stiff after she finished hanging out the bedding, and her toes were stinging from the cold.

With numb fingers she unbuttoned her kidskin boots, slipped them off, and opened the oven door so she could prop her feet to warm them as she leaned forward to let her fingers feel the heat too. She decided she was not going to wash her flannel sheets again until spring. If need be, she would just keep her improvised drying rack set up all the time to dry her linen and muslin towels, her dishtowels, and her underclothing.

That might present a problem, since she only had two chairs. When she was alone, she could pull the rocker up to the table, but what would she do when Ryan came over to eat with her? She was trying to devise a solution when the sharp rap on the back door startled her. Swishing her feet down off the oven door, she bounded across the room to answer the knock, remembering only at the last minute to question "Who is it?" before she turned the key.

A cross voice answered, "It's me, and I want to know whatever possessed you to hang out your laundry on a day like this."

Philippa opened the door as she ruefully admitted to Ryan, "When I started to do the washing, I forgot about the snow. I had the clothes all wet before I thought of it. After I hung them out, I wished I had used the hot water for a bath instead, believe me!"

Ryan smiled at her candidness as he brushed off some snow and stepped inside. His eyes darted to the drying rack of petticoats, panties, and stockings. Clearing his throat, he took hold of the door handle to leave. "I'll just go along, then, if you're okay here—"

He didn't get the sentence finished before Philippa plunged across the room, grabbed up the broom with its intimate apparel flapping wetly against her, and thrust it through the bedroom door. Haphazardly she balanced it unevenly on her washstand and the foot rail of her bed and hurried back to the kitchen. Now that she had eliminated the barrier, she hoped to persuade Ryan to stay for a while. The isolated feeling the surrounding drifts of snow had given her was intolerably lonely, even with Endymion for company.

Assuming the manner of the perfectly poised hostess, she stepped back into the kitchen and announced, "I have a hot pot of coffee on the stove and there is cold turkey for sandwiches. I also have a lot of pie to be eaten up. I do hope you will join me for lunch. It seems only fair that you should have to help eat the leftovers," she added.

Ryan wondered if the girl even suspected what a tantalizing sight she was as she stood there in her stockinged feet, still breathless from her hasty retreat with her laundry. Her cheeks remained rather pink from embarrassment, and she must have had something over her head earlier, for her hair was in an entrancing disarray. He wished he could tell her she was far more tempting than coffee or pie; instead, he began to take off his heavy leather coat, saying, "I'd love to stay, Pip." As he hung his coat on the hook behind the door, he noticed the elegant, fur-trimmed sealskin hanging there and asked, "Don't tell me you wore something like this to do chores in."

"It's all I have except for my lightweight school coat or my good gabardine reefer," she told him, fearing her face betrayed her embarrassment. "In August, one just doesn't think of freezing." Today she wished she had all the out-of-style sweaters, boots, and mittens she had left behind. She would gladly be a teacher in a youthful stocking hat if this was an example of the months to come in Nebraska!

"From now on, I'll do your chores until the weather breaks. You stay inside. I would have done them today, but I had to spread some hay to feed the herd and start rounding up the cows I want shipped. I wish we had arranged to do it earlier in the year. The railroads are making us forget the best times for cattle drives. Luckily, mine don't have to be driven far to the railhead. The Murray boys won't be at school a couple of days next week; they're helping me. Belden, Parker, Radcliff, and his son have also offered to help."

"You sound pleased by their offers. Why shouldn't they help you? Gertrude tells me you always help everyone else out."

"I am still seen as an outsider here in this German-Scandinavian community."

"You should come to the Bluffsview church, then you'd get to know everyone better," Pip said with a guileless look on her face. "Now that you have a buggy, you could save Gertrude and Ole that cold ride over here each Sunday to pick me up."

Since that was exactly the reason he had bought the buggy, he agreed. "I s'pose I could. It's a shame for the Olsens to have to come so far out of their way in the wagon." He wanted to add, "And it would save the pastor a trip out here after church." Of course, he didn't say it, but he was hoping she would want to ride back home with him too.

Reverend Fields seemed to be a splendid fellow.

Ryan didn't know why he always felt so disgruntled when he watched Hamilton help her down and walk her to the door. Why, he should be happy a fine man like that was taking an interest in Philippa. A minister would be good to her and give her the refined, easy life she should have.

So then, why was his pulse pounding so joyously when Philippa added: "—and you can bring me home, too, and save Reverend Fields a trip out here. I must remember to send him a message tomorrow when I'm in town that I won't be eating dinner with him and his housekeeper Sunday. It would be foolish for him to have to bring me home in the cold and snow when you'll already be coming this way."

"Sure would!" Ryan agreed, much too fervently. Philippa was putting the sliced turkey and pie onto the table when he questioned, "You're going into town with the Olsens tomorrow, then?"

She practically slopped the coffee she had just started to pour at the thought of explaining that Calvin was picking her up. But there was nothing to do but admit the truth. She proceeded to tell him hastily, "No. The Olsens won't be going in again until January or February. It's Calvin Lawrence who is coming to take me into town. He says he needs help with his account books . . . but, Ryan, Jasper Clough told me Calvin is an *expert* at mathematics! What should I do?"

Ryan struggled to keep his face straight as Philippa innocently told him of Lawrence's finagling and Clough's retaliation. Ryan had heard the two always teased one another openly in their pursuit of the teacher's affections. Now the deceit and backbiting had started. He was lucky he wasn't on her list of suitors, or someone would be trying to eliminate him too. It was a good thing he had sensibly realized at the beginning that he was beneath her aspirations, even though a downcast feeling wrenched inside him as he dismally tried to help her see her suitor's point of view.

"Perhaps he just wants an excuse to be alone with you. He's using the books for that excuse."

"Maybe." Philippa pondered, recalling last Sunday. "I am sure he intentionally kicked his horse in the side when he saw you coming last week. It wasn't bad enough I had to help Hamilton deliver Thanksgiving baskets. I had no sooner put on my clothes to go for our ride than Calvin came along and practically threw me up on his horse without a by-your-leave!

"Not that you were home anyway," she added petulantly.

Ryan's spirits soared. She had been delivering gift baskets, a duty he knew she wouldn't shirk, and it didn't sound as if she had chosen to go galloping with Lawrence. Trying to keep his rising emotions under control, he replied as calmly as possible, "I went over and got the punkin Gertrude managed to get from Belden for you. Don't you like to have Calvin try to find time alone with you? It's because . . . well, he's partial to you, you know."

"He just thinks he is. He loves Cecilia Clough and she loves him, I'm sure of it. She has never said so right out, but the way she acts when his name comes up, I think she does! In fact, she acts just like my friend Lee Ann did when anyone mentioned Dottie's brother, Roscoe."

Knowing that she had just revealed more than she intended, she hastily continued, hoping Ryan would not question her about her old friends. It was a subject she could not discuss yet, not even with him. There were many times when she wished she could confide in him, but she realized he might stop coming over if he thought she could possibly be a married woman.

"Yes, Cecilia has exactly the qualities any man would want in a wife. She is at ease wherever she is. She talks all the time and to everyone. She can debate on practically any subject."

A nonstop talker? A woman who argued about everything? These were not the qualities most men would look for in a wife, Ryan thought. He was sure that any man worth his salt would find Philippa's sweet hesitation much more endearing, but he didn't quite know how to tell her so, so he just replied, "She may want him, Pip, but I think he wants you."

"As if I'd accept him when the only girlfriend I have here wants him!" Quickly realizing how vain and patronizing that sounded, she went on, "You know as well as I do, Ryan Murphy, that I am a dedicated schoolteacher and that I have to find a way to discourage Calvin Lawrence. Don't just sit there and smirk; help me!"

"You never had any trouble turning into a block of ice where I was concerned," Ryan recalled. "Can't you use that uppity-snippy voice on him that you use on me when you're riled?"

"Uppity? Snippy!"

"Don't git your feathers all ruffled!"

The speechless look of outrage on her face tickled him, and Ryan could no longer resist laughing at her chagrin. He tried to calm her. "Now, little darlin', I admit I was way out of line when you froze me cold. I agree it isn't the way to cool Calvin's ardor."

"I cooled your ardor?" Philippa asked bluntly, her eyes big and questioning. It sounded as if he had at least liked her kisses even if they *had* been uninvited, and yesterday he had actually been the one to kiss her. If she couldn't rope, butcher, or drive a six-horse team, she needed to use every subterfuge possible. She didn't want to be dousing any affection he might be feeling.

Ryan felt that somewhere this whole conversation had taken a wrong turn. How could he answer this question when he was so distracted by her femininity? Hastily he reminded her, "We're not talking about me. We're talking about the estimable Mr. Lawrence. Here's what we'll do: Tomorrow we'll get up and leave very, very early to go to Nebraska City to try out my new buggy and team. You can leave a note that you forgot about an eye examination or something. Don't mention who took you, of course!"

"Oh, that's wonderful, Ryan! You are almost as good a liar as I"—she caught herself just in time and rearranged her answer—"I've always heard that politicians need to be!"

"Maybe I should run for office!" he said, grinning at the clever ruse to cover her slip. One of these days she was going to forget herself and reveal her past to him. Lee Ann and Roscoe: had they been relatives? Why had a sweet innocent like Philippa been forced to lie? He had long since dismissed the idea she had ever been a starving waif, for she cooked as if she was used to an abundance of delicacies. And she was always wishing she had real lemons, baker's cocoa, and freshly ground coffee.

Ryan had made a list of a few of these things and asked his younger brother to pick them up in Chicago for her. They'd be stopping in Omaha to meet Ryan on their way home, to pay him for his share of the sale to the Chicago Beef Export Company, which always eagerly bought Murphy Brothers shipments of cattle.

Calvin was restacking some heavy bags of grain for the second time Saturday morning when Jasper came sauntering in. Without saying a word, Jasper glanced questioningly back at the empty seat by the rolltop desk at the back of the store. Calvin didn't greet him as he usually did; he just continued to restack burlap bags of grain that looked as if they were already neatly stacked.

"The snow is melting, I notice," Jasper finally said casually. "None of the roads must be closed around town, judging from the number of wagons at Hawkins's today."

"Snow probably made 'em think of laying in a supply of stuff for when they do get snowed in. Alec said almost everybody that came in here this morning bought extra," Calvin answered indifferently.

"Oh, you were gone, then?" Jasper questioned knowingly. "I thought I saw your buggy go past my office."

Calvin needed to talk to someone, anyone!—even Jasper! He was so perplexed, and try as he might, he couldn't make things add up.

"Hell, yes, you saw me drive by, and you know damn well you did and prob'ly guessed exactly where I was headed. Well, she wasn't home. Just a note that said she had to go to the optician over in Nebraska City to get her eyes checked. She was sorry she'd forgotten about it.

"But Jas, there was only one set of buggy tracks to her place, and they came from across the road. Murphy doesn't even have a buggy! You'd think

Belden would have taken her in, him being president of the school board and all."

"Nope. Alvena would never let Horace drive that girl anywhere. Stop and think about it."

"You're right. She keeps him under her thumb, and by the way she acted at the Grange Dance when ol' Horace just danced with Philippa . . ." He started to guffaw, but stopped abruptly, asking, "Then who? You're the lawyer. I gave you the facts."

"I hate to suggest it, but it looks as if Murphy bought himself a buggy. Now, the question is, why, when he's always ridden one of those thoroughbred horses of his everywhere before?"

"Ridden with Philippa, in fact," Calvin added informatively in a dejected voice.

"Precisely. Now, however, it is getting too cold for riding, so he has purchased a buggy so he can maintain his advantage."

"You, too? I thought I was the only one who suspected he's seriously courting her. He always seems so quiet and reserved, not her type at all."

"No, possibly not her type, but *there*! Always *there* when she needs someone!" Jasper made his point clear as if convincing a jury.

He certainly convinced Calvin. "Damn Horace Belden!" he exploded.

"Alvena."

"Her, too!"

"So what are we going to do about it? Stand around with our hands in our pockets?"

"No, we'll think of something. Come on home with me for lunch. We can talk about it."

"Cecilia should come, too."

"Why? We can't talk with her there."

"Ceci can give us a woman's point of view. She's

very clever." Jasper was careful not to imply he wished to put his sister in Calvin's mind . . . and heart.

Chapter Sixteen
✦ ✦ ✦ ✦

RYAN'S NEW TEAM was as sensational as his new buggy. He easily taught Philippa to handle the reins before they were halfway to Nebraska City.

The minute they sighted the town, Philippa took the tea towel off her head and ordered, "Our first stop is to be a ladies' ready-to-wear shop. I have to get a velour or plush hat to wear today—and some mittens and a muffler and warm boots."

Ryan wondered if Belden had remembered to pay her recently, or if she had any idea how much this might cost. Just in case she needed help paying the bills, he determined to stand nearby after she made her purchases.

They found a mercantile store where she soon found heavy stockings, long-sleeved undervests, snuggies, and even a couple of union suits. While she inspected the items, he pretended to look at things in the men's department. She was mortified when the clerk held them up to price while Ryan stood there. Although he knew he should leave to keep her from being so embarrassed, he was afraid she would be even more so if she found she could not afford everything.

The order came to nearly twenty dollars, which Ryan knew was practically two whole months' salary for her. Just as he started to reach into his pocket, she handed the cashier a twenty-dollar gold eagle from her tooled-leather handbag. Wordlessly Ryan picked up the package and they left the store.

At the grocery store Philippa was disappointed because cocoa was out of stock and the store did not carry lemons, nor did they have the freshly ground kind of coffee she wanted. But she was ecstatic when Ryan reported he was having the items brought from Chicago.

"You've talked so much about fudge, lemon meringue pie, and eclairs with lemon filling and chocolate frosting that you have my mouth watering too," he told her to explain the purchases he had generously ordered just to please her.

"We'll have lemon meringue pie for our Christmas dinner, and I shall give the children some fudge the last day of school. I'll give them a party with both fudge and hot cocoa. I didn't realize what a treat chocolate would be! I can't remember when we didn't have at least some bars of a Dutch import at home. The boxes of cocoa are so much easier to keep and use, and my aunt Clar—inda always thought it was more economical, too. What a wonderful surprise!"

The surprise was that she would be here for Christmas at all. Ryan had been certain she would go back home for the holidays, as Alexander always had, and he had been anticipating the same bleak, uneventful holiday that he had had last year. At least when he was still back home they had eaten dinner at the hotel in town to celebrate. This year it would be wonderful. Just like Thanksgiving, when she had fixed all those special things.

With a sinking heart, he recalled the amount she had just spent for warm clothing. No wonder she wasn't going home for Christmas—she had no money. Ryan just could not be that selfish, to keep her here when her heart would be elsewhere. Everyone wanted to spend Christmas where their happiest memories were.

"Pip, I know how little you make every month, and Gertrude told me you had to pay for the things for your house yourself. Now you had to buy these clothes you didn't know you'd need. Please, for my Christmas present to you, let me pay your fare to Cincinnati."

"Why ever would I want to go there?" Philippa asked unthinkingly. Her mind was only on the disappointment that Ryan had not promptly accepted having Christmas dinner with her. When he looked at her with a perplexed expression, she reluctantly remembered what she had just said and had to stammer, ". . . I mean, with my father dead and all, it is only full of unhappy memories."

"What about your aunt Clarinda?"

"Aunt who? Oh, Aunt Clarinda. Yes, she's dead too, poor thing. No, Ryan, I never want to go back there," she ended firmly.

"Then nothing in this world would make me happier than spending Christmas with you."

"Really, Ryan?"

"Really, Philippa."

People were pushing to one side of them and then the other as they stood on the board crosswalk. They had been walking from the store when the conversation had begun, and somehow they had become so engrossed in the questions and answers that they had forgotten to keep moving. They began to laugh at their own carelessness as Ryan grabbed her arm and directed her down the block to an eating house.

* * *

Andrew had been avoiding a trip to the house he'd purchased years ago for his mistress, but during the holiday season the empty Van Arder mansion seemed haunted. Most of the gossips would be too busy with their own merriment to notice his comings and goings now anyway, so he cranked up the Mitchell Six after dark and drove to Sampson Street. He was warmly welcomed, as he knew he would be.

"Andrew, darling! I haven't seen you in weeks! Where have you been keeping yourself? Little ol' me has missed your lovin' arms," Lil exclaimed.

"I told you, it's not wise for me to come here frequently, Lillian. My every move is still watched by the harping old cronies," he replied crossly.

"It never bothered you before! Besides, you come after dark . . . after the witches are already in bed. What's the *real* reason?"

Andrew didn't like Lil's presumption that she was entitled to have him answer her, but he had to humor her.

"I've been very busy, that's all."

"Searching for *that* girl?"

"That, among other things. You know it's essential that I find her."

"It's become an obsession with you! You're already a rich man—forget about her."

"And let all that money go to the *temperance league*? Hardly!"

"I want you to stop constantly thinking of finding *her*. It's all you ever talk about. One minute you're lambasting my modiste for selling the girl serviceable clothing; the next you're carping about my uncle and his friends because they haven't located her yet for you. Last month you were angry because her little friends had come up with an idea which not even the Pinkerton agency had suggested—''

''It was a damned good idea, inquiring at all the schools statewide. Too bad nothing came of it . . . nor of my efforts to locate the man who hauled off her things. When the lout turned up to claim the reward, all he could tell me was that he'd taken her to the depot!''

''Did you learn where she got the money for a train ticket? You used to be so certain your mother had kept her penniless.''

''The little conniver must have found all of the coins Mother had stashed away in her room. Mother always did that, even when I was a boy, but when I looked in the coin bank she kept money in, only her ring was there—the one I had given Philippa. We wasted a lot of valuable time investigating jewelry shops where she might have sold it. Oh, she was sharp, all right.''

''Huh,'' Lillian grunted. ''The way your voice sounds, you admire the little sneak thief.''

Andrew pondered a minute before admitting, ''Frankly, Lil, I do. She's a shrewd little minx. Not shrewd enough, of course. The railway connection will soon turn her up. All the destinations of women who purchased tickets for that date are being traced. It's only a matter of days now, and I'll have her back.''

In her whole life, time had never gone as fast as the weeks between Thanksgiving and Christmas, Philippa reflected. She spent every spare moment trying to finish knitting the sweater she was making for Ryan. At school, there was also an expectancy infusing her students. If the children had been unruly the week before Thanksgiving, it was as nothing compared to the festive air that invaded the school before Christmas. Right in the middle of recitation, Lars might dreamily announce, "There's a package on the closet shelf that looks like a Stereoscope."

"No, it's a doll. I know it is," his sister would correct him.

To which Susan would add, "I hope Santa brings me a dolly," and Fred and Roy would look up with knowing grins on their faces.

Isaac John would ask, "If it's a Stereoscope, can I come over and look at the pictures with you the day after Christmas?"

"Children, children, you must finish your lessons or the superintendent will not let me close the school for a vacation. Please resume your work," Philippa would warn them.

Quiet would be restored, but seldom for long. During one study session, the usually quiet Herbert began to hum a German Christmas carol and unthinkingly Henrietta joined in with the words, in German. Philippa determined this to be a learning experience and had the two come to the front and sing it, then translate it. Lars and Ella did likewise in Swedish. The Parker children assured her America was a country just like Germany and Sweden, and the four of them sang their favorite carol. Their voices blended so beautifully that everyone wanted them to sing another. Then they begged Philippa to sing a song she had learned in school, and when she did they all clapped to show their appreciation for her beautiful voice. The rest of the afternoon was spent singing every Christmas carol anyone could think of.

They all enjoyed the singing so much it was decided to have a program for Valentine's Day and invite their families. Lydia soon added a spelldown to the entertainment, and Isaac John said if they had a box lunch auction they could raise enough money for a picnic with ice cream the last day of school. So the plans were laid.

After her first experience at the monthly Grange Dance, Philippa had avoided attending them, but even the children insisted the Christmas party was special and she should be sure to go. Their festive mood was contagious, and she agreed to ride in with the Parkers, unless Mr. Murphy went, which Philippa was ardently hoping he would. Just the thought of dancing with him made her pulse quicken. As her students left the room, she heard Alice Ann say condescendingly to Lydia, "Told you so! She's set her cap for Mr. Murphy, all right." Philippa realized she would have to ride with the Parkers, or Alice Ann might spread her suspicions—suspicions that were much too true for Philippa's comfort.

It was even more dismaying to Philippa to learn the night of the Grange Dance was the night Ryan had to meet his brothers in Omaha on their return from Chicago. Even though he promised her he would only be gone one night, it was most upsetting, and she began to wish she hadn't agreed to go with the Parkers. Therefore, on the day of the big event, it was a relief to watch the snow keep falling and piling and drifting. Being snowbound was preferable to the dance, even though it meant Ryan would have to stay over a second night in Omaha.

* * *

The children loved the unheard-of treat of a
school Christmas party with hot cocoa (heated on
top of the potbellied heating stove) and fudge with
black walnuts in it. Ryan and Philippa had rescued
a bagful of the walnuts from underneath the tree in
his yard before the squirrels got all of them. It had
taken several evenings to shell, crack, and pick the
nutmeats from them, but he had not seemed to
mind.

From her students Philippa received brightly em-
broidered handkerchiefs or homemade candy and
cookies. She also received invitations to Christmas
dinner from every one of them. Even Alvena Belden had told Gertrude that, since it was Christmas,
she guessed she would condescend to have the
teacher at her house.

Calvin Lawrence brought Philippa a silk muffler
with her initials on it for a gift and invited her to eat
with him and his mother. Hamilton Fields gave her
a box of cherry-filled imported French chocolates
and asked her to join him and Mrs. Vail for the
holiday meal. Jasper brought her a new novel from
Cecilia and a book of poetry from himself and went
back as upset as the others had been when they
found that once again she was cooking a holiday
dinner for her neighbor—cooking it with the items
he had had brought especially for her from Chicago.

Sammy Hawkins joined Jasper and Calvin at the
conference table in Jasper's office to discuss what
could be done to block Murphy's much-too-
successful suit. Philippa had not looked to any of
them like a homesick little orphan, blue over her
first Christmas away from home. Indeed, she had
looked radiant. Stern measures needed to be taken.

Calvin growled, "I don't know what she sees

in him. He sure can't cipher worth a damn when he totals up his grain bills. Nope, he's not too smart."

"You should be so dumb," chided youthful Sammy. "I don't see you buyin' up farms right 'n' left and puttin' money in the bank by the bushelful. Why, I heard—"

"That's all beside the point, Sammy," Jasper interrupted. "We're not disputing his abilities at real estate or making money. He's got the luck of the Irish there, it seems. Cal just meant he doesn't seem . . . well . . . highly educated. Not like she is. We just feel she belongs with someone who at least equals her in schooling."

"Shucks!" Sammy told them disgustedly as he got up and walked out the door. "You fellas make it sound like she oughta just cuddle up with a good book to keep warm!"

"Plague take that kid!" Jasper swore as the door slammed shut.

Chapter Seventeen

✦✦✦✦

As soon as the milking was done on Christmas Eve, Ryan and Philippa lit the candles on their evergreen branch. Here on the prairie, one did not chop down the few evergreens that were growing. Ryan had ridden nearly to Auburn to find a family with a large evergreen tree in their yard who were willing to let him cut a lower branch off. Philippa was as delighted with her "tree" as the family had been with the silver dollar he had given them.

"Isn't it beautiful!" she exclaimed when Ryan finished lighting the candles.

It ran a poor second to her, Ryan thought. Her dark eyes were sparking with gold flecks brighter than the candles, and the dress she was wearing seemed to change color as the light reflected against its red/blue/violet color. Tonight she, too, liked the dress, which she had not worn since the Grange Dance. She had worn it that night to look especially nice to impress Ryan, and he had not been there. Tonight he was here, and if the glimmer of emotion in his green eyes meant anything, he was impressed.

"Oh, yes," she sighed, "it's perfect."

"No, it's not quite right." Ryan shook his head, pretending to ponder.

"Whatever is wrong with it?"

"It has one too many of these gingerbread men on it," Ryan announced as he untied one and proceeded to eat it.

Philippa gave him a playful push and vowed, "After all you ate the night we baked them, I don't see how you can think of eating any. You had better not become too full—I have eclairs and fudge made for later, as well as popcorn balls."

"For later? Are we just going to stand and watch the candles burn on the tree until it's time for the goodies?"

"Stop acting addlepated! On Christmas Eve we read Dickens's *A Christmas Carol* and Mr. Clement Moore's poem of "The Night Before Christmas," and then we read the version of the birth of Jesus from the Book of Luke in the Bible. Here, I have all the books out. Do you want to read first, or shall I?"

Ryan practically choked on the bite of ginger-bread he had just begun to swallow. For the first time in days he recalled who and what he was: an illiterate cowhand. He closed his eyes as dread washed over him—he knew he would have to admit now that he couldn't read any but the simplest primer. And he could already imagine the look of disdain on Philippa's face when he made his revelation.

Was there any way out of this coil? Sooner or later, something would happen, and she would guess; but he found himself praying that it didn't have to happen now.

When Philippa saw the look on his face, she announced, "Oh, for heaven's sake, Ryan, don't frown like that! If you're so hungry you may start eating, but *I* am going to read and you have to at least listen. I love these stories, and to me they are a part of Christmas. I suppose with five brothers you could find a lot more fun things to do than to sit around reading, but there was only my aunt and me—and my father, of course," she inserted quickly, "so Aunt always read to me until time for church services at midnight, and I *am* going to read to you!"

She got out a big blue-and-gray stoneware mixing bowl filled with popcorn balls and a platter of fudge and set them on the table. Then she moved the oil lamp to the side of the table where her rocker was and sat down. As she began to read, " 'Twas the night before Christmas, and all through the house . . ." in her soft, melodious voice, Endymion gracefully sprang into her lap and curled up contentedly.

No man in the world could have been happier than Ryan Murphy that Christmas Eve. He loved listening to her read and she seemed to enjoy reading, especially all the roles in the Dickens story. Her voice was gruff for Scrooge and high-pitched for Tiny Tim, then sonorous for the Ghost of Christmas Past.

He could see why she had dreamed of the eclairs, for they were light and fluffy and delicious, even though he was already full of fudge and popcorn balls.

It wasn't so hard to say good night when he knew he would be spending the day with her tomorrow. They had agreed to share the Swedish coffee cake Gertrude had sent Ryan for breakfast Christmas morning, as soon as he finished milking. Philippa had promised he would love the coffee she would make from the beans his brother had brought from Chicago. It was a Java-Mocha blend to which she said she added egg and cream as they did in the South. It sounded fine to him. (She could have served him an okra or gumbo substitute for coffee and he would never have complained if she hummed sweetly as she poured it.)

He began to whistle as he crossed the road back to his own place. The stars were especially bright and a silver moon dipped high in the sky. When he recalled how lucky he had been that Philippa did not find out he couldn't read, he muttered half-aloud, "Thank God!" and looked up into the sky once more before entering his dark, empty house.

As soon as Ryan was out of the door, Philippa quickly took out the sweater she was making for him, to finish it. She had it all blocked and ready to wrap except for embroidering his initials on it. It was brown with a V-neck so he could wear it to church under his suit jacket for warmth, for she didn't think he had an overcoat, and he was too proud to wear his rawhide one. Most of the men at church wore work coats, or sweaters underneath

suit jackets. Only a few from town had topcoats
like the men she had known in St. Louis always
wore.

She began to hum as she worked. Her aunt Clara
Rose had always read to her and bought her a very
expensive present for Christmas. They had enjoyed a sumptuous dinner, for which Andrew· had
joined them. He, too, had always given her a lavish gift, but never had she looked forward to a
Christmas Day as she was looking forward to tomorrow.

Ryan had seemed happy and content to be with
her tonight. Wouldn't that count a little toward her
not being able to assist in roping and branding
cattle? In fact, she didn't think farmers around here
branded their cows. Tilly didn't have a mark on
her, and if they didn't have to be branded, why
would one need to rope them? She hummed a
gayer tune as she took her needle to start the
curlique she was putting on the *R*.

The look he sometimes had in his eyes when she
glanced at him unexpectedly was the same ardent
look Jasper, Calvin, and Hamilton had when they
practically admitted they were courting her.

Perhaps he no longer thought she wasn't his
type. In fact, she was wondering if his type *was* the
prim miss she always tried to be. Just maybe she
should be a little aggressive. He might only have
pretended to be reluctant because he always implied she was too young and innocent. Was Dixie
prim and proper?

Philippa bit her lip as new ideas to attract him
came to her. Since Dixie was leaving him out here
all alone when she knew she was supposed to be
his mail-order bride, Philippa had no qualms about
trying to win him. Dixie was so callous she didn't
deserve him. Why, she'd had plenty of time to get

here—even Swedish and German immigrants made it to Nebraska in three months. Besides, Philippa needed to win him soon to help secure her safety from Andrew's clutches.

Perhaps Ryan would like the sweater so much he would forget himself again and take her into his arms and kiss her. She added a little flourish to the *M*. Lovingly she wrapped the sweater in the tissue paper that had been inserted by Madame Marquette inside her hats to help them hold their shapes. She had ironed it very carefully to use. She tied the package with some bright pieces of yarn from her muffler and held it out to admire, then placed it under the tree, banked the fire, and went to her hard, lumpy bed, still humming happily.

"This is really for me?" Philippa exclaimed joyously the next morning as she took the package Ryan handed her. "It's so beautiful! I've never received a package in shiny silver wrap with a red satin ribbon! It looks like the kind one sees in a store window!"

"That's prob'ly where Halfpint—I mean, my younger brother James—got the idea. I told him what I wanted him to buy; the fancy package was his idea. None of us ever wrapped any of the gifts we exchanged at home, that's for sure, and Ma always just put some little thing or another into our stockings, as I recall."

Ryan was pleased that she liked the looks of the package so much. Halfpint had insisted she would; that was why he'd had the Chicago store clerk wrap it up for her. He had been disgusted because all Ryan wanted to get the teacher was a ladies' riding hat of felt and some heavy calfskin riding gloves, but he couldn't change his brother's mind. They were things Ryan knew Philippa needed, and he thought she'd probably like them all right.

"I just can't wait until after breakfast to open gifts. Here, you open mine first!" Philippa insisted as she handed him the package from under the tree.

"Pip! You weren't supposed to get me anything. You're fixing the dinner."

"With food *you* furnished. Besides, I wanted you to have this. Hurry and open it."

She was like a little girl as she stood there clutching her present from him in one arm while handing him her present with the other hand. He wished he could reach out and crush her and kiss her and swing her around and around to wish her the merriest Christmas ever.

Humbly he took her gift and began to open it. He got so choked up he couldn't even utter a "thank you" when he saw what it was. She had knitted him a sweater. Spent all that time just on him.

She was standing there, watching him, waiting. Oh, hell, he couldn't say it; he'd just have to show her. Jubilantly he picked her up, package and all, and swung her around and around. "Little darlin', that has to be the swellest gift anybody ever got. Even my initials on it, and you made it yourself!" He stopped swinging her and was going to pull her close and give her a big thank-you kiss, but the box she held was between them, so he settled for kissing her forehead and setting her back down on the floor. He took off his suit coat and hung it behind the door, then immediately pulled the sweater on over his starched white shirt.

"The sweater certainly didn't look that handsome before!" Philippa cried, pleased that Ryan seemed so happy with the gift. She started to take her gift to the table to open it carefully, but she already had the table set for breakfast, so, unlady-like, she sank to the floor on her knees and began to unwrap the package meticulously so as not to tear the precious foil paper or snarl the pretty ribbon.

The box underneath was a blue-flowered hat-box. It surprised Philippa that Ryan would buy her a fancy French original hat such as usually came in these boxes, when he had so eagerly sailed hers into the air at the junction the day they had met. She hoped he had not bought her another because he felt so guilty; she had never missed that hat one bit. Gently she pried off the lid and squealed when she beheld the Texas Stetson in her size.

"Oh, Ryan, I love it. A real riding hat to keep the sun out of my eyes!"

She put it on to model for him. It was a perfect fit. "Now, if I was big and strong I would swing *you* around, but since I'm not, all you get is the kiss!" Very properly she leaned toward where he had knelt beside her to watch and kissed him on the forehead.

"Is that all that's in there?"

"You got me something else?" She pulled out a carved wooden ladies' glove box and flipped up its hinged lid to reveal the thick calfskin gloves. Now she was the one to shake her head wordlessly with emotion. He still remembered the blisters she had gotten when she first learned to ride.

"Doesn't two gifts mean two kisses?" Ryan asked, trying to dispel the soft film of tears that he noticed were beginning to mist her eyes. It made him feel damn good that his gift meant as much to her as hers did to him.

Philippa leaned forward to kiss his forehead again, glad for a moment's respite before she would have to say anything. In leaning forward, she lost her balance, and Ryan had to reach his arms out to catch her. Her lips were now aimed not at his forehead but dead-level with his lips, and their eyes were locked. They both kept their eyes wide open as their lips drew closer and closer together until at last they were almost touching.

She parted her lips slightly. He parted his lips slightly. The minuscule space between their lips vanished.

Ryan tried for a moment to make himself remember all his reasons for not touching this girl. Philippa blanked out Decency, Decorum, and Dignity and closed her eyes, applying just a tiny bit of pressure with her lips. It was enough to make Ryan forget all the things he was trying so hard to recall. He returned the pressure, not just a tiny bit, but a lot. He held her face with both hands so he could kiss her more potently. When he had her face positioned where he wanted it, he pulled the rest of her closer to him by putting his arms across her back. She responded by inching forward on her knees and putting her arms around him also. Their thighs were pressed so tightly together that Philippa could feel the hardness that developed between them against her lower abdomen. Her eyes grew wide as she looked into Ryan's questioningly.

Quickly she closed her eyes again and began running her fingers up under the sweater she had lovingly knit for him for this very purpose: to be held tightly against it. Her nipples felt very hard, as if they were all puckered up, and the hardness that pressed against her lower abdomen gave her prickly sensations that both frightened and thrilled her.

When Ryan sought to put his tongue against her teeth, she responded by opening her mouth for it to enter. Tenderly his tongue tasted each tooth, then each corner of her mouth, and at last ended engaged with her own tongue. This time she was not going to be cheated. She wanted to feel those perfect teeth of his. Her tongue escaped his, and when it got a chance, went venturing as his had. She touched each tooth with it, touched the inside corners of his mouth, but now his tongue was attacking hers, grabbing it, holding it as tightly as he was holding her.

She heard him moan low in his throat as he initiated another kiss. Both of them were struggling for breath as the kisses came rapidly, one instantaneously following another.

Gently Ryan pulled Philippa down onto the floor to lie on top of him, managing the motion without breaking the flow of their kisses. The slight weight of her on his chest and loins helped to ease the flames that were engulfing him. The softness of her breasts pulsed against the beat of his heart, causing him to sigh audibly.

The sigh alerted Philippa to her thoughts of last night. Ryan liked this as much as she did. She just might be his type after all. To test her theory she broke their kiss so she could kiss his forehead, his eyebrows, his cheekbones, the tip of his nose. She stopped her tender marauding long enough to join her lips with his for a brief moment, then continued her progression, kissing him firmly on the neck, then under his shirt collar. The sweater she had made him impeded her progress.

Refusing to be daunted, she tugged until she managed to pull it and his shirt up until his bare chest was visible. The sight of it still gave her sensuous tremors when she remembered brushing her fingers through the soft mat of hair the night he had been lying in the hammock.

This morning it was not only her fingers that caressed the muscular chest, it was on her lips as well. Ryan sighed deeper still, then insisted, "It's your turn, lil' darlin."

Philippa was tenderly lifted from on top of him and laid on the floor. Ryan was the one above now. He, too, gently kissed her forehead, her eyes, her cheeks, her nose, but at her mouth his kisses became more demanding. The pressure of his mouth on hers was so vibrant, so stimulating, that she resented it when his lips proceeded to her neck, her throat; but not for long. The scorching kisses he gave her in those areas turned her insides to a quivering jellied mass of emotion. Smoldering, wavering, waiting, wanting . . .

Smoothly, without stopping his onslaught, he unbuttoned the front of her blouse and pulled her chemise aside. Philippa sighed deeply as he proceeded to kiss and massage one nipple and then the other. When he gently drew the fullness of one of them into his mouth and began to suckle it, she cried out in pleasure.

At the sound Ryan raised his face up to hers and she could read intensity in his green eyes as he murmured, "I knew, love." Then he proceeded to do the same thing several times, each time giving her more pleasure until she was sure she was too weak to endure.

He offered her his strength by pulling her tightly into his arms and holding her there until she felt she could breathe normally again, but he did not stop this ardent loving. He threw his leg across hers until she could feel the hard ridge pressing between her thighs, moving and pressing until she knew something was going to break loose inside her. The heat. The power. The unbending desire that seemed as if it might tear her apart. She pushed up with her own hips, matching his movements, wanting to ease some of the pressure building inside her. With a sudden thrust by Ryan it seemed as if they were bonded in spite of layers of clothing between them, and Philippa cried out at the release within her. It was an osculation that gave her a warm, wet feeling between her legs, that caused her to sigh contentedly.

When she opened her eyes, Ryan was looking at her again with a puzzled look on his face. Love and satisfaction were there, but there was something else. Something she didn't understand at all. Wasn't he as happy as she was?

As he looked at Philippa's flushed face, unbidden he heard one of the few maxims his old man ever taught him: "You don't bed virgins, son, you wed 'em!"

"Oh, Pip" was all he could say as he gently put her away from him, out of his arms. He wished he could add "I love you," for he did love her. Painfully he remembered the hands-off policy he had instituted to keep her safe from the likes of him. An illiterate cowpoke had no business making love with a genteel, educated lady like Philippa Marquette.

Her eyes were dark with emotion when she looked up at him from the few inches that he put between them, and her kiss-swollen lips were trembling as she said fervently, "Oh, Ryan, I love it when you hold me and kiss me like this!"

There! She had said something that shouldn't be said, but she wanted him to know just how she really felt for once.

"I'm sorry, Philippa!" he said, regaining control. "Why, I never even think of you in this way," he lied. "I don't know what made me do this." Quickly he pushed her farther away and sat up. Hurt by his sudden actions, Philippa sat back up too, moving several inches away from him.

"I see," she replied quietly as she looked down into the hatbox, trying to hold back the tears. Just when she'd thought he was beginning to care. How could somebody make love that way and *not* care? Philippa could have sworn she felt his heart pounding against her chest, and he'd been as breathless as she had.

Ryan *must* like holding her and kissing her; she was sure of it. So why did he deny it? Because of Dixie? No; Philippa wouldn't allow herself to believe that. No man in love with someone else would have uttered "Oh, Pip!" in such a love-filled way. Perhaps he didn't realize yet that his emotions were love. Somehow he had to be made to see it.

She blinked her eyes to force back the tears, and it was then she saw the last gift in the bottom of the box. At first he was completely shocked as her hands reached in and turned it over unbelievingly. It was undoubtedly Ryan's brother's idea of an embarrassing joke, but it would serve her purpose. After this morning, Ryan Murphy was going to have provocative thoughts about Philippa Marquette —she would swear to it. Provocative enough to make him realize he loved her and maybe even to give him the idea of marrying her.

Looking up from the package, she innocently asked, "You did tell Halfpint—James—*exactly* what to get for me?"

Ryan was grateful for the change of subject as he assured her, "Yeah, I told him just what I wanted, and it looks like he followed instructions to a T. I mean, you like 'em, don't you?"

"Yes, oh yes! I love everything you gave me, but

Ryan, are you *sure* you never think of me . . . in that certain way? Like when you kiss me?"

How could he lie to her when she was looking at him so closely? "Well, I can't deny I think thoughts about you I shouldn't be thinking. I suppose it's because you're so young and beautiful, and we live so close, and—"

"Ryan, you don't have to say any more. I think this nightdress says it all for you." Resolutely she stood up and held up the flimsiest scrap of lace Ryan had ever seen outside of a cathouse. If he knew his brothers, it probably had come from inside one. Damn their hides! He knew his face was sunset red when Philippa held it up against her. It was slit high up the front, and the top had a low, scooped neck with an even thinner lace right where the breasts would fit into it. It was the most seductive thing Ryan had ever seen, even held up on the outside of Philippa's clothes. God! What would it look like with nothing under it?

"Philippa! Give me that this minute so I can burn it. I never ever told him to get that—God's truth!" He dove for it, but she swooped away.

"Oh, no you don't, Ryan Murphy. This is *my* present, and I'll not have you destroy such beautiful lace. Why, it's . . . it's . . . lovely!" She, too, was flushing with embarrassment, but she kept to her purpose.

"Lovely? You'd never wear a thing like that, Philippa Marquette, and you know it!"

"No, not now, of course, but I'm going to save it. If I ever do get married, which we both know I probably won't since I'm destined to be an old-maid schoolmarm, but say, just in case I do: don't you think it would be all right for a husband to see his wife in something like this?"

"Certainly not!" He made another grab for it and missed as she ran into her bedroom and closed the door. The thought of one of those town dudes seeing her in that set Ryan's skin to crawling. Hopefully she would marry the minister. Surely all she'd ever wear with him would be high-necked white cotton nightgowns—nightgowns with nothing under them. Remembering the warmth of her up against him when he held her and kissed her, he felt like punching the pastor.

Just as if everything was all sugar and spice, Philippa paraded back into the kitchen, heading for the door to let the scratching Endymion inside. As she went she was telling him, "I can't wait for you to taste the coffee, Ryan—you are going to love it. The lemon meringue pie turned out perfect, too. This is just the most wonderful Christmas ever, don't you think?" She scooped up Endymion and nuzzled the nape of her neck.

As she handed him the cat and began to prepare breakfast, she asked, "Since it's warmed up, can't we ride the horses this afternoon? I want to wear my new hat and gloves."

He fell in with her banter; truly, it was the most wonderful Christmas ever—except for that gown. As soon as she got engaged to somebody, he'd break in and steal it. He knew just how much he wished he could be the husband who saw her in it, but that could never be.

But nobody else was going to see her in it, that was for damn sure!

Chapter Eighteen

✦✦✦✦✦

THE SNOW SEEMED to be never-ending during the entire month of January. Each night Philippa assigned Roy, Fred, and Bessie June extra homework in case they were snowed in the following day. She was determined to have them pass the Eighth Grade Examination this spring. They must have been equally determined, for even the days they were not snowed in they brought the double lessons back completed.

Near the end of the month a blizzard descended on them rapidly during school hours. The wind changed to the north, and the snow blew so hard from that direction it was almost impossible to see Philippa's house from the school window. They could not see Ryan's house at all.

Philippa did not know who felt the most panic, herself or her students. Her first thought was to dismiss them all and let them hurry home, but the snow had already closed the school paths. What would the roads and the children's own lanes be like?

At noon, no one did anything but nibble at their lunches of johnnycakes with molasses or bread spread with lard and preserves. Even the abundant supplies of apples had run out, and the children ate lunches of cornmeal or flour breads spread with anything on hand and dried fruits. The Murray boys often brought cornmeal muffins topped with cold boiled beans to satisfy their enormous appetites.

The day of the blizzard, even Fred and Roy's appetites were nonexistent. They offered to scoop the paths open, but Philippa did not want anyone to go outside, it had turned so cold and blustery. They added wood to the stove twice as often as usual, and still the room was getting continually colder from the drafts blowing in around the windows.

Ryan arrived shortly after lunchtime, and Philippa knew she had never been so happy to see anyone. He carried Susan, and led Philippa and the girls to her house by tying a rope around their waists; then he took the boys to his own place the same way to keep everyone warm overnight.

By the following morning the storm had blown itself out, and thankful parents arrived by bobsled or on horseback to take their children safely home. The teacher and Mr. Murphy were heroes. These parents all remembered well the blizzard of '88 in which so many schoolchildren had died.

Rural District No. 3's Valentine's Day party became the talk of the community. When February fourteenth finally arrived, the schoolhouse was filled beyond capacity. Chairs had been brought out from both churches in town, but still most of the younger children had to sit on the floor. Horace and Alvena Belden sat in the front row, as Alvena thought befitted the president of the school board. The Lutheran pastor and his wife attended, as well as Reverend Fields. Jasper, Cecilia, and Calvin arrived together. Mr. and Mrs. Hawkins attended along with Sammy. The audience thought the roof might fall in when Alvena Belden looked over her shoulder and spied her old enemy Babette Hawkins here in the Beldens' own school district. Alvena had always been sure Horace had a fondness for

Babette, and she glowered disgustingly, but Babette only smiled sweetly and sat down in the chair her husband politely pulled out for her.

This was going to be some party, everyone wagered. It would probably go down in Bluffsview history, especially once the auction started. The crowd sat back to await the fireworks. All the teacher's beaux were here to try to outbid one another for her basket, and now Alvena's and Babette's husbands would have to offer excessive prices to assuage their wives' well-known temperamental feud, as well.

Tonight Philippa was thankful to her deportment teacher at the Hansen-Tawzer Academy, who had demanded student perfection. While she might be flustered, she was confident she would not make errors in her speech as she stepped up to welcome everyone and to introduce their special guest, the district superintendent, Mr. Niles.

Everyone was still clapping when Mr. Niles stepped to the front of the room. While he was well aware of the fact that they were not clapping for him but for the very popular teacher of Rural School District No. 3, he made the most of the ovation as he announced, "It was with great pleasure that I accepted your gracious invitation for tonight, as it gives me the opportunity to congratulate Miss Marquette publicly. Not only have the students in this district excelled over every other district in the county in progress this year, but she has shown a rare and shrewd judgment for one so young. Keeping her students safe the day of the blizzard was courageous beyond—"

He didn't get a chance to finish his sentence before everyone began to clap and cheer. Obviously they, too, were proud and happy over the teacher's actions.

Philippa knew she was blushing every shade of red and wished she could count on her legs to hold her up and her voice to project loudly, for she needed to correct everyone's assumption that she should have the credit for this. It had been entirely Ryan's idea.

Wide-eyed, she looked around the room until she discovered him standing against the back wall. He must have guessed her intentions, for he was shaking his head back and forth and mouthing "no." She questioningly shook her head no, and he nodded yes. Everyone looked toward the back of the room to see with whom the teacher was having this nonverbal conversation; there were quite a few scowls among the younger single men when Murphy was recognized.

By now the superintendent had the attention of the crowd again as he offered an even more pleasing announcement. "Because of such exceptional qualifications, I am taking it upon myself to offer Miss Marquette a contract to teach District Number Three again next year."

Alvena's pocketbook dropped as she slumped despondently back in her chair while pandemonium broke loose. All the students began to jump up and down excitedly and the parents clapped approvingly. Some of the guests even began cheering and stomping their feet. Jasper and Calvin slapped one another on the back in their enthusiasm, causing Cecilia to duck. Just when Philippa was wishing the floor would open up and swallow her, Susie Murray came running to the front of the room, threw her arms around her teacher, and gave her a big kiss on the cheek. Then she proclaimed, "Oh, Miss Pippa, I'm so glad you're going to be my teacher next year. Will you stay 'til I'm in eighth grade? Mama is so proud of Fred an' Roy, and it's all 'cause of you. Pretty please, stay here forever.''

Philippa hugged the little girl, but she could make no promises. She looked over Susie's head but could not see Ryan, since everyone in the room seemed to be standing up as they continued to clap.

When he could restore order to the roomful of delighted people, Mr. Niles turned the program back over to Philippa, and she introduced the performers in their turn. Since neither Bessie June nor Lydia had family to sing with, they had mended their fences long enough to perform a duet. Philippa noticed with disappointment that they did not sit together when they finished singing. She tried her own method of bringing friendship between the two girls when she declared the spelldown a tie after several words failed to eliminate either of them, the two final contestants. Philippa pinned blue cards on a beaming Bessie June and a frowning Lydia, then gladly let the superintendent take charge once more; he had volunteered to auction off the lunch baskets.

The children's baskets were auctioned first and the results were predictable. Pee Wee spent his entire seven cents on his sister Emma May's basket because he knew what was in it. Lars bought Ella's for the same reason, while Isaac John took a chance and purchased Henrietta's. This meant that the shy Herbert had to pick Susie's or Alice Ann's, when he had been counting on the treats Ma had packed in Henrietta's for him, too. Alice Ann's box looked more special, but Herbert knew she considered herself one of the older girls, so he decided to be safe and pick Susie's. Susie was so happy she giggled, and both of her brothers breathed an obvious sigh of relief that they would not feel obligated to buy their little sister's basket.

The next basket was tied with multicolored ribbons that all the students recognized, having seen them tied in Bessie June Hendee's hair. If the ribbons had not been recognizable, Bessie June's fluttering glances would have alerted them as she looked from Fred to Roy. Then she spied Sammy Hawkins, and her eyes batted even more becomingly as she gave him a sultry smile.

"Who'll open the bidding on this with a dime?" the superintendent asked, already suspecting he would have more than one bidder on this one.

"Me, I guess," Fred offered.

"I'll go eleven cents." Roy glowered at Fred.

"Twelve!"

"Thirteen!"

"Ah, this is more like an auction," Mr. Niles interceded. "How about hiking it to fifteen cents?"

"Okay, I s'pose," Fred agreed, and not to be outdone, Roy offered, "Seventeen cents!" loudly.

"Eighteen."

"Twenty cents!"

"A quarter!"

A suddenly hissed response caused most of the adults in the room within earshot to smile. "Where did you git a quarter? Pa only gave us each twenty cents to bring!"

Before the answer was revealed, a voice came from the back of the room. "A half dollar!"

It was echoed by a high-pitched "Sammy! What are you thinking of, dear?" and a gruff warning, "Son, remember that talk we had?" but the word was "SOLD!" and a red-faced but happy Sammy Hawkins came forward to collect the basket.

Fred spent his twenty cents for Lydia's basket, and Roy paid his for Alice Ann's.

Then the wives' baskets were offered and there was a lot of good-natured bantering and bickering, not between the contestants for the baskets, but between the husbands and their wives. Rafe Parker said he ought to get his for seven cents like Pee Wee had, because he knew the basket had the same things in it. Mr. Murray tried to convince his wife he'd only brought twenty cents, too, but maybe he could get his son's extra nickel. Both men paid a half dollar, as did Mr. Gulickson, Mr. Hubbard, and Mr. Radcliff. Mr. and Mrs. Hendee were the only parents not at the party.

Everybody, even the auctioneer, recognized Alvena Belden's store-bought lunch basket with the brass hinges. The auctioneer held it up, saying, "We have a beauty here, and it's heavy, too. I'll wager I get at least a dollar out of it." Alvena came as close to smiling as Philippa had ever seen her, and Horace stood up, glad to get by for only a dollar. If Hawkins's had been first and he had paid more, Horace knew he would have had to pay as much.

The superintendent evidently decided to help the ice cream social fund along, for he set the basket back down, announcing, "But I'm not auctioning that one yet. I'm auctioning *this* one!" and he held up Philippa's. She did not have a lunch-sized basket, so she had carefully lined the big hatbox she had received from Ryan with a tea towel and put the lunch inside it. Everyone oohed and ahed as the beautiful box was held up. It was well known just who had carried it in here tonight.

Ryan wished that his brother would have just put the hat in a plain old box as the bidding began.

"Fifty cents," from Hamilton.

"Seventy-five," from Calvin.

"A dollar!" Jasper offered, and it kept on going. Will Radcliff dropped out disappointedly after his bid of one seventy-five, but the other three did not seem concerned at how fast the price was climbing.

Ryan felt like stomping out the door; in fact, he was sidling in that direction when he felt a sharp kick in the shin.

The crowd was so involved in the bidding, no one heard his "Ow!" except the administrator of the kick. Ryan looked down into the angry little face of Pee Wee Parker, who pronounced, "Dumb cluck!"

Ryan had always gotten along fine with Rafe Parker's kids, and he couldn't figure out what had made this little guy turn on him. "That's the best basket. I peeked in 'em all. It has apple pie an' roast beef and even popcorn balls. There's some yummy-lookin' things in it with choc'late frosting and yeller insides. Miss Pippa wants you to buy it, Alice Ann said so!" Pee Wee Parker loved his teacher and would do anything to make her happy. His big sister knew everything, so he figured she was right about this.

Naturally Ryan knew that Alice Ann did not know what she was talking about, but he glanced at Philippa anyway. He was surprised to find she was looking at him, her eyes so sad they almost made him cringe. He had never seen her look that way before and tried to think what the cause might be. Lord, she had the three most eligible bachelors in town offering heretofore unheard-of prices for her basket. Could she feel frustrated because she knew all three were her foremost suitors? She always maintained she wanted to remain a teacher forever.

Maybe she was just shy. Shyness he could understand. Come to think of it, Pip did sort of clam up when there was a bunch of people around. She sure wasn't quiet around him, though! Jubilantly he determined to bid, just to keep Philippa from feeling shy and frustrated, of course.

He stepped up to the tune of "Fifteen dollars and fifty cents!" and a big smile from Philippa, which was not lost on the three other competitors. When the bid reached $18.50, the auctioneer warned, "Cash money, gentlemen."

It cost Ryan a twenty-dollar gold piece and two quarters, but the smile he got from Philippa was worth every penny of it. The audience clapped when he came forward to collect the basket, and he found he rather enjoyed the glares he got from the other bidders. They would have their day—tonight she was his.

"His" was scolding as they sat down to eat, "Oh, Ryan, you should never have spent so much. Why, most of it's your own food. You paid for your own food"—she began to laugh softly and then added with honest candor—"but oh, I'm so glad you did!"

"Why?" He still couldn't figure it out.

"I made all your favorite things, that's why! How would I even know what anyone else likes?" She quickly changed the subject before she accidentally told him the real reason. "Did you see Mr. Belden's and Mr. Hawkins's faces when the superintendent said surely those big baskets were worth as much as mine? They both looked stone white when they paid.

"I'm glad Calvin paid twenty dollars for Cecilia's basket, too. Do you realize the school treasury now has nearly ninety-three dollars in it and all the ice cream this whole crowd can eat won't cost ten dollars? We can buy some big desks and a globe and a dictionary—"

"You're gonna have this place snazzier'n the town school. Nobody'll want to graduate."

"They want to graduate, all right. I just hope Mr. Murray lets them remain in school long enough this spring to finish . . .

"Oh! I have to put some of this extra food on the guest table for those who don't have baskets. I'll be right back."

Ryan watched as both Reverend Fields and Jasper Clough liberally helped themselves to eclairs, apple pie, and roast beef Philippa placed on the library table. After he slipped Pee Wee Parker an eclair and a popcorn ball, Ryan sat back and enjoyed the food she'd packed, even enjoyed the antagonistic looks he got as Philippa sat beside him, talking animatedly.

Chapter Nineteen
✦ ✦ ✦ ✦ ✦

SOME OF THE days in March were nice enough to make one start thinking of spring, and others made one wonder if it would ever arrive. Philippa hadn't yet come to a decision about signing the contract for the next term. Alvena Belden had made a special trip to the school one day and related all the reasons that Philippa should seek the comforts of a town school. Rural schools should be taught by men who were prepared to cope with the realities, she said. Philippa thought if she had been a man and lived at the Beldens' home, she would have had very few "realities" to cope with. Politely she assured Mrs. Belden she would think about it.

Actually, all Philippa could think of, in trying to decide about next year's term, was Ryan's fiancée. When was she to arrive? Was she coming at all? Philippa certainly did not want to bring up the subject to him. She hoped he had forgotten to mail her a train ticket, and his Dixie darlin' had married someone else.

To make matters worse, there was really no place for Philippa to go during the summer. The Fitch agency might be able to place her in the fall, but her dwindling supply of coins would not last long if she had to pay board and room for the summer months. Besides, where could she go that would be as safe from Andrew's search as she was here?

Here she was occasionally able to go for days without even thinking of her dreaded husband—if he even *was* her husband. Several times she started letters to the district court in St. Louis inquiring about her legal status, but she never mailed them. Andrew had too many influential friends in high positions—one of them might receive the letter and tell him her whereabouts.

It was equally impossible for her to write to the district court in Lincoln, for Jasper might hear of it, and she never wanted anyone in Bluffsview to learn of her past. What would everyone think if they heard that the laudable Miss Pippa was really a husband deserter and a fugitive! What a catastrophe, if the town's most eminent lawyer or its highly regarded pastor was discovered to have been courting a married woman!

No, her decision to marry, to completely blot out any trace of Philippa Martin, was still her most desirable choice—if only Ryan wanted her. The persistent unease that nudged at her conscience at the thought that such a marriage might be bigamous was promptly stilled by recalling that her marriage to Andrew was against her will and hadn't been consummated. It couldn't possibly be binding, she told herself. Once she had persuaded herself that it certainly could not, she decided to stay in Bluffsview, at least until she knew Ryan was legally married to someone else.

Since spring had arrived, Philippa seldom saw Ryan, for he was busy with calving and did not have time to milk Tilly for her. It was a pleasant surprise when he came to get her one day after school to show her the new colt, Rain.

"He's darling, Ryan," she proclaimed the minute she saw it, "but he has such wobbly legs. Will he be okay? Look at him. His eyes are just like Thunder's, but he has Lightning's coloring. The white even looks the same on his face."

"He's a little beauty, all right," Ryan agreed as he and Philippa stood companionably side by side with their arms on the top rail of the stall door. When they were together like this, Ryan still suffered. He wondered if that first night's burning memory of lying beside her on the hay would ever fade. In one breath he hoped so, and in the next he never wanted to forget it as long as he lived.

Philippa, too, felt the special current generated by standing together this way, and she wanted to stay here until Ryan recalled the memory. Then maybe he would want to hold her and kiss her again, or at least happily swing her around in the air.

"I have some very serious problems I need to ask you about, Ryan," she ventured so she would have a reason to stay longer.

"What's wrong?" he asked as he tried to imagine what might be causing her troubled expression.

"Well, first, it's my chickens. They won't let me have any of the eggs they lay. They just sit there on their nests, night and day, so I can't get any."

"They're setting."

"That's what I said. They just sit there."

"No, I mean they're going to sit on the nests until the eggs hatch."

"Hatch?"

"Yeah, until the eggs hatch."

"What is 'hatch'?"

"It means baby chicks will be born."

"Out of the eggs?"

"Don't you know where chickens come from?" he asked, amazed.

How could she admit to a thing like that? She couldn't tell Ryan, of course, so she just changed the subject. "I need to plant my garden, but the children say I have to cultivate the ground first. I wondered if I could borrow a thing to cultivate it with."

"Such as?" he asked teasingly, certain that she didn't know a spade from a hoe or a shovel.

This kind of ignorance she was perfectly willing to admit to Ryan. "Ryan, I don't even know what 'cultivate' means. All the dictionary says is 'to till, work or break up land for planting crops.' I don't have the least idea how it is accomplished. I've seen the fields that the farmers are getting ready to plant, but I don't know how they turned all the ground over like that."

He was laughing at her as he promised, "I have Grandpa's old horse-drawn cultivator here in the barn. I'll plow for you, but you're going to have to get rid of the rocks first. The ground around here is full of them."

"All right. I'll pick them up today or tomorrow after school and you can plow Friday. All right?"

"Unless you want a mighty small garden, you had better plan on at least a week's time to clear out the rocks."

"No, I need to put the seeds in. The children told me their mothers are already planting some. Am I really going to have baby chickens?"

"It sounds as if you will have quite a flock if all thirteen of your hens are setting. They'll each have half a dozen to a dozen chicks."

"Six to twelve! You mean I might have 78 to 154 babies?"

She could figure in her head so fast it made Ryan's head spin. He had been forgetting about the chasm that stretched between them, but this brought it back with a jolt. He turned away abruptly away and insisted, "I've wasted all the time I can today. I have to get back to work. Until the help I sent for gets here, I'm trying to manage this operation single-handedly, and that keeps me on the move. Thank God it won't be much longer now."

Philippa's heart fell. It sounded as if he was soon going to have Dixie here to help him. What could she do now? She had already signed that dratted contract. Well, she would just be very brave, she resolved, and would keep busy this summer with her garden and her chickens and chopping weeds and canning and a million and one other things until she would fall into bed each night too tired to dream. In the daytime she would keep too busy to think.

She chided herself for thinking of Ryan much too much since he had purchased her basket at the Valentine's Day party. Foolishly she had taken that as a symbol that he cared, along with the holiday season that she had thought he enjoyed as much as she had. Negligently she had relegated the mail-order bride to a far corner of her mind. How mistaken she had been! Now he was practically back to telling her to "git" again.

She'd go, but first she would let him know that she had grown up. In her aunt Clara Rose's most authoritative voice, she commanded, "Be there as early as possible to cultivate on Friday. I, too, am much too busy for chitchatting with a neighbor. Good day to you."

What was he getting the iceberg treatment for this time? Ryan wondered as he watched her march back across the road, her swinging hips making her skirt flounce much too compellingly. He supposed he had been pretty short with her, complaining the way he had because the two men he'd hired out of Nebraska City and sent train fare to hadn't shown up yet. He'd make it up to her by helping her get the rocks out of her garden this weekend. He knew there was no way she could get it done by Friday.

He underestimated Philippa! When she first saw the insurmountable task before her, she wanted to cry and keep on crying for all the disappointments she had had in adjusting to rural life. Darn him—he knew all these rocks were here! Why had *she* never noticed them before?

On Thursday, Rural District No. 3 had a special geology lesson. Each student was to pick up as many rocks as possible within a defined area. Each rock was labeled to show it was shale or limestone

or sandstone or granite and what particular speci-
men it was of its kind. There were prizes for the
one getting the most rocks, the most kinds of rocks,
or the most unusual rocks. Everyone was rewarded
with a cold glass of mock lemonade. (Philippa had
kept all her lemon peels soaking in alcohol to make
an extract Gertrude told her would taste like real
lemonade if she added sugar and cold well water to
it.) It didn't taste very much like real lemonade, but
the children loved it with the sugar cookies she
gave as prizes. Everyone won two cookies—and
the garden was ready to be tilled.

Ryan could not believe the ground was cleared
so completely when he walked across the road and
looked over the fence Friday morning. The girl
must have worked all night long for the past two
nights. Guiltily he admitted he had goaded her
into it, and he felt like hell for it. He didn't know
how to apologize to her, so he just hooked up the
cultivator and plowed the garden twice over so the
soil would be extra fine and ready for her to plant
the seeds.

Ryan and Philippa rode to and from church on
Sunday with only the briefest exchanges between
them. All Philippa could think of was that Dixie
would soon be riding here beside Ryan, while Ryan
tried his darnedest to come up with some words to
tell her he was sorry and get her to stop acting in
this hoity-toity way.

When they returned, the two men he'd hired
were standing by his side porch, so he could only
help her down, briefly say good day, and hurry
home.

Interested, she stood looking over at the two

men. The bigger one looked somewhat familiar,
but she could not place him; someone she had seen
in town, no doubt.

As soon as school was over each day, Philippa
hurried to her garden to get more rows of seeds
planted and any weeds pulled up that dared to
poke shoots through. She was grateful to Gertrude
for explaining about using string tied to sticks to
show where the rows of plants were, so she
wouldn't hoe any of them off thinking they were
weeds. She was also rather proud of the scarecrow
she concocted from her ruined moire dress and an
old tea towel stuffed with corn husks. As Ryan had
predicted, she now had baby chicks to tend, which
created a lot of extra work. As the days went by,
she found little time for thinking about anything
besides the tasks at hand.

Occasionally as she worked in the garden or
tended her chicks she would feel her skin prickle as
if someone was watching her, and she would look
up to see Ryan's big burly hired man staring at her
from the road in a very forward manner. Quickly
she would turn back to her work, and by the time
she was brave enough to look again, he would be
gone. Ryan should have a talk with the bounder
for such rude behavior, and she wished she could
tell him so, but he had not been over all week. She
was grateful for Endymion's company in the evenings as she worked on the children's lessons, but
it wasn't enough.

Saturday afternoon Philippa went over to the
school to water the seedlings the children were
growing for her on the windowsills. Preoccupied

with turning the containers so the sun hit each leaf, she felt the prickling sensation on her skin again and whirled around to see Ryan's hired man scrutinizing her aggressively from the doorway. Looking closer now, she recognized him as the bearlike man who had driven the dray wagon the day she had left St. Louis.

She didn't know if he had just come to greet her or to ask her a question, but intuitively she backed away.

"So ya recognize me now, huh? Don't be backin' off like that. You were eager enough for a favor from me in St. Louie."

Just as she reached the edge of her desk and could retreat no farther, he started toward her. She made a move to dart around him, but he reached out that huge, pawlike hand of his and captured her arm as if the row of desks between them were not even there. Kicking a couple of desks out of the way with a heavy booted foot, he pulled her struggling to a stop. "Now, little gal, is that any way to ree-ward the man who's gonna take ya back to yer husband? Why, they was dee-scriptions of you and ree-ward offers in ever' paper from St. Louie to Kansas City. I got a piece of the ree-ward by tellin' that bastard about pickin' you an' yer trunks up. He only gimme a tenth of what he promised 'cause I didn't know where ya went. I'm bettin' he'll be willing to pay a damned sight more now."

"No! No!" Philippa pleaded, wanting to interrupt his torturous threats and convince him not to take her back. "I'm *not* his wife! He's only saying that—"

"Look, lady, what's between you 'n' him is nothin' to me. That kind of money talks—"

"I'll pay you!" Philippa gasped, hoping to dissuade him.

For a minute he appeared to be thinking that over. Finally he asked, "You got that kind of money?"

Philippa thought of the few coins left in her purse and admitted, "No . . . but—"

"Y' kin git it! Yeah! That Murphy I work for is loaded. He'll no doubt pay to keep a choice morsel like you around!"

Her captor smelled loathsome and his breath was foul. Philippa wanted to scream and kick and run, but there was no possibility of escaping the way he was holding her, and she knew there was no one to hear her screams: she had seen Ryan and the other hired man ride out of Ryan's drive as she came over here. That was probably why the beast had taken this opportunity to accost her.

When his meaning penetrated, she cried, "Under *no* circumstances could I ask him—he'd have no reason to pay you! You mustn't ever mention it—or any of this—to him." The mere thought of Ryan's knowing the truth about her made her violently ill. "Please . . ." she begged.

"Then how are ya gonna pay me?"

"I'll give you all the money I have now . . . and you can have all my salary . . . for a year . . . two years!"

"Ha! What would that amount to, a couple a hundred? Y' gotta be crazy! Why, yer old man's offerin' thousands! Yep, reckon we're on our way to St. Louie—just the two of us." He leered at her with a sickening smirk.

Philippa's mind was reeling. She had no choice but to go quietly with him if this whole community wasn't to find out about the sordid picture of her godawful predicament! Yet if she went, what punishment would Andrew have devised for her after all this time? Torture, no doubt—as would be the trip with this beastly man! No, she couldn't go back, yet there seemed no escape. Her arm was already throbbing from his fierce hold on it. It would have bruise marks for weeks.

Her frantic thoughts were interrupted by a growled command. "Git the stash yer school took in on that box lunch thing ever'body's talkin' about. We'll be needin' travelin' money."

"Don't be ridiculous!" In her most authoritative schoolmarm voice she automatically asserted, "You can't take *that* money—it's for the school."

"Who sez I can't? Not you, I hope—fer yer sake!" With his other hand he twisted her arm behind her back until the pain was excruciating.

Philippa couldn't hold back an anguished cry of pain, pain so deep she felt as if she might pass out.

When she cried out so piteously he loosened his grip, saying, "That's more like it. Now, just git that money—NOW!"

All he had to do was begin to tighten his grip again. Philippa knew she couldn't stand it and headed unwillingly toward her desk. When they reached it, she nodded. "It's in the bottom left-hand drawer."

"So, git it out!"

"I can't," she informed him with a tinge of satisfaction. "It is hid behind the drawer. The whole thing must be removed." When she'd been given the responsibility of keeping the school treasury, she had conscientiously hidden it in the most difficult-to-find spot she could think of.

The brute let go of her arm, commanding, "Stand there, or you ain't felt no pain compared to what I'll be dishin' out!" Then he knelt down and yanked the big bottom drawer out, upsetting its contents as he did. When he leaned forward to reach way in to the back, Philippa lunged toward the big black cast iron stove poker, positive this would be her best chance.

The big, heavyset man was used to moving fast in street brawls. He was already beside her when she raised the poker, wielding it with all her strength.

"Oh, no, you don't!" He made a grab for it, but Philippa managed to step back. Instead of the poker he accidentally grabbed the ruffled shoulder of her dress, rending it clear down to below her hips. The sound of the ripping fabric fueled Philippa's anger, and she aimed the heavy stove poker at his head, bringing it down with all the force she could muster.

The blow staggered her attacker and he swore vehemently. "Goddamn bitch! Now yer gonna get it! You'll be goin' back to St. Louie tied, gagged, and out cold!"

At this gruesome threat, Philippa raised the poker to hit him again, but he was too fast. He wrenched the poker away from her, clenched it in his beefy fists, and swung it toward her. Her own scream pierced her ears when she saw it coming at her.

Susan Murray had found some early-blooming crocus in their yard, and she had picked them for her very own special Miss Pippa. She had ridden her pony to bring them to her teacher's house, but on the way had noticed the schoolhouse door was open and decided to investigate. When she realized her teacher had been attacked, she screamed again and again.

"Quit that screamin', kid, an' git the hell outta here," the villain yelled, but Susie just stood there, too terrified to do either.

Realizing he'd have to get rid of the kid before he could bind and gag the unconscious teacher, he headed toward Susie. But at the sound of hoof-beats, he ran cursing to the rear of the room and kicked out a back window to escape.

Coming in from the bright sunlight, Ryan could not assess what had happened. Susie stood in the doorway, clutching some yellow flowers in her hand, and continued to scream piercingly. She looked to be unharmed, but something had fright-ened her badly.

Then Ryan saw the man crawling out the back window. Susie must have come upon someone who knew of the school's ninety-dollar treasury and caught him in the act of stealing it. On second glance, Ryan saw it was his own hired man, and he ran back out around the building and met the burly fellow at the side.

Furious that he'd hired a thief, Ryan doubled up his fists and knocked the big man to the ground. He pounded him continuously with more angry blows, enraged that the fellow would frighten a child this way and try to steal the school's money. When he became aware that his temper was out of control and he was beating an unconscious man, Ryan pulled himself together and ran back inside to take the poor little girl home to her mother.

It was as he knelt in front of Susie that he saw Philippa lying on the floor between the desks, her dress top torn completely away. He bounded across the room to her and felt pain sear through his body at the sight. All he could think was that she had been raped and killed, when he saw the huge swollen gash on her head and her torn gown. He reached for her wrist to find a pulse.

As he pulled the bodice of her dress together he

thankfully saw the light rise and fall of her breasts. Somewhere at the back of consciousness he heard Thunder galloping off, but it didn't matter now. Nothing mattered but getting help for Pip.

He went back to tthe doorway and began shaking poor little Susie like a rag doll, shouting at her, "Susie! Your Miss Pippa has to have help. Go get your mama! No . . . wait!" Ryan feared that the man might still be out there somewhere, and anyone vile enough to do this to Pip would harm Susan. "You stay here with Miss Pippa. I'll go to town and get Doc!"

"No, Ryan! Please, no!" It was Philippa's voice, a soft, pleading whisper. "I'm all right now." She reached for the huge lump on the side of her head and rubbed it softly, wincing with pain. "He must have knocked me unconscious, but I'll be fine. Don't get the doctor. Oh, please, try to understand. I'll die if anyone hears about this."

The mere thought of the questions she'd have to answer about why she hadn't just let the man get away with the money made Philippa quiver. She knew she could never conceal her past if a lot of questions were asked, and she went on to try and convince a doubtful-looking Ryan. "He was . . . was . . . more than just a thief, though he did take all the school's money, but . . . there was . . . he was . . . Oh, God! I can't even think of it, much less speak of it . . . Please, please try to understand. Don't ask me to. . ."

Watching the terror in Philippa's face and seeing her tremble made Ryan certain he knew what she had been through. He didn't have to guess what had happened to her, seeing her ripped dress and the way she was pleading with him not to get Doc. He knew the gossips would crucify her, no matter how popular she had been up to now. When a woman had been raped back home, half the town ostracized her because they were sure she'd done something to lure her attacker, and the other half pitied her but treated her like the carrier of some vile, contagious disease.

He looked down into Philippa's frightened, pleading eyes and knew he could not deny her, but he had to make one more effort. "You should see Doc Eberle. I'll bring him out here. He's a good man, Pip; he won't tell anyone."

Mournfully she shook her head. "He can't do anything for me; no one can."

Her teacher's grieving voice made Susan stop whimpering and hiccuping, and she seemed to come out of her trance as she walked on into the room, saying, "I can, Miss Pippa." She sat down cross-legged on the floor and took hold of Philippa's hand. "I can magic you well. I magic my dolly all the time." Susan lovingly patted Philippa's swollen head where she had been hit and gently touched the cut on her forehead, proclaiming in childish singsong, "Magic, magic, do your spell! Magic, magic, make Miss Pippa well!" Then she stood up, pronouncing, "You'll be fine now. I have to get on home or I'm gonna get a spanking. I'm not 'lowed past the pasture gate. Promise me true you won't tell I was here?"

"I promise true, my very own special magic maker, Miss Susan Murray," Philippa whispered.

Susan had already started to run out the door when Ryan recalled, "I'll have to make sure she gets home okay, Pip. Promise me you'll just lie there. I'll lock the door and be back as soon as I can! The fellow could jump down from that high window in the back, but he won't be able to make it back up. However, to make you feel better, I'll leave you my pistol."

As soon as the two of them left, Philippa tried to sit up and pull her clothing together. She had been trying to tug her dress together since she regained consciousness.

That awful man! Thank God Susie had come along and Ryan had heard her screaming, or by now Philippa would have been abducted. How long would it have been before anyone missed her? Ryan would just have assumed she'd gone into town with the Olsens.

She gulped deep, trying to keep down the bile in her throat, but the pain was so terrible she couldn't keep some of it from her mouth. As she forced herself to keep swallowing hard, another debilitating thought struck: that man would probably be back! With thousands of dollars at stake, a desperado like him would take the chance.

The thought that that horrible, vile man might come back for her was so frightening, especially when she viewed the broken window, that she began to shake violently.

Frightened equally by the man and by Ryan's gun, she quaked with indecision, but in the end she picked up the weapon. If he came back now, Philippa knew she would kill him if she could. She wanted to! She grasped the gun tighter and propped herself against her desk, waiting to kill.

Chapter Twenty

✦✦✦✦✦

When Philippa awoke to find herself once again lying under Ryan's walnut tree, it was as if she was in some sort of recurring nightmare. This time there were no leaves, only buds on the branches, and Ryan was not in sight. Painfully raising her head to look around, she saw him hitching the team to the buggy. Where was he going, and why was she lying here like this?

The throbbing pains in her head brought her narrow escape cruelly back to torment her again, and she let her head fall back to the ground. She cried out the only word she could think of that would ease her pain or help erase the memory of this terrible ordeal.

"Ryan!"

It did not come out as the loud cry she had meant it to, but it was enough. He heard her hoarse plea and was instantly beside her, pulling her up into his arms as he knelt down. She began to sob hysterically, and clung to him as if she were drowning in a flooding river. Back and forth, back and forth he rocked her on his knees, trying to soothe her as one would a child. Rhythmically he brushed her hair away from her forehead and crooned, "Don't fret now, little darlin'. It'll be all right. Cry your eyes out if it helps. I'm here now. You're safe, little darlin'."

Hiccuping, she whimpered as her sobs subsided a little, "Why were you leaving me?"

Aghast at this assumption, he answered, "I wasn't! I was gonna take you in to see Doc Eberle."

"I told you, I don't *want* to go. I thought you understood!" She began to cry again.

"I did . . . until you aimed at me with my own gun when I came through the door."

"I didn't shoot at you, did I?" Philippa asked, gulping back tears.

"Nope, but you looked ready to."

"Why would I shoot *you*? You rescued me."

Ryan chuckled slightly, partly in relief that she was all right and partly because he recalled the other time she'd unexpectedly clobbered him and in his shock and surprise he'd failed to duck. "With you that don't mean much. I've been hit in the head before for trying to rescue you. I admit it was different this time"—once again he was serious—"that's why I was takin' you to town. I thought the shock of all that happened was too much for you."

Philippa tried to comprehend, then added more assertively, "Yes, it must have seemed that way. But I'm all right now. I just want to go home and take a hot bath. My head hurts." She tentatively ran her fingers over the swelling. "My, what a lump! I must be a sight. What will everyone think when they see me?"

"They'll think," he said as he raked her up into his arms and started walking toward her house, "that once again the teacher is a heroine. She saved the box social money from a thief. My own hired man, 'Big Louie' McDermott."

"Wherever would they get an idea like that?" Her mind wasn't able to absorb anything so far-fetched. She'd seen Big Louie shove the cash into his pocket before he lunged at her to grab the poker.

"Well, that's what I told Mrs. Murray. I found out Susie had panicked when she came to the school door, and the way you were down behind the desks, she saw nothin' of what actually happened. You must have moaned or cried out in pain or somethin' and that started her screaming. I promised Susie she wouldn't get a spanking if she told her ma the truth. Then I convinced Mrs. Murray I saw you go in the schoolhouse door just seconds before Susie rode up. Susie and I figgered you must have happened on the man while he was stealing the money and tried to stop him. That's when he hit you. I came running when I heard her scream, and . . .

"I think it'll work, Pip. Susie believes it happened that way, and a kid can be very convincing."

"That's a marvelous evasion of the truth you concocted, Ryan." She squeezed him tighter around the neck and shoulders as she balanced herself in his arms. "Thank you very, very much." Her voice was pathetically grateful. "But let's face it: the money is gone. They'll know I didn't prevent him from stealing it."

Ryan was so taken aback he couldn't even speak. She had been through a horrible experience, yet here she was, thanking him for doing the little he had been able to do to help her, putting a lousy ninety bucks in the drawer so that everyone would be gabbing about that instead of the attack.

Philippa herself was not sure why Ryan had put his own money in the drawer. He couldn't know the real reasons why she couldn't answer questions about that man. Was it because it was his own hired man and he felt guilty? Or was it because she'd implied she didn't want to, couldn't, in fact, talk about the vicious crime beyond the theft of the money? He didn't suspect anything, did he? No, it was just his wonderful generosity. Now everybody would be so busy lauding her bravery for saving the money they would forget to question the details.

Once again Ryan carried Philippa into her home, but this time he laid her gently on the bed. She vaguely heard the noises of him fixing her bath water as she drifted in and out of a pleasant semi-darkness. In the mists there were no thoughts, and she willed her mind to stay there. Away from Big Louie. Big Louie, who was probably already on his way back to St. Louis to tell Andrew where she was. What could she do . . . where could she go . . . ? Her head hurt so badly and these devastating worries tore at her so fiercely that when the blackness came, she eagerly allowed herself to slip into it.

Philippa seemed in a sort of semiconsciousness when Ryan picked her up to carry her into the kitchen, for she was utterly limp in his arms and unable to sit alone in the chair he'd placed beside the tub. It appeared she was too weak to balance herself, so he started to carry her back to her bed, but her hair and her body were wet from perspiration. Ryan hesitated. He knew how much she had wanted a bath, wanted to wash away the filth of the touch of that bastard's skin against hers. At the thought of that scum feeling Philippa's soft skin, Ryan became unmercifully furious all over again. He, too, wanted her washed and scrubbed *now*.

Without thinking of propriety or decorum, he laid Philippa on the floor and took off her torn dress. He walked to the stove, where the fire was still blazing from heating water, and stuffed the torn garment in. When he removed her knit undervest and saw the large, inflamed bruises on her arm, he doubled up his fists with hatred for Big Louie and wished more than ever that he had killed the bastard when he had the chance.

He burned the vest too. Slowly Philippa opened her eyes as he slammed down the grate on the fire chamber. When he knelt beside her again, she murmured, "Thank you," and then seemed to drift off again. He was glad he'd done what she evidently wanted to do herself, and he repeated the action with her pink knit snuggies and silk stockings.

Carefully he lifted her into the tub of water and gently scrubbed her as he'd wash, Halfpint on Saturday nights when they were kids. He shuddered at the thought that later he was going to visualize seeing her beautiful bare body and remember this, but today it was a totally different emotion that consumed him. Taking care of her was all that was important.

He dried her off and carried her back into the bedroom, where he found a flannel nightgown folded neatly on the shelf under the washstand. After he dressed her in it, he started to tuck her into the bed, but at that moment she opened her eyes, and he saw how tear-filled and pleading they were. Ryan's heart pounded heavily against his chest as he felt the agony he saw revealed there. Gently, wordlessly, he picked her up and carried her back into the kitchen. The way she was shivering, he suspected she might have a chill, and her big tears were falling much more freely now.

With a booted foot he hooked the rung of the old rocker and pulled it nearer the cookstove. He sat down in it, still cradling her in his arms. Leaning forward, he opened the oven door so more heat would come into the room, then leaned back in the chair and pulled her tightly against him, beginning to rock softly and wishing for all the world he could bear the pain of today for her.

In all her life Philippa could not remember anyone who had shown her such deep, loving care. While her aunt had never abused her, she had been a cold, austere woman, incapable of any loving actions. To have someone hold her and comfort her this way tore at her innermost being, and the tears she shed were for all the love she had missed in her life. To feel as protected as she did right now in Ryan's arms ripped through her with such deep yearnings that she could not stop crying. Wistfully she envisioned telling Ryan how much this meant to her, how much *he* meant to her. But of course she could not. Now she knew him well enough to realize that his sometimes arrogant bravado masked his tenderheartedness; it would embarrass him to have her say such things when he did not love her in return, when he was going to marry another.

As the image of marriage crossed her mind, the unbearable memory of Andrew shaking her viciously in the judge's office came to her. The tumultuous fears that he would find her and be even more cruel overwhelmed her, and she began to sob, great, racking, uncontrollable sobs.

"Lil' darlin'!" Ryan said gently. "Please stop torturing yourself this way. Try not to think of what happened. Please try, my love." He pulled her tighter still against him and began to rock faster, certain she was reliving the horrors of this afternoon. "It's all right now. It's all right . . . I'm here, you're safe, sweetheart! You're safe," he crooned over and over.

Philippa was certain he was using the endearing names to try to calm her, but this once she needed to believe he meant them. Somehow her benumbed mind imagined he might really care for her, and at last she was able to stop crying and fall into a peaceful sleep.

For a long time after she had quit sobbing, Ryan continued to sit and hold her, vainly wishing he had the right to do so forever. To hold her, protect her, and especially to love her openly. To tell her of the burgeoning love that filled his heart and his desires to take care of her always. But he had no such rights. God, how appalled she would be at the mere thought of being married to some illiterate! To snuff out his torment, he made himself carry her back to her room and carefully put her to bed. Standing looking down at her, he noted the increasing swelling on her head, so he tenderly put a cold wet compress on it, then went out to do the chores.

Forgetting she had baby chickens, he opened the door to the henhouse too wide and three of the little devils got out. He ran them down and put them back with their disgruntled mothers. What a damned nuisance chicks were! He had to go back to the house and get the buttermilk for their crockery feeders. They were so thick everywhere on the floor he could hardly find a place to step to fill the hens' feeder. The rooster stood up on the perch looking cocky as all get out. Ryan figured it had a right to be proud with this many offspring! On the way out he had to rather rudely boot Endymion out of the way as the cat tried to slink past him to get into the henhouse.

"Demon,"—his own name for the cat—"out!" The cat picked itself up and looked at him warily through lidded, aloof eyes. "Oh, all right, Pip would probably kill me for booting you. Come on,

you can have your saucer of warm milk after I milk
the cow." Keeping its distance, the cat followed
him toward the shed.

When he went back inside, he wondered what to
do now. He couldn't just leave Pip here alone. He
should have asked Mrs. Murray to come over and
sleep here—but there was no bed.

As it turned out, that didn't stop Mrs. Murray.
She came up the drive shortly after dark, riding
one of their workhorses, saying as she climbed
down, "Evenin', Ryan. I knew you'd stay 'til I
could get m'family fed an' settled in fer the night."

"Yes'm, I stayed, but I sure am glad to see you!"

"You shoulda knowed I'd come. A sensitive girl
like Miss Pippa must'a been frightened outta her
wits, comin' up on a thief like that and then him
hittin' her that way! My Susie told me her teacher
was braver'n all git out!"

"I think she's okay, just scared. She said she
would take her bath while I did chores and then she
was goin' to bed. I hated to leave her here all alone."

"I'm here to spend the night."

"There's no extra bed."

"Won't be the first time I slept sittin' up all night
with a sick child in the house. I used to sit an'
steam Susie over the stove a lot when she got the
croup. It's the least I kin do fer her, Ryan, after all
she's done fer my boys."

After she heard she wouldn't be left alone in her
house tonight, Philippa didn't stay awake to hear
the rest of the conversation.

Dreams plagued her all night long. In one dream
a sneering, snarling Andrew and a smirking Mrs.
Carpenter looked down at her in her ruffled cano-
pied bed in the rose-mauve bedroom back in St.

Louis. When she cried out, Mrs. Murray was immediately beside her bed to reassure her everything was fine.

Only everything *wasn't* fine! Philippa had to leave here early tomorrow. Where could she go . . . and how? For a brief moment she thought of confiding in Ryan with her plight, but she immediately rejected that. Ryan was so good he might jeopardize his own life to save her. No, she couldn't tell him, or anyone! She had to find a way by herself.

Again her dreams took her to a nightmare. Big Louie was dragging her toward Andrew, who stood there haughtily with a bag of gold coins in one hand and his buggy whip in the other.

"Here she be, at last. Have at her! Just gimme my money'n I'll be off!"

Philippa struggled to get away, but Louie had tied and gagged her and she lay crumpled in a helpless heap. When the buggy whip came toward her, it turned into a cast iron stove poker.

Once more her piercing scream brought Mrs. Murray to her. "You poor little dear! What awful things must be runnin' through yer head. Maybe it'll help if you tell me ever'thing that happened. Ever'thing that thief said or did!"

Everything! What a relief it would be to tell everything; but Mrs. Murray was such a good soul, she would never believe anyone could be like Andrew . . . nor that their schoolmarm—in whom they had such pride—was a runaway wife with a reward on her head. No, Mrs. Murray wouldn't understand.

"I keep seeing that stove poker coming at me . . . over and over! The man said very little to me after he ordered me to get him the money . . . but he hit me so hard!"

"Yes, that's a terrible lump you have. Why, you could have been killed. I sent my boys to tell the sheriff the whole story as soon as I heard it from Ryan and Susie. They'll have him behind bars in no time. I'll wager there's a posse after him right now."

"A posse? You mean they might catch him . . . yet tonight?"

"I wouldn't doubt it a whit, so you just try to go back to sleep, Miss Pippa. You're safe now."

Safe? When they caught Big Louie he'd tell them why he was trying to capture her. Why, the law might even be on his side and come to help him take her back.

Chapter Twenty-one
✦✦✦✦✦

IF THE NEXT day had not been the sabbath, perhaps not so many people would have heard the story so soon. Philippa might have been spared the steady stream of visitors, who were so proud that she had dared to defy a thief and so appalled at the sight of the big swollen gash on her forehead.

So that Philippa wouldn't be left all by herself, Mrs. Murray stayed until Mrs. Parker arrived. The young woman tried to assure them she was fine this morning, except for her still-throbbing forehead. She was determined to get a few things packed and slip away. But how could she, with Mrs. Parker chatting away as she rolled out biscuits? What was she to do?

Meanwhile, one person after another came to call, to praise, and to sympathize.

When Jasper Clough arrived, he took one look at his beautiful Philippa's face and, speaking as a lawyer, guaranteed a conviction that would keep the assailant behind bars for a long time, if the man could be found. So far, the posse had had no luck, but Philippa feared her time was running out, because everyone said a Bluffsview posse always got its man. She hoped this once they didn't. Everyone was being so kind! She wanted to be gone from here before they found out the truth, before Andrew arrived. How long would it take him to get here—three or four days?

Late that afternoon, the sheriff dropped by her house with several of the men who had ridden in his posse. They had picked up the man's trail early last night. Unfortunately he hadn't stopped once, and they'd had to ride all night to try to catch him. Only minutes before they had him in their sight, he was shot and killed by a stray bullet from a hunter's gun. They hadn't even been able to question him, although Thunder was returned to Ryan.

At least it had been an accident, Philippa thought; he hadn't been killed because of her. Andrew's blood money had filled the man with heinous greed, but Philippa still didn't want to see him die. What a blessing he hadn't had a chance to stop at a town to telegraph Andrew. It was as if a huge weight had been lifted from her. She was safe again—for now.

After everyone but Jasper and Cecilia had gone, Philippa sighed with deep relief. She had pretended she felt fine in front of all her students and their families this afternoon, but now the combination of the pain from her throbbing head and her tremendous weakness finally drained her reserves.

Doctor Eberle had left some laudanum for the pain, but he had warned it would make her sleepy, so she hadn't taken it. Conscientiously she had wanted to be awake to thank everyone who was so concerned about her that they had made special trips out here to see how she was.

The central source of her misery was that Ryan had not come over all day to find out how she was doing. He must have been thoroughly revolted, having to clean her up when she looked so awful. Once again she'd proven herself totally inept. Instead of rendering her assailant unconscious, he'd used the weapon on her! She recalled how angry Ryan had appeared when he had burned her clothing. Surely he didn't think she had arranged a clandestine meeting with that awful man? When he had bathed her, rocked her so lovingly, then put her to bed and talked with Mrs. Murray, he had seemed so caring. He cleverly had contrived the story about her saving the funds, even supplying them from his own pocket to make her a heroine again, instead of just a victim of a thief. Couldn't he stand the sight of her now that he'd had more time to think about it? She couldn't really blame him; she herself was revolted by it all.

"Please, Philippa, don't try to talk," Cecilia was telling her. "It must make the pain in your head even worse. I am coming to teach your classes for you for the next few days. If you prepare the lessons, I'm sure I can guide the children through them. I'd like to be a teacher."

Jasper candidly informed his sister, "You'd make a terrible teacher, Ceci, unless they need a class in oratory or debate. Besides, I don't think Cal will want you to teach school, at least not for any length of time. He'll need someone to do those account books that give him so much trouble!" He winked at Philippa.

"Calvin probably wouldn't let me touch his books. He excelled in math, Jasper, and you know it."

"Only kidding," her brother informed her. He didn't want her to find out that Calvin had tried to lure Philippa to straighten out his records. Especially since Cal and Ceci had discovered, after the Valentine's Day party, that they had a great deal in common, just as Jasper had theorized they would. They had seen one another frequently since then, and Friday night at Grange Hall Calvin had danced every dance with Cecilia. Afterwards, he had proposed, which surprised no one who had been at the dance and seen the two of them together.

The news excited Philippa, and she tried to express how happy she was for her friend. "Made for each other" was one of the barely intelligible words she uttered.

"Don't try to talk, Philippa," Jasper warned her again. "We know what you're trying to say. You already suspected they were in love with each other, didn't you?"

Philippa nodded her head yes as Jasper continued, "And you've suspected I'm in love with you as well, haven't you?" He was looking at her with such penetrating eyes that she could only truthfully nod again.

"While you are unable to change the subject as you always manage to do, and now that you have practiced nodding your head up and down, I have another question for you." His businesslike tone changed as he said beseechingly, "Philippa, will you marry me?" His gaze was still penetrating, and

Philippa's eyes became large with surprise and questioning.

Cecilia chuckled softly. "I would have expected a much more romantic proposal out of you, Jasper. Something from those poetry books you adore, but . . ." She turned and saw Philippa's questioning face, and the tone of her voice changed from chiding to conniving. "He does love you, and I would *adore* having you for a sister. You would make such a wonderful wife for a lawyer, especially one who hopes to run for the state legislature next term. I can see you now, graciously presiding over big state dinners. You have so much poise and refinement."

Philippa's eyes grew bigger than ever, now with trepidation. The very thought of elegant dinners where she would have to talk to many strangers upset her. She started to shake her head no, but Jasper quickly stopped her.

"Don't answer me now, Philippa. Just think about it, please.

"Are you upset at the idea of living in a big city? After the sad experiences you had in one, I can understand that. We will wait until you feel more at ease in a big town again before I run for office.

"Please, give your answer some thought. I will ask you again . . . and next time, poetically. All right?"

Up and down went Philippa's head. This she would do. Jasper was a good friend and so very interesting and fun-loving. She would try hard to think of loving him . . . after Ryan's bride arrived.

His bride! Maybe Dixie had arrived today and that was why Ryan had not been here. He had implied last week he was expecting her to be here soon to help him. Perhaps he had gone to meet the early-afternoon eastbound train at the Bluffsview junction. Her head began to throb harder than ever.

Ryan sat in one chair with his feet propped up on another and watched the last buggy pull out of Philippa's driveway. It looked like Clough and his sister, but it was too dark now to tell for sure. Wagons, buggies, men on horseback, and children on ponies had been arriving and leaving since early this morning, especially after church. Susan and her brothers must have told everyone in the congregation.

He breathed a sigh of relief. They had all rushed in eagerly to see how she was faring and to congratulate her on her bravery. Even the county sheriff had commented on it after he talked to her and then came over here to ask questions. None of them had guessed it was more than an attempted robbery.

Last night after he fell into bed, still too overwrought to sleep, the ultimate degradation of the brutal assault on Philippa had come to him with a shock: she might be pregnant! The enormity of this possibility was so sordid that Ryan felt sick.

There was only one answer: she had to get married within a week or two. Ryan reckoned the minister would be the best choice because he'd be good to her even after he found out. Clough or Lawrence probably would be too, when she explained why she was not a virgin bride. They would love her in spite of everything and they'd be understanding. Who wouldn't, for the chance to marry a beautiful, loving, educated lady like Philippa Marquette?

Ryan felt the old despair steal over him, and as

usual it began gnawing at his insides. If only he had a halfway decent education and a few genteel qualities, he'd go on his knees and beg her to marry him. If she did have a baby, he would be as good to it as if it were his own, so she would never feel he didn't love her enough to love her child.

But he was an illiterate clod, he reminded himself, and could only make her miserable. Now he had to love her enough to make her marry someone else at once.

Hamilton Fields came on Thursday to visit the school. It was Philippa's first day back, and she was immensely pleased with his thoughtfulness. He always seemed to know when she needed someone to help her through a difficult situation. The children had had so many questions: "Where were you standing when you saw the thief?" "Where was he?" "What did he hitcha with?" and on and on. With Hamilton's support, Philippa ran through a brief description and then gave them special assignments because the school had a visitor. They would have a spelldown, a ciphering match, and a morning recess to go out and play "Red Rover, Red Rover," or "Duck, Duck, Goose" since it was such a lovely spring day. Bessie June won the spelling bee, but Lydia could not be beaten at ciphering on the chalkboard. Philippa commented that her eighth-graders no longer played games during recess but sat on the woodpile talking instead.

"It's true," Hamilton concurred. "You've done a wonderful job," he continued. "You have not only helped them to be ready to pass their exams, but you have helped them to mature tremendously. The ones going on to town high school are properly prepared, and the others will take their places in the community confident of their ability—the ability you gave them."

More softly he continued, "I wish I could persuade you to take *your* place in the community, a place you more than have the ability to fill: the place beside the minister as his wife, his helpmeet, and his beloved. I care about you, my dearest Philippa, as I believe you know, and I would always be good to you."

Caught off her guard, Philippa did not know how to avoid answering this without hurting Hamilton's feelings. Although she held him in the highest regard, it was not in the way he wanted her to. Hesitatingly she stammered, "I . . . I . . . just don't know! You told me I must be very sure it is love and not infatuation. I know I admire you . . . I respect you . . ."

"But you don't love me? Don't you think there is a chance you might learn to care for me, Philippa? I will give you as long as you need . . . Or are you in love with someone else?" he softly pressed, asking the questions from his heart.

"I think I am, but he does not return my love. He is going to marry someone else, and that has been difficult for me to accept," Philippa answered him honestly, sadly.

Hamilton wondered who the foolish man was who would cast away a treasure like Philippa Marquette. Surely she wasn't in love with Calvin Lawrence. The look on her face when Ryan Murphy purchased her basket the night of the school box lunch auction came to him, and he questioned, "It's Ryan, isn't it, Philippa?"

His eyes were still looking at her so intently that she decided to admit it. It would feel good to say it out loud one time in her life, and she could trust

Hamilton not to reveal her confidence. "Yes, I'm sure it is love I feel for Ryan."

"Then perhaps, Philippa, it is just as well he does not return your love. It would be a very unsuitable match."

"Why do you say that?" she cried in perplexity. "I know I can't rope a calf or do branding or drive a six-horse team, but we like a lot of the same things. I can talk to him so easily. He makes me laugh a lot and when he . . . that is, when I think of him, I get a warm, wonderful feeling deep inside me."

Hamilton was a man of God, but he was also very human. He cringed inwardly at the way her face became radiant when she spoke of Ryan Murphy.

"For your sake, I am glad he does not return your affections. The man is practically illiterate, Philippa. It would never do for a highly educated lady like you to marry a man who can't read any but the simplest of words. I discovered this quite by accident when I took him his grandmother's Bible. She had left it at a missionary meeting shortly before she passed away; I found it later and returned it to him because it had family birth and death records in it. I don't think he realized I became aware of the fact he could not read, and until now I've never told anyone."

"Ryan can't read?" Philippa asked, unable to perceive what Hamilton had told her. "But Ryan can do anything!" It didn't seem believable. Why, he was brilliant! He knew all about raising crossbred cows and thoroughbred horses and marketing them and . . . and true, he never actually discussed books and poetry or politics or religion. Was it because he wasn't interested in those things,

or hadn't he read up on the subjects? Well, he'd
certainly proven the three R's weren't the necessity
Philippa had always deemed them to be. He was
very successful—possibly without them.

Just then the door flew open and Pee Wee Parker
came hurtling through, shouting, "Miss Pippa!
Miss Pippa! It's Lars an' Herbert—they're fightin',
an' Lars has a bloody nose. They both got back to
the empty space where the duck was at the same
time, but they both wanna be first!" Philippa was
on her way out the door as he finished the sentence.

The fight was over before she got there, and both
boys stood repentant, expecting a scolding. They
didn't know their teacher wanted to give each of
them a big thank-you hug for rescuing her from a
conversation she did not want to continue.

She bid Hamilton a good day as he got into his
buggy. It was obvious he was waiting to hear her
say more, but there was nothing she could say. He
would know her answer soon enough, for she
would be gone. She'd been saved from the threat
of Big Louie's telling Andrew, but the experience
had ingrained fear into her again. It would not be
long until another of his ilk found her. Anyone
would turn her in for "thousands of dollars." She
had to get farther away from St. Louis.

Chapter Twenty-two
❖❖❖❖❖

ALL WEEK RYAN had procrastinated. Repeatedly he'd put off seeing Philippa for one reason and then another. He knew she was being taken care of, for Ole came and did her chores and Cecilia Clough stopped at her house before and after school each day.

He excused his own absence with such meager pretexts as extra work; a trip to Nebraska City to make sure the sheriff there had buried her assailant, since they had no leads on Big Louie's family's whereabouts; or the need to fence in more pastureland for his growing herd. By Saturday, he knew he could wait no longer. Philippa had to be convinced to marry, and soon! He dreaded the confrontation, but by now she was undoubtedly worried about the possibility herself. What an abominable fate, to have to persuade the one girl he'd ever loved that she had to marry someone else . . . but it had to be done.

The weather had turned unseasonably hot, and Ryan unjustifiably blamed it for the fact that he was perspiring profusely just from the small exertion of walking across the narrow dirt road. Behind her house, Philippa was hoeing her garden, looking reasonably cool and composed, and he marveled at the girl's inner resources. Many women would have remained indisposed for weeks after such a heinous crime had been perpetrated.

At the sight of Ryan coming across the road, Philippa almost threw down her hoe and ran to him, but she controlled the impulse by recalling that he now thought her more undesirable than ever. She presumed it was his lowered opinion of her that had kept him away all week, for she'd seen no signs of his bride. She tried to go on hoeing nonchalantly, being especially careful to chop off weeds, not vegetables, in her jittery reaction to Ryan's presence.

Ryan walked carefully between Philippa's rows of tiny sprouting plants to the center of the garden while she continued to work, not even speaking to him. It showed how small her regard was for him, which was understandable since he had hired the man who had ravished her. He didn't blame her. If she used that frigid voice she sometimes adopted and treated him with cold aloofness, he might be able to accomplish the intolerable job he had undertaken today. Philippa had to get married!

Saying "hello" or "good afternoon" would be too ordinary for this conversation, so Ryan broke right into the center of it without preliminaries. "Pip, we have to have a talk."

"We do?" She was relieved to let the hoe fall at her feet, and pleased by the urgency in his voice. He didn't sound too repelled by her at all.

"Let's go sit on the log by the gate."

"All right."

Without further words, they went over and sat down. Glancing into her questioning eyes, Ryan looked quickly away and busied himself with petting Endymion, who had waltzed up unconcernedly as they seated themselves. He wondered how to go about broaching the subject. She wasn't acting high and mighty at all, just sweet, almost as if she was glad to see him. Well, there was nothing to do but lay the cards on the table, so he asked bluntly, "You've had a lot of company this week. Did anyone propose to you?"

"What kind of question is that, Ryan Murphy, and what if someone did? It should be of no con-

cern to you! I don't query you about Dixie, do I?"
she replied in astonishment. Endymion, startled
by her voice, bounded away around the corner of
the house.

"Who?"

"You know—Dixie!"

"Oh, her." Ryan vaguely recalled the story he
had made up, but it was irrelevant now. "She up
and married Stuart this winter."

"She married your own *brother*?"

"Yeah. She always was partial to him. Look, Pip,
Dixie is beside the point. We have to git you married to one of those suitors of yours right away."

As far as Philippa was concerned, Dixie was anything but beside the point. Her heart was going at
a triphammer rate, and she wanted to throw her
arms around Ryan thankfully. The last part of his
statement didn't register for a moment, and when
it did, she wanted to cry her eyes out. It was heart-
rending to hear him insist she had to be
married—to someone else. Unfairly, he must have
decided it was the only way to keep her from being
a nuisance to him. He was so conscientious he
probably considered it his duty to keep her safe,
and this was his way of eliminating the bother-
some burden.

Ryan could not bear to watch the emotions that
played over her face. He had learned to read her
expressions too well; at first, she appeared happy
at the idea of getting married, then she looked
suddenly sad and her eyes misted over. He hurried
on to reassure her, "Why, you could prob'ly still
teach school. You could ride out here every day.
I'd even give you Lightning."

"You'd give her to me?" A mare he'd told her
more than once was invaluable to his plans for

raising thoroughbreds? This was unbelievable. Either Ryan did not really want her to get married and move away, or he was awfully anxious to be rid of her. Philippa chose to think it was the first possibility and asked pointedly, "What would become of my chicks and my garden?"

"Most folks in town have gardens and chickens."

"My proposals were from Jasper and Hamilton. That means the gardens would already belong to Cecilia and Mrs. Vail. No, Ryan, I am going to stay right here." She sounded as if her mind was firmly made up.

"No, you have to marry Clough or the reverend right away!" Ryan's voice was hard, but he knew he had to be firm with her.

"Immediately? Why?" Philippa asked, innocently puzzled.

The words hung heavy between them, as heavy as the air had become all around them. The stillness was echoed everywhere. How could Ryan delicately bring up the consideration of pregnancy? Could it be possible she had not perceived it herself? He recalled her surprise that chickens hatched from eggs. Was Pip that naive? If so, how could he explain? He looked helplessly this way and that, as if the answer would pop out from somewhere. He even glanced back across his shoulder.

A rising breeze was moving black thunderheads and white, wind-filled clouds toward them much too fast. The stillness around them became almost unreal, and the sky was suddenly overcast. The sudden coolness of the breeze indicated a hailstorm was nearby. Ryan watched the black clouds twist and swirl for a few seconds. As the storm came nearer, one cloud began to break away from the mass, spiraling off on its own.

Practically jerking Philippa's arm from its socket, he hauled her up, ordering, *"Run!"*

The tone of his voice left no room for doubt or hesitation. Philippa tried to hold up her skirts with one hand while Ryan kept a tight grip on her other as they ran toward his house. There were a dozen questions that popped into Philippa's mind, but she was too breathless to ask them. She tried to tug on his arm to get him to slow down. He only yelled, *"Don't stop!"* and pulled her faster. When he paused for a second, it was at the door to his grandma's cellar, which he swiftly flipped open and started down, grabbing her hand once more to drag her down the steps.

This was too much! She was *not* going into that rodent-infested hole with its spiderwebs everywhere, whatever the reason!

As she started to tell him so, her voice was drowned out by the vicious roaring sound of the wind as it descended with a velocity and force that petrified her. She stood and stared numbly in the direction of the raging, turbulent onslaught.

Not waiting, Ryan seized her around the waist and threw her over his shoulder so both his arms were free to pull down the old door against the force of the wind. As soon as he had it in place, he carried her down into the depths of the cave and back into the far corner of it before he let her slide off his shoulder and down into his arms. They clung tightly to one another as the deafening roar passed overhead, rattling the old boards on the cellar door as if to tear it to splinters. A corner of the door gave way, and Philippa could see rain and hail pounding the ground with powerful fury.

In their corner of the cave the air was close, near

suffocating, but neither of them released their tight grip on the other. The power of nature had welded them together with its bonding strength of terror.

As suddenly as it had approached, the roar of the storm receded, but the rain and hail continued to beat upon the wooden door for several minutes more. Soon the hail subsided, but the rain continued to shower down in torrents.

At last Ryan's voice returned, and he began to reassure the girl quivering with fear in his arms. "It'll be all right, little darlin'. We're perfectly safe down here."

"What kind of storm is this?" she asked shakily.

"Oh, wind, rain, 'n' hail," he told her, not mentioning his fear a tornado might have struck not too far away. The twister had been heading toward the ground the last glimpse he'd had of it. He'd been relieved because it looked as if it was whirling away from where his herd was pastured.

"Goodness! That was the strongest wind I've ever seen . . . and the way the rain is coming down now is beyond belief . . . but Ryan, why didn't we just run to my house? It was closer."

"This is safer." He tried to sound matter-of-fact.

"Safer? This place has cobwebs and mice . . . and I shudder even to think of what else."

"The wind above could be a lot worse—it could even blow out windows."

"It's that strong?"

Ryan didn't want to frighten her by explaining how strong tornado winds could be, so he changed the subject. "I figured you might need more jars, so I swept down all the cobwebs and left the door open to air this place out. The cats took care of the rest. You're safe, all right."

Philippa's arms tightened around his shoulders as she admitted unthinkingly, "I always feel safe with you. Why, it's as if I don't have a worry in the world. You can't even imagine what a wonderful relief that is."

Her voice sounded sad and very worried indeed, and Ryan tightened his hold on her. If only for a minute, he wanted to dispel those worries. Soon they'd be taken care of, but for now he needed to console her. This was no time to bring up Clough or Reverend Fields. "You're safe now, lil' darlin'," he promised.

Oh, how Philippa wished those words were true! Would it hurt for just one minute to pretend that they were? She would be gone very soon now. She needed one final loving encounter with Ryan to last her the rest of her life. Forcefully she reached her hands up and pulled his face down so her lips could conquer his. She kissed him with all the passion that had welled up inside her since Valentine's Day. Her fingertips ran invitingly up his cheeks, across his temples, to rumple the hair she loved. She was almost glad the wind had blown his Stetson away, so her fingers could joyously mess up his hair.

Ryan met her needs with those of his own. He poured himself and his love for her into the kiss, feeling as though he was giving her his whole self.

His hands played across her back for a few moments, but as one fervent kiss ended and another, then another, began, his hands could no longer obey his resolve to control them. They began to cup and tenderly massage her shoulders, her waist, her delectable breasts. Within seconds he had heedlessly unbuttoned her shirtwaist, and his hand had ventured underneath it and under the loose chemise to carefully lift one of the tantalizing mounds hidden there. His thumb stroked her nipple until it formed a hardened, irresistible peak that his mouth was at once drawn to.

As he began to gently draw on her breast with his warm lips, she was swept by an intense giving sensation such as she had never known before—never knew existed. She wanted to push her body closer to him, to crawl inside of him, to keep this glorious dream from stopping. Her hands pranced from his hair, down his back, and onto his buttocks, where she could get a firm grip to pull him toward the flame burning inside her.

The hardness she felt as she held him against her focused some of the violent pressure, and she snuggled her own hips closer to his, tighter, tighter still. The pushing made her feel all warm inside, too warm. It was as if she needed to burst free, and she tried to push against him harder still.

By now Ryan's resolves were lost, boggled somewhere in his burning need for this lovely woman. Slowly his hands went from her breasts to her skirt, to begin inching it up from the floor. When he had it high enough, his hand automatically went to massage the warm skin on her inner thighs. It felt tender even though covered by silk panties, and he rubbed one side and then the other, repeatedly wishing her bloomers didn't reach down to her knees. He had only let his fingers drift to press against the entry to her womanliness when he felt her own hand on his hardness. Her fingers had been pulled away from where she had been nestling them against his buttocks before this last maneuver of his. Her hand grasped his manhood tightly. It was the only incentive he needed.

His fingers stole up and down, up and down over the delightful creases that he found between her legs, gently parting them as best he could through the silk that was becoming more and more soaked with moisture as his fingers continued to forage. He was muttering softly, "Oh, my dearest, my darling girl," and her murmurs were equally endearing. "My beloved, I worship you."

Philippa felt as if she were drifting on some high, far-off cloud. Her entire body was awash with a heat and a passion no poet she'd ever read would be able to define. It was beyond all her dreams. She sought a tighter hold on Ryan's hardened manhood and began to stroke sensuously as he was stroking her so that he, too, might be engulfed in this plunging, burning fire that raged within her. While his fingers gave some relief, she began to feel as if there was more to this and she sighed with unrequited longing.

A brief moment later, the thought of Andrew came back to her. *Andrew!* She had to stop this. The storm had made her forget her circumstances, forget that this could never be, and she began to struggle against him, trying to push him away. She knew how hard it was going to be for her to leave him. She was better off not knowing the fulfillment she suspected he could give her.

"Pip . . . darling . . . what is it?" Ryan asked quickly, dropping the hem of her skirt to the floor.

As she rebuttoned her blouse, Philippa stammered, "There is no way . . . I mean I can't . . . I just can't . . . never!" Her voice was sad and piteous as she thought of her circumstances. Andrew had ruined her life.

Ryan was instantly angry at himself for what he had nearly done to her. My God! After the rape, of course, she couldn't think of being taken, not even in love. Angry at himself, he warned, "No matter, Pip. I know this is abhorrent to you, but you must marry one of your suitors . . . soon! Then you'll be safe."

This? Abhorrent to her? It was wonderful! Marvelous! She'd never wanted to stop. What was he saying about her suitors and her being safe? What did he know?

"Why?" was all she could mutter.

"You need a man's name," he insisted.

He *did* know something. "What are you saying?"

"Think about it, honey. With a man's name, in his home . . . nothing and no one could touch you."

It didn't sound as if he knew any details, only that she had reason to be frightened. Was he right? He might be. If she went to another school she would still be Philippa Marquette, since her records said that. As a Mrs.—Mrs. Ryan Murphy, for instance, living in her husband's house—why he was right! Andrew or his hirelings would never find her then!

Both of them noticed at the same time that it was now quiet outside.

Carefully Ryan removed Philippa's clinging arms and went to the front of the cave. She followed right on his heels, as if she was afraid of allowing any space between them. He could feel her breath on the back of his neck as he tentatively pushed up what was left of the door, hoping it wouldn't splinter from the beating it had taken. He raised it a few inches. "Mary, Mother of God!"

"What, Ryan? What is it?" The shock in his voice resonated and she tried to anticipate what could have caused this kind of reaction.

There were no words to describe it. Ryan could only fling the door open, not caring now if it broke into shreds. He reached for Philippa and pulled her close to his side to give her some support when she saw the utter havoc the whirlwind path of the tornado had wreaked.

It must have touched down at the corner of his pasture, for fence posts were uprooted and lay snarled in their own barbed wire out in the middle of what was left of the debris-piled road. The schoolhouse had been next in its path, and now it lay as a grim reminder of what had once been. Only the foundation of the building remained standing.

There was no sign of the chicken coop or cow shed at all in Philippa's yard, only sticks and boards everywhere. The storm's path had missed the house itself, but the backlash of the wind had torn its roof half off and flattened the front part of the crumbling old place.

In a daze, Philippa tore free from Ryan's arms and walked slowly across the road. Her adorable baby chicks lay dead everywhere among the mother hens and boards and shingles and pieces of straw. The straw had been blown about with such force that pieces of it had been forced through boards with the strength of nails. Poor Tilly lay lifeless several feet from where she had been tethered outside this morning. Hail had flattened nearly every tiny shoot that had poked through the ground in the garden. Endymion was nowhere to be seen, nor was the rooster.

Now it was Ryan who followed on Philippa's heels as she walked around viewing the devastation. She did not utter a word or shed a tear. It would be a miracle if her mind did not shatter from a shock like this on top of last week's assault, he thought, wishing she would turn to him and cry or do something to release the emotions he was sure must be building up inside. He thought about reaching for her, but she continued to walk gravely to the back of her house, the only edifice on her side of the road that remained standing.

For a moment Ryan feared she planned to go inside and he knew it wasn't safe, but she didn't open the door. Instead she turned to face him, her desperate sadness reflected in her words. Sounding completely broken, she grieved in a near-whisper, "Everything is gone! I have nothing! No one! Nowhere to go! Now you are going to force me to marry Jasper or Hamilton, aren't you?"

Ryan could not stand the sad bitterness or the accusing ring in her voice, and he promised as he took her into his arms, "No, no, Pip. You don't have to do anything you don't want to. We'll work something out. I'll help you any way I can, I promise!"

"But I still have to get married?" she asked, remembering their conversation from before and during the storm and needing an answer for his unreasonably insistent statement.

"You know it would be best, Pip," he had to tell her sadly.

"Then will you marry me, Ryan?" she blurted. Her words electrified him. He was afraid she must still be in a trance, yet when he looked into her eyes they were not glassy, just pleading. Then the truth became painfully evident to him. He was the only one who knew what had happened to her. She would be sure he would understand her repugnance at having a man touch her after being raped. Oh God, yes! He could promise her that! He could promise her anything if she truly wanted to marry him. Just to be around her and take care of her forever was all he could ask.

"Little darlin', I give you my word. We'll be married as soon as we can get to the county courthouse. That is, if you still want to marry me on Monday mornin'. And Pip, I swear to God I won't touch you!"

Philippa looked at Ryan in bewilderment, for she had thought if he married her he would hold her in his arms and that he'd kiss her often. Now, upon discovering he didn't even want to touch her, she felt very foolish for begging him to marry her.

The way he had offered to give her Lightning was such an endearing gesture that she had read things into it which evidently weren't there, and when she had witnessed the gruesome spectacle all about her, all she could think of was turning to the solace only Ryan could provide. Unthinkingly she had turned his generous offer to help her into a weapon to obtain her own desires, and she vowed not to trap him this way, no matter how great the temptation to do so was to her at this moment. A line from one of Terrence's poems came to her: "You believe that easily which you hope for earnestly." This was exactly what she had done, wanting so much to have him love her that she had permitted herself to believe that he might.

The firm conviction that marriage would permanently shield her from ever being found by Andrew and the strong love she felt in her heart for Ryan had perverted her judgment. Imagine! The shy, reserved, well-brought-up Philippa Martin asking a man to marry her—and for purely selfish reasons! No, she could not have him making this sacrifice just because he was good and kind, the most wonderful man in the whole world.

Forcing her words to a notch above a whisper, she tried to sound convincing as she declared, "You don't have to marry me, Ryan!"

"I want to!" He, too, nearly whispered, but still very assertively.

Philippa's voice was noticeably stronger now, and she was looking into his eyes, trying to read signs of truth, trying to erase her own qualms. "Are you positive?"

"If you really want me to." His voice had become firm.

"I really want you to, but I don't want to force you to do something you don't want to do."

"Oh, little darlin', if only you knew!" he answered as he tightened his arms about her, forgetting the noble vow he had just taken not to touch her.

Here and now Philippa made a vow of her own. True, she had trapped Ryan into a marriage only because he felt sorry for her, but she would make him love and respect—and touch—his wife.

A pathetic yowl came from the front part of the house near the door. Breaking away from her, Ryan went to investigate. In just a few minutes he returned, beaming, and extended his arms to her.

"Look, Pip! She was hidin' under the house all through the storm! Not even wet, just confused, I'd guess!"

"Oh, Endymion!" Philippa cried, taking the cat into her arms and cuddling against its warm fur. Tears of joy began streaming down her face, and suddenly she was both laughing and crying at the same time and he was trying to blot tears away with his handkerchief. Ryan almost felt like crying along with her, he was so happy. Instead, he hugged her again.

At that moment Buzz came riding into the yard, shaking his head at the gruesome sight. Ryan released Philippa but kept an arm around her waist as they walked to meet the hired man.

"Jaysus! I was afraid I wouldn't find either of you alive!" Buzz swore. "I saw that twister dip down from the hill over yonder in the north pasture where I was workin'. I took cover under m' saddle an' poncho, but I watched the tail of it sweep through here. The air was sure black over this way, an' I never heard such an unholy roar!"

"It was unbelievable, all right," Ryan muttered. How could he feel so happy as he stood in the midst of such a catastrophe? Philippa was going to marry him! Only because she had to, of course, but he would do everything in his power to make her happy. He pushed back his qualms about his illiteracy.

Buzz walked around shaking his head and calling out, "Look at this!" or "Can you believe that?" He found the rooster a hundred yards away from the chicken coop, huddled in the middle of what was left of a chokeberry bush. The bird squawked and pecked angrily as he returned it to the area where the henhouse had been and then began scratching at the ground in disgust.

The Murrays' wagon was the first to pull into the yard, the horses in a lather from being driven hard. The Murrays had just climbed down when Jake, Will, and Lydia Radcliff rode in on horseback. The neighbors were soon followed by people from town who had watched the tornado touch ground and knew it had struck near here.

Everybody stood around exclaiming about this or that and remarking what a miracle it was that Ryan had seen the tornado tail break loose and had got them to the root cellar safely. After they finished expounding on the storm's ravages, everyone pitched in to clean up. By comparison, all their homes had sustained only minor hail damage.

Philippa watched, sobbing quietly, as the men picked up her hens and chicks and threw them into a blazing fire they had started from the splintered wood and shingles. The rooster had been put into a makeshift crate in the back of the Murray wagon because it kept pecking at the men trying to help clean up the debris. They dug a deep hole to bury Tilly so her carcass would not draw wolves and coyotes. Some of the men shored up the house so it would be safe to go in and pack Philippa's things. Children forlornly picked up pages of their readers and favorite storybooks, trying to put them back together. A few books were scattered about, wet but otherwise unharmed. The old cast iron stove lay in the center of the rubble.

Cecilia, Mrs. Olsen, and Mrs. Murray all stayed protectively close to Philippa. Mrs. Belden sidled up after a brisk turn about the yard and pronounced, "We can't afford to rebuild the school, you know, not when there are so few children left in the district. No, they will have to finish the semester in town." She sounded almost as if she was pronouncing herself victor in an ongoing battle.

Mrs. Murray, Mrs. Radcliff, and Mrs. Parker all spoke up at once.

"No!"

"Absolutely not!"

"I never heard the like! Only time will tell whether we may be able to rebuild, but the children are going to finish their term with Miss Marquette and graduate as planned!"

"They can use our parlor for classes," Mrs. Gulickson said, entering the fray.

"Or ours," Mrs. Radcliff asserted.

Once again, Philippa was grateful that she had found a place like Bluffsview, a place full of such good people. Now she would be staying here forever, unless Ryan changed his mind. She could not hold him to a promise she had forced him to make.

"Now you will have to move into Mrs. Crafton's house," Cecilia stated matter-of-factly. "We might as well have the trunks and things they brought out of the house tied to the back of our buggy."

Philippa did not know how to answer. She did not dare tell anyone about the forthcoming marriage, in case he had changed his mind. While she hesitated, Ryan was listening alertly for her answer. Would she still tell all these people that she was marrying him, or had she come to her senses at the sight of the preacher and Clough? They had both been hovering near her all afternoon, giving her devoted understanding and loving sympathy for her plight.

Quickly Philippa looked around until she spied him. He recognized the questioning in her eyes. Well, if anyone backed out, it would be her, never him. He nodded his head up and down. Philippa smiled then and nodded her head jubilantly. Everyone looked from one to the other, wondering what they were nodding about.

It was Philippa who spoke. "I just need somewhere to stay for two nights. Ryan and I are being married on Monday."

Reactions to this proclamation were mixed. The children considered this man who had repeatedly rescued their beloved teacher a hero, especially since he had kept them safe during the blizzard. In addition, he was the best horseback rider they'd ever seen, and he wasn't a plain old farmer like their fathers. Their parents all thought highly of

Murphy and were so glad the sweet, hardworking young teacher was to remain among them.

Cecilia Clough embraced her and kissed her cheek, for she was in love herself. Quietly she wished it had been her brother that Philippa had fallen in love with, but she rejoiced in Philippa's happiness despite the fact that it wasn't.

Within seconds, Jasper's spirits had cascaded from the heights to the depths. He had been happily walking over to load her trunks, elated she'd be moving into town; then she'd made her announcement and he felt his insides twist as if a knife had been plunged into them. He reluctantly congratulated Ryan and sincerely wished Philippa happiness with habitual politeness.

Hamilton gave them his overt blessings, but inside he too was torn by his own loss. Alvena sniffed haughtily. It was about what she could have predicted this itinerant Irishman and an immigrant from the city tenements would do.

The Hawkinses had stayed in town to mind the store, so everyone could only suspect how Sam Senior would rant when he found out his Sammy wasn't to have Miss Marquette's hand in marriage. Most of them thought Sammy would be relieved. He really liked that little Hendee girl, and now that she was graduating, who knew?

One thing that the group would not assent to was a quiet wedding in the office of the justice of the peace in Nebraska City. The children wanted to attend the wedding of their two favorite people, and their mothers wanted to prepare a wedding meal and have a dance after it. Reverend Fields insisted they should be married in the church.

Most of the crowd left the site of the disaster with thoughts of the happy event that was to take place on Monday. The Parkers insisted that Philippa stay with them until her wedding. She turned around on the wagon seat where she sat with Mr. and Mrs. Parker and waved at Ryan, who stood by the road holding Endymion, watching. Lovingly, tentatively, they waved good-bye to each other, then he turned to walk to his lonely house.

Chapter Twenty-three

✦✦✦✦

ANDREW VAN ARDER stood looking out disconsolately from his office window, not even seeing the coachman-driven carriages, the drays, the buggies, nor the occasional automobile that passed by. His thoughts were far from the late spring scene before him. St. Louis had come alive with its usual bounty of early-blooming flowers, but this year the Van Arder residence was not the customary showplace it had always been. In spite of his constant haranguing and the innumerable gardeners he'd hired, then fired, the place did not have the laudable lawns and gardens his aunt had achieved. It irked him unreasonably.

If that damnable little cousin of his was here, she could have taken over that chore for him. Presumably his mother had trained her to grow flowers and to prevail upon gardeners to do as they were instructed. Mrs. Carpenter wasn't competent with the house either, and Sadie's meals had become atrocious. Philippa would undoubtedly be skilled in planning menus and ordering delicacies. Surely she'd taken classes with a French chef at the academy. The elegant, ostentatious house he had planned to use for entertaining influential people was in a shambles. With his bride still missing, he hadn't even been able to organize a dinner at his club for a few cronies who could do him some good. Everyone still seemed to think he should be spending every free minute trying to find her.

Strangely, this was exactly what he *had* done—or almost. Naturally he'd allowed himself a few evenings for entertainment at a gambling establishment in the exotic new brothel he'd discovered, but on the whole he'd followed society's expectations of him for once and searched for Philippa. Soon his perseverance would pay off at last.

Would his creditors hold off for another week or so? That was the question. He'd gotten seriously into debt at the bank and with some high-percent loan companies he ordinarily would not have dealt with if his capital had not dwindled. Loan sharks would take stern measures to collect. None of them would hesitate to sue him—or worse—and he was in deep enough now that they could just about clean him out, house and all. Andrew knew he had to find a way to get that Fitch fellow at the employment agency to open up, but first he'd try talking to Judge Timpton one more time. Thank God they'd finally traced a purchased ticket to that agency. It had taken weeks longer than he'd expected; weeks in which he had gotten deeper and deeper in trouble financially and hadn't been able to coax funds from any of his wealthy friends to forestall bankruptcy.

*   *   *

"Timpton, you are being the most obstinate, stubborn . . . My father helped you get this position as a judge, and by God, I can help see to it that you get ousted from it!"

"Who would 'help' you, young man? I am a well-respected judge. I've never used this office for personal gain."

"Oh, now listen—"

"Well . . . seldom, and the few times I have, everything's been well covered. No, my boy, you would have a deuce of a time disposing of me. If you do it with anything so unpleasant as murder, you would be an immediate suspect. Besides, you might get worse treatment from another judge—at least I'm giving you time. I could declare your marriage null and void; then the will would be revoked."

"You'll be well paid for waiting, and you know it. Damnation, I need some of those funds *now*. At least make me a conservator. You can finagle a way to make some of that money available to me now. It's mine, for God's sake!"

Judge Timpton rubbed his fingers thoughtfully across his jaw as if deeply pondering, but after only a brief moment he replied, "I could, but I won't, Andrew. I gave your dear mother my word. It's true your father helped me, but I don't think this would help you. Clara Rose wanted you to change your ways, to become an upstanding community member, as she and your father were."

"Dammit! I have *commitments*. This wretched search has cost a bundle—"

". . . and the purchase of a house for your mistress, as well as expenses for her upkeep."

"I didn't buy her an elaborate residence, only a

small bungalow in a shabby neighborhood, and I've cut off all her accounts," Andrew said, quick to defend himself.

"There have been rumors of gambling losses . . . and other women, lately."

"I have to keep busy. Keep my mind off everything. For Christ's sake, Timpton, be reasonable!"

"No, *you* be reasonable, Van Arder. Until that girl comes here to my office and vouchsafes she is agreeable to being your wife—yes, and *willingly* resigns that forgery on the certificate—you won't see a penny. Not one cent! I won't be giving you forever, either. I'm already having the statutes checked. I feel guilty as sin for my part in that sweet little thing's disappearance. For both our sakes, I hope no ill has befallen her."

"That 'sweet little thing' was a shrewd manipulator who covered her tracks superbly. However, I have a new lead: the Fitch Employment Agency. So far they have refused to cooperate with my efforts, but they will. The money will soon be in my hands, and after this refusal of yours today, Timpton, your portion will be smaller."

"It's of no import. I don't care much for blood money."

Andrew scooped up his hat and angrily stalked from Judge Timpton's chambers. The judge was becoming soft and addlepated. Soon he would be of no use whatsoever. The way his personal guilt was eating at him, he might even turn on Andrew. That would be a disaster. Finding Philippa immediately had become imperative. He decided to go back to that employment agency and try once more to squeeze information from that tight-lipped bastard who operated it. Today he'd use threats if necessary.

* * *

On Sunday night after she had the children in bed, Mrs. Parker fitted her own altered wedding gown onto Philippa and volunteered, "I'm gonna have a talk with you tonight just as if you were my own Alice Ann or Emma May being married tomorrow." Then she proceeded matter-of-factly to tell Philippa the facts of life. The young woman so appreciated the frank talk that she threw her arms around Mrs. Parker and thanked her with a light kiss on the forehead.

In the middle of the night Philippa awoke smelling the slight scent of camphor in Pee Wee's comforter. Lying in the darkness, thinking of everything Mrs. Parker had told her, she grasped the real reason Ryan had said she had to get married. He thought that she'd been raped, and he was preparing to sacrifice himself to protect her from the possibility of having a baby without a father. It made her love him more than ever, and she surmised that if he would do this he must love her, too. Guiltily she nudged the thought aside that he should be told the truth. If she told him, he might not marry her, and then she would never get the chance to convince him that he *did* love her. She knew him well enough to realize he would continue to insist she was too young and too citified.

But would he love her enough to understand about Andrew? Someday soon he would have to be told. When she knew they were safe from anything Andrew might do, she'd tell him everything. Surely the time was up that her aunt had allowed before the money went to the Temperance League. Then there would be no reason for Andrew to find her. Not that he could now, anyway. She was safe at last. No one would ever think of looking for a young farm wife.

Philippa stared at the ceiling and continued to worry as she lay awake anticipating her wedding day. Ryan must care for her since he was willing to do this, but he still didn't love her the way she wanted him to, and he'd said he'd never touch her. Hadn't he liked it the times they had shared loving encounters? He must not, or he would want to hold her as much as she wanted to be held in his strong arms. Wouldn't it be possible to make him love her and want her? Mrs. Parker had made it sound as if men needed the loving of a wife. Now that Dixie had married his brother, he might want *some*one someday, and if Philippa was there . . .

Yes, she told her guilty conscience, she would be there for him, always. Deep in her heart, she hoped that when he saw her in the beautiful ivory satin dress Mrs. Parker was loaning her to wear tomorrow, he would forget all his reservations. He would take her home after the dance and make love to her. And then everything would be fine.

Chapter Twenty-four

◆◆◆◆◆

THE PARKER KITCHEN was surprisingly quiet when Philippa went downstairs the following morning. She had lain awake so long during the night that she had overslept, but she did not think it was late enough that all the dishes and chores would be done. She had never been at the Parkers' when there was a serene moment.

Mrs. Parker looked up from stirring the contents of a large mixing bowl and offered, "There's hot coffee a-plenty for you and some biscuits and jam. I'll be right glad to fix you some fried salt pork 'n' an egg if you don't mind waiting 'til I get this in the oven."

"Please, don't even think of it. Coffee and biscuits and jam will be fine. In fact, I'm so nervous I may not be able to eat at all."

"Bride's nerves. Perfectly normal, dear. Don't fret it."

"I had hoped the children would be here to help me quell my jitters," Philippa said as she poured her coffee. She hoped she sounded more casual than she felt.

"Here? With their teacher's and their hero's wedding today? Goodness me, no, they were up and had their work done and were off before Rafe and I had a chance to count noses at the table this mornin'."

"Oh, I see."

"No, you really don't yet, but you soon will. I imagine weddings here are very different than the ones in the big cities. I hope you'll like all the surprises there will be for you today."

"I'm sure I will; in fact, I'm excited just to think

that they are happy about all this. Now, if you will excuse me, I had better return to getting that crate of wet and torn books and odd pages into order."

"Tsk! Tsk! I still can't believe such a catastrophe could happen, but, well, it did and all we can do now is make the best of it."

Philippa went back to mending books with flour-and-water paste, but her mind was not on her task at all. She was glad when it was time to go upstairs and dress for her wedding. It had been a wise decision not to have school today, she thought, for the children certainly would have had an absent-minded teacher.

When she entered the church, she was amazed by its changed appearance. Large crocks of fragrant berry blossoms were sitting everywhere, and twined ropes of daisies decorated the end of the pews on the center aisle. Lydia was waiting inside the door to give her a huge bouquet of spring wild-flowers tied together with one of Bessie June's hair ribbons. All of her pupils grinned broadly at her.

The ceremony was brief but meaningful, and Philippa was positive that there was a most sincere tone in Ryan's voice when he took his vows. She knew she had never seen him look more handsome. For a second she recalled seeing him in that suit for the first time, on Thanksgiving Day, when she was so sure he wore it because he had married someone else. Her heart gave an extra thud at the thought, and she turned to smile gratefully at him. He returned her smile with one that made her heart give her several more hard thuds, and she felt a little short of breath, too.

The Grange Hall was decorated even more lav

ishly than the church had been, almost as if the children had had some adult help here, and the table was loaded with things everyone had made and brought for the wedding feast.

"Have you ever seen anything more beautiful in your life?" Philippa whispered as she looked up at Ryan.

"No, never." Ryan looked thoughtful as he studied the decorations.

"The flowers are so lovely . . . why, I can't believe you found so many blooming this early."

Isaac John proudly interrupted them. "You just gotter know where to go, Miss Pip—I mean Mrs. Murphy. Down by where me 'n' Lars fish there's a bunch, and the Murrays knew some good spots too."

Mrs. Murphy. Philippa beamed at the wonderful sound.

When Ryan saw her expression, he asked, "Sounds kind of funny, huh?"

"I like the way it sounds," she replied, smiling at him.

After all the food was eaten and the wedding toasts to happiness given, the dancing started. Ryan reluctantly gave Philippa up for a few dances but claimed every one of the waltzes for himself. He held her so tightly in his arms that she just knew everything was going to be all right, and she nuzzled ever closer to him. He reciprocated by kissing her on the top of her upswept hair—only discreet little butterfly kisses, but she felt them. They jarred her already sensuously taut feelings. The wedding dance was wonderful, of course. It was something she would never forget, as were all these people who had helped to make it so, but the best part was when she and Ryan got into the buggy to drive home afterward. Home . . . to Ryan's house.

"Can you believe how many miles those kids must have walked today to gather that many flowers?" Ryan asked.

"And all the cooking and the baking," Philippa added. "Everything was so good, especially the Swedish wedding cake Mrs. Olsen made."

"They all like you a lot."

"Me? Ryan Murphy, this was for *you*. Everyone thinks you—"

"Nope, little darlin', it was for you."

Philippa saw no reason to argue this point. She had other things on her mind. They were almost to Ryan's house now. Would he forget all that silliness he had mumbled on Saturday about not touching her? Surely he would, after the sincere way he had spoken his vows. And oh, the way he had held her during that last waltz! She had felt as if they shared heartbeats.

When they turned into Ryan's driveway, his remaining hired man, Buzz, came out to take the buggy. Buzz had left the dance early to come home and do chores. Ryan took Philippa's small bag to carry in for her after they thanked Buzz and wished him good night.

At the back porch he stopped and handed her the bag, just remaining by the door, not saying a word.

Was he hesitating about carrying her over the doorstep, she wondered, since the circumstances of their wedding were a little different than most? She hoped to encourage him when she asked, "Aren't you forgetting something?"

Ryan looked at her sharply, trying to read what she meant in those words. She had seemed so loving all evening, so pliable in his arms, he'd honestly hoped she had forgotten that vow he had made. That maybe she wanted more than a marriage, in case she was expecting a child. Evidently she didn't, or why would she be asking if he had forgotten something?

"No, ma'am, I haven't forgotten a thing," he growled. "My clothes have already been moved to the other room above the barn."

"You've moved to the barn?" Philippa was appalled. She had assumed they would at least share the house companionably, if not the bed.

"Only to sleep," he told her brusquely. "Buzz and I will be in for breakfast around six-fifteen."

"So," Philippa snapped, angry now, as she watched him walk down the steps, "the bride does not get carried over the threshold, but she is permitted to cook for her master. Well, that suits me fine too!" She slammed the door shut to emphasize her words.

"*Damn*," Ryan swore under his breath. So that was all she had meant by asking if he was forgetting something. He felt like storming back in there and sweeping her up in his arms and carrying her a lot farther than across the threshold. He wanted to carry that little firebrand he'd married in and toss her on the bed and . . . But as he started to turn back, he recalled their circumstances. Oh, sure, tonight she felt all romantic, and he knew how easily he could ignite her, but tomorrow would she feel the same way, or would she hate him for taking advantage of this marriage of convenience? Ryan knew how much he wanted her tonight, but he also knew he wanted all of her love forever, and this wasn't the way to win it. He turned back and walked slowly to the barn. Buzz stood in the barn doorway, nodding his head in disbelief.

Was she the only girl in the world to have *two* unconsummated marriages? Philippa wondered to herself as she sat at the kitchen table in her new house—Ryan's house, which, after three weeks, was now very much hers, too. Ryan had bought her a beautiful New Home sewing machine and she had made curtains for the kitchen and bedroom. He had also had a deluxe new range with double warmer ovens and enamel trim brought by freight from Omaha. Most exciting of all, he had sent clear to Chicago to get a Chickering piano for her when Philippa mentioned she missed having one to play. He was so good to her . . . but he *still* slept in the barn!

Philippa would have sworn there was love in his eyes when he reverently stated "I do!" at their wedding. But it had all been an act. When it was time for the regular Saturday-night Grange Dance the following week, Philippa had looked forward to going, just to be held in his arms once more. But no, Ryan had said he was expecting another mare to foal, so they couldn't go. That was two weeks ago, and that horse hadn't had her colt yet!

After putting in a late garden and fixing up the house, Philippa did not know how else to try to win his affections. She cooked his favorite foods and even offered to help him in the fields after school and on weekends. He only laughed at her and then told her seriously he wasn't going to have *his* wife dying young from a heavy workload, as his mother had. Philippa recalled the very capable Dixie he had been set on marrying because she'd be a help with his cattle operation. Unhappily she feared maybe he was heartbroken over the loss of his childhood sweetheart to his own brother.

When her monthly menses arrived, she burned the telltale rags she used in the stove before she left for the school in the Radcliffs' parlor. He had married her because he thought she was pregnant. If he found out she wasn't, might he leave her?

By subtle questioning, Philippa had learned from Cecilia that an unconsummated marriage could be set aside. Perhaps Ryan was waiting to have the marriage annulled when he was sure she was not in the family way. She had to deceive him for just a little longer, to give herself more time to make him love her.

Angry at herself for her scheming machinations, Philippa tried to forget about Ryan and concentrate harder on the assignments she was preparing for her younger pupils' last week of school. All the eighth-graders would be at the town school for final examinations to determine if they would graduate from School District No. 3. Philippa was confident they would pass the tests.

Ryan let Thunder lope along at the horse's own gait. His mind was elsewhere as he rode toward town. He had a disquieting suspicion that something had happened to his hired man. Buzz had gone into town the first thing this morning for some nails they needed to finish building Philippa a chicken coop, and he still had not returned. The fellow was probably just having a beer or two before he started back, but it wasn't like him. He'd always been very reliable.

Soon Ryan's thoughts shifted from Buzz to Philippa, where they seemed to dwell all the time. He

had had to move out to the barn to ensure that he
kept his promise not to touch her. It was a vow that
was getting harder and harder to keep, but he had
made it to her and he wouldn't break it until she
released him from it.

Other than her brief hint about being carried
over the threshold, she had not given him any sign
of encouragement. She wasn't the cold Miss Hoity-
Toity, but in everything she did she was extremely
fastidious. It must be because she had the rape
engraved on her mind and found it revolting to
think of a man touching her. From past intimacies
he knew she had a warm, sensuous disposition,
and maybe someday . . .

Rounding the curve in the road, Ryan noticed
there was a crowd in front of Hawkins's place and
lightly nudged Thunder in the flank to hurry him
to the center of town. Obediently the horse took off
at a gallop, while simultaneously the crowd in front
of Hawkins's parted and a motorcar banged,
chugged, and spluttered toward the horse and
rider. At the sight of such a contraption, Thunder
reared up onto his hind legs in fear. Only Ryan's
expert horsemanship kept him from being thrown
and enabled him to get the frightened animal under control. The car hissed and screeched to a stop.

The dusty but luxurious Mitchell Six was the first
car that had actually stopped in Bluffsview, Nebraska. A few automobiles had passed through
town, frightening horses and dogs. One had even
hit a chicken that had found its way out onto Main
Street, but this had only helped to enforce the
town's ordinance that chickens within the town
limits were to be kept penned. There had been cars
on display at the county fair for the last two years,
so most people had closely looked them
over—looked them over and decided they weren't

made for the deep-rutted, often muddy or snow-drifted roads of southeastern Nebraska.

This was not at all the same as having an automobile stop in the middle of town. Its driver wore a touring hat, coat, and goggles, which impressed the townspeople even more. The most impressive fact, however, was that this stranger had the county sheriff with him, and they'd asked several questions about Philippa Marquette Murphy.

It seemed they were trying to determine her exact arrival date in Bluffsview. Someone had pointed out Ryan Murphy's hired man, Buzz, to them and they had stood and talked to him for several minutes down the boardwalk, out of earshot of the crowd. The stranger appeared to give Buzz some money, then they had climbed back into the car after the driver cranked the engine. The automobile coughed and the exhaust banged a couple of times as fuel reached the motor and the engine sputtered to life. It began to chug and growl when the gear was set, and then it started off with a lurch. The motor had barely begun to purr when Murphy's stallion reared up in front of the vehicle and it had to come to a screeching halt.

The crowd moved from the front of Hawkins's store closer to the scene. Murphy looked like he'd lost that Irish temper of his from the way he swung agitatedly down off Thunder, and the man in the car stepped out, pompously belligerent.

Too bad the sheriff was here. There probably wouldn't be a fight. All bets would have been on Ryan, though. The other man was as big, but he looked soft. Murphy didn't look a bit soft, and from tales they'd heard from friends and relatives out around his hometown, he was tough as whang-leather. The rare times he'd lost his temper and got into a fight, he'd always come out victorious.

The sheriff intervened before any confrontation could arise between the two glowering men, whose only conversation had been foul.

"You stupid bastard!"

"You ignorant son of a bitch!"

"Here, now, both of you," said the sheriff, trying to placate the two. "It was just one of those unfortunate things that are bound to happen when automobiles and horses share the streets," he maintained, then abruptly added, "Why, Van Arder, this is the man you want to see."

"See me? What the hell for?" Ryan was getting a gut reaction to this fellow he didn't like at all.

"Not here, Sheriff! Not with all these yokels gaping and eavesdropping." Van Arder's voice was loud, commanding, and demeaning. "We'll go out to his place and talk there."

"There's no need for that. We've got nothin' to say to each other, mister," Ryan informed this self-important stuffed shirt disgustedly. "I'm goin' on in and hunt up my hired hand." He turned away, annoyed with this puffed-up man who was so insulting to the townfolk.

Andrew knew the weapons for verbal battle well. He jeered, "For openers, cowboy, I have just paid the estimable Mr. Buzz Yates one hundred dollars for some information about your so-called wife that was very valuable to me. I don't think you'll be seeing him again, do you? Do you want me to divulge that information here? I also paid Louis Dermot, better known as Big Louie, for other pertinent facts."

Ryan had to clench his knuckles until his fingernails chewed into the palms of his hands to keep from smashing his fist into this man's smug face. If he hadn't wanted to protect Philippa's reputation, he would not have been able to refrain.

Why was this man paying for information about Philippa? He would find out, and then he would punch him out, sheriff or no sheriff. This bastard was not going to drag Philippa's name into the mire.

"All right!" Ryan growled low in his throat. "We'll go out to my place, but we'll talk in the road. Step one foot on my property and I'll nail you."

Before Andrew had time to answer, Ryan swung up onto Thunder, whirled him around, and galloped out of town.

The town residents relished Murphy's splendid riding ability and enjoyed a knee-slapping laugh when the arrogant fool's car wouldn't start no matter how hard he cranked it. He got the water can that was strapped on the back and poured some in, red-faced and totally disgruntled. The car banged, chugged, and spluttered into action once more. It left a curious community behind it.

Philippa heard Ryan gallop into the yard and hurried to finish preparing lunch while he stabled Thunder. She had made an apple pie for him with one of the few jars remaining from last fall. It was still his favorite pie, and she hoped to garner a kiss from him for making it.

In fact, she had made the decision to boldly ask for one. When Ryan had kissed her in the past, it had often led to more. She ardently hoped he would kiss her today. She had made him forget his reservations about her youth and innocence before, and she was determined to do it again. Enough was enough! She was convinced now that he truly did love her, but for some ridiculous reason he was holding tight reins on his feelings. The love and emotions they had shared in the past were too real to be denied, even by this most stubborn Irishman.

When he didn't come in, she looked out the window just in time to see him walking to the road. Curiously she ran to the lace-covered glass pane in the parlor door and watched to see what he was going to do, thinking perhaps she should go out and tell him his lunch was ready.

When it appeared he was going to walk out the gate, she quickly unlocked the door and started to open it so she could call to him. Before she had a chance, there was the unmistakable sound of an automobile cresting the hill from town. Not knowing why, she instinctively stepped back into the house and locked the door. Staring out the window, she watched the car stop in front of their house. Unexplained jitters enveloped her entirely.

The sheriff and another man climbed out of the big black car, and when the stranger took off his driving hat and goggles, Philippa immediately recognized the dreaded Andrew Van Arder.

Oh, dear God in heaven! Merciful Lord above! She had been positive he would never find a Mrs. Murphy in the sparsely populated countryside around the small town of Bluffsview, Nebraska. For a moment she feared she was going to faint. If she fainted she could not fight going back with him, and she was going to fight it every way she knew how!

In her benumbed mind Andrew became associated with Big Louie, and regretfully she recalled that the heating stove had been taken down and stored in the toolshed behind the barn for the summer, along with its ugly black stovepipes and its cast iron poker. Having to eliminate the poker as a weapon, she hastily looked around for something to use and thought of her cast iron frying pan. This might suffice, but it was not the kind of weapon to accomplish her purpose.

She watched the expression of shocked disbelief that registered on Ryan's face as Andrew began to talk. It was the spur she needed to galvanize her into action.

Ryan stood unbelieving, furious, heartbroken . . . How could so many emotions pour over a man at one time? he wondered. Philippa Marquette—no, Philippa Martin Van Arder—was married to this man? Big Louie had helped her escape from her lavish home in St. Louis?

He was shocked that a high-principled girl like Philippa would break her wedding vows, not only break them, but commit bigamy. He was angry because he had kept his vow to the letter and not allowed himself to make love to her when he had wanted to so badly because he had thought she was so prim and proper. Ha! She had made a complete fool of him!

Most of all, he was hurt—hurt that she had used him this way when he loved her so much. No, he could not believe this of Philippa. He was furious at himself for the way he felt now, but there was no use denying it. In spite of it all, the heartache was there. It would probably be there forever. Agonizing as it was, he knew he'd always love her.

". . . So," Van Arder was droning on, "the detectives traced all the women who purchased tickets departing from St. Louis that day, after that rotten, good-for-nothing drayman admitted to hauling her trunks to the depot . . . The man was a fool; he knocked me unconscious and robbed me when I didn't pay him the reward he thought he should have.

"I don't take that from anyone. I put a few men on his tail and one of them shot him four or five weeks ago near Clay City. He never saw the man or the bullet." Andrew Van Arder suddenly recalled the sheriff's presence and assured him, "There was a list of 'Wanted' posters out on him for other crimes, and a reward. I may have been wrong to encourage bounty hunters, but—"

"Naw, never mind. Clay City ain't my territory. It don't concern me none what happens down there." The sheriff put his badly chewed cigar back into his mouth. He still didn't relight it, but just went on chewing it, moving it with his lips from one side of his mouth to the other as he continued to listen intently.

"Yes. Well, then, as I was saying, unfortunately Philippa did not buy a ticket that day, so tracing it took a lot longer than it should have. They finally traced a ticket that was sent to the Fitch Employment Agency. We didn't get any cooperation there until I threatened to have their office closed. They learned you play ball with an alderman if you don't want to be blacklisted. Finally they came through with the information.

"However, Murphy, the most valuable piece of news I got was from your hired hand, Buzz Yates. He said he could vouch for the fact that for some reason you and my wife never consummated your 'marriage,' " Andrew said with a sneer.

He got no further before Ryan hit him. With one blow, he knocked Van Arder off balance and came in with a left that flattened him. Ryan dove on him astraddle and was ready to pummel this man's face, this man that he now hated with a black anger more potent than he'd felt even for Big Louie. Everything about Andrew Van Arder was despicable. Or perhaps it was his frustration with Philippa that made him want to beat this pompous billy goat senseless.

His doubled-up fist never reached its goal. Two big, hairy hands clenched it and the county sheriff ordered, "Don't cause no problems, son. You're harboring a runaway wife, and this here man's willin' not to prosecute if Mrs. Murphy—that is, Mrs. Van Arder—goes back with him quiet-like." Seeing the look on Ryan's face, the sheriff continued, "Now, come on. She is *his* wife. He's got the papers to prove it."

Slowly Ryan got off Andrew, still filled with bitterness, rage, and grief. He picked up his hat and strode toward his house. The sheriff reached down and helped Van Arder to stand, then the two of them tried to keep pace with Ryan, but couldn't. They were both panting when they got to the side porch. Andrew was trying to brush the dust off his jacket and trousers while Ryan continued to pound on the door.

"Philippa! I know you're in there! Unlock the door! I know the truth, Pip. Open the door or I'll bust it in!"

The door opened and Philippa exclaimed, sweetly apologetic, "Sorry, darling. I was trying to get my hair braided and pinned up when I saw you had guests." Her hair, which had been neatly braided up before breakfast this morning as always, looked seductive, half up and half down.

Ryan was puzzled by the way she was acting. She had called him darling! She must not have seen who the "guests" were. Angrily he stepped aside to reveal them as she continued, "Good afternoon, Sheriff," and finally said, to Andrew,

"You've wasted your time and money tracing me and coming after me. I'm married *legally* now and I won't be coming back." This last was delivered in her starchiest, most frigid voice.

Andrew could not believe how attractive and mature this girl had become. In the dress she wore she looked as if she could seduce a saint. He couldn't wait to get her back to St. Louis. He admired spunk. The girl his mother had chosen for him was going to be perfect. For once, Clara Rose Van Arder and her son agreed on something.

Andrew determined to reason with her first. By now she must have had her fill of this primitive lifestyle. He looked around the cozy kitchen with disdain as he began, "Your duties are in St. Louis, Philippa. You have a beautiful home to supervise and a place you are expected to fill in society. The expensive gowns you ordered at the dressmaker arrived shortly after you left. You will dazzle everyone at the mayor's dinner party next week."

"The gowns *you* ordered, Andrew, not I!"

As if she hadn't spoken, he continued to drone on. "Your housekeeper and cook and even the day maids miss you and send their regards. They are eager for you to return." At this Ryan tried to leave, but Philippa quickly grabbed his arm, keeping him beside her.

"You just can't accept it, can you, Andrew? I am a *married* woman. This time I *took* the vows and *signed* the certificate and I'm staying with my husband! I won't *ever* come back, and you can't make me!" She picked up the frying pan in her free hand and held it like a weapon.

"Oh, I can make you come back, Philippa. It will be very easy." He grabbed her arm and cruelly twisted it until she dropped the heavy pan to the floor.

Dammit! No one was going to harm Philippa as long as he was around, Ryan swore, no matter whose wife she was or what she had done! No one! He pulled his arm free from her and grabbed Andrew's wrist, twisting it unmercifully.

"Cease that at once, damn you." Andrew's voice echoed with pain. "Sheriff, control this man with your pistol, if need be. I showed you my marriage certificate. Now I am within my rights to take my wife home."

"I never signed that paper!"

"So?"

"So I am *not* legally married to *you*. I signed papers in Otoe County, Nebraska. Sheriff, surely you uphold marriages that are registered right here in your own courthouse, don't you?" Philippa pleaded.

"Yes, we do, Miss Marquette . . . I mean, Mrs. Murphy . . . I mean . . ." the sheriff stuttered.

"See, even you know I am Mrs. Murphy, Sheriff," she gloated.

"No, ma'am, you ain't. I mean, it ain't legal. It ain't . . . well, you never . . . you an' Murphy don't sleep together. Your hired hand told us so."

Philippa moved provocatively over to stand beside the sheriff, saying pointedly, "You didn't really believe such nonsense, did you, Sheriff? Come now, look at me! You don't truly think a red-blooded man like Ryan Murphy would fail to . . . to consummate our marriage, do you?"

Philippa knew Ryan was probably furious with her. He hated it when she acted this way, but she wanted to stay with Ryan and she would do anything she had to do to make it possible.

The sheriff was getting a little mixed up. He looked at Murphy and he looked at Philippa. No, he couldn't believe they'd lived in the same house for nearly three weeks and not— "But the hired man said Murphy sleeps in the barn!" he finally managed to spit out.

"In the barn?" Philippa chuckled. "Hardly."

Andrew had heard enough. Philippa was just trying to dupe this fool sheriff. He was acquiring more respect for her all the time. She would be a tremendous asset to him; she could wrap politicians around her finger whenever he needed a favor.

"Get your things, Philippa," Andrew ordered, reaching for her arm. "I'm taking you home, where you belong."

She pulled out of his reach. "No! I *won't* go. I won't, I tell you! Ryan, tell him we're married." Philippa needed to know if Ryan did or didn't want her. She was determined to stay one way or the other, but this might be an opportunity to find out if he really wanted to have her with him, or if he had just been concerned that she was pregnant. If it was the latter, he could easily turn her over to Andrew now. Philippa anxiously awaited his answer.

The pleading in Philippa's voice, the beseeching look in her eyes were all it took for Ryan to forget she was accused of being someone else's wife. With wild fury he ordered, "Leave her alone! Pip is not going anyplace with you if she doesn't want to. Now get the hell out of here!"

"She's coming, you bastard!"

"She's not, you son of a bitch!"

This was the way all this had started, the sheriff thought in exasperation. There must be some way to resolve it.

Philippa resolved it herself. Now that Ryan had indicated that he wanted her to stay, she couldn't wait to spring her trap. She tugged on the sheriff's arm, pulling him through the parlor and to the door of the bedroom, talking in that soft, husky voice of hers all the way.

"It seems to me, Sheriff, that you are only obligated to uphold the law in your own county and state. Ryan Murphy and I were married in this county by the laws of this state. We live here and we sleep here . . ." She threw open the bedroom door.

Ryan heard the sheriff from clear out in the kitchen as he exclaimed, "I shoulda known that Buzz fella was a shyster. You're right, Mrs. Murphy. I'm gonna uphold the marriage in this county until we get to the bottom of things and find out just what's what!"

When Andrew heard the sheriff's decision, he marched into the parlor, blustering. "I'll have your badge for this. You back me up or else!" Then he, too, must have looked into Philippa's bedroom, for Ryan heard him curse.

"*Damn!* Damn you!" Then there was a long pause before he said in a menacing tone, "I'll grant you've won this round, little Philippa, but don't think for a minute this is the end of it." He turned on his heels and stomped back through the kitchen, giving Ryan a menacing look as he passed him. The sheriff followed close behind, grinning.

Chapter Twenty-five

✦✦✦✦

His CURIOSITY AROUSED, Ryan walked through the parlor and peeked into Philippa's bedroom. The covers on her bed were twisted every which way and both pillows obviously looked slept on. Ryan's shaving mug and razor lay on the nightstand, looking as if they had been recently used there from the residue of soapy shaving water, while her hand lotion sat open beside his shaving mug.

The floor was strewn with clothes—one of his dirty outfits and one of hers. It appeared somebody had got out of them in a hell of a hurry. His drawers lay suggestively on top of her pink silk underpanties, and over the foot of the bed, laid out ever so seductively, was the nightgown Halfpint had put into her Christmas box.

If a room ever revealed it had been used as a lovers' tryst, this one did. The conniving vixen! Ryan couldn't believe it of her. *This* was what she had used to convince the sheriff? This scene she had hurriedly rigged up was completely unlike the prudish young virgin he had thought he was married to. Her and her "touch me not" airs! Red. Blue. Black. All the colors of darkness, death, and destruction shadowed the towering rage that engulfed him.

When he noted she'd stepped softly into the room, looking tormentingly vulnerable, he began to shout, furious at her acting ability, "Why in the name of God and all the saints did you do this, you tramp!" He yelled to wipe out any softness he felt at the sight of her stricken face. The face of a consummate actress, he reminded himself. "Why did you want your husband and the sheriff to believe you were unfaithful? My God! And you made a jackass of me—not to mention a bigamist of yourself—with your treachery."

"Ryan—" she pleaded, but he was too enraged to be interrupted.

"I know why you picked me. You needed to find someone so head over tail in love with you that he'd be willing—and stupid enough—to go along with your scheming. Who better than a dumb cowboy? A lawyer or a minister or a store owner . . . even a young clerk might have gotten wise to you . . . but me, Lord, me! I was blind to any plot you devised, wasn't I? *Wasn't I?*" he shouted again before she had time to plead.

"No! No! Oh, Ryan, no!" Philippa could not bear the wounded look on his face, and she tried to take hold of his arm, to turn his face toward her with the perspiring palm of her hand, wanting to look him straight in the eyes to convince him. "That's not true."

He jerked his arm away and knocked her hand from his cheek, almost violently. It was then that she saw his tortured eyes. They penetrated to her very soul as he rasped, "Christ! I idolized you, girl." Then he turned and practically ran from the room. The kitchen door slammed behind him before she caught up with him.

Yanking it open, she cried, "Please, *please*, Ryan! We have to talk. Please hear me out . . ." But he didn't stop walking, just continued his long, angry strides in the direction of the two men waiting in the center of the road.

Feeling too weak to stand for another minute, Philippa turned to the kitchen table and sank helplessly into a chair, sobbing great, heart-wracking sobs. Sobs of hatred for Andrew, and fear of what might become of her now that he'd found her; but even more soul-rending were the tears for what she had done to Ryan by her selfishness. Dear Lord, she had never meant for Ryan to be hurt, not Ryan!

How long she sat there crying she did not know. She tried to quash the flow of tears when the sheriff stepped back into the kitchen, embarrassedly clearing his throat to politely draw her attention, but it was impossible. They continued to course unabated down her face as she watched him walk toward her.

In his most official lawman's voice he proclaimed, "The two aggrieved parties have agreed, ma'am, that I should take you on into town. Murphy's gonna loan me his buggy. He staunchly refused to have you jailed as Van Arder wanted. Insisted he'd go any amount of bail necessary. Said he knew you wouldn't run, at least not 'til the end of the term. Right dedicated to your students, he says. That'll speak well of you to the court . . .

"Wall, anyhow, there's a widder in town, a Mrs. Crafton, who's got a spare bedroom. That's where I'll be takin' you fer now. If you'll just git together what things you'll need, missuz, he's hitchin' up the team now."

"—But Sheriff," Philippa managed to stammer, "you said you'd honor the vows I took in this state. I am wedded to *Ryan*, not Andrew. You agreed!"

"No, ma'am, I didn't agree to nothin'. I jist decided that feller wasn't takin' you back . . . the way things turned out here 'n' all." He was blushing furiously but forced himself to continue. "You didn't come up with no papers provin' Van Arder's document of marriage ain't valid, so . . . Believe me, missuz, this is fair. I could charge you with bigamy—I could haul both you an' Murphy in."

"*Ryan!* He's guilty of nothing!" This threat stemmed her tears as she begged, "You can't charge him with anything! He didn't even know of Andrew. Oh, please, promise me! Ryan mustn't come to any more harm or grief because of me."

Regretfully the stocky sheriff admitted, "I won't have no say-so in this matter. It'll be up to the court to decide. Just git your stuff now, will you? Please, ma'am!"

With the possibility of Ryan's being implicated or even jailed, Philippa gripped the tabletop, forcing her weak, still-shaking body to stand as she meekly assented, "I'll be out as soon as I pack a valise."

Chapter Twenty-six

✦✦✦✦

PHILIPPA AWOKE THE following day with firm resolutions to act like an educated adult instead of the weeping nincompoop she had proved herself to be. Thank heaven it was Sunday and she did not have to confront her students! Any thought of attending church was promptly dismissed. Even the most educated adult would not be brave enough to face *that*!

"Good to see you a little more the thing this morning," Mrs. Crafton's voice intruded into her thoughts as she walked into the kitchen. "I knew you were a plucky girl. It took spunk to run from that bully who forced you to marry up with him, and that same spunk will pull you through this, too."

Philippa wished she could feel some of Mrs. Crafton's confidence.

"Incidentally," Mrs. Crafton announced, "Jasper Clough came by last night after you were abed. Told him to come over this mornin' while all the busybodies are at church. You need to talk to him."

Philippa walked to the door with a sense of doom engulfing her when Jasper arrived.

Jasper took one look at his sweet Philippa's ravaged countenance and, heedless of propriety, held out his arms to her as he murmured, "You should have trusted me enough to confide in me, love."

Gratefully she accepted the solace of his words and his comforting arms as she softly swore with deep sincerity, "I couldn't bring myself to tell anyone, I was so afraid I'd be found."

"Now that you have been, perhaps it would be best to tell me everything, right from the start."

Philippa sat on the edge of the fainting couch in Mrs. Crafton's cozy parlor and told the entire story, ending with, "I'm right, aren't I? It's not a legal marriage. It can be annulled, can't it?"

Slowly, warningly, Jasper shook his head. "Your friend—and Cecilia, too, I'm afraid—were referring to the marriage of a minor without the consent of her parents or guardians. In such instances, yes, annulment is possible if the marriage has not been consummated. However, in most states, fourteen or sixteen is the age of consent for a female, so that law would not apply to you."

He had adopted his most impressive practicing attorney's language to answer her, hoping to spare her as much embarrassment as possible.

"Here in Nebraska there are other grounds for annulment, such as mental illness or retardation—"

"Retardation?" Philippa interrupted. "That surely applies to me. I've done nothing but stupid things for months now."

Jasper chuckled, pleased to note she was becoming more her old self now, then continued, "—retardation at the time of the marriage . . . and incidentally, that is a hard case to prove, as is force, which is also grounds. Others are bigamy, impotence, fraud . . . but unfortunately, we are talking about the grounds for annulment in Nebraska. You were married in Missouri and they don't recognize any."

"None?"

"None," he affirmed. "But incestuous or bigamous marriages, or instances where one spouse was without mental capacity at the time of marriage, or there was no license obtained, are void."

"I still say I fit the one about lack of mental capacity," she lamented before asking, "Then he can take me back? Doesn't it mean anything that the document was forged, or that I took no vows?"

"Both will be hard to prove after this long, but no, he cannot . . . force you to go back to live with him, that is. Philippa, didn't you know that even Missouri law gives the woman the right of consent?"

"Yes, but they forced me into the marriage! After the ceremony, who would have believed my word against Andrew and the judge? No one! I told you, they're wealthy, powerful men in St. Louis. Both of them."

"I see." Jasper seemed to be in distant thought. "Even divorce will be difficult, then, for a wife's domicile is her husband's home. The case would be tried there, I'm afraid, and your grounds are flimsy at best."

Jasper Clough took another look at her woebegone face. He took a deep swallow before promising, "We'll get you and Ryan back together. Somehow we'll work this out, legally, this time. We'll beat them at their own game."

He'd hoped the promise would make her happy. He wanted to see her lovely smile light up her face, but she only shook her head sadly. "I've botched everything. Ryan hates me, and I may have caused him a lot of legal troubles. They can't arrest him or do anything to him when he didn't even know, can they? I swear, he knew nothing, nothing at all. Oh dear heaven, Jasper, the look on his face yesterday when he learned of my past . . . I'll never be able to forget what I did to him, nor forgive myself for it."

"Trust me, please?" Jasper pleaded, hating to see her reproach herself this way. He knew Murphy was no fool; he'd come back to a love like this. Any man would. Time would cool that stubborn Irishman's temper.

The last week of classes was most eventful. On Monday Philippa rose and dressed early, allowing herself adequate time to go to Cecilia's house and ask to borrow her horse, but Mrs. Crafton said it wasn't necessary; she'd be getting a ride. Since she was already jittery because only the small children would be having classes today, this was a relief. She had been very apprehensive about riding out alone on Cecilia's horse. The Murray boys had obligingly informed her last night, "That car's parked down by the hotel." Andrew was staying in town to guarantee she did not escape again, or perhaps to try to take her back forcefully. It would be typical of Andrew to offer to drive her to the Radcliffs' but abduct her instead.

With relief she found Sammy and Calvin waiting by the front porch in Hawkins's surrey to drive her out to the Radcliffs', where school was being held, and they picked her up after classes each day too.

Mr. Radcliff and Will were painting the house when she arrived. Philippa knew this was unplanned, since Lydia had said nothing about such a noteworthy project. "It'll take us all week, ma'am," Will assured her. As to the reason for their rifles sitting on the front porch, Mr. Radcliff insisted, "The missus has been complainin' of rabbits eatin' off the tops of vegetables in her garden. We're gonna keep an eye peeled for 'em."

Several times that day she heard the Mitchell Six roar past and was thankful to her benefactors. Late in the afternoon it stopped. Loudly the rifle pinged, then Will yelled, "Hey, sorry 'bout that tire, mister. I was aimin' at that big ol' jackrabbit that just ran across the road."

Even from indoors she could hear Andrew cursing.

Andrew finally realized he had to keep this legal-like if he didn't want to jeopardize his plans again. This hick town had made abducting Philippa impossible, but she *had* to go back with him. Once in St. Louis, if she didn't settle down he'd have her committed to an asylum. He knew of several where he could easily incarcerate her—for a price—and after a few weeks in any one of them, she'd be begging to live with him. She'd accede to anything. He had to have the money she represented! Two or three of the ventures he was involved in were floundering worse than ever, and without cash input they would bankrupt him.

To make matters worse, that old coot Timpton still wouldn't let him touch a cent of that inheritance until Philippa actually returned. He kept threatening to go ahead and give it to the Temperance League! The old fool had recently developed stomach problems and blamed booze. Now he was a teetotaler and favored prohibition. Tried telling Andrew the money would be going to a good cause! He ought to be committed, too, but even the Van Arder fortunes weren't enough to hatchet such a powerful political figure as the judge. Philippa had to be taken back, and soon.

Sterner measures were called for, so he went to the town's most outstanding attorney—there were only two to choose from, and he'd already discounted the older one as less manipulable. He'd made the right choice, he determined as he looked around the young man's small office. The shelves were lined with dog-eared volumes of poetry and only a few new-looking law books. Undoubtedly he could be bought.

"Let me understand this," the solicitor said after Andrew had briefly outlined his situation. "You are of the opinion that because of her aunt's untimely death the girl was temporarily . . . upset, confused? Distraught enough to merit the charge of 'temporary insanity'? That is why she deserted you and married this other fellow?"

"Precisely."

"You're certain that once she is back in her familiar surroundings she will be amenable," the young lawyer pressed.

"Absolutely," Andrew insisted.

* * *

On Saturday afternoon Ryan had stood in the shadows of the barn and watched as the Nebraska City sheriff drove out of the yard, escorting Philippa into town. Damn! Beneath his fury, he hadn't hurt like this since he was a kid.

In the first place, he couldn't figure out why someone like Pip had married such a pompous galoot and then chosen to run away from him. Maybe he should have listened to her explanation at least, given her a chance to tell him about this, even if it was a pack of lies.

And if it wasn't? Why hadn't she confided in him, if it was the truth? God, she must know he'd do anything to help her, and if she was as frightened of this man as she appeared to be in the kitchen, when she'd wielded that skillet . . .

Well, hell, he couldn't just let her be whisked back to St. Louis if she was unwilling to go, could he? He saddled Thunder and headed for town. From the back door of the blacksmith shop he could see Widow Crafton's house, front and rear, so he found reason to stay there until dark, but Van Arder didn't approach the place. The sheriff must have laid down the law to him. Still, Ryan didn't trust that pompous ass and determined to stay on guard all night. He slept out behind the smithy after everyone went home so no one would guess he was such a fool as to care for that husband deserter–bigamist he'd married.

Before long those terms had become so unpalatable, so unbelievable of the Philippa he loved, that Ryan knew he would go to her and listen to her story, whatever it was, the minute she sent for him.

On Sunday he hung around town, watching and waiting, only going home long enough to oversee his chores. His wife, if she was his wife, sent for

Clough, but not for him. Even when he got desperate and asked the Murray boys to give her the message he would come if she needed anything, she hadn't asked for him. Once again he spent the night out behind the blacksmith's.

By Monday morning it was evident her loyal former suitors had arranged for her to be protected by the whole town. Now that they knew her marriage to Ryan was illegal, they were probably trying to win her favors once more.

And with their chivalrous, educated ways, they might, too—if she didn't go back to St. Louis with old moneybags, that is.

Chapter Twenty-seven
+–+–+–+

"I DON'T UNDERSTAND, Jasper. Why do I have to come to the church with you right now?"

"The sheriff and the judge from Nebraska City are here, Philippa, to hear your case. In lieu of a courthouse, Hamilton has graciously offered them the use of his church. Come along, now. You look fine."

"No!" Mrs. Crafton, who had been standing quietly inside the front hall of her house until now, intervened. "Let her change into one of her prettiest dresses. The whole town's going to be there. Why, the Hawkinses even closed the store."

"For my hearing?" Philippa asked, unable to believe such a happening.

"You've seen how they all stood by you. They'll be there to lend their support. It may sway the judge," was Mrs. Crafton's matter-of-fact explanation.

"Oh, I see," Philippa said softly, not at all willing to have all these people witness Andrew's accusations, yet she did not want to face him and a judge alone again. He might own this one too. She decided to change her dress, just to have some time alone before this upcoming ordeal.

The church was packed with people, and everyone turned to look as she walked in with Jasper and Mrs. Crafton, but only one pair of eyes caught hers. The questioning green eyes of Ryan Murphy captured hers and she stopped, brown eyes as quizzical as the green ones that tightly held them. The whole room was silent as the two stared beseechingly at one another.

The judge broke the spell by ordering, "The court will now proceed with the case on the docket," and Jasper nudged her to walk on down to the front pew and be seated.

Clearing his throat, the judge began, "In the court action of recognizing the voiding of the marriage of Van Arder vs. Van Arder, we are now in session."

"*No! No!*" Andrew lurched to his feet. "The marriage being voided is Murphy vs. Murphy!"

The judge peered over his spectacles, warning, "I'll tolerate no more of these outbursts in my courtroom," then looked back at his docket carefully. "The marriage which has been legally voided by reason of the temporary insanity of the bride at the time is that of Andrew Van Arder and Philippa Louise Martin, which took place in St. Louis, Missouri. This court is recognizing only the action of the district court there to verify whether Miss Martin's marriage to Ryan Murphy is bigamous or legal and binding."

"You bumbling baboon!" Andrew was on his feet once more and waving an accusing finger at Jasper. "What have you done, you ignorant fool? I'll have your license revoked for this!"

"Order!" the judge was shouting. "You were warned." But Andrew was out of his seat now and stood towering over Jasper threateningly . . . but only for a moment. When Jasper Clough stood up he dwarfed his enraged adversary, and his firm words indicated he was not the least bit intimidated by the other's dire threats.

"I did exactly as ordered. I had the marriage voided as we agreed. You yourself wrote the deposition Judge Timpton honored: the statement verifying the girl's temporary insanity at the time of the marriage due to the sudden death of her aunt. The judge seemed pleased to carry out your instructions. He even donated the fee you paid to the same worthwhile fund that Clara Rose Van Arder's money will now go to."

"Why, you . . . you jackass! You unprincipled bastard! Not *my* money! I swear I'll find a way to stop this—"

"Sheriff, remove that man from this room. Cite him with comtempt of court, obstruction of justice, and whatever else you need to until I have time to thoroughly check his background and his current records. Get him out of here, *now!*" the judge shouted, drowning out Andrew's continuing barrage.

The sheriff didn't seem to mind that he had to restrain Andrew by force and use handcuffs to subdue him. He was taken from the courtroom at gunpoint, muttering obscene threats as he went.

Once again the judge cleared his throat to call

attention to the proceedings, but this time there was too much chatter among all the people gathered and he had to resort to his gavel. Receiving silence at last, he pronounced, "Since the marriage of Van Arder vs. Van Arder has been duly voided by the state of Missouri, the state of Nebraska does not consider its existence. Therefore, the marriage of Philippa Martin and Ryan Murphy is legal and binding, unless it is learned one of the parties consented to it under duress, fraud, or false pretense." He paused and looked from one Murphy to the other, trying to get courtroom demeanor from the happy crowd again. They were clapping their hands and stomping their feet, and he had to pound his gavel repeatedly to bring some semblance of order to this solemn place of worship.

Philippa peeked over her shoulder to the opposite corner of the room, where Ryan was sitting. She *had* forced him to marry her, and certainly he could protest on the grounds of fraud or false pretenses. What would he do or say now to this pertinent question of the judge's? He was sitting there staring stonily into space. "Please, God," she prayed silently, "let him love me enough to give me another chance."

As for Ryan's thoughts, all the words Reverend Fields had said to convince him to come here today flew out the window: "Stand by her, Ryan. It's your Christian duty at such a time as this. You took vows! Vows in the name of God. You meant them, didn't you?"

Lord yes, he'd meant them, but to what avail if she wanted to be free of him? The old inferiority stole through him and he was oblivious of the unruly, happy crowd as he sat waiting to hear Philippa's answer.

After he finally managed to bring the room to

order, the judge turned to Philippa and demanded, "What is your answer? Did you consent to this marriage to Mr. Murphy or not?"

"Oh, yes." She whispered softly, but Ryan could hear the ring of sincerity in each word. "I consented wholeheartedly."

"And you, young man," he asked, turning to Ryan, "were you agreeable?"

"I sure was." Ryan spoke firmly, turning to Philippa.

It was Hamilton Fields who stood up this time, bringing the crowd to the appropriate reverence by offering a blessing for the reunited Murphys.

"You know all about . . . everything?" Philippa asked as Ryan drove them back to the farm. It had taken over an hour to get away from their well-wishers and to pick up Philippa's things from Mrs. Crafton's.

"Clough came out and talked to me before he went to St. Louis to pay off that crooked judge there and get him to void your marriage. Later, Hamilton came for a long talk."

Ryan wanted to ask why she hadn't come to him herself. He could understand their explanations of her fright that she might be found, but it couldn't disperse the hurt he felt when she had not trusted him to help her, especially when she had not sent for him after she was found out.

"Do you still hate me, then?" she asked innocently.

"Hate you? I *never* hated you!"

"The things you said . . . and you sent me away. I thought you never wanted to see me again."

Ryan's spirits soared. She hadn't sent for him because she'd thought he was angry, which he had

been when he'd first learned the truth, of course.
"I s'pose I *was* mad. Mad as hell, to be honest, but
after I cooled down, well . . . I know you too well,
Pip. I just knew there had to be an explanation. I
waited for you to tell me."

"Oh, how I wanted to! Oh Ryan, I've needed
you so badly this week. No one can make me feel
comforted and cared for and protected the way you
can. I cried myself to sleep every night."

Teasingly confident again now, he tried to
lighten her mood. "At least you slept. I tossed and
turned in the haymow."

"You slept in the barn?"

"I couldn't bring myself to go into your bedroom. There were too many memories of you in
the house."

They were turning into the drive now, and Pip
answered him with heartfelt testimony. "It's so
good to be home. I never want to leave here again!"

Chapter Twenty-eight
✦✦✦✦

As WAS HIS habit when he was feeling on top of the
world, Ryan whistled a frisky tune while he unhitched the team and hurriedly did the evening
chores. Pip was back!

Philippa, too, hummed softly as she prepared
their supper, using her last jar of apples to make
Ryan his favorite pie. He loved her! He'd missed
her! He'd just the same as said it today. The way

her heart was throbbing, it felt as if it would rend the seams of her bodice.

Finishing his chores in short order, Ryan practically ran to the pump to wash up so he could go inside and make sure his dreams were real—that his beloved wife was back. The words she spoke as he entered the kitchen were real enough.

"I made an apple pie especially for you."

Ryan felt the suggestion in her voice tickle through every nerve of his long-strained body.

"Especially for me, little darlin'? That's terrific! Can you think of any way I might reward you for it?" he asked, hardly daring to hope.

"Well . . ." Philippa pretended to ponder. "A hot apple pie should at least deserve a kiss, shouldn't it?"

"It sure should!"

Each one took two giant strides to meet the other at the center of the floor. Ryan lovingly folded her in his arms, and Philippa followed suit by wrapping her arms tightly around his waist as he bent to kiss her upturned face. First her forehead, then both eyes, both ears, her nose, and at last her mouth. Philippa's lips clung to his with her long-pent-up desires. Ryan matched her with his own urgency. The kiss flared into a passionate merging of lips as each of them poured months of yearning ardor into it. For so long now both of them had held their emotions in check, for reasons that neither cared to recall.

Their caressing arms signaled the cravings that burned so deeply inside. When Ryan tenderly raised his lips from hers and looked into her dazzling, brilliant eyes, he was swept away by the intense adoration he read there. His heart soared as he bent to kiss her again. Within seconds their tongues were touching, tasting, savoring ravenously.

A stream of new sensations was playing havoc with Philippa's inner self. Her heartbeat seemed to be on a rampage, and she was inflamed with unnamed, unfulfilled fantasies. A longing to submit to temptation scuttled her prim and proper self, and she began to unbutton his shirt. She wanted to touch, feel, see the muscular frame she had glimpsed lying nude on the hammock so long ago. Ryan stepped back to ease her exploration.

Winsomely she unfastened each button, her eyes shimmering with anticipation. She held her breath as she pulled the shirtfront apart so she could look at the expanse of his chest. She was entranced by the thick mat of auburn hair she found there, and she tiptoed her fingers through it softly.

To him her touch felt like a full-fledged stampede. The room seemed to surge around him with a furor he could not control. The unslaked needs that had plagued him with sleepless nights since Philippa had arrived at the Bluffsview junction swallowed him. He picked her up and carried her into the bedroom with vivid impatience.

Philippa's eyes flared into their deepest brown, and the gold sunbeams in them were flickering incredibly. She held one hand firmly against Ryan's chest and looped the other around his neck to balance herself. The hand demanded more than balance. It soon pulled Ryan's face down to hers and vaulted the two of them into the clouds with the intensity of the kiss. Cherishing each second, he stood in the middle of the room, holding her, never wanting a kiss like this to end, a kiss that made his life whole and his world perfect. It was a kiss that consumed every part of his being. He idolized this girl who could turn his insides from iron to jelly and back again with only a kiss. Tenderly he stood her on the floor. Now it was his turn.

He unbuttoned her dress, kissing each new opening every tiny button revealed. When he kissed the valley between her breasts, Philippa mounted a sublime precipice. Her breasts felt as if they were firmer, harder, and the nipples pulled tautly at her whole body. It was as if she was languishing for some precious dream to come true. She tried to nestle against him, but he cuddled her for only a moment and then he stepped back and continued with the buttons.

Now he was below her waist, still kissing each new opening. Philippa quivered with a sensation she had never before known.

After he finished undoing the buttons, Ryan slid the dress off her shoulders and pulled her chemise over her head. Then he knelt and unrolled her stockings, frequently stopping to kiss her thigh or knee or calf or ankle as he did. He slipped off her shoes and then her stockings.

Only then did he look up into her eyes. He was struck by their full force of passion. She reached down and twisted her fingers in his hair, then let them fall to rest on his shoulders, her eyes still clinging to the radiant sheen of his. Ryan reached up to her waist to lower her knee-length silk panties. Only as he slipped them over her hips did he let his eyes draw away from hers. He leaned forward and kissed her stomach inch by tender inch as he pulled down the bloomers.

When he reached the patch of light hair between her legs and stopped the descent of her panties to kiss her there, Philippa thought her entire insides were going to break loose. She was hot, then cold, then it felt like she had turned to molten lava as she began to shiver with ardent anticipation for she knew not what: Something that would extinguish this fire within her!

Slowly Ryan rose up off his knees, kissing and nipping here and there on the way up as he had on the way down. Ever since the night he had given her a bath, Philippa's beautiful body had tormented him. He had never allowed himself to seriously dream it would be his. Yet here she stood before him in naked splendor. Surprisingly, she did not act as if this was repellent to her. Perhaps enough time had elapsed since the rape; perhaps that was why she stood here now, seeming to relish each new sensation.

Nonetheless, she was trembling like a virgin. He wanted to go slow with her so she could forget her past tragic experiences with men, but at the sight of her nude before him, his breath shook and he knew he could not keep much longer from possessing her.

Philippa wondered why Ryan had stopped kissing her. Was he going to stop now, as he had every other time they had ascended this peak of wanting? Now that Mrs. Parker had explained everything to her, Philippa yearned to know the fulfillment that Ryan's love could give her. She reached out for him as she had always done. Where Ryan was concerned, she was truly a vamp, and before this afternoon was over, she was determined to become a fallen woman, too.

She started to kiss his chest, going lower and lower, inch by inch, as he had done to her. When she came to his belt buckle she undid it and pulled his shirt loose. Gently she tugged it off, kissing his arms and shoulders and even his nipples as she did. Then she bent to kiss right below his navel where she had managed to get one of the metal grips of his trousers undone.

That seductive, sensuous kiss was the final straw that drove Ryan over the brink. He laid her down on the disordered bed and quickly divested himself of his sharp-toed boots and socks. Then he lay down beside her on his stomach, took her in his arms, and kissed her again, a long, turbulent kiss that left both of them gasping for air. He let his face fall to her breast then and began to kiss it, nibble it, pull it into his warm mouth. Philippa was writhing up and down, side to side, squirming and quivering as he did the same to the other. She couldn't stop. Unable to wait any longer, Ryan stood up beside the bed and let his dungarees and drawers drop to the floor.

When Philippa saw the large emblem of his manhood she expected to be upset, but instead, she was only fascinated by it. She stared at it, her eyes large and intense. The sight was causing those hot tremors between her legs again.

Ryan saw Philippa's expression change and he was afraid she might not want him to continue. Oh, Lord, if he had to stop now! If Philippa wanted him to, he would, but holy hell, he'd have to make a run for the creek and hope it was possible to cool off a blaze of passion like this. He looked at her puzzled eyes again to see what he should do, and miracle of miracles, Philippa held her arms up to him, welcoming him to her. With a deep sigh of relief he lay down on top of her, allowing their intimate parts to barely touch one another. He was using every ounce of reserve he could muster to continue to go slow with her.

She was the one who slightly, tentatively, spread her legs apart to allow him to enter her. All his restraint faded and he invaded her with the full force of his staff, hard and fast. He couldn't believe it when he felt the small blockage, but he could believe her painful cry. She had not been ready for this. If only he'd known, he could have entered her slowly. He held her tightly in his arms, saying soothingly, "Oh, my precious little darlin'," but they could not stop and talk about this surprise now. As the initial pain subsided, Philippa began to move against him in a rhythm that felt right. It felt too good to Ryan. He kissed her over and over again between the deep breaths of air he was gulping.

Philippa tried to hang on to his body as he vaulted and descended in the full force of his passion, but her arms failed to hold her where she wanted to be, so she wrapped her legs around him too. It was an ultimate victory for both of them as they crested the heights together and slowly floated back to earth. For long minutes they lay in each other's arms, too exalted by what had happened to move.

It had been too perfect. Ryan could tell that where his wife was concerned, he was going to be insatiable. He would want her again and again. He already wanted her again now, but she would not be ready for him, she'd be too tender. He tried to cool his ardor by asking the question that was foremost in his mind.

He rolled off of her and pulled her tightly against him. "You were a virgin, Pip!"

"Of course I was! I tried to tell you those ideas you had that I was fast were just your imagination, or"—she giggled intimately—"maybe I always *was* a little too forward around you. I couldn't help myself, Ryan. You've always done things to me that . . . well, I'm just glad I'm a fallen woman now!"

Ryan chuckled at her outburst. "That's not so, love. You aren't a fallen woman, you're very much a married lady now . . . But the rape?" he asked, still bewildered.

"Do you mean Big Louie?" she asked, comprehension finally dawning. "Ryan, he didn't try to . . . rape me. He recognized me, and he was going to take me back, bound and gagged if necessary, to get the reward Andrew was offering."

"Pip! You were in grave danger. Why didn't you warn me? What did you think you were going to do?"

Shamefaced now, she admitted, "Run away . . . again . . . but when I heard he was dead, I thought I was safe again. And Ryan . . . I wanted to stay here with you."

Although Ryan was pleased by her confession, he still had questions. "Where did you ever get the dumb idea I thought you were fast! I took liberties I shouldn't have, I know. I couldn't seem to help myself, but I've always respected you, little darlin'. Don't you know I considered you above my touch?"

"Why?"

Ryan began to feel the jaws of the trap clenching shut around him. He shuddered slightly as the shadow of his ignorance and shame stole across him, obliterating some of his happiness.

"Why, Ryan?" She wasn't going to drop the subject. She had to know. Did he feel guilty because he wanted her physically but still loved his childhood sweetheart? "Nothing could make me above your touch. Nothing in this whole world. You are so wonderful, and you've taken such good care of me, and I love you until I actually ache inside." She hoped her love could obliterate any feelings he still carried for that traitor Dixie.

At Philippa's intense declaration of love, Ryan could no longer deceive her. She had to be told the godawful truth. She was waiting for his answer, looking sad and perplexed by his silence.

"I can't read or do arithmetic, Pip. I'm practically illiterate." For the first time in his life, Ryan Murphy had actually spoken aloud the inner burden that he had carried since childhood. He turned his face to the wall, unable to bear the look he would see in her eyes.

He didn't expect a disgusted, matter-of-fact "I *know* that!"

"*What?*"

Philippa raised herself up in his arms and looked into his face with sympathy and understanding. She replied consolingly, "I've known for a long time, Ryan. What difference could that possibly make to a schoolteacher? I can easily teach you to read and write. I taught the Murray boys, didn't I? You're so intelligent, Ryan. The way you've successfully built up this place, it will be simple for you to learn to read!

"No, I'm much more concerned that *I* can't handle a team and help you run your farm the way Dixie could have. I don't think I can stand it if you're sad about losing her to your brother."

Now it was Ryan's turn to puzzle. Why would he care if Stuart married Dix? They belonged together. Dixie would keep Stuart in line or bust his thick skull for him, one or the other. The sincerity in Philippa's voice told him she had honestly believed that tale he had contrived, and still did.

Someday he would tell her the truth about that,

but not now. All he wanted to do now was kiss her again, so he said briefly, "Unlike Calvin, I really do need help from you to straighten out and keep the account ledgers—until you teach me to read and cipher, that is!

"As for Dixie, I told you: we grew up together, but I never loved her. I love *you*, Pip!" He bent down to demonstrate, reminding himself this had been her first time and he had to wait a day or two until she would feel like making love again. It was a difficult thing to remember with the passionate way she was kissing him back. He pulled free from the kiss while he still could.

Breathlessly Philippa asked, "Is it possible to consummate our marriage again now, my love?"

"Yes, little darlin'! It sure is!"

Epilogue
✦ ✦ ✦ ✦

HORACE AND ALVENA BELDEN stood on the makeshift platform in the town square to receive the plaque of honor for having the most students in the top ten percent of the district's eighth-grade graduating class. Rural District No. 3 had never before received the honor.

After Superintendent Niles's lengthy congratulatory speech, he presented the framed award to Horace Belden, who only muttered "Thank you" and nodded. His wife, however, had much more to say. She stepped forward and announced in her precise, clipped words, "An award like this comes to a district that is selective in hiring its teachers. We have always hired ours through the very dependable Fitch Employment Agency in St. Louis, Missouri.

"This year they outdid themselves in sending us a highly educated, genteel young lady from one of the finest old families in St. Louis. She is a graduate of the select Hansen-Tawzer Academy for young ladies . . ."

Philippa barely listened as Mrs. Belden droned on, listing all of Philippa's estimable qualities and indications of culture. It was almost laughable. By now her true past had been revealed in bits and pieces to the whole town. In fact, she finally told most of it herself. Alvena Belden, upon hearing she was the adopted niece of the wealthy, well-known widow, Mrs. Clara Rose Van Arder, had practically prostrated herself with apologies and excuses. She had sent Philippa and Ryan a hand-painted set of Bavarian china as a belated wedding gift. Not to be outdone, Babette Hawkins had sent them a thirty-six-piece set of crystal goblets, cordials, and sherbet glasses.

Philippa was proud of all her students as they came forward to receive their diplomas and then stepped to the side of the platform where she was sitting with Ryan. Lydia and Alice Ann had thrown their arms around her, in tears at the frightening prospect of town high school and a bevy of new teachers as well as pride at their own achievements. They had scored first and second on the superintendent's exam. Fred and Roy had stood before her awkwardly, bashfully trying to stammer out their appreciation. At last Roy managed to blurt, "You're the best, ma'am," and Fred shook his head in agreement.

Ryan leaned over and whispered suggestively to her, "You sure are, ma'am!" and made her blush.

Bessie June Hendee, the most articulate member of the class, proclaimed, "Mrs. Murphy, I owe you a lot more than I can ever say or repay. I know now I can do anything, or be anybody, thanks to you. You deserve the best!" Then, with her old brazenness, she boldly winked at her teacher and concluded, "And I think you got him, too."

Both Ryan and Philippa nearly laughed aloud as she turned and walked off the platform, head high and hips swinging seductively. Everyone noted that her parents were not in attendance, but that she sat by a proudly beaming Sammy Hawkins.

When the ceremony was over nearly everyone came up to congratulate Philippa. Calvin and Cecilia were holding hands, and after congratulating her, they told her they had set a wedding date. Philippa threw her arms around Cecilia and wished her happiness, saying, "I know you'll be as happy as we are!"

It was a lie; no one could be as happy as she and Ryan were, she thought with a smile.

"What's that smug little grin for, sweetheart?" Ryan whispered, glad they were alone for a moment.

Philippa was happy she no longer had to lie anymore; she could tell Ryan everything. "Oh," she admitted complacently, "I was just thinking how clever I was to make you fall in love with me."

"I think I loved you the day I saw you at the junction with that silly little hat half on and half off. If not, then for sure the next night when we kissed in the shed!"

"Ryan Murphy! You loved me all that time and didn't tell me? You let me worry night and day how I was going to learn to ride horseback, rope and brand calves, drive a six-horse team, and butcher a steer before your mail-order bride arrived?''

Ryan laughed loudly at her mock angry-tirade, causing the bystanders to smile understandingly at the happy newlyweds. When he stopped laughing, he asked her seriously, ''Were you really willing to do all that for me, little darlin'?''

''Of course!'' she answered with unqualified assurance.

No one was too surprised to see Ryan Murphy sweep his wife off her feet and kiss her just as resoundingly as he had at their wedding ceremony when Reverend Fields had said, ''I hereby pronounce you man and wife.''

Reading—
For The
Fun Of It

Ask a teacher to define the most important skill for success and inevitably she will reply, "the ability to read."

But millions of young people never acquire that skill for the simple reason that they've never discovered the pleasures books bring

That's why there's RIF—Reading is Fundamental. The nation's largest reading motivation program, RIF works with community groups to get youngsters into books and reading. RIF makes it possible for young people to have books that interest them, books they can choose and keep. And RIF involves young people in activities that make them want to read—**for the fun of it.**

The more children read, the more they learn, and the more they **want** to learn.

There are children in your community—maybe in your own home—who need RIF. For more information, write to:

RIF
Dept. BK-3
Box 23444
Washington, D.C.
20026

Founded in 1966, RIF is a national, nonprofit organization with local projects run by volunteers in every state of the union.